I0563789

DESCEND

JEN LYON

ALPHADU
PUBLISHING COMPANY

COPYRIGHT © 2025 JEN LYON

ALL RIGHTS RESERVED.

NO PART OF THIS BOOK MAY BE REPRODUCED, STORED IN A RETRIEVAL SYSTEM, OR TRANSMITTED IN ANY FORM OR BY ANY MEANS—ELECTRONIC, MECHANICAL, PHOTOCOPYING, RECORDING, OR OTHERWISE—WITHOUT THE PRIOR WRITTEN PERMISSION OF THE PUBLISHER, EXCEPT IN THE CASE OF BRIEF QUOTATIONS USED IN REVIEWS OR SCHOLARLY WORK.

ISBN (PAPERBACK): 979-8-9929445-7-0 D2D

ISBN (EBOOK): 979-8-9929445-9-4 D2D

LIBRARY OF CONGRESS CONTROL NUMBER: PENDING

PUBLISHED BY ALPHADU PUBLISHING COMPANY

BERKSHIRES, WESTERN MASSACHUSETTS

PRINTED IN THE UNITED STATES OF AMERICA

FIRST EDITION

COVER DESIGN BY ALPHADU PUBLISHING COMPANY

THIS IS A WORK OF FICTION. NAMES, CHARACTERS, PLACES, AND INCIDENTS ARE PRODUCTS OF THE AUTHOR'S IMAGINATION OR ARE USED FICTITIOUSLY. ANY RESEMBLANCE TO ACTUAL EVENTS, LOCALES, OR PERSONS, LIVING OR DEAD, IS PURELY COINCIDENTAL.

SALES OF THIS BOOK WITHOUT A FRONT COVER MAY BE UNAUTHORIZED . IF THIS BOOK IS COVERLESS, IT MAY HAVE BEEN REPORTED TO THE PUBLISHER AS "UNSOLD AND DESTROYED" AND NEITHER AUTHOR OR PUBLISHER AY HAVE RECEIVED PAYMENT FOR IT.

CONTENT WARNING: THIS BOOK CONTAINS SCENES INVOLVING SWEARING, EMOTIONAL TRAUMA, GRAPHIC AND WAR-RELATED VIOLENCE. ***READER DISCRETION IS ADVISED.***

To Those
Who Came
Before…

You Are Not Forgotten

Energy cannot be created or destroyed,
It can only be changed from one form to another
-Albert Einstein

CHAPTER

ONE

The fire consumed the second floor of the house long before the ground floor began to burn. The flames broke through the bedroom windows, hurling skywards into the frigid November night. At first, the crackling from the heat was a low hum, but by the time the roof began to fall in on itself, the fire grew into a loud roar, rumbling throughout the quiet residential street.

Watching the monitors, Sarah kept her eye on the front door of the house, willing it to open and see the occupants flee to safety.

It did not open. It could not. The door was locked and barricaded from the inside. As black smoke thickened downstairs, the wail of the rescue sirens was heard in the distance. But by then, it was already too late.

The little girl planned it this way. Sarah would swear she saw the girl press her face against the downstairs bay window, smile and wave right at her before the glass shattered outward from the heat building inside.

"She did it again. Damn. I really hate her." Sarah reached out and shut the monitor off before turning to her computer analyst, Jess.

"What do you expect? That one is never going to learn. She's a bad seed. Cube her already and move on." Jess clicked on her keyboard and checked the data. "She's already arrived. I could send Bunny to meet her?"

Both women smiled at the thought, but Sarah waved it off. "No, I'll go and tell her, but you're right. She's a lost cause, no more second chances."

As Sarah pressed the button for the elevator, she glanced back to Jess, who was shaking her head disapprovingly.

"If it was up to me, she'd have been taken out a hundred lives ago. You're getting soft."

The elevator dinged. Sarah got on and hit the button down. Right before the doors closed, she flipped off Jess who responded with a hearty laugh.

Sarah took a deep, steadying breath as the elevator plunged the 500 feet to the ground floor. Jess was right and Sarah knew it. That little girl was never going to change—none of them would—and time was running out. If Sarah failed, humanity was doomed, with no second chances left for anyone. Maybe everything she was planning was pointless. Maybe humanity deserved extinction—they certainly seemed eager enough to race toward it.

The elevator slowed to a smooth stop and doors slid open. Sarah left the Ascend Control Tower, turned left on the pathway, and headed towards the green fields in the distance. As she walked, Sarah glanced at the stream of new Arrivals on the way to their dorms.

Despite the tranquil setting, the campus was populated by the worst souls humanity had to offer. She watched as they shoved each other, punching and jeering. Harsh laughter followed if anyone fell to the ground, where they were inevitably kicked by the victor.

Pulling her long, blonde hair back into a loose ponytail with an elastic, Sarah squinted upwards towards the pale blue sky. It was warm, but not too hot out. No clouds meant her light complexion would soon be sunburned.

She spotted Tiny, who sat in the shade near the path, leaning against a massive oak tree. Even from a distance, Sarah could see he was deep in thought, ignoring the shrieks and taunts of the newest group of rancid souls passing by him.

Tiny was, in reality, the very opposite of his nickname. Standing over eight feet tall, his broad shoulders and massive frame made him easy to find in every crowd—not to mention the fact his skin was as strong as armor. He looked like the unlikely offspring of a turtle and a pangolin, standing tall on two muscular legs. Thick brown intersecting plates cascaded down his back, creating a blunt ridge at the tip of his short tail. His yellow-and-black stomach mirrored the under shell of a tortoise. But his formidable build didn't hold a candle to his brilliant mind.

"Hey there, big guy," she called as she approached. Tiny had his eyes closed and was tracing patterns in the air with a sharp claw that protruded from one of his wide, six-fingered hands. He kept his talons short. "What are you thinking about?"

Tiny opened his eyes and smiled. "Just the task at hand, as I am sure you are doing. We must have overlooked an important factor, I just do not know what it could be. I would like to access the Library database and search a few nearby quadrants. I doubt we are the first to encounter this type of problem with a host species."

Sarah nodded. "We need all the help we can get. Let me know what you find. I'm heading over to Arrivals to deliver a message. I'll catch you later."

She turned down the walkway, continued towards the four story structure that sat on the edge of the high grass fields. Arrivals was the first place the humans returned to after their death.

An attendant in pale purple scrubs held open a door for Sarah. She stepped into the cooled reception area with high ceilings and glass walls. As she walked across the wood floors, the scent of the plants and flowers nestled in the corners filled the space. She took in a deep breath and enjoyed a brief moment of calmness.

The attendants moved quickly, assisting the newly deceased within their predetermined sections. Lo-Reps - short for low repetitions - were people who had lived less than fifty lifetimes, and were located on the left side of the building. Their section held several cots to accommodate newer souls who passed away and arrived in Descend. Dim lighting helped ease the transition between Earth and Descend. In here, attendants would pass out water and snacks to help the returning deceased adjust. Incense and soft music wafted through the rooms to keep the mood relaxed.

Across the lobby, on the right side of the building, were the Mid-Reps. Here were those who lived from fifty to one hundred and fifty lives. This room had recliners instead of cots for the deceased as they arrived, with the same soothing music and low lighting. Mid-Reps transitioned much faster than a Lo-Rep, they'd been there plenty of times to remember how the system worked.

The largest section, directly behind the lobby, belonged to the Hi-Reps—souls who had returned more than a hundred and fifty times without successfully Ascending. This section was vastly different than the others. Harsh industrial lighting shone down onto wooden chairs that were scattered about on a vinyl tile floor. The only smell was of bleach with a tinge of urine. No attendants waited to give snacks or words of encouragement to the Hi-Reps when they awoke. That is to say, if they awoke.

Typically, a Hi-Rep would die on Earth and immediately land back on their feet in Arrivals, already complaining about their previous life. They had no problem adjusting to this level. They had been part of this cycle for thousands of years and often knew they would be heading back to Descend before their mortal bodies ceased operating.

People were streaming out of the doors, like teenagers leaving a concert. The Hi-Reps let the doors slam into people's faces, while they hip-checked others out of their way. It was always easy to spot a Hi-Rep in Descend from their deplorable behavior.

"Even death doesn't deter them from being an asshole for too long," she muttered as she pushed through another door, bringing her into the holding area.

Sarah heard a young voice rise from the crowd.

"Oooh, lookie here. Queen Bitch is gracing us all with her fucking presence! Shall I bow?"

Sarah gritted her teeth as she spotted an innocent looking six-year old stroll up to her. The little girl had dark red hair twisted into twin braids, her cheeks dotted with freckles and a wide, defiant smile plastered across her face. She was the spitting image of Wendy's restaurant icon. While this little girl looked sweet, Sarah knew the truth, after all, she just witnessed her work.

"Ginnie, back so soon? Tell me, did your hosts realize that you're an evil spawn and cut your visit short? Because if they did, I'll reward them with a fast track to Ascend." Sarah said, crossing her arms and staring back at the malevolent child.

"Fuck no, I got them first. I burned them. I burned them all!" Ginnie let out a series of giggles that crescendoed into maniacal laughter, the kind typically heard from unhinged serial killers. Only this time the sound was coming from a little girl's mouth.

"Pleasant. As always. Well, I'll let Bunny know you're back. You're one of his favorites and this time, you two are going to have lunch together. He's going to Eat. You. Up." Sarah grinned at Ginnie, whose own smile slid off her face, replaced with a look of dread.

As she left Arrivals and headed back to her office, Sarah thought of the early days, when so many humans easily Ascended. That was until the balance shifted, causing millions of humans to be caught in an endless loop between Earth and Descend.

She walked up the pathway past Tiny, who was now deep asleep in the shade. Her smartest Demon needed his rest. So did she. They had been running themselves ragged trying to find a solution for the humans before it was too late.

She opened up her office door and flipped the light on. Time was running out. Her plan to save the human race was now underway.

CHAPTER
TWO

"Are you a Demon?" the human asked, trying to keep his voice steady.

Sweat dimpled his forehead and his collar was soaked from perspiration. He was trying to appear calm, but his shaking hands betrayed his fear.

The Demon Keeper sat across from him, unblinking.

"I'm just asking what the hell is going on here," he said, his voice wavering despite his efforts. "I think it's only fair for you to tell me why you brought me here."

The Demon Keeper's emotionless grey eyes continued to pierce through him.

The man looked around at his surroundings and saw nothing that would help him. The small room was bare concrete - walls, floor, ceiling - with a single overhead light and one closed door. There was no other furniture except for the two chairs in which they were sitting.

The Demon Keeper was small and lean, her dark blond hair pulled back in a loose ponytail. She wore jeans, low boots, and a black long sleeve shirt. The man considered attacking, strangling, or knocking her unconscious so he could escape.

"Have you ever been to a zoo?" she asked, finally breaking the silence.

Surprised, he nodded slowly.

"Well, at the zoo, have you ever seen a flamingo keep the other flamingos in their pens?" Her left eyebrow raised minutely.

"No!" He scoffed. "That's stupid."

"What did you say?" her voice deepened slightly.

A chill shot up his spine as he felt the temperature in the room drop. "No. No, I haven't."

"Right," she leaned back in her chair, her eyes firmly set on his face. "You don't see one elephant feeding the other elephants, do you? Otters trotting around and giving the other otters medications? Perhaps you've seen a zebra in a park uniform, giving tours about their migration across the plains?"

"I get your point." He cast his gaze to the concrete wall.

"Look at me," she said quietly.

His eyes remained fixed on the wall.

The Demon Keeper rose out of her chair, looming over him. "I said, look at me."

He turned his head back in her direction, but only far enough to look at her waist.

"Look at me!" Her voice now reverberating off the walls. His body convulsed involuntarily with fear. She leaned in close, their noses nearly touching. She blinked slowly and when her lids opened again, her bright grey eyes turned coal black.

The man screamed so violently, he tore one of his vocal cords. Then he fainted, sliding off the chair into a crumbled heap on the floor.

The Demon Keeper chuckled. From the corner of her eye, she caught movement through the tiny window in the door. She stepped out into the hallway.

"Ooooh, is he a bad one, Miss?" Luis asked, gesturing towards the room. Luis was holding onto the long handle of a mop and pushing a cart of cleaning supplies.

"Luis, I keep telling you, call me Sarah." She took his arm and led him away from the cart and towards the bench in the hallway. She turned to him with a huge, toothy grin.

"That one in there? Luis, he's had four hundred and seventy nine repetitions."

Luis' eyes grew large. "Oh my, Mis- oh my, Sarah." He squeezed her hand.

"Four hundred and seventy nine repetitions! Can you imagine? No one has ever been that high. He was never supposed to get past three hundred. He should have been yanked the moment he pushed that blind person in front of a bus when he was eleven years old. The Elgets refused to Recall him. Same old tired argument, 'What about his poor parents? They won't understand, they think he's a normal child,' blah blah blah."

Sarah rolled her eyes. "I guess it might be hard to explain to a parent that their precious kid is actually an unredeemable psychopath that hacked the afterlife. That piece of shit went on to murder twenty more people and countless animals before the humans finally pulled his ticket." Sarah bit at her lip. "That's only counting his last round."

Luis shook his head. "What a shame. How awful. So terrible. I hope his next training is very difficult."

Sarah laughed, "Oh, he's not going back to ReTraining. Ever. That's the best part. No, no, no. He's done." She leaned in. "And this time, the paperwork will not be mishandled, I promise you that."

A grunt from inside the room caught their attention. The man was trying to sit up. He looked confused as his gaze darted from Sarah to Luis standing in the open doorway. He became enraged, slamming his hands against the floor, soundlessly yelling as his face blossomed into a deep crimson blush.

Sarah and Luis both watched as he struggled, but the harder he fought, the more his limbs stuck to the floor. He kept glancing back at the door, and each time it prompted a new bout of laughter from Sarah and Luis. His petulant grimace was unintentionally comical.

"Ohhhh Bunny! I have something for you. A Treat. Come get your Treeeeeat!" Sarah called down into the dark hallway.

The floor and walls began to shake. The man frantically redoubled his efforts to free himself, but to no avail. He tried again to scream for help, but no sound came from his damaged vocal cords.

Then the room stopped shaking. The man could see the Demon Keeper tilt her head back, looking at something over her head. "Yeah, you have been really good. You deserve a treat! He's all yours!"

Then the doorway stretched impossibly wide, its frame distorting as the wall stretched open to accommodate the massive demon who just stepped through it.

Bunny.

The demon stood at least fourteen feet tall, covered with spikes, scales, and thick, oozing slime pouring from every crevice. The demon appeared to be two halves of other creatures, mismatched and joined together at the waist. The upper half had a round, wide chest, with arms the length of its entire body, and dragging on the floor beside it. The head was too small for the size of the beast, with several jagged teeth jutted upwards from the misshapen skull. On the very top of its head were two long bony protrusions, resembling a rabbit—but only in someone's nightmares.

The lower half narrowed dramatically below the barrel shaped torso, into meaty haunches and talons that scraped against the floor with every lurch forward.

Bunny's black, lifeless eyes wandered the room before settling on his treat.

Two pink tongues rolled out from the jaw and flicked into the air, tasting the man's fear.

The Demon reached forward and sliced the man's arm cleanly off at the shoulder.

Bunny plopped the limb into his mouth and swallowed it whole, his eyes rolling back in his skull to savor the taste.

Somewhere, far away in the background, the last thing the man heard was laughter.

CHAPTER
THREE

"That guy, his face was all big like this!" Luis pulled his eyes wide and the corners of his bushy mustache up in a garish gesture. "Oh, it was such a mess too! Miss, I mean, Sarah, Bunny had such a good time. I haven't seen him so happy in, well, I don't think I've ever seen him so happy!" Luis wiped the tears of laughter from his eyes.

Sarah leaned back in her chair, clasping her hands behind her head. "Yeah, it was so good to see him really dig in like that, with complete abandon." She glanced over at Luis, and they both started howling again, tears streaming down their faces.

When their laughter finally subsided, she added, "Well, he deserved it. He really did."

"Who? Bunny or the bad man?" Luis asked, dabbing his face with a handkerchief.

Sarah considered this and shrugged. "Both, truly a case of win-win on this one."

Nephemerus appeared at her office door and saw Sarah and Luis wiping their faces.

"What was a win-win?" he asked, leaning against the doorway frame with his arms crossed. The latest Descend Elget was tall and lean, his ink black hair falling messily over his intense eyes. Dressed in a dark button-down shirt, tucked neatly into his black jeans, he exuded an effortlessly sharp presence. His dark features will help sell the humans on his new role, Sarah mused.

"Uh-oh, the Devil's here, you're in trouble now, Chica." Luis teased, pointing at Sarah and winking.

Nephemerus sighed dramatically.. "The Devil? Really? Can we pick another moniker? Even Lucifer feels played out."

"If we change the name, we have to put out a whole new series of books, then update all the stories, statues, fanboy sites, blah blah blah." She gestured for him to take a seat.

"Blah, blah, blah, oh yes, the stories," he mocked. "Humans and their coveted stories. How…what is the word I'm looking for?"

"Primitive? Barbaric?" Sarah offered, sitting up in her chair. "You know the deal. Most worlds this young go through their god stage, but eventually they figure it out."

"I should go, I still have work left to do." Luis said, excusing himself as he headed toward the door, "Oh, before I forget!" He reached into the front pouch of his overalls and took out a small, obsidian cube. "Bunny left this for you."

Luis placed the cube on Sarah's desk. They both stared at it for a moment, before another burst of laughter erupted between them.

Nephemerus watched the exchange, puzzled. Luis bowed his head and walked out, closing the office door behind him.

"Should I ask?" the Elget inquired.

Sarah looked at the cube and then back at Nephemerus. "Oh it's nothing. One of those 'you had to be there,' things," she said, brushing off his question.

He reached out and started to pick up the cube. His hand hovered over it as his eyes met Sarah's. "May I?"

She shrugged nonchalantly, but felt her jaw tighten as she waved him on. The Elget picked up the cube and examined it thoughtfully, not saying anything. When he was done, he put it back down on her desk and studied Sarah.

"What is that exactly?" he finally asked.

Sarah glanced back down at the jet black cube, perfectly measured at two inches on all sides. "That? Oh, yeah, that's probably something you should know about, but so does the other new guy."

She picked up the phone on her desk and waited. When a voice answered, she said, "I need to speak with the new Ascend Elget. Yeah, about twenty minutes. Uh-huh, and I'm bringing the Devil too."

Nephemerus dropped his head in his hands and groaned. "Stop saying that!"

Sarah hung up the phone, swept up the cube and dropped it into her pocket, feeling the weight of what it represented as she moved from behind her desk. She held the office door open as they exited.

"What would you expect me to call you?" she asked.

"My name? Try using my name?" he said, exasperated, as he walked past her.

"I am using your name…Satan," she said, winking at him.

CHAPTER

FOUR

E arth. Such a disappointment. Desi had known he would be coming to this remote planet for the past eight centuries, but now that the time had finally arrived, he fully regretted accepting this assignment. Truth be told, it felt more like a punishment than work, which was unfair. He had been doing exceptionally well in all his postings since he became an Elget for the Multi-Dimensional Galactic Council. He should have his pick of the best assignments - not been relegated to such dour places like Earth.

It's fine, he told himself. He would only be here for two thousand human years. After all, the longest anyone ever had to stay on Earth was Galloyde. Granted, all that time had driven Galloyde mad to the point that he created his own race of monsters. When the Council found out about the creatures, they banished him, never to be seen again, although Galloyde's wild creatures still roamed the planet.

No one really knows why Galloyde was left on Earth so long. Some say it was because he refused to leave, others believed it was a punishment. Some even suggested he had simply been forgotten because let's face it, no one cared about Earth. It was just a tiny planet in a remote galaxy, located in a solar system tucked inside a black hole. You couldn't design a worse location if you tried.

If the Multi-Dimensional Galactic Council or "Muldigal" Council as it was called, could get away without staffing Earth, they absolutely would. Yet The Verisian Treaty was clear. Once a species became self-aware, it was the duty of the Council to provide oversight until that species Ascended to the Higher Consciousness or became extinct. They were simply stuck with Earth, whether they liked it or not, and no one liked it.

The Council sent two Elgets to Earth on rotation every few thousand years to provide the oversight. Desi only needed to get through this assignment, and then he would be off to bigger and better things. He consoled himself with the thought that at least he was going to be serving his time here with Nephemerus.

Desi had known Neph since they both attended Elget training together more than fifty millennia ago. They had been on assignment together twice since, but they had always gotten along. Their last assignment was for the equivalent of twelve hundred Earth years outside the Neba Solar Array on a moon-like planet called Iitka.

The inhabitants of Iitka believed that day and night were ruled by separate god-like entities, who were constantly at war fighting for the right to illuminate or darken their skies. The species did not understand how the angle of their planet relative to their sun was the reason for their daylight or lack of it.

They had built large monuments to celebrate and appease their gods of Day and Night. The Iitka shared stories of how, with enough willpower and offerings, Day could overcome Night and rule for all eternity, never allowing the sun to set again.

There were a few Iitka who suspected there could be other reasons behind the shifting light, but they were beaten and often killed when they expressed those opinions. The belief in gods was not unique to the Neba Solar Array. Many new species would develop grand mythical stories to explain what they had yet to discover with science.

During their assignment, Neph represented the entity of Day, while Desi embodied Night. Now, on Earth, Desi was assigned to Ascend, while Neph had agreed to work as the Descend Elget.

Desi couldn't understand why the Council was investing any effort into Earth. Humans had once been on track to achieve Higher Consciousness within thirty-two thousand years. Meaning, they would become part of the cosmic order, officially becoming part of the evolved races in the Multi-Dimensional Galaxies. Those races who had already Ascended reaped the benefits of their lives lasting several millennia. They could travel amongst the trillions of galaxies and dimensions, sharing their experiences with other species, and shape the expanding fabric of the Universes.

Unfortunately, due to their innate self-destructive behavior, humans were now predicted to self-eradicate in less than three thousand years. Every model confirmed it. There were no other probably outcome for the little barbarians.

Hence, no Elget wanted an Earth assignment. It was like jumping onto a sinking ship. Desi feared this extinction event would happen during his watch. That would adversely affect his perfect portfolio. If he was lucky, he could keep the humans alive long enough for the next guy to deal with the fallout.

If the humans did end up wiping themselves out from existence, there was little he could do about it, except minimize the impact of the destruction.

Some from the Muldigal Council had kicked around the idea of using Earth as an emergency shelter, but retrofitting was cost-prohibitive. The planet had been so trashed at this point that no one has expressed any interest, except the Gigla, but they wanted it for strip mining.

No, Desi would serve out his time on Earth, perhaps catch up on his correspondence. Maybe he would even catch a glimpse of the creatures Galloyde created, the ones they call Daemons? Or was it Demons? Humans had such a peculiar ear for language.

This reminded him to reset his mirreáge to the Earth quadrant. The bracelet altered his appearance into something humanoid for those who looked upon him. Each mirreáge took on the unique physical attributes of the wearer and turned them into a palatable version of the assigned species. This eased culture shock to the inhabitants and aided in gaining the trust of the native inhabitants.

Desi touched the squishy pink protrusion sticking out beneath his two green eyes. Two holes sat at the bottom of the fleshy mound, lined with soft hairs. Below that, the human mouth—filled with rows of unnervingly hard, white nuggets. He studied his reflection, stretching his new features into various expressions.

This was fascinating. The mouth could move in countless directions, and when paired with other muscles, it allowed for an array of emotions he had never been able to display in his natural form.

Granted, Desi's people used telepathy in combination with occasional speech to communicate. Human beings had a fascinating array of communication cues to give each other and Desi found himself enthralled as he tried out his new face. Perhaps Earth wouldn't be so terribly boring after all.

CHAPTER
FIVE

The elevator ride with Sarah up to the Ascend Operations Tower felt shorter than Nephemerus expected, especially compared to his first visit two weeks prior. That had been a blur to him. His predecessor was thrilled to be leaving, and kept chanting, "Enjoy this shit show," while laughing maniacally at no one in particular. Nephemerus didn't know what to say and felt wildly out of place.

Usually, someone was on-site to ensure the Elgets transitioned in and out of their roles smoothly. Unfortunately for Nephemerus, the Earth transitionary, Aramik, was off-planet completing one of his many duties and would not return for several days.

Nephemerus figured he would just wait until Desi arrived. They would work out how they wanted to operate this assignment. They would be fine once they learned the little idiosyncrasies of this particular planet. After all, it's not like they could mess up a species that wasn't even intergalactic yet, right?

Sarah had her eyes closed and was humming to herself as the elevator shot up the fifty floors to the Control Room. Nephemerus knew very little about the Demon Keeper other than she held an extremely powerful position within the realm of Descend. She was much smaller than he in stature, but carried herself with unwavering confidence. That, and she carried a jeweled dagger strapped to her thigh that would give anyone pause should they cross her.

Both Ascend and Descend operated under a corporate structure, with Elgets serving as middle management reporting directly to the Muldigal Council. Their function was to keep the peace and make sure whatever species that became self-aware would Ascend and join the collective Higher Consciousness.

Yet no other worlds had someone like Sarah, because no others required one. Demons didn't exist anywhere else in any of the universes or dimensions. Nephemerus had yet to see any of the monsters since he arrived and hadn't wanted to appear too eager by asking to see one. Secretly, witnessing Galloyde's Demons was the only reason he was looking forward to his assignment on Earth.

He thought about Galloyde's race of experimental creatures. From what he had heard, the Muldigal Council had no idea what to do when they first learned of them. A few of the creatures apparently possessed extraordinary intelligence, and some did not. All were terrifying in their appearance, but after lengthy discussions, the Council had decided their survival would fall under their jurisdiction. Had they done a better job in tracking Galloyde, or rather, hadn't forgotten about him on this remote outpost—he probably wouldn't have created them, Nephemerus mused. Galloyde's experiments now belonged to the Council and would be protected as such, hence the need for a Demon Keeper.

The elevator finally arrived at the top floor. The doors slid open, revealing a pretty but severe-looking woman with a sleek dark brown ponytail and yellow eyes waiting to greet them.

"Where have you been?" Jess snapped. "We have been waiting for almost five…five…five…five - " The woman seemed stuck on her words.

Sarah gave the brunette a weary look and slammed her hard in the side of her head with an open hand. Jess stopped stuttering and finished her sentence. "Five minutes. Thanks, Sarah."

"No problem. How come Aramik hasn't fixed your verbal processing chip yet?"

Desi blinked rapidly, trying to process this new revelation. Jess was indistinguishable from the other living beings he'd observed on this strange little planet. Neph furrowed his brow and narrowed his eyes as he studied the droid from a few feet away. He didn't like missing details, and he certainly hadn't picked up on Jess' origins when he first visited the Tower.

Sarah snickered. "She's so lifelike right? That's Gigla manufacturing for you. I had to pull some serious strings to get this droid. You didn't know? Don't sweat it, she would never told you, and to be fair, the last Elget never knew."

"Neither did the eighth or eleventh Elgets, but thanks for telling everyone, Sarah." Jess pouted.

"I didn't tell 'everyone,' Jess. I told your bosses. They need to know. So did the other Elgets too. Well not number sixteen, the last one. He was such an idiot." She glanced at the new Ascend Elget. "Sorry, but he was a complete imbecile. You've got a lot more work on your plate because of him."

"No, no, I've been getting that feeling. No apology needed." Desi held out his arm awkwardly in an effort to offer a handshake. I am Desimidor, although you can call me Desi. I am Ascend Elget number seventeen, reporting for duty." Sarah readjusted his wrist, grabbed his hand, shook it twice, and released it.

"I'm Sarah, Descend's Demon Keeper. Nice to meet you. That's how you do an Earth handshake, but trust me, neither of you will have to do too much of that here. You can shake hands with staff if you want to, but we keep it pretty casual around here with each other. With humans, though, it's not casual."

Desi inhaled a deep breath. "Ah, humans. Yes. I haven't really met any humans yet. Granted, I've only just arrived, but still, maybe I should pop on down-"

"No!" Sarah and Jess yelled at the same time.

"There will absolutely be no 'popping' anywhere." Jess said. "Haven't you read the books I assigned to you?"

Desi looked at the floor like a scolded child. Nephemerus stared straight up at the ceiling, the perfect co-conspirator.

"Oh great. Neither of you read any of them? I can't blame you, they're rough to get through." Sarah said, collapsing into a leather chair at the head of the conference table just off the computer operations room. The others followed suit and found seats around the table.

"Well, it's hard to know where to start," Desi admitted. "In one religion, the first book said one thing, then the second book in the same series was completely different, but both were supposedly written by the same author? How can that be true? One religion says a single being created an entire universe in only six days, yet the same books outlining this achievement have tens of thousands of editorial changes from one edition to the next? No one questions this?" He raised his eyebrows quizzically.

"Oh," Sarah laughed. "You did read some of it."

"It was all the contradictions that got me." Nephemerus groaned. He slyly pulled out a digital story card out of his back pocket and tossed it on the conference table. "It didn't even matter which religion it was. None of them made sense. Does anyone really buy any of this?"

Jess added, "They buy it, and they love it. Can't get enough. These are their favorite bedtime stories. They laugh, they cry—"

"They kill over it," Nephemerus interjected.

"They definitely do that," Jess admitted. "But you both need to know that a lot of humans arrive in Descend believing these stories are real. If you see them wandering around, you can talk to them, but don't act like anyone from their books. If you do, it'll be pandemonium."

"Got it, don't encourage their fantasy role-play. Not a problem." Desi said, rolling his light green eyes. He had short, curly auburn hair that whirled around his head, looking almost cherubic. Sarah mused that they both resembled the human's ideology for one particular religion a bit too well. She let her mind wander to their mirreáges, wondering if their outward appearances were influenced by their job assignments here.

She snapped herself back to the conversation. "You two are just here for the typical Elget oversight, deal with any administration issues, send your reports back to the Council, and if the need arises, relocate the surviving animals. According to our prediction models, at least 97% of the animal species will survive when humans self-eradicate, so that's something...yay."

A slight pause and then everyone slowly joined in with a meek, "Yay."

"Don't worry," Jess said. "It won't be armageddon, all the time. I'm sure some of it will be fun, some drinks by the pool before the end of days."

Sarah stood up. "So this might not be the very best time to announce this, but since you mentioned fun and drinks by the pool, I should let you all know that I am officially leaving for a vacation."

CHAPTER
SIX

"Can she even do that?" Desi asked, pacing and breathing erratically. "I mean, can she just leave? Doesn't she have to stay here?"

Jess was staring out the window of Ascend Operations Tower towards the mountains in the distance. The computer analyst had never left the campus since she arrived on Earth. No one had ever entertained the possibility of Sarah leaving Earth and her Demons behind for any reason, business or personal.

"She isn't a prisoner here. She is free to leave. I suppose she is phenomenally overdue for a vacation, although soon, she won't have the humans to worry about anymore." Jess turned back and looked at the Elget. "It was Sarah who requisitioned me from Gigla. She pre-dates my arrival to Earth by several millennia."

"When did you get here?" Desi asked.

Jess accessed her data, "I was put into service 113,614 years, 298 days, and approximately 38 minutes ago. Upon my arrival, the humans had reached self-awareness. They needed sorting for Ascension and Re-training in accordance with the Multi-Dimensional Galactic Counsels' directive for new species. No Elgets had yet arrived. Sarah had already located, transported, and contained all of Galloyde's creatures. She was working on creating what you see now." Jess gestured out the window, where Desi could view the Descend campus sprawling below, surrounded by lakes, fields, and mountains in the distance.

"Is she the only Demon Keeper? There must be others? What do we do? Can we make her stay? That sounds terrible. I don't want to say that but - "

"But you are scared, as you very well should be," Jess interrupted. "The Demon Keeper's responsibilities in Descend are essential to smooth operations. An Earth without a Demon Keeper is…hold for calculations. Human self-destruction increases by 9,824.87% without her direct oversight. Humanity will be in shambles before she reaches for her first drink by the pool."

Desi considered this, wondering if the humans self-destructing might not be such a bad thing. After all, why wait for the inevitable? Then he reconsidered, how would it look on his record if the planet imploded mere days after he arrived?

"Wait, who trained Sarah?" Desi's knuckles paled to white as he clasped his hands tightly together.

"He is no longer on this planet," Jess replied flatly, looking back out the window.

Desi stared at the android in disbelief. His eyes shifted from left to right as he searched for a new approach. "That's fine. We'll get him back here so Sarah can take her break. We all need time to recharge ourselves. That's perfectly understandable. We can ask him to perform her duties until she returns. Voilà, problem averted," Desi stated with a flourish, and sat back in his chair, clearly pleased with himself.

Jess watched the new Ascend Elget revel in his plan. She began calculations on the odds of his actions increasing the timeline on the human extinction event. She had too little data to determine if he would speed up the outcome.

"We cannot do that I'm afraid." She told Desi.

His face fell. "Why not? Is he on another assignment? I'm sure we can request a transfer based on this being a high priority."

Jess sighed. "I don't think so. The original Demon Keeper - the one who taught Sarah how to handle the creatures - was Galloyde."

CHAPTER
SEVEN

S arah squeezed the cube in her pocket, thinking of her plan. The first step was now complete. She had told them she was leaving. They didn't try to stop her, not that she would have listened to them if they had tried. She had to leave and it had to be now.

She was in the elevator with Nephemerus heading back down towards the Descend campus. He stared at her. He knew something was off, but he couldn't be sure exactly what it was.

"You can call me Neph by the way. No reason to be formal. Certainly no reason to call me those other Earth variations for the head of Descend. Just 'Neph' would be great."

Sarah glanced up at him, nodded and gave him a little smile, then stared at the elevator door.

"So, a vacation!" Neph continued, a bit too enthusiastically. "That'll be exciting. Any place special in mind?"

Sarah's fingers traced the sharp edges of the cube. She opened her mouth to answer just as the elevator landed. She was interrupted by the loud ding and the doors sliding apart.

Sarah quickly rattled off her answer as she stepped out. "Oh, you know, all the hotspots. I've been hearing so much about Galaador, so I'll probably head there for a bit, or take a tour around the Omega quadrant? Maybe go somewhere a bit more quiet. I probably will just visit family, who knows? So many possibilities." She was moving fast on her way outside the building, but Neph was just as quick and he easily stayed by her side.

"Right! Of course, of course. Well, we still need to talk about the details. How long will you be gone, what kind of transport will you require for travel, and is there anything else you think we should all…know?" He let that last part hang in the air.

They were outside on the pathway heading towards her office. Sarah did not respond to his probing. She was walking as fast as her legs would let her, trying to put this conversation - and Neph - behind her, but the Descend Elget was a foot taller and his long legs had no problem keeping pace with her.

"Oh, and before I forget. That cube." He said pointedly. "You were going to tell Desi and I something important about that cube. We all were distracted with your news."

Sarah stopped walking. She had been hoping he had forgotten about the cube. Why did Luis have to hand it to her right in front of him? She glanced back up at him and found Neph staring intently into her eyes. She felt herself shifting uncomfortably under his gaze.

He studied her carefully, and in a low voice said, "We'll discuss that cube tomorrow, when we go over the details of your hiatus."

She forced a smile. "Sure! Yeah, of course. Sounds great. Tomorrow." Her hand closed around the cube in her pocket once again, this time hard enough to cut into her skin.

CHAPTER
EIGHT

GilGerg ran haphazardly down the hallways, knocking over the trash cans. The smallest of all the Demons in Descend, he was approximately the size of an Irish Wolfhound with a similar type of mud-brown shaggy coat. The bulk of his body formed one massive lump perched atop five gangly legs. GilGerg seemed to lack eyes, ears and a mouth. There was no way to tell which end was which. He moved with absolute uncertainty, bounding forward with unabashed enthusiasm while his legs frantically attempted to catch-up but always failing, hence his constant crashing. Yet the staff loved GilGerg. When he was happy, which was almost all the time, a gentle thrumming sound emanated from the center of his body which felt hypnotic to those near him.

Luis would patiently upright each trash can after GilGerg knocked them down every single day. They were the best of friends, often spending hours together, traveling around the maze-like corridors of Descend. GilGerg loved to visit the ReTraining classrooms where he served as a type of mascot for the ReTrainees. Luis spent his days cleaning up the messes whenever lessons with the other Demons went poorly.

Professor Chronny was one of Descend's tenured ReTrainers, having been at his post for over 20,000 human years. His classes were often the most challenging because of the nature of the students he had. Professor Chronny taught only the high repetition ReTrainees. Most remembered him from their multiple returns to Descend and while most didn't like what he had to teach, they respected him enough to listen. After all, the punishment for not cooperating was a visit from one of the Demons. No one was interested in that, so they sat through the lectures whether they wanted to or not.

Yet on this day, the Professor had a particularly vocal group of ReTrainees in his class when Sarah appeared at his door. He clocked her presence right away. She would often stop by his classes to usher in Seglee, the Triplets or Bunny were needed to convince a student to behave. She hadn't been scheduled to come in today and a drop-in visit was highly unusual for her. She sat in the back row while Luis entered through the side entrance, pushing his cart of cleaning supplies, GilGerg faithfully wiggling at his side.

Professor Chronny's classes focused on moral and ethical choices humans faced by presenting real-life scenarios. Instead of debating the teachings of philosophers such as Hobbes, Locke, Hume, and Kant, the Professor believed that presenting realistic scenarios would train the humans to make better decisions in their next life.

Chronny had a full head of red and grey wiry hair, heavy-framed glasses and a penchant for houndstooth blazers, which gave him the physical likeness of many of the philosophers he struggled not to constantly quote. He often lost those battles and found himself blurting out sayings from Plato, Aristotle, Korsgaard or Mele to a sea of blank faces. But Professor Chronny excelled at turning the ancient words of wisdom into something the modern-day humans could find relatable.

There was a large screen set up at the front of an auditorium classroom. Eighteen ReTrainees sat scattered about the room watching the film that just started. The camera angle was from the point of view of the ReTrainee and designed to put them in the middle of a hypothetical situation.

In this scenario, they were in a grocery store line, getting ready to check out. They had a full cart of groceries. As they approached the check out line, they could see an elderly man having trouble walking and holding one loaf of bread with a can of soup. He was trying to get into the same lane as they were in, he was limping severely and appeared to be in great physical pain.

A message appeared on the screen with a choice. A) Let the man into the line before you or B) Make him go to the back of the line.

The ReTrainees looked down at their keypads and made their choices. The majority chose A. The scene showed the elderly man smile into the camera and hobble into the line in front of the ReTrainee's full grocery cart.

Luis watched from the side with a smile on his face. GilGerg was leaning against his side thrumming in bliss. The next scene continued as their cart was now unloaded, but the belt stopped moving. The elderly man was speaking with the cashier. He had forgotten his wallet. He explained to the clerk that he had taken the bus to the store and was by himself. The cost of his groceries was $4.65.

New choices appeared on the screen;

A) Pay for the man's groceries.

B) Do not pay for the man's groceries.

The ReTrainees voted. The overwhelming response was B.

Luis slumped forward and rubbed his forehead. GilGerg reached up and tried to nuzzle his face.

Professor Chronny asked the class why they chose to not help the elderly man. Several felt the old man had the money, but he was running a con game. Others believed that the man wasn't as old as he pretended, while two of the class thought he didn't even have a limp and he was faking it for sympathy. A smattering believed the man was old, and that he did forget his wallet, but that simply wasn't their problem.

Not one person in the class understood the concept of paying for the man's food as being the right or kind thing to do. Everyone in the class had lived over one hundred and fifty lives on Earth and each one struggled with this moral question.

"Could any one of you put yourselves in this man's shoes?" Professor Chronny asked. "Imagine working your whole life. You are old, you're tired, you need to eat. Every day is a struggle. Your back hurts, your legs hurt, your feet hurt," Chronny acted out each move for the ReTrainees. "You comb your hair. You get dressed, trying to find clean clothes to wear. You're so hungry. When you check your cabinets, you find you have nothing left to eat in the house. You only have a few dollars. You walk outside to the corner and catch a bus. You travel for who knows how long - maybe you don't even get a seat. Finally, you get to the store, find what you can afford, only to realize you forgot your wallet at home. Wouldn't you hope that a stranger would be kind enough to help you out for just a few dollars?"

"Hey man, he should have checked his pockets when he checked out those cabinets!" One ReTrainee shouted.

"He had the money for the bus, where did that come from, huh?"

"That's not my fault. Why do I have to pay for some old man? Look at all the food in my cart. What if I pay for him and then don't have enough money for all my food?

"Will some guy behind me pay for all my food too?"

A cacophony of increasingly selfish excuses to not help the man rose up in a chorus. Their voices built into a low roar, drowning out the Professor's words.

"This is why you will never Ascend!" A voice boomed from the rear of the class.

The class turned. Everyone stopped talking as soon as they saw who had spoken.

Sarah let out a long, withering sigh. She slowly stood up and walked to the front of the room. GilGerg shuddered and whimpered as she passed him. Luis pulled the tiny Demon close and whispered kind words into his brown fur to let him know he was safe.

She wore the same blank expression she'd shown the man who had lived 479 lives. She meant business. She picked out one unlucky person in the front row, hovered over them and whispered, "You will never Ascend."

She walked further along the row, pausing and staring at another ReTrainee, then stated again with authority, "You will never Ascend."

She reached the ReTrainee seated at the end of the row, who began to stutter as she approached. Sarah slammed the desk with her fist and shouted, "I did not give you permission to speak!" She scanned the room and among the cowering faces, she found one bold ReTrainee staring back at her defiantly, arms crossed. Sarah climbed up the three rows towards her and leaned over the desk, getting nose-to-nose with the defiant woman.

"What's your problem?" the ReTrainee spat out, as tough as she could manage.

An audible gasp was heard somewhere in the classroom. Luis grunted and stood up, grabbing his mop as Sarah's face lit up in sheer delight.

CHAPTER
NINE

Professor Chronny leaned against the counter in the break room, sipping his tea. "I didn't know GilGerg could do that."

Sarah was at the sink, washing her hands. She stopped to check the bottom of her shoes, just in case she hadn't made it out of the way in time.

"Oh yes, he certainly can. I hate to ask him to do that type of thing because he's so sweet, but at the same time, I think it's good for him to really stretch out those muscles once in a while."

Chronny continued to stare off into the distance. He was struggling to comprehend the horror he just witnessed in his classroom. He gave her an absentminded, "Yeah, stretch those muscles…"

The door to the break room opened and Luis walked in with GilGerg bounding into the room with unabashed joy. The Professor visibly stiffened as GilGerg headed straight towards him, both ends wiggling. The small demon missed and crashed straight into the wall, hitting the nearby trash can and knocking it over. GilGerg recovered, shook his wooly, matted coat, wiggled all over and headed straight towards the Professor again, who held out a cautious hand to pet him, as if this was the first time they had ever met.

Luis and Sarah sat down at one of the café tables, watching Chronny's interaction as Nexar entered the break room. The ReTrainer in charge of History, saw how Professor Chronny was gingerly petting GilGerg, as if he were made of glass. Nexar frowned and walked up to the fuzzy beast and gave him a hard whack on his side. The Professor let out a yelp as GilGerg launched himself towards Nexar and nuzzled against her, wiggling and thrumming. Professor Chronny's normally ruddy complexion was now pale and waxy.

"What's your problem?" She asked Chronny, who looked ready to vomit upon hearing the exact same words that set off the scene of utter chaos in his classroom just moments before. "You look like something crawled up your trousers and got into your bits." She watched him with her bright purple eyes as he squirmed to make his escape.

Chronny ignored her question. Sarah and Luis watched as he pressed himself against the walls of the break room and slid his way towards the door, his eyes never leaving the panting, woolen, matted beast. Just before the Professor could reach the door and could make a break for freedom, Sarah pushed a chair into his path and blocked his escape.

"Sit. Down." She said darkly. He took the chair and sat, still staring at GilGerg, who was now lying down flat in the center of the room, all five legs splayed out.

Nexar grabbed a sandwich from the fridge, a bag of chips from the basket on the counter and three candy bars from the bowl next to it. She suffered no fools. Nexar cut to the chase, every time. She didn't worry about your feelings and expected the same in return.

"Well, I'd love to stay because this looks like a lot of fun," she said, eyeing the clear ambush, "but I've got to be anywhere else." With that, she slipped out the door and let it slam shut behind her.

Professor Chronny watched in horror to see if the loud bang woke GilGerg. It did not. Sarah hooked her toe under the edge of Chronny's chair and despite him being twice her size, she easily pulled him forward to her table.

Luis faked a cough and started to get up in an effort to leave, but a quick glance from Sarah told him he wasn't going anywhere. He readjusted his position in his chair and sat back down, now wearing his pleasant smile.

"I'd like to talk about your class today," Sarah began. Chronny couldn't stop staring at GilGerg, who was now snoring. She snapped her fingers in front of his face to break his gaze.

"Hey" Sarah shouted. He blinked a few times and looked at her, as if waking up from a nap.

"I'm sorry, I just didn't know - I didn't know he could do that. It was so...unexpected." Chronny said in a daze.

Luis smiled like a proud father as he looked lovingly at the snoring Demon.

Sarah nodded. "I know. I'm sorry. That was unfair to do to you. I hadn't planned on having that demonstration today. Here's the thing, you have all the Hi-Reps with you. 150 through 225 right?"

Chronny thought for a second. "The highest we have on campus right now is a 224."

"Well, because you have all the Hi-Reps, you know that they remember Bunny and Tiny, Seglee, Clara, and the Triplets. No one thinks of GilGerg as anything but a cute, little mascot."

Chronny's eyebrows narrowed as he looked back at GilGerg, who was now chasing something in his dream, legs prancing in all different directions.

Sarah continued, "So today, when that ReTrainee got the balls to challenge me, I had GilGerg put the class into a rapid state of contemplation over their cumulative life decisions that keep leading them back to this campus." She laughed heartily. "Frankly, the idea only occurred to me when I ran into those two on my way to your class. I had wanted to see how the Hi-Reps were doing, if any of them seemed salvageable. You know how we're looking to revamp the program?"

Chronny leaned forward in his seat. "Yes, and you know that any Hi-Rep over 150 is absolutely not salvageable in my opinion. Not one person that high has passed any morality test in the past six thousand years. Not one single person! We're chasing our tail on this because we keep retraining the same rotten humans to send back over and over again."

Sarah held her hand up. "You are singing to the choir on this one, my friend. You don't have to make that argument with me, I'm with you. Anyways, we have two new Elgets to discuss this with and before I leave-"

"Wait. What? Leave? You can't leave!" The commotion caused GilGerg to raise one end of his body, wiggle all over, then lay back down.

"Relax. I'm not leaving for good. I'm just taking a break." She smiled at the Professor. "I'll be back before you know it."

"Vacation." Luis jumped in. "She needs a vacation. She's never taken one. Miss, I mean, Sarah, needs a vacation. She must go."

"Thanks Luis. I'll be gone for a short time, but before I go, I need to bring the two Elgets up to speed. Your Hi-Reps today confirmed what we have been thinking. Plus GilGerg here showed them they need to stay in line, no matter who is around, right little fella?"

GilGerg stood up and shook his wooly coat, then stretched from end to end. As Professor Chronny watched in horror for a second time that day, GilGerg's entire midsection opened from the bottom and revealed several rows of rotating razor sharp teeth. A guttural hiss escaped from a dark hole in the center of the teeth and a wave of nausea passed through Chronny. He felt like he could vomit and faint at the same time. GilGerg's body folded back over on itself again, turning back into his normal cute, playful lump of shaggy hair.

"How did you think he ate? All this time and you never wondered?" Sarah laughed. Chronny, who was no less traumatized after seeing this a second time, held his head in his hands and groaned.

Luis hugged his furry friend and whispered words of encouragement about how well GilGerg did with the class that day.

"Chronny? Hey, you did better than 99% of those who first witness GilGerg do that. That's why Luis was there ready to clean up. Go hydrate and rest. Listen, don't hold any of this against GilGerg either. I mean it, he's sensitive. I don't normally ask him to do this type of work because he doesn't like it. It's not in his nature, but he needs to build up his confidence. Plus, you know every shit head in that class deserved it. A little vomit and pee on themselves after the generations of misery they've imposed on others is a small price to pay."

"Yeah, yeah, you're right. I'm sorry. I'm just so used to seeing Bunny or Seglee or the others do that type of thing. Not GilGerg. That was just so—"

"Unexpected." Sarah interjected with a smile.

"Unexpected." Chronny agreed, his color still pale, but slowly beginning to return.

"It had to be that way. Sorry. Won't happen again." Sarah stood and started to head towards the door.

"Hey, when are you leaving for this vacation?"

She paused, reaching into her pocket and feeling the cube. The stakes were impossibly high; everything depended on her plan going perfectly - and nothing ever went perfectly. If she failed, every soul that has ever lived, and every soul yet to come, would cease to exist. Nothing mattered more.

"Soon. Really soon." She said through clenched teeth.

CHAPTER

TEN

S arah cut across the courtyard that led into the west woods
and towards the old stone classroom building that was now
only partially visible from Middle Operations. This building
was originally used for Demon encounters before they expanded the
current campus. New buildings and designs were needed to handle
the increasing number of souls returning to Descend. The original
Demon interrogation rooms had been so difficult to keep clean,
given all the unpleasant substances excreted from the humans.
Polished concrete holding rooms had become the practical solution.

Sarah had been planning on using the old stone classrooms for
additional housing, but the Council was currently denying any
budget requests for renovations based on the pending 'End of Days,'
outlook.

Sarah walked around to the back of the building to followed a thin
path leading towards an old fieldstone well. The well was mostly
covered with ivy and weeds and a decaying wooden lid to prevent
anyone from falling in. She pushed the cover off to the side and she
sat on edge of the well, swung her legs inside and without hesitation,
pushed off the edge and fell straight down into the darkness.

Inside, she landed with a hard thud. These underground caverns were a forgotten part of Descend for most who lived above on the campus. Sarah knew these tunnels well as did her all of her Demons. She picked up a torch that was hanging nearby and dragged it against the rock. The flint in the tip rained sparks down and lit the oil in holder below. The resulting blue flame gave Sarah a warm glow in the gloomy tunnel. As she made her way along, admiring the beautiful scroll work carved into the walls, she noticed the long, dragging claw marks in a few crumbled portions of the tunnel. Thousands of years were taking their toll and she wondered how much longer these passageways could survive.

She walked for several minutes, turning back and forth through the tunnels as if she walked them every day. The blue flame from her torch remained bright and unwavering. Finally, she arrived at her destination, a round wooden door at the end of the tunnel. It blended in with the darkness and was difficult to see. Easy to miss if you didn't know exactly what you were looking for, as it was designed.

She pulled open the door and stepped into the chamber just beyond. The room looked like it belonged in a 19th-century mansion. A beautiful brick fireplace was the main focal point of the room. Carved wooden moldings with 40-foot high ceilings were among the high end finishes that were notable in this comfortable space. A long, blue paisley couch stood in the center, appointed with ornate pillows. A few armchairs and vintage tables filled out the room. Books were piled high in stacks throughout the comfortable space. The room felt lived in, now and in the past.

The high, arching plaster walls held intricate etchings carved into every visible bit of open space. The glyphs began down in each corner of the room and stretched across each wall, reaching as high as she could see. With each symbol curving and falling into the next, the effect was mesmerizing. Up close, Sarah marveled at the detail. The grooves had a sheen to them and at the right angle, appeared to glitter in the light. She set her torch down in the center of the room to illuminate her workspace as she took off her jacket.

Grabbing her notebook out of her bag, she picked up where she last left off, trying to decipher the message.

She was writing furiously when she felt the hairs raise on the back of her neck. She started to turn, but it was too late. Before she had time to react, she was hanging upside down by her ankles.

"RAAAWWRR!" The snarl was accompanied by a blast of hot breath against her skin. Sarah found herself high in the air, face to face with a panting, snarling Demon.

"Oh no, don't hurt me." She responded in a monotone voice.

"I've got you!" The Demon growled and roared a second time menacingly.

"You so sure about that?" she gestured downward. They both saw a thin rope on the ground glowing bright green around the Demon's feet. Sarah whistled sharply and the rope rose upward and bound the Demon tightly around the knees. He yelled out as he started to lose his balance. Sarah whistled again and the rope fell loose to the ground.

Tiny set Sarah down gently. She looked at him with a huge smile. "That was the best you could do?"

Tiny gave her a good natured laugh as he stepped out of the rope. "A Whistle Rope hidden under the dust? Nicely done."

Sarah found her water bottle and took a sip before turning back to the wall, gesturing to the newest etchings. "You've been busy."

Tiny's eyes climbed up and down over the scrollwork as if he was just seeing it for the first time. "I wake up every morning standing here with more questions than answers. No matter how hard I try, I cannot make sense of this."

Sarah grabbed Tiny's massive arm and gave him a reassuring squeeze. "You know that's not true. You picked up the first clues. I wouldn't have any idea of what it meant if it wasn't for you. Oh! I have something to show you."

Tiny watched as Sarah reached into her pocket and held her hand in front of him. She opened her fingers and showed him the cube.

"How many?" he asked quietly. The cube was as black as he's ever seen.

"Four hundred and seventy nine." She waited for a moment before looking at his expression and repeating. "Tiny, four hundred and seventy nine!"

Excited, Tiny asked to see the cube. He studied the obsidian mass as he walked over to the wall and held it up next to a symbol on the wall. Countless hash marks surrounding a cube was prominently carved into the vast scroll work. He looked back at her in wonder and said, "This is it. This could do it."

Sarah's smile faded. "I know... I know, but— the Descend Elget saw it. Luis gave it to me right in front of him, and he saw it. Now I have to tell him.

Tiny sat down on a pile of cushions that he had pushed up against the wall. His mind racing through all the calculations, just as Sarah had been doing ever since Nephemerus saw the cube. What if she got a cube from a different Hi-Rep and swapped them out? What if she ran away before telling them about it? Finally Tiny looked at her and nodded. "You have to tell them, there is no other option."

Sarah flopped down onto the cushions next to her Demon, laid her head against his massive bicep, and nestled against him. Tiny curled his arm around her, cradling her protectively.

"I know." She groaned and took the cube back from Tiny. "I have to tell them the truth. I just hope they'll listen."

The giant Demon hummed his agreement, giving her a reassuring squeeze. He also knew the weight of their plan and what it meant if they failed, or if someone tried to stop them.

CHAPTER
ELEVEN

Among the numerous stories the humans covet regarding life after death, the common theme emerges that "Heaven" is located high above in the sky and "Hell" is buried deep within the core of the Earth.

In reality, the campus for Descend included the ReTraining classrooms, bunks, cafeterias, staff quarters, and surrounding buildings exist on a parallel plane to the living humans, shielded by multiple portals.

At any one time, nearly half a million human souls are active in the afterlife, either preparing to enter Descend, participating in ReTraining, or returning for another chance at life on Earth.

The Ascend campus bordered Descend, consisting mainly of one tall tower and a few open grass fields. The fifty-story tower housed the Operations Center at the top, where the current Ascend Elget works with their team. That team includes Jess, the computer analyst who monitors the flow of the humans, along with any anomalies that arise on Earth. She was assisted by Aramik, who worked in research, kept Earth's records up to date for the Council, and supported the Elgets in their transitions, as well as obtaining interplanetary supplies and information. The rest of the Tower was dedicated entirely to the Ascend Elget's personal housing. Since no humans ever stayed in Ascend, no additional housing was needed.

Situated between the Ascend and Descend campuses stood Middle Operations. This small, two-story building sat neatly in the center of the courtyard and was designed for Elgets who refused to cross into each other's territories. Not every team assigned to Earth got along with one another, and when they didn't, they typically remained immersed in their own assigned campus. Middle Operations existed so meetings needing both Elgets could be conducted in neutral territory.

Middle Operations also worked for practical applications such as when crisis events took place, which required the attention of both Elgets to monitor the situation and determine what, if any, assistance might be given. Intervention from the Elgets or the Muldigal Council on primitive planets was highly unusual, but dual oversight was part of the promised services that Quadrant Representatives insisted upon when negotiating on behalf of the primitive species.

Neph found his way to Middle Operations. He was greeted in the lobby by an android far less lifelike than Jess, who directed him to the Conference Room on the second floor. He jogged up the flight of stairs in the open lobby and found the room easily.

As he walked in, Neph saw Desi seated next to Jess at a large round table. Also at the table was Sarah, who was seated next to a sharply dressed woman with an air of inherent confidence. Her dark complexion made her purple eyes almost glow and added to her mysterious allure. Neph helped himself to a glass of water and a pastry from the banquet table before he found a comfortable seat.

Sarah noted Neph's arrival. "Ahh, good timing. We just got here. Nexar, I'd like you to meet the Lord of the Underworld."

"Nephemerus or Neph is fine. Just not Lucifer, the Devil, Lord of the Underworld, and definitely never Satan. She says those things to be a wiseass." Neph reached over to shake Nexar's hand. "Nice to meet you."

"Nice to meet you too," Nexar grinned. "And I'm glad you already know she's a wiseass; that will shorten your learning curve here."

Desi announced in a deep, booming voice, "You may call me Brahma, Ukko, Oh Mighty God, Krishna, Śakra, Muhammed, Jah, King of Kings, The Redeemer, Yahweh, or Elohim." He winked and shook Nexar's hand, in the manner he learned the day before.

"That's it? You don't want to keep going? Hit all 18,000 named gods?" Sarah asked dryly. "Or you could add the names of all of the 33 million Hindu gods. Actually, they are still naming a bunch more, so there's a few hundred million more gods you could add to your collection."

Jess looked at Desi, pleased. "Someone finally read all of their assignment, I see!"

"Oh yes, I read 83 different religious tomes last night." Desi responded in his normal voice, nodding towards Neph, who rolled his eyes.

"Yeah, I'm not going to call you any of those names." Nexar laughed. "How about Desimidor or Desi?"

Desi acted like he was pondering this when Sarah interjected. "I have some ideas of what you can call him-"

"Desi will be fine." He answered quickly.

Sarah continued, "Let's get started. Obviously we can't cover every single thing before I leave, but I need to get you both up to speed on the basics so that you're good for a bit."

Jess leaned in towards Sarah, her fingers tapping below the table. "Yes, and I need to know how long is that going to be?" Tap-Tap-Tap.

Sarah evaded the question. "I won't be gone long, but part of my vacation will be picking up a part that I think will help you stop the tapping caused by your gravitational inverter, which is fried. You also need a computational processor. Those were designed to last about 100,000 years, so they're way overdue for an upgrade. A lot of your parts are shot. Sorry sister, you need a major make-over.

Jess rolled her eyes and stared down at the conference table, running her own internal calculations on the lifespan of her parts.

Tap-Tap-Tap

"Alright. To start this off, I asked Nexar from the Dalubar system to discuss pertinent Earth history with both of you. She comes from a long line of Harivaskers, so she is far more qualified than I am to cover any historical references. Desi, I believe you spent some time in Dalubrai?"

"Ooooh yes I have! I'd love to discuss your thoughts on the ruins of the...OOW" Desi grabbed his shin with a pained expression blooming across his face.

"Sorry, was that you? I thought it was the table." Neph grinned. "My foot must have slipped." He struggled not to laugh. He was used to distracting Desi in the past and wasn't interested in a long list of inconsequential questions today.

Nexar took over and thanked Sarah for the introduction as the Demon Keeper made her way over to the banquet table. She nibbled on a few snacks as she watched the Elgets, who both surreptitiously watched her, while listening to Nexar.

CHAPTER
TWELVE

O nce Nexar wrapped up, Sarah took over and dismissed
the history teacher with her thanks. "I think you know
the basic outline of our post-life system here from your
intro packages, but I'll go over it again so it's clear. Stop me if you
have questions. As you just learned, humans had finally evolved to a
point where they reached a level of self-awareness, so now we
needed to address their afterlife component. When the first two
Elgets arrived, we quickly realized that we couldn't allow everyone
to Ascend.

"We had to figure out how to separate those who were ready to
move into Higher Consciousness and what to do with those who
needed more time to ehh…evolve. That's when we decided to create
Descend. This way, one Elget would oversee one division and the
other Elget would oversee the other."

"The Elgets decided this or the Council?" Neph asked.

"Great question. That was Qeraa and Liro, they were first two
Elgets here on Earth. The decision came from them."

"Interesting," Neph glanced at Jess, who was still tapping, but had
moved her hand onto her leg so the sound was muted.

Sarah continued, "Our thinking was that when a human performed sub-optimally during their life, they would arrive at Descend and receive counseling. They would be ReTrained and given another chance to repeat life on Earth. They would be faced with a similar challenge that they faltered with before. Of course they wouldn't be consciously aware of it, but with better training, tools, and support, they would be prepared to overcome their prior deficiency."

"Buddhism?" Neph offered.

"Oh, look at you. Someone has been doing their reading!"Sarah said. "Close, but not quite. Life wasn't meant to be constant suffering. Although some do seem to go out their way to suffer, which is super weird, but no, we don't recommend it. You read eighty-three different versions of those books, do any of those sound like fun ways to live to you?"

Both Elgets shook their heads no.

"For whatever reason," Sarah shook her head, "some of these guys make the conscious choice to wake up in the morning and punch a kitten in the face, while others are late to work because they are helping turtles get across the street."

"Because humans are assholes." Jess piped up.

Sarah pointed to Jess. "Yeah, some of them are, but not all of them. Not in the beginning at least. Ok, let me back up. We started Re-Training the ones that didn't Ascend on their first attempt. We thought they would come through Descend one or two times and we'd give them a little help. Then 'voila,' they would understand the errors of their ways. They would slow down for the turtle, they would call their mothers, they would stop punching kittens in the face and they would finally Ascend."

Sarah pointed to a graph showing a circle on the display above the table which outlined the "Life Cycle of a Human in Descend."

Desi cleared his throat, then briefly touched his teeth, as if to check to see if they were still there. Neph watched his friend in amusement. "Excuse me Sarah," the Ascend Elget said, "but isn't this a departure from the Core Belief Values? There's nothing in the directive that states that a soul should be 'ReTrained' or counseled. A soul either Ascends or doesn't. The cycle is simply repeated until they figure it out themselves."

Sarah and Jess exchanged brief glances. "You're right," she agreed, leaning forward in her seat. "There is no mention of any intervention. But we found that when the flow to Ascend started to slow, and souls going through Descend increased, that if we provided some gentle guidance, we could decrease the number of repeated lives."

"Until you couldn't," Neph interjected.

"Until we couldn't."

"And now here we are, hundreds of thousands of years later and all of humanity is about to self-destruct." Desi said, standing up and walking over to the banquet table to grab a muffin. "So what happens to all these people who keep rotating through?"

Sarah reached into her pocket and pulled out the cube. She placed it on the table near Neph.

Desi came back to get a closer look, wiping his hand on his pants before picking up the cube. "What is it?" he asked.

"That is what happens to a soul who keeps rotating through."

Desi threw the cube down and Sarah quickly caught it before it fell off the table.

"Was that a human? All crushed up or something?" Desi asked, horrified.

Sarah and Jess stifled their laughter, while Sarah handed Jess the cube to inspect.

"No, that's not a human in the way you're thinking of one." Sarah explained. "We keep ReTraining these humans over and over and over again. They could go back fifty times, maybe even a hundred, sometimes more. Remember how in the beginning we had planned on only ReTraining them once or twice? Right now we have a system where people have returned hundreds of times - "

"And now you have an Earth filled with assholes," Neph quipped, before pausing and adding, "I like the idea of second chances though. For the ones who listen."

"Yeah, we get a sprinkling of decent people who Ascend, so we know our program can work. It's worked for nearly 67.4% of the total human population so far, but that's still a far cry from the required 78.92% required for Species Ascension per the Council's regulation."

"But if they keep failing, they turn into this cube?" Desi asked. "How does that happen?"

Sarah took the cube back from Jess and placed it in the center of the table. "This person went through four hundred seventy-nine lifetimes." Sarah pushed the cube closer to the Elgets. "When someone fails that many times, we know with certainty that they will never, absolutely never, Ascend. We have studied this, we have tracked this. This was a mistake, he should not have been allowed to go back to Earth that many times."

She picked the cube up and held it in her palm. "When we have someone this unredeemable, well, a Demon gets to..." She fought the urge to smile, thinking of how happy this made Bunny. Unable to restrain herself, she blurted out, "a Demon eats them."

"What?" Neph shouted. "I was told they only scare the living shit out of people. Quite literally the living shit, vomit, urine, whatever. No one told me they actually eat people!"

Sarah rolled her eyes. "Oh come on. It's so rare that they get to do it."

"Get to do it? Get to do it? What if they just decide to do it all the time? What if they go on an eating rampage?" Neph looked around anxiously as if a Demon was going to pop out from under the conference room table.

Sarah stared down both Elgets before taking a long, steadying breath. She stood and walked towards them slowly, until she reached their seats.

She leaned down and quietly said, "My demons will not cube anyone unless I instruct them to. They are not mindless beasts. I assure you that they are not the most dangerous thing you will find in Descend - not by a long shot." She breathed into their ears. "They are quite intelligent, but I will ask you once and only once, to never - ever - judge their intellect based on their appearance. If you do, that mistake will surely be your last. Are we absolutely clear?"

Jess' incessant tapping had stopped. Both Elgets nodded silently.

"Good!" Sarah snapped back into an upbeat tone and returned to her chair. "Bunny ate this sad excuse for a human and had a grand time doing it. He pooped out this cube, which is the remains of the consciousness of a horrible, fucking miscreant that we wasted a millennium on trying to rehabilitate. This monster killed countless animals, raping and killing as many men, women and children as he could get his hands on. Getting eaten by Bunny was far too quick and far too good of an ending for him."

The depth of the depravity of the soul, now crushed into cube form, finally dawned upon the Elgets. They exchanged glances with each other and shifted in their seats, avoiding Sarah's gaze.

"When we get to the point of creating a cube, and to be fair, only a Demon who is willing to do so, can create a cube, we take it to be Re-Cycled. I'll have Jess explain that part."

THIRTEEN

J ess explained the transport of a cube to the Elgets, and pointed to a rendering of two solar systems which appeared on the displays above the table. "As you see here, once a cube is ready, we pick a planet which is still in their early stages of evolution. Enceladus, Saturn's moon, had been a great spot for us for quite a while. It is right in this solar system, still uninhabited. We have chucked so many cubes onto that mass for tens of thousands of years, it's going to be overflowing with humans one day!" She let out a hearty laugh and then composed herself.

"Alright, well, when humans started getting better eyes in the sky, we had to disguise our transports, as you both know from when you arrived. That reminds me, Sarah, how are you planning on traveling?" Jess looked to the Demon Keeper expectantly.

Sarah took a long swig of water. "A better question is how are we getting Aramik back early? We can't use our usual methods because the Aurora Borealis isn't scheduled until later. If he just flies back, he'll be seen by the humans. We need him here ASAP. Have you reached out to him?"

Jess said she had spoken to him, but hadn't arranged his travel yet.

"What about a solar flare?" Desi suggested. "He's currently in Lossinia, correct? He could approach from behind this sun and sneak in using a solar flare for cover. Judging from their level of technology, they still can't seem to properly map space in this quadrant yet, so I assume the humans would believe any emissions they see from that direction were from a solar flare?"

Sarah and Jess exchanged looks again. Sarah agreed, "Yes, that's excellent. Perfect actually."

Neph looked puzzled. "So let me get this straight. The cube is just jettisoned into another primal planet? That's it? Back to square one?"

"I suggested panspermia, but no one would listen." Jess pouted.

Sarah frowned at her. "Yep, randomly shooting their consciousness out into space in the hopes that they would just happen to come across a hospitable planet or asteroid wasn't the most responsible plan for their future development. I'd think the highly advanced Gigla droid would know better than that."

Jess responded by sticking her tongue out at Sarah.

Sarah turned to Neph. "The human DNA has to a near-exact match to life that would naturally develop on that planet without the presence of a cube. We wouldn't want to introduce something untoward into any planet's ecosystem, but yes, the cubes will have to start over at a single-cell level. It will take hundreds of thousands of years to evolve into a human again. During that time, their consciousness, being, or "soul," since you two just read your autobiographies last night, remains present. By the time their self-actualization occurs again, their poor decision-making that is currently ingrained in their thinking, will be eradicated."

"If it isn't, they won't evolve. They cannot genetically advance if they aren't both lucky and intelligent." Neph mused.

Desi considered this then turned to Neph, "Would you do something different if you designed this system?"

Neph took a moment and said thoughtfully. "I don't know. This system has been in place for hundreds of thousands of years. I'm not sure I would have a better idea. Perhaps more civilizations should utilize being eaten by a Demon and shat out."

They both laughed heartily at the thought.

"Told you Earth would be fun!" Neph grinned.

"So what of the oversight?" Desi asked. "Is it the same here as it was in Iitka? You said you were familiar with that assignment. Do humans have the same internal mechanism as other species or are we actually 'watching and judging them' like their books say? If so, how and why?"

"Ahh yes, well, no one is watching them all the time." Jess laughed. "That's called paranoia and no one has that kind of time or interest. Who would even want to know every single move each of these little primitives are making?"

Sarah poured a glass of juice from the banquet table when Jess finished speaking. "They possess a moral compass, like most others this early in their evolution. The trouble with the humans is that their moral compass is a bit fragile at best. It doesn't hold up for very long."

Desi looked to Neph, who returned his look of concern.

"What does that mean?" Neph. "Why is it so fragile? Does it have to do with the number of repetitions that they go through?"

Sarah returned to the table with a muffin and her juice. "Yes, that's exactly what it is. We're running into an issue where their compass seems to basically stop working after a certain point. We can have a human successfully Ascend at 90 repetitions, or lives, whichever you want to call it. They can even Ascend as high as...what?" She glanced at Jess. "130 reps right?"

"It's been awhile since we've seen that." Jess muttered.

"We really haven't seen anyone Ascend once they hit 150

repetitions. It's never happened actually." Sarah said as her face darkened.

"How many do you have in Descend that are over 150 repetitions currently?" Desi asked.

Sarah sucked in a sharp breath and looked to Jess. The droid checked her display and calculated. "Today we have 8,045,311,447 humans alive on the planet. 6,841,962,019 of those people are Descend repeats. Of those, 5,398,424,190 are currently over 150 repetitions.

"Fuck me." Neph groaned.

"So," Sarah exhaled slowly, "now it's easy to see why there's going to be a pretty quick implosion soon. I know most models predict the eradication at three thousand years but -"

"It won't take that long." Neph jumped up and grabbed himself a muffin. "These guys will tear themselves to pieces long before that."

Desi leaned in over the table and looked intently at Sarah. "Tell me about this compass. Why is it falling apart so easily? Do you know?"

Sarah rose out of her seat and started pacing by the window. "Humans have understood the concept of what is right and wrong well before they officially reached their self-actualization stage. They hit that hallmark the Council looks for in a species a long time ago. When faced with a moral dilemma, we know they possess the ability to decide to make the right choice or wrong choice."

She walked past Neph, who was now leaning up against the wall, listening intently.

"Initially the humans didn't have rules to dictate good behavior. They depended on straight-up, self-guided morality. 'Should I take this animal's life so I can eat and survive another day versus should I kill this animal for funsies?' Ideas like that never even occurred to them. They simply didn't do things like that. So at this point, their moral compasses were dialed in tight, and working the way they should."

Desi was getting excited and wiggled in his seat. "Yes! Yes, so initially they were balanced. They have an innate sense of right and wrong. How were you able to track that? Wait, I want to know that, but first, how did it break? Or did it break? Is it just a fault in humans? Or is that how they are built? Maybe they are just... immoral beasts?"

When Desi was finally done asking his dizzying array of questions, Neph pushed himself off the wall and slowly walked back to his seat. "I have a question to add to Desi's long list of inquiries." He gave Desi a sidewise glance filled with the fake annoyance that longtime friends share. "Is it even possible to fix their little broken ways?"

Jess let out a harsh laugh and Sarah gave her a weary look to which the android rolled her eyes in response.

"Jess tracks their moral compass readings, but she needs a system update as you can see." Sarah said as Jess began tapping again under the table. "We had to get a Gigla droid immediately once we realized that the human's internal guidance systems were based on a moral compass."

"Or should be," Jess added.

"Fair." Sarah continued. "The issue we found with the humans is they will ignore their own moral compass. All the time. At will. It's both fascinating and horrifying to witness."

Neph leaned in. "Wait a minute. What? Say that again?"

"Oh, you heard me. Humans will be faced with a decision, something clearly right or something clearly wrong. Black and white. No grey area, and let's be fair, life is mostly grey area, but for the purposes of this conversation, let's say the situation is black and white, clearly a right or wrong choice."

"Go on," Neph pressed, now sitting on the edge of his chair.

Sarah mirrored him on the other side of the table, leaning forward. "A human will chose the wrong thing, knowing it's wrong, feeling like it's wrong, aware of the fact the outcome will be bad. Knowing they will feel bad, but they'll choose to do it instead of doing the right thing."

"Why?" Desi cried out.

"Because humans are assholes!" Jess shouted.

"Because sometimes, or a lot of the time, it's just an easier choice," Sarah sighed. "Because they feel like they have to punish themselves, because they want to see what happens. Whatever it is, humans choose the wrong moral choice at an alarming rate. Even though it causes so many more complications in their lives, and so many more problems for others, they keep making those wrong choices and eventually land back here in Descend."

"That's insane," Desi remarked. "Absolutely insane."

Neph started to speak and Sarah held her hand up. "To answer the rest of your question, we have tried to figure out how to fix this, of course. It appears that humans equate this idea of 'free will' with making poor decisions and-"

"Free will?" Neph interrupted.

Desi groaned. "You really do have to read more of their books Nephemerus. I cannot do all the work."

Neph smiled, "You like reading the books Desi, I do other things you don't like. Remember the Pockula uprising? Who dealt with all of that? Who always deals with the wars and battles? Who always deals with the yelling and screaming and the crying -"

"Yes, yes, yes, very well," Desi relented. "Fine, someone came up with the concept that their gods gave humans this thing called 'free will.' So now the little primates can do anything they want and they will be forgiven for it. Clean slate. Free pass. They simply have to say they are sorry and repeat a few nonsensical phrases, and they are absolved to repeat whatever criminal immoralities suit their fancy."

Desi shifted his focus back to Sarah, "There's several issues with this, depending on which stories you choose to read, defining what free will truly means. It might come from a religious text, philosophical, theoretical-"

"Wait, just wait!" Neph interrupted. "So these guys believe they are free to do whatever they want? Free from all moral implications because these books say it's ok to do?"

Neph sat back in his chair, running his hands through his hair and then rubbed his face.

Desi nodded and smiled back at Neph, "Yes. That's free will."

"But the books are written by other humans! Why would they think any of it is real?" Neph shouted. He buried his face in his hands and offered a harsh laugh. Then he looked up and motioned to Sarah, "Sorry, you were saying?"

"So free will and their moral compass have been at odds ever since. They know the right thing to do. In their hearts and heads, they have an inner consciousness guiding them towards what is morally right. But then, somewhere from outside themselves, they started following an arbitrary set of rules created by other people instead of following their own compass."

"Because some genius told them they can just do whatever they want and they'll always be forgiven, no matter how heinous the act. That's how you sell books, people!" Jess added.

"Fuuuuuck," Neph groaned, rubbing his face, again.

Desi laid his forehead down in front of him. "I can't believe they don't listen to their own moral compass," he said, muffled by the table. Then he popped back up. "Hold on. Wait, how come some people still Ascend right away? I mean, not everyone is repeating, so there are still humans that have a working moral compass, correct?"

"Some people are just wound a bit tighter than others." Jess answered, blinking rapidly at Desi, the edges of her mouth turning up in a half smile.

"Oooo! The Droid's got jokes!" Neph shot back, laughing along.

Sarah joined in, "That's what you get when you get a Gigla. The best that money can buy, but she's not wrong. Some people still manage to follow their moral compass. When they do, they Ascend. Arms Others refuse to make the right moral and ethical decisions, so they end up here. Then round and round we go. Where we stop-
"

Jess interrupted the rest of what Sarah was saying by playing a video of the Earth exploding into oblivion on all the display monitors.

CHAPTER

FOURTEEN

They broke for a quick lunch to eat and digest what they had been discussing. Food was prepared by the Ascend Elgets' chef and brought to them. They nibbled and made small talk until Sarah stood up and signaled it was time to continue. She explained how Jess was in charge of tracking the humans as the droid pulled up complex graphs and data points on the monitor displays.

"We can flag unusually high activity from Ascend Operations anywhere on Earth," Jess started, "but we aren't tracking anyone move-for-move. Again, no one is watched or monitored for daily activities. We only pick up anomalies, such as if someone who has a 86.47% positive morality flow suddenly begins to regularly choose negative moral outcomes. That's when we notify Descend and the intervention teams are activated."

Sarah nodded. "Basically when a ReTrainee is going off-plan, we try to nudge them back in line. Hopefully it works before they end up back here."

Jess pulled up another display filled with long sets of numbers. "Here we can see the quadratic expositions to the relationships of outcomes for positive grey decisions versus negative grey decisions. Sorry, I know this is really rudimentary stuff, but you'll see this broken down for you in your operation reports. Got it?"

"Got it!" Neph answered quickly. Desi coughed hard while rolling his eyes. Neph sat back in his chair grinning, intentionally not looking at his co-worker.

Jess continued on. "What you two really need to understand is that the system is essentially self-governed."

Sarah cleared her throat and gave Jess a hard stare.

"Almost self-governed," Jess retracted. "Ideally, humans would follow their moral compass. When they die, electrical impulses from their compasses dictate their status of morality and lets me know if they Ascend or Descend, as you already know."

Desi grunted, "Yes, that one we actually do know." He cast a sideways gaze at Neph, who still had the same blissful grin plastered across his face.

"The trick-trick-tri-tr-tr-t-t-t-t-t."

WHAM. Sarah kicked Jess in the side of her thigh. The hit was hard enough to do what it needed, to jar her stutter loose.

Jess didn't acknowledge the kick, she simply continued speaking. "The trick with the humans is that their signal is initially quite strong, but once they reach over a few dozen repetitions, it becomes very weak."

Desi furrowed his brow. "Weak? The transmission? Does the data get corrupted? Is it hard to discern whether they are meant for Descend or Ascend?" He looked alarmed at his own question.

Sarah jumped forward. "No! No, not that. Never that. Trust me. It's more like…imagine a thin wire spring being pulled straight over and over again. At some point, that wire isn't going to snap back into a coil anymore. You know what I mean?"

Both Elgets nodded slowly.

"Right, so to answer your earlier question regarding their compasses - can they be fixed or are humans just immoral creatures? I think the answer is their moral compass is like a thin metal spring. When humans keep choosing to make the wrong moral decisions, they wear out that spring. This is the problem we've been facing for a very long time. We can't seem to tighten or fix the spring once they are past 150 reps, because they've made so many bad decisions. They have worn out their spring. They have broken their own moral compass."

CHAPTER

FIFTEEN

As the afternoon sun began to slip towards the horizon, everyone voted to take a break. Jess wanted to reach out to Aramik and coordinate plans for his immediate return. Sarah said she would take Desi and Neph for a walk through Descend to stretch their legs and continue their discussions.

They made their way down the elevator and out into the courtyard. Turning right, they moved onto the paved winding path, leading past a group of short buildings. Sarah explained that the number of repetitions a person had dictated where they lived within Descend.

They were walking through the low repetition, aka Lo-Rep area, located on the surface near the Middle Operations. Lo-Reps tended to be less confrontational and less likely to be problematic, she explained.

"The majority of our time with Lo-Reps is spent explaining what happened to them and how they move forward. Initially they are in a state of shock, once they understand they are just here for some helpful tips and not an eternity of torture, things go pretty smoothly."

Desi noticed an old man walking slowly on the pathway in front of them, stopping occasionally to glance back at the two Elgets and the Demon Keeper.

"How involved have the past Elgets been? Not working directly on Earth as I'm understanding, but here in Descend or Ascend? Have they been more hands-on with the people?"

Sarah thought for a moment. "Well, many humans come here expecting to see the different gods or devils reflected from whatever religion they invested their time and money into while they were on Earth. It's a primary directive from the Council's Core Belief Values to only teach the truth. When the humans Ascend, they naturally come to understand the nature of the cosmos, but for anyone still in Descend, they haven't reached that level of evolution yet. Forgive me for the easy pun, but I'm preaching to the choir on this one. You guys know this - encouraging a false belief system would only hinder their ability to Ascend."

Sarah walked a few minutes quietly before continuing. "In the past, the Ascend Elget usually just hung out in the Tower. They'll work on their apartment, sometimes pick up a hobby. Most of them have just keep to themselves. We did have one who liked to travel on Earth quite a bit. Undercover of course. She thought this little world was quaint. I think she mainly enjoyed hanging out with the baby animals."

"How about on my side of things?" Neph inquired. "Are the humans all scared of running into the King of Hell? Will they faint if they see me?"

"Well, none of them know who you are unless you tell them or start wearing insane costumes. Don't do that. I'm not kidding." She gave Neph a warning look as he lifted an eyebrow. "I mean it. They actually think you're going to start pulling off their limbs or eating their faces because you're the Devil."

Neph inhaled a long breath and looked towards the sky. "I really wish you would update your vernacular," he said wistfully.

She ignored him. "Let's remember that for a few of these belief systems, you two used to be besties. You only hate each other because you had a fight. So now one of you is stealing souls while the other is saving them."

"Aww," Neph put his hands on his chest and pouted. "Points for originality."

"Listen, these little barbarians still wholeheartedly believe that in a universe in which they have never traveled, where they don't even know they are stuck in a black hole, and are blissfully unaware of other dimensions," at this part, Sarah stifles a laugh, "that they are the only form of intelligent life that exists, in all of the cosmos."

They all looked at each other and exploded into gasping laughter, struggling to catch their breath. Desi had to sit on the grass to recover from a coughing fit that followed from laughing so hard.

When he was ready, Desi took a hand from Neph and was pulled to his feet. "Oh my, I think I pulled something. You have to warn me when you are going to say something like that, Sarah." He winked at her and adjusted his shirt.

Neph started back down the path. "What exactly are their offenses here? Will it be one big travesty like killing someone or a collection of smaller slights? How does that work?"

"Ahh yes," Sarah took the lead on the path, taking them towards the lake. "Well, it's never just one thing. Honestly, they could kill someone and still Ascend because of circumstances beyond their control. Maybe someone stepped in front of their car on a rainy night. They couldn't see them to stop in time. Their intent was never to kill someone. We know that and they know it. Their moral compass recognizes it was an accident, so that wouldn't stop a human from Ascending."

"How about him?" Neph pointed to the old man, who was now seated on a bench, watching them walk by. "What did he do?"

Sarah glanced at the man, then she closed her eyes for a moment while the Elgets watched. Her eyes flicked from left to right under her lids, as if reading something only she could see. When she opened them, she said, "He didn't do anything."

Both Elgets stopped walking and looked at the man, then back at Sarah.

"Well, hold on." Desi pointed to the man on the bench. "You mean to tell me, he's here and he didn't do anything to deserve to be here?"

Sarah cast a withered look at Desi. "No, that's not at all what I said. I said he didn't do anything. He absolutely deserves to be here. In fact, if he doesn't figure it out on his next life, he will be transitioned down into the Lower Platforms. No more of this!" She gestured to the trees and the lake.

"Wait. I don't get it. How could he do nothing yet end up here?" Neph asked.

Sarah led them both over to a bench, overlooking the water and far away from the old man. They all took a seat. "He didn't do anything like I said. He didn't do anything when he was 9 years old and the boys in his class picked on his little sister on the bus every single day after school. She would cry and beg for his help, but he made the choice not to help her.

"He didn't do anything when he was 14 years old and he saw a man rob his parents' corner deli. The man looked straight at him and then ran down the street with all their money. He knew the robber. When his parents asked who he saw, he didn't say anything. When the police asked him if he saw anyone, he stayed quiet, choosing not to help his parents get their money back.

"He didn't do anything when he was 17 years old and a girl asked him to go to the prom. She had been his closest friend. They would do their homework together and play records after school. She showed him how to dance, both fast and slow. One day when they were dancing, she asked him to take her to the prom. He didn't answer her. He just walked away and went into his room and closed the door. She went home crushed. She didn't get to go the prom that year or any year after that. She died in a car accident that same summer.

"He didn't do anything when he was 28 years old and was walking down the street when he saw one of his friends surrounded by a bunch of street thugs. One kid had his foot on his friend's chest while his friend was gasping for air. His friend looked right at him and begged for his help. He just walked away. He didn't try to help his friend, he didn't call for anyone else to help. He didn't do anything.

"He didn't do anything when he was 41 years old and saw a young boy attacked outside of his store, the very same store his parents used to own. The boy had been stabbed and was lying on the sidewalk, bleeding out and crying. He chose to pull down the shade and walk away. He didn't call an ambulance. He didn't go outside. He let that boy die, because he refused to do anything to help.

"He didn't do anything when he was 54 years old and had rented out the apartment above his store to a young family. He heard them fighting every night when the father would come home from work. He saw the bruises on the little girl's arms. He saw the cuts and black eyes on the wife's face. He saw her limping after those loud fights. He didn't call the police or social services. He didn't ask if they needed help. He didn't tell the husband to stop. He didn't do anything.

"When he was 77 years old, he was in a nursing home sitting in the corner of the recreation room when he felt dizzy. He felt a sharp pain shoot down his left arm. He struggled to breathe. Then he tried to call for help. He pressed the emergency button he carried around his neck. The young aide on duty was scrolling on his phone and heard the Call button alarm in the background, but he didn't do anything."

Sarah paused for a moment. "Those experiences I just shared with you were ones that he chose after forty-nine full lifetimes. For each new life, he was given specific training and counseling on principles, ethics and morality. He has not taken action once in any of his lives.

He has never stood up for what is right. He has never been courageous. He has never protected a loved one. He has never once...tried." She looked over her shoulder at the man on the bench. "We can do our best to explain what is right and why, but there are some humans who will never get it. If I had to wager, I would safely bet that he would not Ascend given a hundred more lifetimes."

Desi stood up exasperated. "Then why bother? Maybe this system doesn't work!"

Sarah nodded. "It works for some, just not everyone, but we do know it works for some."

CHAPTER
SIXTEEN

The three of them stood up to leave when they heard an odd bubbling sound coming from the lake. The audible gulping grew louder as the center of the lake sank downwards.

Neph pointed over to alert his companions, "What's going on over there?"

Before he could finish his question, a long, graceful winged creature burst out of the water. She flew straight up in the air about forty feet before coming down in a magnificent belly flop. Just as she landed, a high shrill scream of terror emanated from her stomach. She rolled sideways on top of the water, revealing deep blue and green scales on her stomach that glittered in the sun. She had the long legs of an osprey that she tucked under herself as she continued to barrel roll on top of the water.

When her belly was turned upwards towards the sun, her scales became translucent. The shrill screams were the loudest at that point. Finally, she stopped rolling, swam to the edge of the lake where Sarah was now standing with the two Elgets. The regal creature stepped out of the water and unceremoniously opened her crimson beak and let out a sharp squawk. Simultaneously, her blue and green tail feathers splayed open and a human dropped from her rectum onto the ground, covered in a clear, thick goo. The screaming stopped as the human fainted in the grass.

"Hello Seglee! Good of you to come visit. I'd like you to meet the new Elgets. This is Nephemerus." Seglee bowed her head deeply to the ground, showing great reverence. "And this is Desimidor." Seglee raised her head straight up and bobbled it, as if eating a fish, then did another bow.

Both Elgets stood in stunned silence for a moment, looking at each other and then back at Seglee with wide eyes. Sarah gave a short, harsh cough and they snapped out of their daze.

Neph nodded and stepped forward. "It is my absolute honor to meet you, Seglee. I very much look forward to working with you." Neph ended with his own deep bow.

Seglee gave him a beak shake in the air punctuated with a high squeal.

Desi stepped forward, one eye on Sarah at first who gave him a slight nod. "Seglee, it is my distinct honor to meet you. I hope to spend more time with you. I am at your service as well." He also finished his greeting with a formal bow.

Seglee squawked one more time, then nudged Sarah, who pushed her away. Seglee turned and in one smooth action, launched straight up into the air and then dove back into the water. She did not come back up again.

The human on the bank started coughing and spitting out goo. "What just happened to me?" he gasped, looking ragged.

Neph went over and yelled into the human's face, "A giant bird just shat you out because you're a fucking prick."

With that, he smiled and joined Desi and Sarah who were already walking back up the path. "I think I'm going to like this gig after all."

CHAPTER
SEVENTEEN

W here did she put it? It was the morning after her walk with the new Elgets and she was back in her office. Sarah was on the floor and pulling open the drawers to all her filing cabinets, looking for a small box that she was sure she tucked away somewhere in there. She wasn't sure if she would need to bring it with her, but better safe than sorry.

"Where is it?" she mumbled as she continued her search, now in the back of the closet. She pushed aside boxes that had lived there for decades. "I know you're in here somewhere."

"Ahem. Knock, knock," A voice said behind her.

Two boxes that were teetering precariously fell as Sarah tried to bend herself backwards to see who was at her door. She saw Neph leaning against the doorframe, taking in the chaos. "Taking a little bit of everything, I see?"

Sarah crawled her way out of the closet until she cleared the mess. "Oh, you know, just looking for vacation stuff."

"Uh huh…and you think you left your bathing suit in your office closet, do you?" He took notice of the strange variety of items she had piled in the chair next to the door.

She quickly tossed a coat over the pile. "Well, I don't own a bathing suit, so it's safe to say it's not back there."

"Are you going on a vacation Sarah, or somewhere else? Is there something perhaps I should know about? " Neph pressed, leaning against her desk now, his dark eyes intently locked on hers.

Sarah looked at him and took a beat, but did not give him an answer. He was not expecting one. He continued, "I need to speak with you about something, and I fear my opportunity with you is running short. Could we speak today? It's important."

Neph was staring at her in a way that Sarah had never experienced before. He was summing her up, assessing her.

"Absolutely. We do need to talk. I have to tell you something important as well. I just need to do something first. Then, I promise that you and I will have the rest of the day to talk. Does that work for you?"

She knew he didn't believe her, but there was also something else that she couldn't quite put her finger on. She could feel her face flushing. It was part of her job to make others feel uncomfortable, not the other way around.

"Fair enough," he said coldly. "Do what you need to do, but then we talk. No distractions. This must happen today."

She agreed. "No distractions. I'll see you shortly."

CHAPTER
EIGHTEEN

L uis was cheerfully enjoying his lunch in the Lower Platforms with GilGerg begging for his scraps. He would toss the fuzzy Demon a tiny bite onto the floor and GilGerg would straddle the food and a giant tongue would dip out from underneath his belly and snap up the morsel. Each time, Luis would cheer and tell GilGerg what a smart boy he was.

Sarah found them performing their daily ritual in the break room and waited until they were done. She watched quietly from afar.

When Luis had arrived at Descend for ReTraining, Nexar asked Sarah to review his record. This was a rare request, but when Nexar first met Luis, she believed he was inappropriately assigned. Sarah assured Nexar that those types of mistakes simply did not happen, but she granted the favor. When she read Luis' record, she had to agree. It appeared he was misplaced in Descend when he clearly should have Ascended.

The Multi-Dimensional Galactic Counsel is similar to many corporate entities with endless protocols for everything you could imagine, including misplacement. Sarah had Jess perform a confirmation check on the electrical pulse from Luis' moral compass when he arrived. Nexar was correct, Luis had been assigned incorrectly. His moral and ethical record was spotless, there was no doubt that he should have been assigned to Ascend.

It should have ended there. That is what should have happened. That is not what happened.

The 16th Elget, an idiot by all measures, had just began his assignment on Earth. Sarah brought the matter to his attention and he stated if the system assigned Luis to Descend, then he must stay in Descend until he earned his Ascension.

Sarah, Jess and Nexar used various methods to explain to the 16th Elget that even though the system is accurate within a trillionth of a percentile, at this point in human history, a pico miscalculation resulted in a singular incorrect assignment. Fortunately, they had caught it. Luis had a clean record and the Muldigal Council protocol said he should be sent immediately to the correct destination based on the review of his record.

The Ascend Elget disagreed and ruled Luis had to stay in Descend until such time he Ascended on his own.

Sarah had wanted to appeal this decision to the Descend Elget, but he had spent time with the Ascend Elget during training and again during the travel time to Earth and hated him. Upon his arrival on Earth, Descend Elget immediately put himself into hyper-sleep with the strict instructions not to wake him unless they wanted total and complete Armageddon. He didn't care for the planet Earth and would have no compunction in destroying it himself.

So Sarah kept Luis in Descend. She sat him down and explained the entire situation to him. She offered to send him back to Earth immediately, have him Re-Called immediately after his birth, where he would automatically Ascend. He asked her if he could think about it. She agreed and told him to take as long as he would like.

That was 12,314 years ago. He has since remained by her side as her friend, confidant, and trusted advisor since that day. During that time, he appointed himself in whatever capacity he felt was needed, but mostly, he preferred to travel the halls with his cart of cleaning supplies and pick things up. He liked when everything was tidy.

Sarah constantly told him he didn't need to do any of that, but he said it kept him busy and he enjoyed keeping watch on everything that happened within Descend.

Over time, Sarah had taught him almost everything she knew about each of her charges and all their eccentricities. He was kind and respectful to them and they to him in return. She couldn't make Luis an official Demon Keeper. He was only a human after all, but she knew they would listen to him while she was away.

Luis caught sight of Sarah watching them outside the break room. He tossed the last bit of food to the floor and told GilGerg he would be right back. He made his way out over to her, his smile fading when he saw her face.

"What is it mija?" he asked in a soft voice. Sarah motioned him to follow as she walked around the corner to a quiet spot.

Her eyes were shining and her voice started to waver. "I'm going to be leaving soon Luis, and I…I've never left them." Hot tears started to flow down her cheeks.

Luis pulled her into his chest as she tried to catch her breath. The harder she fought to stop crying, the faster the tears came and soon, she was sobbing against his shoulder.

He patted her back and told her they would all be okay.

"You have to keep checking on them to make sure they're ok, like every day," She said between choking sobs. "You have to make Bunny rest if see him starting to get a goopy nose, not his normal gooey nose." She wiped her eyes against his shoulder. "Make him eat carrots too. He won't want to, but he has to if his nose gunk runs green."

"Shhh, shhh, it's ok, I know, I know mija." Luis said into her ear.

"And be sure to let Clara scare all the little kids, you know how much she loves that. And - and feed Seglee cattails if she ends up swallowing a vegan."

Luis pulled out a clean handkerchief and wiped her face. "They will be ok. I will take good care of them for you."

Sarah sniffed hard and pulled back a nose full of snot. Her eyes welled up once more. "I just have never left them. Not once, not even for a day. I promised I wouldn't ever leave them alone with those monsters and now…and now -"

She collapsed to the ground, gasping. "I can't do it! Luis, let all the stupid humans die. It's their own fault anyways, no matter how hard we try. They are all so horrible, they deserve it. I don't care. I don't. I just don't care."

Luis sat down on the ground next to Sarah. He put his arm around her shoulders and let her sob.

Finally, when she was done, she wiped her face clean with his handkerchief, and stood up. She then pulled him up to his feet and gave him a hug.

She unclasped the leather holster that held her dagger around her thigh and handed it to him. He paused for a moment, taking in the beauty of the golden weapon. A large green jewel adorned the handle. The dagger itself was about 15 inches long. Luis didn't dare pull it from the leather sheath. He knew of the dagger's power and he feared it.

He took the blade from Sarah and nodded. She kissed him on the cheek and walked away without saying another word.

CHAPTER
NINETEEN

A blue glow of light shone from the chamber entrance. Tiny must be here early, she thought. As Sarah entered the room from the tunnel, she stopped dead in her tracks. Standing in the middle of the chamber room, staring right at her was Nephemerus.

"Four hundred and seventy-nine," he said gravely. "I'd like to know exactly what is going on here. The truth, Sarah."

Sarah was shocked to see him standing in the middle of the chamber room. No Elget had ever entered this space. She willed her body to move forward towards his. "I don't think you'll believe me, Neph, but please, give me a chance to explain. I had every intention in telling both you and Desi about all of this when we talked later today."

Neph stared at her without expression, giving her no indication of whether he believed her or not. He could read her, and she was telling the truth. Still, he remained steadfast, letting her unravel the mystery before him.

"There's so much to say. Although, right now I'm pretty sure you if you found this place, you might already know some of it. I only know one way to tell it, and that's from the very beginning. This will take a while," she said, moving over to a long couch in the center of the room. She sat on one end and Neph sat down on the other end, waiting.

"Galloyde of Terevia was born a talented young mage with dreams of becoming so much more. Before he came of age, he had already exceeded the capabilities of most fully trained Elgets. We know eventually those powers of unknown origin grew and what he eventually became was legendary."

"An Overseer?" Neph asked.

Sarah smiled. "Certainly sounds like it, but I don't think anyone knew that at the time. He was sent to Ala Mia to officially train and be inducted as an Elget. There he was personally taken under the wing of the Grand Precipice, Algetia, who was your own teacher. Algetia recognized immense power in young Galloyde. He invested countless hours personally training his young charge."

Neph raised an eyebrow. "I heard Galloyde was pretty good before he went mad. I never found out what set him off though."

She took a long look at the etchings before continuing. "The Grand Precipice trusted Galloyde with the most sacred texts of the Elgets. He believed the young mage would one day succeed him. Over the years of training together, Algetia came to love Galloyde like a son, but the Grand Precipice was not a young man, and as you know, he holds one of the highest political positions within the Council. His position granted him many benefits, including a wife. In this case, a very young wife. Olethia was the product of an arranged marriage."

"Oh shit," Nephemerus grumbled.

"Oh shit is right. Algetia was not terribly interested in Olethia, as he believed she was not intellectually fit to meet his needs. She was not at all interested in him, for too many reasons to name."

Neph scoffed. "That's putting it kindly."

"I don't think I need to lay the groundwork for you to know what happens next. As much as Galloyde loved working with Algetia, his heart belonged to Olethia. From the first moment they saw each other, it was-" She paused, looking for the right words.

"Love? True love?" Neph offered with a hint of condescension.

"It was more than love. It was something far more binding. They were pulled into each other, they couldn't function apart. I don't know what to call it, but the closest word I have is love." Sarah paused and bit at her lower lip, lost in thought. "Olethia couldn't leave the Grand Precipice legally, so she and Galloyde gave up everything they had to run off together. They tried to start a life as far away as they could get from Ala Mia. They knew it would mean a lifetime of living in the shadows but, well…I'm sure you've heard the rest of that story."

Neph nodded. "Of course I have, who hasn't? They were found, the Council sent Galloyde to Earth as a punishment. He went mad and created a race of monsters. He was guilty of breaking natural law and rightfully banished. But all of this began because he ran off with the Precipice's wife? That's a bit dramatic, isn't it?"

Sarah nodded in agreement. "I hear you. I don't think it makes sense. I'm just telling you what I was told…by Galloyde."

"Wait, hold on. You knew him? Mad Galloyde? You've actually seen him? Talked with him?"

Sarah pursed her lips into a thin smile. "You could say that. When Galloyde came to Earth a little over 700,000 years ago, the humans weren't exactly the most exciting company to keep, because let's remember, he's an Overseer. At some point along the way, he discovered that he either could see the whole future or at least glimpses of it, like all Overseers can do, right? Finally, life on Earth advances to a point where he - "

"He interfered!" Neph huffed, "That's against the rules, everyone knows that!"

"You're getting upset," she said softly. "I'm simply relaying to you what happened." He took a breath and apologized.

Sarah continued. "We do know that at some point he tampered with a species. You've seen it for yourself in Descend. An Athecierian vessel came here around 150,000 years ago. They saw Galloyde with Tiny, Seglee, and maybe some of the others."

"Athecierians were here? On Earth?" Neph was alarmed. "What were Athecierians doing way out here?"

Sarah was taken aback by his reaction. "They came to fight. They dropped bombs and tore up the planet. They were looking for something. Apparently, they found it because they left soon after they arrived, but not before killing a lot of the primitive humans as well.

The 'Angels,' she laughed mirthlessly. "That's what the surviving humans called them. They started drawing pictures of the Athecierians with their long feathered wings, bloodless skin, and jyras on rock walls, in the dirt, and in their little caves. Over the years, the humans seemed to forget about the part where the Atheciery were brutal murderers as they retold these stories to one another. Over time, these images got stuck in their collective consciousness, but the actual truth of what happened didn't survive from generation to generation."

Neph started pacing. "Hold on! Just hold on. You're telling me an Athecierian War Ship came all the way out here, looking for something and then just left? There's no way that would happen. Absolutely no possible way. If they came all the way out here, they would have destroyed this entire planet. They wouldn't let anyone survive - that's how they operate."

Sarah paused. "I don't know about the ship or their intent. I do know they ran to the Council and said that Galloyde had created monsters on Earth. Then suddenly, Galloyde was gone. Not like, oh 'they sent a transport-ship' type of gone. I mean, he was gone - like that." She snapped her fingers for emphasis.

Neph thought about this. "Where do you think they sent him?"

"Where? I have no idea where he went. It had to be somewhere that he isn't able to escape from, he can't just come back from wherever it is on his own." Sarah looked up at the etchings and coughed. She grabbed her water bottle and took a sip.

"Right before he disappeared, he told me there were more Demons spread out all over the planet. It took me almost 500 years to locate them all and get them back here. When I was done, the Council decided to send the first Elgets here and as you just learned, that's how this system started. Flash forward to now, and we have our world filled with assholes."

Neph looked up at the etchings. "So what does a black cube containing an evil soul and that etching with four hundred and seventy-nine separate hash marks around it have to do with the destruction of this human race?"

"You counted? How did you get up that high?"

Now it was his turn to be coy. "You have your secrets, and so do I. Tell me what the cube really does."

Sarah looked around the room for Tiny - he should be here for all of this. "About 2 years ago, Tiny began to carve these etchings. At first, we thought they were just fancy doodles, but then some of them repeated. We finally realized it was a code, more than that. It's a message."

"Who's Tiny?" Neph asked.

"Oh." Sarah let out a little chuckle. "Oh yeah, you haven't met Tiny yet. He supposed to be here right now. He's one of my- well, he's a Demon, but he's different, very different than the others."

"So you think Galloyde is communicating messages through a Demon?"

"What do you know of Overseers?" Sarah asked. "Aside from the myths and legends. Factual knowledge, what do you actually know?"

"What do I know for certain? I know they can move objects of almost any size with their minds. They can see the actions from the past, present and future, some can do it completely; others in bits and pieces - hence the name 'Overseer.' They can read minds, even better than most Elgets can," he gave her a sly smile. "I've heard some other things too, but for facts, I guess that's about all I've heard consistently enough to say it must be real. I have never met one myself, so I cannot say any of it for certain."

"That's a fair assessment. Do you think communicating across dimensions would be possible for an Overseer? Through a being that an Overseer created? Perhaps with the intention to communicate through him all along?"

Neph considered this. "That is a lot to consider without any proof."

She gestured towards the walls. "There's your proof."

Just then, Tiny stepped out of the tunnel and into the dim blue glow of the lantern. Neph was speechless at the sight of the Demon, mouth agape. When he recovered, he quickly stood at attention to greet the Demon. Sarah noted that his stance was reminiscent of a military salute.

"Greetings. I am Nephemerus os Clorria. It is my honor to meet you." He bowed deeply, as he had for Seglee. Tiny approached and gave Sarah a rueful glance. She tilted her head in acceptance towards Neph.

"It is an honor to meet you as well. I am Thrinythidor, but you may call me Tiny. I must apologize, I was listening to both of you without announcing myself." Tiny responded. "This-" he gestured widely to the room, "has been quite a journey for Sarah and me. Naturally, we have concerns about sharing it with someone new. Please forgive our hesitation."

Neph nodded and took a long moment before speaking. He looked like he wanted to ask several things, but finally landed on one. "How do you know with certainty it has been Galloyde communicating with you and not someone else?"

Sarah looked to Tiny, who answered.

"At first, we didn't know for sure until here." He pointed at the far left wall down towards the bottom corner. There was an etching of a figure reaching up towards the sky, standing next to multiple figures that did not match each other. "This is Galloyde, there is no doubt in my mind."

Sarah nodded. "You can tell by the constellations above it. This is definitely Earth and Galloyde. These are the demons next to him. This figure repeats throughout. That's him, that's Galloyde."

"Ok. So what does the rest say?" Neph asked.

"That part took us much longer. Essentially all of this is a location map and instructions on how to reach him. This tells us where he is and how we can travel through the Galactic Ripple to reach him."

"The Galactic Ripple? You think he's in a Galactic Ripple?" Neph said incredulously. "You think they really exist?"

Tiny and Sarah exchanged glances. "We know they do," Sarah said, reaching into her pocket. "That's why we needed this." She held the cube out in the palm of her hand.

"479." Neph narrowed his eyes. "That is going to get you through the Ripple? How?"

"Yes, how exactly is using someone's consciousness going to rip open the fabric of space? Could you please explain that to me?"

Everyone turned to see Desimidor standing at the door to the tunnel, holding a torch and looking quite angry.

CHAPTER
TWENTY

After being introduced to Tiny and getting caught up to the point when he entered the chamber, Desi leaned back in the dark green armchair and prepared himself to hear the rest of the story. Tiny was seated on the floor in front of the couch, propped up by the cushions he pulled over from the pile in the corner. Sarah and Neph remained on the couch.

Desi stared at each of them, trying to decide if this was an elaborate hazing ritual or not. The look on Neph's face told him what he needed to know.

"So you believe that Galloyde has been communicating with Tiny and you're positive it is him? Second question, why would he want to come back here?" Desi inquired.

"We have no doubt that it's Galloyde behind these etchings. We do have doubts about how the transmission is coming through. Is he communicating through Tiny via a sort of inter-dimensional telepathy? Are others hearing it? If so, has Galloyde already been rescued? And..." Tiny and Sarah exchanged glances before she said, "Worst-case scenario, what if it's a dimensional echo?"

"A what?" Desi asked.

Tiny explained. "A dimensional echo is where a powerful transmission is sent out blindly through a dimension. It may trickle out through a black hole or during the implosion of a star or any major cosmic event that can pass through a dimensional wave. If that's the case, any signal transmitted through may be delayed anywhere from milliseconds to well over a gigayear.

Neph sighed. "He may already be long gone from this location, and there's no way to know for sure."

Both Tiny and Sarah quietly nodded.

"You haven't answered the 'why' portion of my question" Desi pressed.

Sarah leveled her eyes at him. "You come from a long lineage of Elgets, which is extraordinarily rare. Elgets hardly ever come from the same planet more than once. Seven have come from your family alone. Add to that, your maternal line has both Firvian and Clorrian blood lines. The Firvian bloodline is brilliant in their cunning, while possessing a strong, universal altruism. The Clorrians also joined your ancestral line and no species is better equipped with inherent strategy and deduction. An excellent combination for an Elget I should say."

"Natch" Neph cried and sat back amused.

A smile stretched across Desi's lips. "I see you have done your due diligence."

"I have," Sarah responded. "That is why I petitioned the Council for the two of you to be assigned here right now. I arranged for this nearly 20,000 years ago."

This revelation shocked both Elgets who did not see this coming.

She continued. "Your assignment on Iitka was a trial run for Earth. You exceeded my expectations."

Neph rose to his feet and exclaimed. "Hah! Well now, this is getting interesting!" He patted Tiny on the back and said, "I can't wait to hear what is next."

"Why would the Council grant your request?" Desi inquired. "Not to be reductive, but in the larger scheme of things, you are-"

"They owed me," Sarah responded coldly. "This was what I chose in return." She brushed the memory off and continued in her normal tone. "So, with your backgrounds and extensive understanding of strategy, history, connections, experience in primitive cultures, and political awareness of the Council, you tell me why Galloyde has been communicating with Tiny, why he needs to return to Earth, and what this cube is for, because if you cannot, all of this has all been a mistake and you two are the wrong choice."

Desi gave Neph a concerned look, before they stood and began to study the etchings in earnest. They pointed out the different symbols, moving slowly, consumed by their discussion.

Tiny pulled Sarah aside. "We may have risked too much by telling them any of this," he whispered.

"No," she disagreed. "Neph found this chamber. He counted the dashes around the cube you etched into the wall. Did you know there were literally 479 hash marks? I don't know how we missed that. No, no, they're the right ones for this, I'm sure of it." The Elgets moved back into the center of the room and gestured for Sarah and Tiny to join them.

Neph began first. "The desire that humans have to use stories of outside forces to explain what they cannot yet understand is not uncommon in primitive species. This is the very foundation of our assignments as representatives to the Muldigal Council. What is uncommon is you, Tiny. You are not what we encounter on our assignments. You are an immensely intelligent being, capable of grasping the complexities of the multi-dimensional galaxies, and extricating the most difficult theorems, without any prior eduction in the subject. That is extraordinary."

Tiny nodded and bowed his head with humility.

Neph continued. "The Council had informed both of us, along with the rest of the Galaxies, that Galloyde took it upon himself to create you, Bunny, Seglee, and the others," he glanced at Desi as he said the next part slowly, "that we are incorrectly calling 'Demons.'"

Tiny's head snapped up and looked at Neph in surprise.

"This is wholly incorrect. Neither Desi nor myself see any of you possessing the attributes that are associated with the human definition of a 'Demon.' I'm rather surprised that this moniker has remained, but as you can tell, I'm not a fan of incorrect or outdated titles." He slyly winked at Sarah, who gave him a faint smile.

Desi jumped in. "As far as we can ascertain, there was only one creature, whom you called 'Kevin,' who had questionable Demon-like qualities. He was banished from Earth, am I correct?"

Sarah nodded in agreement.

Neph sat down facing Tiny. "The next part is going to be difficult. We- well, the entirety of the cosmos have been led to believe that Galloyde was banished from Earth for breaking natural law, the one absolute rule we all must abide, which is to never tamper with the evolution of a species. The Council didn't bother to come to Earth to investigate the allegations against Galloyde. They simply took the word of an Athecierian who reported that 'creatures' were roaming the planet. They blindly believed that Galloyde went mad, but Tiny, you are not the creature that Galloyde was banished for creating."

"It was something you said, Sarah." Desi broke in. "When you were cautioning us against judging your...what should we call your charges?"

It was Tiny who answered now. "Regulators." His deep voice said with unwavering confidence.

Desi nodded, "Your Regulators. You said something along the lines, 'they are not the most dangerous thing in Descend." At the time we had assumed you meant, well, yourself. You can be quite, ehh-"

"Scary. You're fucking scary sometimes." Neph offered with a huge smile.

"Thank you, I try," she demurred.

Desi pressed on, "We don't believe that Galloyde was banished for creating the Regulators. We believe he was actually banished for the humans. He tampered with their evolution. We were all led to believe that he created this arcane race of, apologies," he nodded to Tiny, "'monsters' while in fact he did. Just of another variety."

Tiny's eyes flooded with tears. They flowed down his face as he grinned. They knew. They understood.

Sarah rose and started pacing. "Ok, you've done good so far. Galloyde did interrupt and change the evolution of man - well, part of it." She drew in the dust on the ground, making a large circle with several branches coming out of it.

"He tinkered with one small line of their genus, not all of them. Just as you observed, Neph, it takes luck and intelligence to propagate, to thrive, to evolve. The outcome seems to be that those who would have naturally been weeded out through evolutionary means have now made it across the finish line."

"And could ultimately Ascend. And we can't have that." Neph added.

"And we definitely cannot have that." Desi grunted. "So the Council banishes Galloyde, but not before bringing you in to learn everything you can to oversee the Demons...I mean Regulators. Which is fascinating to me. Why didn't the Council just destroy this little planet? They could have had an asteroid or virus eliminate the problem, but they made you clean up their mess."

Sarah nodded. "The Regulators were self-aware and now an established species. 'No matter the origin, population, creed, or locale, the Council will protect each as their own throughout the known Multi-Dimensional Galaxies without prejudice.'"

Both Desi and Neph chimed in to finish this well-known Muldigal proclamation.

Neph narrowed his eyes. "Is that why they owed you? For taking his place here? Taking over indefinitely with the Regulators?"

Sarah evaded the question with a shrug of her shoulders. "Something like that. It's just important you two are here now."

"Ahh yes, because now the humans are going to self-destruct." Desi mused. "You think that if you can bring Galloyde back, he can stop it? That's a pretty big bet."

Tiny looked at Sarah and grinned. "You win."

The Elgets looked questioningly at her, and she explained, "Tiny bet you wouldn't be able to figure it out without us explaining it to you. I bet you could and oh man," she laughed hard. "I really bet on you, you have no idea. Now let's go eat before we talk any more. I'm starving!"

TWENTY-ONE

"Ahhh, the Demon Keeper graces our humble abode tonight! We shall give her a feast so she joins us more often than what? Once a decade?" Frath beamed as Sarah walked onto the patio and asked if he had room to accommodate their party.

He laughed at her question and sat them at the outdoor patio under a canopy of wisteria vines. The long wooden table was surrounded by comfortable wicker chairs and a long stone bench, which easily held Tiny's considerable frame. Torches and candles added to the cozy ambiance in the private space. A screen door from the patio led inside the small cottage restaurant, where there were another dozen tables for the Descend support staff who often came here to eat and drink. This was one of the few places that served as a social gathering spot for those who dedicated themselves to the human afterlife, but were not originally from this planet.

As soon as they were seated, Frath stroked the long red braids of his beard and looked at Sarah thoughtfully. "Pasta, wine, fish." He looked to Tiny and grinned, "Snails, picked fresh today my friend." Then he turned his gaze to the Elgets, seated comfortably around the large table.

"Frath, I'm sure you haven't had a chance to meet-" Sarah began to say.

"Nephemerus, I've a lamb chop waiting for you that will make you cry for your homeland." Frath interrupted, with a twinkle in his eye.

"Don't you get around quickly?" Desi looked at his friend, eyebrow arched.

Neph chuckled. "While I was waiting for you to arrive, I found this little place and Frath has been very kind to me. I originally wandered in, thinking it might be my office or something, based on how they name things around here." He pointed to the sign, "The Devil's Cup," which hung on the side of the building. Neph narrowed his eyes at Sarah, who pretended not to notice.

Frath examined Desi. "Let's see, the new Ascend Elget. Firvian Volle would be ideal for you, but alas, not a delicacy we have available on this planet, unfortunately. I think I can whip you up something you will like though. Please, relax and talk. Wine will be out shortly."

Frath reappeared with mountains of food almost immediately. Cases of wine were stacked by the table, and Tiny pulled the tops off the crates with no effort. Bottles passed down the table and talk began innocently, starting first with Desi's home planet, then Neph's first assignment as an Elget, and eventually turning back to business.

"I have to admit Sarah, my suspicions peaked when you said you might vacation on Galaador," Neph said, enjoying his second glass of wine. "You don't strike me as a Ryhol-Mist dancing fiend."

Sarah took a long sip of her wine before answering. "I had just been given the cube from Bunny, so I was riding high. I couldn't even think straight. We had been hoping to get a Hi-Rep around 250, but I never dreamed of getting one as high as 479. This miscreant was apparently hacking our system. Each time he came through Descend, he swapped out his assignment card with a Mid-Rep. I can't believe it."

"You can't believe someone didn't use the honor system? In Descend?" Desi raised an eyebrow.

"Shut it, Firvian." Sarah quipped. Tiny let out an uproariously loud bout of laughter.

"Diabolical," Neph smirked. "What happened to the person he swapped with? What about them?"

Sarah pursed her lips together. "Not a thing. We don't check assignment cards after they're here. Basically those cards are just so they know where to bunk."

"Wouldn't they be treated more harshly though? If you really thought someone was at 400 or more Repetitions?" Desi asked.

"That's the problem," Sarah said. "479 did it so many times, we didn't even know we had someone racking up reps that high. Sure, we have outliers that are high, but nowhere close to that number. People are cubed once we know they aren't salvageable and that's long before they reach 300 reps. This guy was operating in the shadows, outside of our system."

"Hang on, so someone could just trade assignment cards and you wouldn't know where they belong at all?" Desi let his fork slip back into his bowl of chana masala.

"That is not what we are saying." Tiny answered. "When the humans are ready to return to Earth, their levels are confirmed. We discovered that 479 would physically pull the plug out of the terminal when he needed to be confirmed. Then he would present his assignment card as a back-up for confirmation. This worked every time. The staff wrote down the number of the repetition on the card for when the system was back up and sent 479 on his way back to Earth."

"Seems like the system isn't as finely tuned as it could be." Neph noted, pouring himself and the table another round.

"Well Mastema," Sarah said to Neph, "you're here now. Your predecessors didn't really pitch in and help too much. They just laid about, so feel free to work on a new operational tracking system while I'm off saving mankind. That would be grand. Thanks!" She toasted him with an obnoxious wide-eyed smile and drained the full glass of wine he just poured for her.

Neph smirked back at her and immediately refilled her empty glass. "Mastema? Really? Fascinating choice. I might have to do just that."

"Let us all remember when the person he traded with died again, they came back in their correct levels, or they Ascended." Tiny added, opening up a new case of wine that Frath brought to the table.

Neph took a moment to savor his lamb chops. "Yes, tell me more about this. You can get Hi-Reps to Ascend? This really works?"

Sarah's mouth was full and she looked to Tiny to answer.

"It isn't one clean life if you've accumulated multiple lifetimes of failures," Tiny explained. "Think of it as a chit system, like a voucher. In Life 1, you go through, you do some good things, you do some bad things. If the total sum is good, you Ascend. Now good and bad is subjective, but we usually can boil it down to basic morality. Don't kill. Don't cheat your fellow human. Treat others kindly. Be of service to others, things like that."

"There is also intent, as we discussed before. If you do something accidentally or had something forced upon you by the downstream actions of another, that's not counted against you," Sarah added.

The Elgets nodded and continued to drink their wine and nibble at their plates of food.

"A major good deed could be outweighed by a lifetime of small, almost seemingly inconsequential slights. For example, let's say you are a surrogate. You volunteer to carry a baby for someone. That's a huge chit. If you died shortly after completing that deed - boom! You would most likely go straight into Ascend.

"Ehhh, but let's say you live another 50 years, and during that time, you volunteer at the library, you have your own kids, you raise them without fear or violence. Give them a roof over their heads and food every day. You make cookies for their team bake sales, you do all these things. Sounds good right?"

Neph shook his head knowingly. "Ahh ha hah, there's definitely a catch here."

Tiny grinned back at him. "She never holds a door for someone, she speaks poorly about every person she meets behind their back. She poisons wild animals that cross her lawn. She won't talk to her neighbors. She refuses to help her significant other do any tasks outside their home, but expects him to do chores with her inside. She picks who her children can play with and she won't allow them to have pets. See the pattern?"

"She's selfish, narcissistic, petty, and doesn't understand or care about her place in the larger scheme of the universes." Desi sighed, looking down to his plate.

Sarah continued, "So that human would gather about 50,000 chits. She would not Ascend despite her great sacrifice early on. She would go to Re-Training, where she learns what mistakes she made and why they weren't in the best interest of humanity.

"Now, here's the thing, in Re-Training, humans typically understand the lesson, they recognize the problem, and admit to it. They have to or they won't be given another chance to redeem themselves. So, back to Earth she goes!"

She poured everyone another round of wine. "So let's say our lady starts her next life, minus 50,000 chits. Buried in her mind, she knows she has to work on being more giving, on being kinder to others, being more tolerant - don't be an asshole - all of that.

"If she continues to struggle, we get alerted through Jess, who monitors her moral compass. We have our department on Earth reach out to nudge her back on track through a variety of ways. We can put people on the ground for seemingly innocuous interactions. Plant little reminders in her mind, create coincidences or "synchronicities," as the humans like to call them.

"Now that the little barbarians finally have rudimentary technology, we can place ads, television shows, movies - whatever we need - right in front of them to push them in the right direction. They get clues all the time, really, if they bothered to pay attention.

"If all that somehow fails, we will do a dream intrusion."

"Whoa," Desi said, swaying just slightly. "That sounds exciting."

Tiny stood up from the table and proceeded to sit down onto the cool stone floor, carrying three bottles of wine with him. He lifted one to his mouth and drank the entire bottle in one gulp, leaning against the wall of the restaurant. He had a pleasant smile on his face.

"They have to be pretty far off course for a dream intrusion, that's a lot of work." He grabbed another bottle, popped the cork with the tip of his thumb claw, and drank the whole thing in one swig.

Sarah reached for her wine, then reconsidered and picked up her water. "So now they have to reconcile two full lives, but remember, they have already been counseled with Re-Training. Somewhere in their little minds, deep down, they know what they are supposed to work on, plus you know- maybe follow your fucking moral compass?" She hiccuped, and Neph laughed at her. She shot him a look, but he ignored her and raised his own glass to drink.

"They're getting help from us," Sarah continued after the hiccups eased a bit. "They're nudged in the right direction if they veer off course, so they just need to try. If they can pass a few challenges related to their weaknesses, then they accrue chits like crazy."

"And then, with enough chits, they'll Ascend?" Desi asked, watching Neph clean the rest of his plate and then look for more food off of Desi's.

"Correctamundo!" Tiny shouted from the floor. The Regulator had pulled several more bottles of wine down under the table with him.

Sarah laughed, "Kinda, yeah. It's a combination of their moral compass which ultimately tells us if they are ready to Ascend, and the accumulation of chits. You can have no chits and still fail on your moral compass, which is all you. Remember, no one else is judging you. At the end of the day, you know if you are doing the right things or not," she poked at her heart, "in here."

"Unless you don't have a heart, like 479." Neph quipped, as he took another long pull from his wine glass.

"Let's pick another example." Sarah continued, waving Neph away. "We placed one of our own people on Earth to guide a young man on his 34th Repetition. We wanted to give him a solid foundation and see if we could get him to Ascend if we pulled out all the stops. This was a controlled experiment to see if, when we throw every advantage we have at a subject, could we change the results? Our insider played his "Mom," and she was on the ground with him, teaching him to be kind to others, telling him to always consider other people's struggles, reminding him to be empathetic - all the things which prevented him from Ascending in the past. This way he wasn't relying on lessons we taught him while he was here - they were being reinforced with him every day during his living experience."

"Every day!" Tiny seconded. Another cork pop was heard from below the table.

"The young man gets a job at a clothing store when he's about 22. This sweet, kindhearted girl from one of his college classes had come into the shop to see him one day. She would walk by pretty often, too shy to stop in. She liked him a lot and he knew it, but he wasn't interested in her. Well, one day she finally worked up the nerve to go in and strike up a conversation with him. He doesn't say anything mean or unkind to her. He's actually quite nice - smiling and laughing, even charming, I would say. They have a fun, easy chat as she looks around the store. She's feeling so good about their conversation, she even picks out this cute little dress to try on, hoping in the back of her mind that he would ask her out so she would have a reason to wear it."

Sarah paused and picked up a bottle of wine, drinking directly from it now, not bothering with her glass.

"This girl goes into one of the fitting rooms and tries the dress on. They're still chatting away, but she's taking a long time in the room. He asks her if she needs anything. She does - she needs a bigger size - but she's too embarrassed and doesn't want to say anything to him. She wants to go get the right size herself, but he keeps insisting he'll get whatever she needs. Finally, she relents, thinking that he sees her for who she is, not a number on a tag."

"Oh no," Neph whispered.

"Oh no is right. Our boy goes to get the dress for her, except he deliberately gives her a smaller size, then puts a tag on it that says the size she asked for. The poor girl gets stuck trying to put it on and she can't come out of the stall. She's absolutely mortified." Sarah finishes quietly. "The memory of that day haunted her for the rest of her life."

"That coward. That absolute piece of -" Neph slammed down his glass and ended his sentence with a growl.

"Couldn't you just ReCall him right then?" Desi slurred. "I would smite him! That's what he needed. There should be more smiting. Humans. Guhh. Hateful beasts." He poured the last of the wine from the bottle closest to him.

Tiny lifted himself up onto one elbow so he could see everyone over the table. "He was placed with our people right at his side. We constantly reinforced what moral lessons he needed to face. We gave him the biggest advantage we could on that life. Bringing him back to Descend early wouldn't have helped. He collected his share of chits for that little stunt. Plenty, as I remember."

"Ultimately, he took 96 repetitions to finally Ascend," Sarah continued." He could have made it on that 34th repetition. He should have made it then. I asked him about the store incident when he died, I think he was about 74 years old then. You know what he said? 'I knew it was wrong, but I thought it would be funny so I just did it.'"

Sarah pushed her wine bottle back towards the center of the table. "I think that's where you see the clearest difference between the humans that evolved naturally without Galloyde's interference and these modified ones."

"Do you...do you think Galloyde can...can fix 'em?" Desi hiccuped his way through his question, but no laughter came from Neph, who was busy shuffling more bottles of wine to Tiny under the table.

Sarah rested her head on the cool table. "I really hope so."

"Hey, so does everyone go back? Do they all get another crack at it?" Neph asked.

Tiny shouted. "Not the ones we cube!" This caused a hearty round of laughter. "We try to counsel as many as possible, so they can eventually Ascend," Tiny continued, "That's our goal. They have to understand why they have failed and express real regret for their actions before being given the opportunity to return."

Sarah jumped in, "Some lie, of course. I mean, that's how they got here in the first place. They'll lie, say they completely understand, thinking we buy their bullshit. They want a free ticket back to Earth so they can continue their reign of chaos because, for a few of them, they like it. They don't want to change."

"What? So what happens to them?" Neph leaned in, intrigued.

"We bring in a Regulator to help remedy their thought patterns. Depending on what their malfunction is, determines which Regulator we use. The other day, you saw Seglee bringing a particularly stubborn fellow for a ride." Sarah pointed out. "He was a Hi-Rep, around 168 repetitions, I believe? At this point, every time he returns to Earth, he does the exact same thing. He invents something that he remembers seeing in Descend and makes a boatload of money. Then he lives like a fucking king until he ends up right back here."

Sarah leaned back, putting her feet up on the table.

"He acquires chits like he's plucking fucking daisies in a field. He doesn't give a fuckity-fuck-fuck about hoarding his money, sticking it to the poor, murdering others to get ahead, price-gouging medications, or anything else he needs to do to sit on his pile of gold. So this time when he showed up, we gave him to Seglee. She swallowed him whole, where he sat in her belly looking out so where he can see exactly where he is, deafened by her wings so he can't even hear himself screaming. Then he gets knocked around when they go underwater. She flips him all around and then she evacuates him before he pukes." Then we do it again and again, and we'll keep doing it until we think he might change his perspective. Nothing else has worked on him. If he doesn't change soon, he'll get cubed."

Neph pounded the table. "I think it's fucking brilliant. I love it! I want to go scare a terrible human for being like that shitbag from the store! Where is he?"

"Yes, count me in too!" Desi added his own fist pounding, albeit much more delicately than his co-Elgets display. "I'm down to have him meet his maker! Or at least who he thinks is his maker - I can pull it off with the right robes, I think." Then he laid his head back and stared at the tiny white lights that lined the wisteria overhead.

Sarah could feel the wine getting to her and the overall relief that she had two Elgets on her side. She might have a chance of getting this plan of hers off the ground.

"Too late, he Ascended, remember? But you are The King of the Underworld, so go ahead and be your bad self. Go scare some Hi-Reps. Want to bring Tiny? He's a great wingman for that type of thing."

Tiny was lying on his back against the cool stone tiles, surrounded by sixty-two opened wine bottles. He gave a thumbs-up. Neph cheered and helped pull the two-ton, inebriated Regulator to his feet.

Sarah looked over at Desi who was already out cold in his chair. She left *The Devil's Cup* and stumbled back to her place, finally looking forward to the next day.

CHAPTER
TWENTY-TWO

G alloyde stared into the coal-black sky as he had done for countless centuries.

He had seen the entirety of planets forming, life beginning and becoming part of the vast universes, and sometimes, the same planets dying. He had witnessed the birth of stars, their explosive deaths, and their equally surprising return to life once again.

Galloyde had seen galaxies shift throughout the cosmos - incredible species - terrible races, black holes, wormholes, dimensional folds, and even lived upon the Galactic Ripple itself, a phenomenon most did not believe existed.

He had seen much in his long years.

Alas, he had missed even more. Olethia flooded his mind. She was always waiting in the shadows for the rare moments when he let down his guard. His love for her remained strong, but the anguish he still felt from her absence was so painful that it made remembering her a torture rather than a comfort.

He saw her as she used to be, in Algetia's house, sneaking down the stairs as he worked alongside his mentor. She would bring them a hot drink or a small bite to eat. The Grand Precipice never pausing to notice, but Galloyde never failed to catch her eye.

He had never wanted to run away. They could have stayed, they didn't have to leave, but he had no choice but to follow her. His intent was to find her and bring her back but -

"But nothing can change the past," he sighed, brushing away memories from countless lifetimes ago. They only made him feel sad, frustrated, and lonely.

He closed his eyes. Today he would go somewhere happy. When he opened them, he was in Cartika. The sun was bright upon his face. He looked down to see he was riding a Lupa, the six-legged desert animal, who had a wide, comfortable back. He saw a busy market ahead and could feel the heavy bag of coins banging against his leg.

Galloyde smiled. Today would be a happy day.

CHAPTER
TWENTY-THREE

It was late the next morning when the two Elgets met with Sarah back in the conference room in Middle Operations. Neph was wearing sunglasses, but walked with pep in his step. Desi looked tired. Sarah pushed the water pitcher towards them.

"Earth wine can be dehydrating. Drink."

They both took glasses and obliged. Neph was smiling broadly. "Ahh what a great day! Let's get out of here and scare some more humans!"

"Ok, slow down there. I heard about your exploits last night. You had quite the time. Even got the Triplets involved?" She gave him a half-smile while taking her seat.

Neph clasped his hands together in a wistful expression. "I love them, I love them all!"

He turned to Desi. "Did you know The Triplets can smell, hunt, and find a specific human anywhere on Earth? Anywhere! The heads of a lion, eagle, and bear combined to form the perfect hunting beast. They are absolutely incredible. And Clara...oh

Clara! She took this child and flew her up way into the air and dropped her -"

"A child? How old?" Desi asked, his face revealing shocked horror.

"Old enough to have locked her siblings and parents in their house and set it on fire on purpose, that's how old. That fucking little shit. Anyways, Clara- what a beauty! She dropped that little bitch from at least 500 feet up in the air, let her fall straight down and almost smash into the ground, right before swooping her up and doing it again and again and again! Ahhhh, her screams! So great. So deserved. It's all just so wonderful to watch. Great fun."

"Quite the change from when we were here yesterday and you were afraid of being eaten." Desi observed dryly.

"Well, yesterday I was ignorant. I have since learned and I am the better for it." Neph snapped back.

"Sarah," Desi asked, changing the subject. "I was thinking, if Galloyde can communicate with or through Tiny, is there any chance that Tiny can communicate back to Galloyde?"

"We tried that," she answered. "Tiny goes into this type of fugue state, so he isn't really aware of the communication. We tried everything we could to communicate back in any kind of telepathic relay," she sighed. "Tiny has tried to focus on messages or symbols to send to Galloyde, but so far, we haven't had any confirmation on our end to let us know that he's received any of our messages."

Desi nodded. "I am trying to look at all angles and it appears you have already done that. Of course you have, but good to ask, just in case. You say you need to go soon. I assume that has to do with the etchings and the cube. The timing of this must all be coming to a head?"

Sarah explained what they understood from the etchings. Galloyde had been banished to the Galactic Ripple, a wave of energy that traveled throughout the Universes. She and Tiny believed they had calculated the location of the Ripple and where it would appear next.

She had to leave the next day if she was going to have a chance of making it in time.

There was no indication how long the Ripple would be within reach. Humans still didn't have any transport that could travel at the speed of light, never mind having the ability to jump to other dimensions or to fixed locations in the Universes. This made traveling to the Ripple location nearly impossible without a Clorrian Cruiser or a Council Traveler - either of which were capable of traveling directly to any location, anywhere in the Muldigals. Neither option was available on Earth.

Desi raised an eyebrow. "Oh no! Do you think I have a Clorrian Ship?"

Sarah stifled a laugh. He pursed his lips in embarrassment. "No, no, I'm sorry. I know you have Clorrian in your bloodlines, but I didn't think that meant you had access to a Clorrian Cruiser."

"I've heard of the Galactic Ripple." Neph said. "But only as a legionnaire's tale. Nothing more."

Desi looked inquiringly at him. "Story goes that every few thousand years, a Ripple churns across all the dimensions, opening up a portal to each one at the same time. Only an Overseer can see the Ripple and pass through for the price of a-"

He stopped cold, jaw agape, staring at Sarah.

"Well you can't stop like that." Desi pleaded.

Sarah put the black cube on the table. "For the price of one thousand souls, as the saying goes."

"But that isn't a thousand souls. That's just one shitty human." Neph pointed to the obsidian mass.

Sarah picked the cube back up. "When a human who is 'cubed' under 100 Reps, the color is a light grey. Like a stone left in a running stream for centuries. The darkest cube I've ever seen before this was someone who completed 268 Reps. His was the color of charcoal. This one here is the blackest of black. The midnight of the soul. Every time he killed someone, he collected a tiny part of them. This doesn't contain one soul Nephemerus. This is thousands."

They all stared at the cube.

Desi broke the silence. "I still don't understand how that will get you into the Ripple.

And even if you did make it in, what if Galloyde is not there? How do you come back?"

"She doesn't." Neph said quietly.

"No! Then no! No, no, no. You do not go." Desi stood up. "I hate to pull rank, but I have to say no. I forbid it. No."

Sarah looked up at him, amused. "I appreciate that, but the alternative is what? If I don't go, then the humans die. Their species will disappear. There's nothing we can do to change that. It is an absolute certainty. I don't know what Galloyde can do, if anything, to stop it, but if I don't try, then I'm no better than that old man who chose to do nothing."

They sat in silence for a moment.

"Did you practice that? In front of a mirror or something?" Neph asked Sarah, wearing a slight grin on his lips.

"Too much?"

"A bit. I mean it was good, but slightly over the top. I personally like a little more subtlety in my hero-rescue speeches," he said, winking at her.

"No one listens to me. We just got here and already, no one is listening to me." Desi ranted under his breath.

"Not this time, my friend." Neph stood and put his hands on Desi's shoulders. "We'll have to play this one out. It's the best plan we have, even if there's really no plan at all."

CHAPTER
TWENTY-FOUR

Galloyde blinked and found himself back in his body. The time was drawing near. She was preparing, and the Elgets were going to help her. Soon he would be returning to Earth to fix his tragic mistake. His mind went back to his time there, before Sarah, before it all changed.

He remembered the time on Earth when the barbarians clumsily chipped away at dull stones, trying to make tools. Some tribes did this with ease, learning quickly. Others struggled and failed. Those who failed would grow angry and throw rocks at one another, steal food from children to feed themselves, not even caring if their own children starved and died. They would kill each other randomly, without reason or provocation. Each human fended for themselves instead of sharing food and resources with the tribe. Galloyde watched in awe at how this group of barbarians constantly made such poor decisions.

Would it be the worst thing if he just helped this one small group of primitives? Just so their offspring could flourish? Surely their children could learn to be better. They could evolve into a stronger tribe and learn the best ways to hunt. They could develop ways to build better tools, like the other tribes had. They too could learn the value of sharing resources within the group as a whole for success instead of hoarding, which only leads to failure.

They only needed a little more time, Galloyde told himself. Not every tribe should be weeded out by natural evolution. Maybe this tribe would succeed if they only had a little more time to learn. After all, how could his helping them survive be a bad thing?

How wrong he had been. Galloyde stared into the vastness of space and pondered just how wrong he had been.

CHAPTER
TWENTY-FIVE

I n the end, Sarah decided to pack as little as possible. A compass, the hologram of Descend, details of the etchings, a few clothes, and her essentials. Just before she walked out the door, her hand automatically went to her right thigh - no dagger. Her heart raced briefly before she remembered she had already handed it over to Luis.

She closed her door and locked it. *They'll be fine*, she told herself. Luis will take care of all of them while she is gone. She had shown Luis what to do. She knew they would all be on their best behavior for him in her absence.

Sarah walked towards Middle Operations. As she got closer, she saw a large group gathering on the lawn. Bunny was standing there next to the Triplets. The middle lion head snapping at Bunny's face, while The Triplets' bird head was caught between the exchange, squawking and snapping at both sides. Sarah's eyes narrowed. *This can't be good.* Then she saw Seglee with GilGerg riding high on her back. *What the fuck is going on?* Tiny spotted Sarah and whistled to her loudly, causing everyone to stop what they were doing and line up.

Luis was standing at the beginning of the line with all the ReTrainers. Behind him was the support staff from the entire campus. Sarah approached him, quickly blinking. "Luis is there a drill, did something happen? What is going on here?"

Luis stepped forward and grabbed her hands. "No, no, mija. It's all ok. We are here to wish you luck." Sarah looked back to all her charges, who were beaming and standing as straight as they could. Even GilGerg's constantly matted hair was now brushed and shiny as he tried to stop wiggling and stand still.

Jess stepped forward out of the line. "I guess I'm not getting my processor after all, huh?" She laughed, approaching Sarah. "Saving this crap planet is a decent excuse though. Hey, be safe." She hugged Sarah hard.

Chronny stepped forward and formally shook her hand. "I want to wish you the best. You'll get this done. If anyone can do it, it's you. Probably. I mean, I'm sure you'll do it. Good luck."

Nexar was right after him. She threw her arms around Sarah and hugged her tight. "I had no idea! You're going to save the world! Go get 'em! Literally, go get him. Hah!" She stepped back into the line, jumping up and down like she was watching a parade.

Sarah looked to Luis with a questioning face. He smiled broadly, showing no willingness to acknowledge her confusion. Her eyes drifted to Tiny, who was standing next to Desi. Tiny looked as confused as she felt.

More people hugged her and shook her hand as she slowly made her way to her Regulators. She murmured to each, hugged them and gave them a pat. Finally, she made it to Desi and Tiny. "Well?" she asked flatly. "Who told?"

Desi sighed. "It was Nephemerus. He said that everyone should know what was happening. He wasn't going to spend the whole time you were gone lying to everyone, saying you were on Galaador when you were facing certain death." She grimaced. "His words, not mine. It's better they know Sarah. I do agree with that."

As the crowd started to dissipate, she heard a voice call out. "Hang on hero, you're not going anywhere yet." She turned to see Neph walking up the path with a pack on his back, sunglasses on and coat in hand.

Desi raised an eyebrow. "What do you think you're doing?"

"Well I'm not going to let my Demon Keeper - sorry, my Regulator Wrangler? We'll work the new title out later. I'm not going to let Sarah do this alone. I'd be a shitty boss if I did. I'm going with her."

"No you're not!" Desi and Tiny cried in unison.

"Oh yes I am. I'm King of the...I'm Lord of the Underworld or something. I'm going. I am technically your boss, you know." He said to Sarah.

She rolled her eyes at him.

Desi led Neph a few steps away, so they could have privacy. "Are you certain about this? There are risks."

Neph patted Desi on the arm and turned back to the whole group. "Listen, the last Elget for Descend went to sleep for over 2,000 years. I'm willing to go out on a limb and say the Descend Elget hasn't done too much around here. She's done it all." Pointing at Sarah, who kicked at the dirt on the ground.

"I'm not needed here. It was fine without an Elget before me, it will be fine without me. You," Neph pointed to Desi, "will not go mad and start creating monsters or flying trees or whatever craziness while I'm gone, agreed?"

Desi grunted. "Well now I won't."

"Good." Neph turned back to Sarah. "Now, you seem to know a lot about my friend. I'm betting you know just as much about me?"

She stared into Neph's deep brown eyes for a moment, then quickly looked away. "Born in the Vecuraus Galaxy to a native Vecurasian mother and a Balksen father. You were sent to be raised by your uncle when you were eight because your parents were killed in the

Recusuvo Wars. Then sent to Veris before arriving in Toomot." She paused. "The man who raised you, your 'uncle' wasn't a blood uncle though."

Neph's eyes narrowed. "Go on."

She took a deep breath. "You had been sold into slavery when you were discovered to have the powers of an Elget. The slaver told people he was your uncle, but in truth, he kidnapped you in Veris where you were supposed to meet your real uncle.

Desi gasped. "Stop! Sarah stop it! Nephemerus, you do not need to talk about this."

Neph waved him away. "She does. Go on."

Sarah swallowed hard, "He used your insight as an Elget to cheat merchants and other traders in the yards at Toomot until...well until I assume until you said you wouldn't do it anymore. I couldn't find any record of the slaver after you turned twelve years old. My best guess is, when he couldn't cheat anyone without your help, they probably came to collect on his debts and killed him. By then you had already fled the planet, on a Clorrian ship."

"On a Clorrian ship! Why didn't you ask me about it yesterday when Desi brought it up?" he asked Sarah, "when you know I have a connection to the Clorrians?"

Tiny considered all of this. "Neph, could you access one of their ships?"

Neph dropped his pack down on the ground. "Hang on a minute," he said to Tiny, and then moved close to Sarah.

"I need to know something first," he said, holding her by her shoulders. "I need to know if you can be honest with me. Can you do that?"

She looked out at Descend, towards the buildings, out toward the lake. Her eyes drifted over Luis playing with GilGerg, Bunny lying in the grass, sunshine warming the his belly, Clara flying high above in the distance. Finally, she looked back at Tiny and Desi. Then she looked into Neph's eyes and nodded.

"There's a lot on the line. More than you know," she whispered so the others couldn't hear.

"Oh, I think I do know," he countered.

"Wait a minute. Even if you can get this ship - which is ridiculous - I mean, how in the world would you get a Clorrian Cruiser? We would still need an Overseer to find this Galactic Ripple, correct? Do you have one of those up your sleeve?" Desi asked Neph. "Don't tell me you're also an Overseer and you didn't bother to tell me that either."

"I'm not," he answered. "But she is."

Sarah glared at Neph and stepped back, pulling out of his grip.

"What?" Tiny exclaimed. "Sarah, what is he talking about?"

"The truth, Sarah." Neph pressed.

"Yes. Yes, it's true." She pushed past Neph and started walking up the path towards the clearing at the top of the hill.

"Sarah! Sarah, where are you going?" Tiny called after her. She turned around and pointed straight up into the sky. Tiny and Desi looked up to see a Clorrian ship closing in on the clearing.

"You knew I would call them. You knew!" Neph shouted over the roar of the engines as the ship slowly landed.

"Yes I knew!" She shouted back. "I knew you stowed away with them. I knew you joined them before you went through your Elget training. They are your family. Not the one you were born to, but the one you chose. You are a Clorrian, Nephemerus. I also knew that you wouldn't want to miss a huge adventure like this, because that runs in your Vecurasian blood. That's why I needed you here!"

The ship's engines were drowning her out, so she yelled louder. "I need you to help me Neph. That's why I picked you!"

"Well, all you had to do was ask!" He picked up his bag and walked past her, grinning. He turned to wave goodbye to Desi and Tiny and then entered the ship through the loading platform.

Sarah went to Tiny. They had already said everything they needed to say to each other earlier that day. She squeezed his giant claw one last time before she approached Desi.

"Take care of my friend. Bring back Galloyde. Both of you get back here safely. I - I command it," he said to her in a wavering voice.

Sarah hugged him fiercely and boarded the ship.

CHAPTER

TWENTY-SIX

Raka greeted both of the travelers with open arms. This was something Sarah had not expected based on what she had read about the Clorrian race. Known for their fierce fighting and espionage skills, she was apprehensive about what she would find when she boarded. As soon as the entry door closed and they started to lift away from Earth, she felt the harsh adrenaline rush of panic - for leaving her home, her demons and for blindly walking onto a ship belonging to someone she had never met.

The ship was far smaller than she expected, just seating for the pilot and three others. Raka stood in front of her with a build that looked like an upright reptile. His overall features looked eerily similar to Tiny, if Tiny wore an intricate military uniform, and was smaller in stature. She began to feel less tense though. This stranger looked just like a version of her best friend. Perhaps this was why Neph took to Tiny as quickly as he did.

"Raka!" exclaimed Neph, as they exchanged a hard embrace. "It is so good to see you, Chriska!"

"Good fortune brings us together yet again. Are we fleeing? Must we move quickly? Shall I engage the shields?" He teased Neph, adding his deep, booming laugh.

Neph chuckled. "No, not this time, we're fine. Take it easy. We'll have time to talk more soon. Let me introduce you to someone very special. Raka, this is my…"He paused, then gingerly placing his hand on the middle of her back. "My friend, Sarah. I'd like to introduce you to Raka os Clorria. He is the 7th Captain of the Lisceraa Force."

"Ahh Saraahhhhh." Raka bowed deeply. "I am honored to meet you. I have never had the opportunity to meet one of your kind before."

Sarah gave Neph a quick glance. He held his hands up and shook his head in surprise.

Raka let out another baritone laugh. "Oh forgive me for being so blunt. I have never met a human before. You are human?"

Sarah relaxed and laughed along with him. "Oh no, no, I'm not. I'm sorry, I was just caught off-guard. I understand, they are certainly unique and haven't been seen in the universes yet, but no, I'm not a human. Just on Earth for work."

Raka put his arm around Neph. "We have much to discuss, chriska. First, there are many who need to remind you of shared times." He looked to Sarah. "You will get to see Nephemerus with his family. You are part of his family now. We eat. We talk. Then we travel to where you need to go."

Sarah could hear heavy metal objects moving outside their craft. She glanced out the window. She no longer saw blue sky, but the inner mechanics of another ship. Of course, she thought. A Clorrian Cruiser must hold hundreds of soldiers, if not more. She was merely on a shuttle to the Cruiser. She was about to find out just how large a ship it was.

TWENTY-SEVEN

Desi was back in the Ascend Operations Tower with Jess. He was staring out the window at the clearing where the Clorrian ship had just left, his eyebrows furrowed.

Jess put a hand on his shoulder. "They'll be ok. I know Sarah, and she always gets the job done - no matter what it is. She'll bring him back. Both of them."

Desi nodded his head. "Yes, yes, I'm sure you're right. I've known Nephemerus since Elget Training, and he was always good about getting out of tight spots. It all makes so much sense..."

"What does?" asked Aramik, who was just walking into Operations and getting his workstation set up for the day. He had a slight build, considerably shorter than his android counterpart, with short cropped brown hair and a hesitant nature. Aramik spoke in a pattern that sounded like he analyzed every possible outcome - unlike Jess, who actually did, but she often sounded so human, you had to wonder where the Gigla got her template from.

"That Nephemerus should go with Sarah to save the humans!" Jess responded. "He had this secret past living with Clorrians, so he can take her to the Galactic Ripple. Oh, and guess what? Sarah's an

Overseer! You really need to keep up with everything that's happening around here."

Aramik waved Jess off and logged onto his station, showing little interest in the news of the day.

She turned back to Desi, who was wringing his hands and mumbling to himself. She sat him down at the conference table and made him a cup of tea at the tiny kitchenette set up along one wall of the meeting room.

"Tell me what you worry about the most in this situation," she asked him. Her programming included vast collections on psychology and therapy.

His hands wrapped around the mug and held it tightly. "I worry they don't come back and I never know what happened to them. I worry they come back without Galloyde and we fail to stop the humans from destroying themselves. I worry they *do* come back with Galloyde and we *still* fail at stopping the humans from destroying themselves. I worry that -"

"That's enough, let's stop there," Jess interrupted. "You've administered enough planets to know that some species do not survive. That's natural selection. Them's the breaks."

Desi stared into the mug. "I agree. Honestly, I'm not even sure why she's going, of all people. Why would she go? Why would she even want to try to save the humans from destroying themselves?"

Aramik turned around in his seat and looked at Desi. "What do you mean?"

"Well, not to be insensitive, but she's the Dem...Regulator, the Regulator Person. She has spent her entire time here on Earth dealing with humans who have done terrible, just awful things. Why is she risking herself and now Nephemerus, to save them? Of all people, she should be the very last person to want to save this horrendous species."

"Oh," Aramik replied flatly. "I really wish I was here when you first landed." He said quietly. "I should have been here." He turned back to his monitor.

Jess stared at Desi with her head cocked to one side. "Sarah had the impression that you were quite intelligent. I'm not sure I share her observation." She then used a voice that was far more robotic than her normal tone. "On the 3,748th day prior to your arrival, Sarah the Demon Keeper stated, 'Desimidor Vas Qulas Zyrla ranks as the second-highest intellect of all Elget trainees in Logic, Strategy and Emotional Quotients.' She stated you were the most intelligent Elget that Earth had ever received to date. The Demon Keeper's pulse rate increased by 28 beats higher than normal and her pupils dilated by .22 mm wider each time she spoke of your impending arrival."

Desi turned to Jess, puzzled. "Why are you telling me this?"

Jess resumed speaking in her normal voice. "You questioned why Sarah would save the humans? You truly believe she despises them? Let me ask you this - as the most intelligent Elget that has ever graced our presence here on Earth - why would anyone spend several millennia dedicated to training and counseling the worse of humanity, in hopes that humans would Ascend to the Higher Consciousness if deep down, she hated them so much?"

Jess didn't wait for Desi to answer before continuing.

"Since Sarah is not going on a vacation - and certainly not picking up my service parts - I placed an order with Gigla. The fact I had not scheduled those updates prior to the needed maintenance schedule reveals my system failure. I have now updated my programming to order parts automatically in the future. I will receive this order on a drop delivery during the next Perseid Meteor Shower. The humans will not notice the container drop." She left Desi and returned to monitor her station.

Desi sat in silence considering what Jess said. Of course Sarah cared about the humans. She planned on having Desi in place here on Earth long before he knew of his assignment. She orchestrated a plan that took tens of thousands of years to bring them all to this moment. Right now, his real fear was that he could do nothing while his friends were risking everything.

She brought him here for a reason. Maybe he didn't have to wait for Galloyde to come back before he could help. Maybe he could work on his own plan to help the humans, from right where he was sitting.

CHAPTER
TWENTY-EIGHT

S arah was led to her room by a young soldier through a maze of pristine white hallways. The walls were roughly textured under her fingertips, dampening the sound of the soldier's boots on the hard surface. Above her, lighting was integrated into where the wall met the high ceiling, glowing brighter as they approached. Glancing over her shoulder, she noted the lights dimmed after they passed. Each hallway seemed interminably long, with few doors between the start and end. Symbols adorned a placard next to each door, none of which she could read.

The soldier suddenly stopped and gestured for Sarah to enter her room. She looked left and right before entering, trying to see anything she could use as a landmark, but found none.

The young Clorrian told Sarah to prepare for dinner and promptly left with no further instruction. The door slid closed behind her, as her breath seemed to slip away in her chest. She felt panic wash over her, beads of sweat breaking out on her brow. What was she doing? How did she think any part of her plan was going to work?

Closing her eyes, she leaned back against the door. She reminded herself that she had no choice. If she didn't try, the humans were sure to perish. All of the souls that ever were or ever could be would be lost. Everything was just coming at her so fast, now that the time was here. She'd never been on a spaceship, met a Clorrian warrior or traveled anywhere beyond the confines of Earth.

She opened her eyes and took in her accommodations. She was standing in a small ten by ten foot space. It felt more like minimalist train car than intergalactic quarters. The room itself was well-designed for the amount of function it had. In front of her was a drop down mattress, just long enough for her to fit on. *How in the world would a Clorrian ever squeeze onto that?* Her mind wandered as she inspected the rest of the room. To her left was a sliding door which stood closed but a quick peek revealed what she believed to be a toilet. To her right was a small closet, sink and mirror.

She dropped her pack onto the shelf and found a long, flowing white garment resting on a hanger in the tiny closet. Since she didn't bring any dinner wear - or any special clothes - so she chose to wear the wrap.

At least it fits, she thought as she washed her face and brushed out her blonde hair. She took a long look in the mirror and smiled at the thought of being mistaken for a human by Raka. How funny was that? she mused.

She unhooked the mattress and let it drop open. Sitting on the surprisingly comfortable bed, she waited, relieved that some of the tightness in her chest was lessening. She began to fidget with her necklace, a gift from her father when she was about eight years old. The silver pendent looked Celtic, with intersecting loops. He told her it would help her fit into her surroundings. Now, as an adult, she understood it was her mirreáge. This was how she could understand Raka and the other soldiers.

She, as well as anyone who worked for the Multi-Dimensional Galactic Council, wore a mirreáge to alter their appearance. Her mind began to drift, wondering how others looked in their original form. She was shaken from this thought when there was a knock at her door.

She opened the door and found Neph standing there, dressed in the same clothes he left Earth in. Strangely, he appeared much taller to her now - imposing. Perhaps it was because of the size of the hallways?

"Are you alright?" he looked concerned. "I wanted to check in on you. See if you needed anything?"

She gestured for him to come in, but the room was so small, they both couldn't stand in the center of the room. Neph stepped in, sat at the edge of the bed, and leaned back while she slid the door closed. Then she sat down next to him, the only place left to sit.

"I feel like you're unsettled," he said to her quietly.

"Are you reading me?"

His face flushed and he coughed to cover it up. "No. No! That would be the obvious reaction when you're in a strange situation." He paused. "Ok yes. I am. I can't help it. I'm not trying - it's just there."

She tried to hide a smile and looked away. She did feel nervous. She wasn't used to not being in control of the situation.

"I'm sure you're right. This is all a strange environment for me. I don't know how Raka is going to take this whole story about the cube and the Ripple and bringing Galloyde back-"

Neph gently took her hand into his warm grip and held it softly. "Shhh. It's going to be alright. Breathe. Right now, you are much further than you were yesterday. One thing at a time. It's a lot to take in, but you're going to be alright. All you have to do is breathe."

He leaned slightly against her as she closed her eyes and took in a slow deep breath, held it, then slowly let it out. She repeated this a few more times. When she opened her eyes, Neph stood in front of her and helped her to her feet. "

Time for dinner. And I think you are going to love this!" He said with a mischievous grin.

CHAPTER

TWENTY-NINE

The dining hall aboard the ship was several decks away from her room. They walked the long hallways that Neph knew by heart. She half-jogged to keep up with his stride. Had he walked this fast on Earth? She couldn't remember, but she thought she would have noticed if he had.

She almost asked for him to slow down when they finally arrived at the dining area, which was spectacular. She tried not to stare at the various soldiers moving to and from their tables. Each and every one of them looked like younger, leaner versions of Tiny in their splendid military uniforms. None matched his size, but each had a distinct attribute that her best friend also possessed.

They entered a room located off the main space. As soon as they stepped in, soldiers called out Nephemerus' name fervently from each side of the room. The arched room was adorned in green, red, gold, and black, with torches illuminating the alcove with warm light. Rich aroma filtered through the room, signaling to Sarah that she was indeed, quite hungry. They moved towards the center, where two large wooden tables were set up, able to hold twenty Clorrians each.

Neph said hello to a cacophony of voices shouting and laughing, while Sarah tried to catch her breath from her jog over. Could there less oxygen on these ships than Earth's atmosphere? That would explain her panting and slight dizziness.

Then, a singular voice rose above the others and said, "Nephemerus os Clorria, you come over here right now!" He turned to see where the voice came from and broke into the widest smile she had ever seen on him. He placed his hands on her shoulders and guided her past the throng of warriors anxious to say hello to their long-lost friend. Expertly weaving past them while also serving them a quick greeting, Sarah felt exhausted by the time she sat down on a bench with Neph. Her water glass was filled and she quickly remedied her thirst.

She smiled and said hello to all the new faces at their table as Neph called out to each Clorrian by name, adding a funny quip and raising his glass as he introduced everyone at the table. She was confident she could remember the first eight names - but after that, between the toasts and complexity of their names - she soon was lost.

Neph was halfway through his introductions when he leaned over to her and whispered in her ear. "That's not water. That's Kasyli. It's an alcohol, similar to mead, just much more, uh…potent."

Her face dropped. She was almost finished with her second glass and hadn't eaten yet that day. He grinned and continued to introduce people, but motioned to her slyly. He was bringing his glass of Kasyli to his lips, just not drinking. She followed suit but it was too late. She was feeling giddy.

Overflowing baskets and plates filled with food piled high on the table from the kitchen staff who appeared out of nowhere. Neph casually put a basket of something that looked like bread in front of her. She tore it open and chewed it down. She heard cheering. She took another bite. Again, she heard more cheering. It took a moment for her to realize it was related to her eating.

"Oh, should I be waiting for everyone? Am I doing something wrong?" she whispered back to Neph. He shook his head and grabbed something that looked like a potato and took a huge bite. Everyone cheered.

"This is what happens. You'll get used to it. Keep drinking and you'll start doing it too."

More plates and more baskets of food kept arriving on the table. So did the drink. Both Neph and Sarah ate a considerable share, cheering for those eating, while laughing at stories for what felt like hours.

Suddenly a voice boomed out and cut through all the chatter. "Ey Girl! You know my Mery?" An older Clorrian woman, whose husband was already dozing next to her, was pointing at Sarah from across the table. "Let me tell you of Mery."

"No! No, no, no, Qualla, she doesn't need to hear your made-up lies," Neph winked at Sarah.

The woman stood up and threw a piece of bread at Nephemerus, hitting him square in the middle of his forehead. "I do not lie Mery. You shut up, boy. Let me tell this girl who she has taken up with."

Sarah listened intently as Qualla told the story of finding a skinny, dirty, scrap of a boy hiding in the laundry chute of this Clorrian Cruiser they were on now.

"I go to toss in the wash and - AHH! There is this face - much younger, but still so handsome…that face poking back out at me. What could I do?"

Nephemerus groaned and rubbed at his cheeks, having heard this story so many times before. Sarah reached up and gently squeezed his bicep reassuringly. She was loving Qualla's story and his well-practiced reaction.

"This boy, I make him crawl out. Filthy. Lanky. No meat on the bones, like now. Why don't you eat Mery?"

Suddenly she realized this was the voice they heard when they first arrived at the dining hall, demanding they sit at this table.

"I bring him back to my quarters, making sure he isn't seen because back then…uh, uh, oooh, if they found him, they would have sent him-"

"Right out the airlock." Both Neph and the woman's husband said together.

"So now you are awake?" She nudged her husband, who smiled at Sarah with a huge toothy grin. Sarah smiled back at him, warming to the familiarity in his face.

"Then we raised him, give him a good home, fed him, just so he can leave us and become a big deal. He never comes home, he forgets we exist. The end." Qualla picked up her cup, gulped down all the Kasyli and slammed back into her seat with a colossal thud.

Neph moved his hand down under the table and found Sarah's hand. They brushed their fingers together for a moment before intertwining them. She felt a warm tingle flow through her body as he squeezed her hand gently. She looked up to see him watching her intently. She smiled and leaned against him.

"Qualla look, he's right here, sitting across from you. He's here. He takes care of us, he comes to see you as much as he can. He talks with you often. He hasn't forgotten about you. Stop with this, especially in front of the girl," pleaded the husband.

Qualla stood up again, swayed, then grabbed her husband's drink off the table and finished it. Neph moved quickly out of his booth and over to steady her. Others tried catch Qualla, as her large framed weaved from side to side, but she pushed them all off, except for Neph who - as tall as he was - still had to look up at his adopted mother. She grabbed his face rather roughly.

"This face, so handsome…you should have seen it!" She shouted at no one in particular. "Almost dead in the laundry chute. Now look at you! Ok, go with the girl, I have to go to bed. Ishonna, my dear Mery, even though you drive me crazy." She let go of his face and her husband caught her as she fell backwards. With the assistance of two others, they carried Qualla out the door. More cheers erupted from the crowd as they left.

Neph slid back into the booth next to Sarah, pushing right up against her and wrapped his arm around her shoulders. It felt comfortable and natural. Like a missing puzzle piece she didn't realize was gone. She rested her head on his shoulder and took a deep breath, taking him in. His arm pulled her even closer to his chest. Soon the stories faded into the background as Sarah looked up to see Neph's eyes darting from her eyes, to her lips and back. She closed her eyes as he leaned in and they kissed .

CHAPTER

THIRTY

They had reached Neph's room from the dining hall far more quickly than the trip from her room. He carried her the entire way. Sarah remembered leaning into his kiss, not letting go. She still didn't want to let go, but he was trying to open his door and her toga dress was getting wrapped around his hands.

She giggled as he put her down. She gathered the extra material in her hand as he opened the door. She was shocked to see he had a massive cabin compared to hers. Her jaw dropped as she saw an entire wall of windows lining one side of the main room.

Neph stripped off his jacket and told her to get comfortable, that he would be right back. She looked around and wasn't even sure which hallway he disappeared down. Her own room didn't even have a chair, she thought.

Walking over to a nearby bar cart, she found a carafe filled with clear liquid. She sniffed at it, trying to determine if it had the slight scent of cinnamon found in Kasyli. She couldn't tell. She poured two glasses and waited to confirm with Neph that it was water and not more mead before trying it.

She left the glasses by the couch and walked over to the wall of windows and pressed her forehead against the cool glass. She couldn't believe how big space was…and suddenly, just for a second, she thought of her charges back home.

"They're fine. They're more worried about you, and you're fine. And yes, that's water." Neph reappeared in loose black pants and a robe wrapped around him. "Sorry, I felt so sweaty and just wanted to rinse off quick."

She took a long drink of the water and knelt next to him on the couch, staring at him. She could see his eyes looking back and forth into each of hers. His lips softened and he leaned in to give her another warm, deep kiss. She sat leaning across his lap as he brushed the hair out of her face.

"Was this part of your 30,000-year plan?" He asked, studying her face. She smiled at him, taking in his dark features and tracing her finger along the back of his neck, playing with his hair. She could feel doubt rising from him.

"20,000 years - and no, this was definitely not part of the plan. You were not supposed to be debonair or charming. I was banking on connected, helpful…slightly repulsive."

She could feel his unease lift and replaced with excitement. She kissed him for a long time, holding him tight, then pushing him down on the couch.

"Not here." He got up off the couch and swept her up in his arms again. "Unlike your little closet, I have a nice big bed. Want to see it?"

Sarah cried out yes, and not for the last time that night.

CHAPTER

THIRTY-ONE

N eph awoke first and watched her sleeping. She had one leg wrapped over his thigh, her head resting on his chest. Her arm was stretched across him, with her hand resting on his forearm. *She's got me pinned*, he mused.

He played with her hair with his free hand and nuzzled against her forehead thinking of when he started to feel something for her. It was in the chamber when he first suspected, no, when he first knew she was holding back on the cube. He had gone to her office and asked to meet with her. He needed to speak with her about the Regulators, let her know they were not Demons, but she refused to talk then. She said she had something more pressing to do, and he was surprised to find out he couldn't read her. She had blocked him, which was something he wasn't used to. In fact, he had never been blocked before. Reading others, and developing his intuition for their actions was one of his strongest skills. That's when he knew she was different, and when he decided to confront her in the chamber.

The look on her face when she walked in and saw him standing there was perfection. He smiled to himself. She was so shocked, and then genuinely apologetic. Any attempt to block him fell away, and he could feel that she had every intention of telling him everything…well, almost everything.

That was when it happened. The way she looked at him - so open in her heart, her grey eyes pleading to give her a chance to explain. He could read that she was trying to do something good, something right, although he didn't quite know what it was just then.

There was a sudden knock on his door and Sarah jolted awake. "What's happening?" she asked, disoriented and trying to get her bearings. Neph knew she was not going to like what would happen next.

He grabbed a thick blanket and tossed it over both of them just as his bedroom door burst open. He held the blanket tight against her.

"Ahhh good morning Admiral! I hope you slept well! Sarah, nice to see you again. Dinner was wonderful last night. I enjoyed your stories about Earth. Admiral, the Captain is requesting both of you to join him as soon as possible on the Bridge." A Clorrian who had drunk heavily at their table the night before was now standing at the foot of the bed, smiling at the two of them. Two additional guards stood alongside him, acting casually, as if everyone was seated in a conference room and not lying naked in a private bedroom.

Sarah was frozen, her eyebrows raised high on her forehead with a death grip on the blanket. Neph quickly responded, "Of course, thank you, Lieutenant Nimi. We had a wonderful time as well. We will dress and be ready very shortly. Thank you for the message."

Neph gave a curt bow of his head, dismissing them. As they walked out through the bedroom door, Neph called out, "Do you mind-" and before he finished, the last guard turned and closed the door. A moment later, they heard the second door to the outside hallway shut.

"I'm so sorry-"Neph started.

"What the fuck was that? Is that some sort of Clorrian wake-up alarm ADMIRAL?" She yanked at the covers and moved towards her side of the bed.

Neph swept her and the covers back towards him and grinned down at her. "You didn't like that? I ordered it special for you."

"Ass. Move. I have to pee."

"I'm sorry," he started to say. Sarah wasn't interested in his apology and yanked the blanket harder. He pulled her back again, making eye contact, and repeated, "Really, I'm sorry." He punctuated this with a kiss on her forehead.

Sarah stopped, untangled herself from the blankets, crawled on top of him, and gave him a deep kiss. "That was fucked up. We'll talk about the early morning peep show later, but I really do have to pee." She rolled off the bed and trotted toward the bathroom.

CHAPTER
THIRTY-TWO

S arah and Neph left his quarters and followed the same three Clorrian soldiers through the hallways towards the Bridge. Sarah was dressed in the clothes she had brought with her. All of her things had been delivered to Neph's suite while they slept. She had her small bag slung across her chest and her hair pulled back in a bun.

Neph was dressed in his full Admiral uniform, which was splendid - to say the least. Sarah did a double take when he walked out of his dressing room. Her face flushed bright red, and she tried to look away before Neph saw it. He pretended not to notice her reaction, but he definitely did. The Clorrians prized comfort and utility in everything they wore - except their military regalia. That fashion fell in line with most cultures, with the intended purpose being to impress and intimidate, and, depending on the audience, make them swoon. In this case, it was working, and Sarah couldn't stop stealing glances at him.

They moved through the halls at a slower pace than the night before, walking behind one soldier in front of them with two more following behind. Did the Clorrians really believe that Neph needed protection on this ship, Sarah wondered. They turned the corner and encountered two workers fixing a panel in the hallway. They stopped as soon as they saw the guards approach and saluted Neph as he passed. He gave the men the slightest nod and continued on. She glanced over her shoulder to see the two Clorrians still watching Neph with fascination as the guards passed.

"What does Raka already know?" she asked, as three very young girls came bounding out of a door unexpectedly. They jumped back and made a high-pitch tittering sound as she and Neph passed by their door. They were thrilled to see him, she thought.

He covertly took her hand, squeezed it and just above a whisper said "Nothing. He knows absolutely nothing about why we are here."

They arrived at their destination and Nephemerus cleared his throat as they pulled their hands apart. Her palm felt sweaty, but she wasn't nervous. She wondered if he was anxious as the doors to the Bridge opened.

The guards announced his presence, "Fleet Admiral Nephemerus os Clorria on Booooard!" All crew stood and saluted. Nephemerus returned their salute in full and turned to Raka. "Captain Raka, permission to board the Noneru?"

Raka saluted, then returned, "Permission granted Fleet Admiral. She is all yours." The crew resumed working, and Neph motioned to Raka, who led them to a private room off the Bridge. This appeared to be a strategy room, with maps along the walls and a large round table with a built-in display in the center. Sarah had no idea if there were active battles happening with anyone right now. Her intergalactic knowledge was woefully limited in her primitive world.

Both officers removed their caps and sat down, but did not drop their formality. Sarah sat next to Neph and gave Raka a slight wave and smile.

"Sarah, I am glad you are here, and I am eager to help you and the Admiral." Raka began.

She suppressed her instinct to laugh at the mention of Raka calling Neph an 'Admiral,' especially after how they greeted each other yesterday. Now she realized it hadn't just been an old friend coming down to get them in that small transport ship. The Captain of this Clorrian Cruiser came down to pick up the Fleet Admiral. That might have been their only opportunity where they could be themselves with each other. The thought made her both happy and a little sad.

"Captain," Neph began, "our mission is complex. There are a number of concerning factors to overcome, but I believe we have planned the best possible approach. With your assistance, I'm sure we will achieve our goal."

Raka nodded. "Whatever you need, Admiral. What can I do?"

Neph inhaled slowly. "There is so much to discuss, and parts of it I cannot get into fully right now because there's not enough time, but we need to locate and cross the Galactic Ripple."

Sarah braced herself for the loud, boisterous laugh she had heard from Raka yesterday, but it did not come. Instead the Captain remained serious and pensive. He thought for a moment before he responded. "Admiral, we have no way to predict the appearance of a Galactic Ripple. We have no way to locate or track a Ripple with our current instrumentation. There are no accounts of any being traveling into the Ripple and surviving. There are no records of ships entering a Ripple and reporting back. If this is your mission, we could travel to the coordinates if you know when and where one might appear, but even then, we would have no way to ascertain if the Ripple is actually present. No one is capable of directly viewing a Ripple, except for a Traveler or an Overseer, neither of which we have onboard."

"I believe I will be able to see it." Sarah offered.

Staying true to his training, Raka gave no indication of surprise that he was sitting across from an Overseer. He nodded as he processed this information for a brief moment before moving onto the next part.

136

"The legend of the Galactic Ripple states it requires a toll, a payment that is…I'll say steep," he said gravely. "Of course, as Admiral, it is your discretion to use the enlisted service personnel as you see fit -"

Sarah pulled out the ink-black cube from her bag and slid it across the table. "That is your payment." Raka stared at the cube and then back at the two of them questioningly.

"Captain, I would never sacrifice one thousand lives of your men, of our men," Neph emphasized. "I'm not here to ask you for that. As I said, we are as prepared as we can be, and we believe we can enter the Ripple using this as payment."

Raka stood and moved over to the window, looking out into space for a moment and let out a low but audible sigh of relief.

He returned to the table and started to pick up the cube, stopping with his claw just above it before asking Sarah, "May I?" she nodded and a grin escaped her lips as she remembered Neph doing the exact same gesture in her office not long ago. Raka grasped the cube, studying it closely.

Neph leaned in. "What we know about 7298 is so different than what we were led to believe. The Council is putting out wholly incorrect information, as is…" He broke into his familiar grin, "The Grand Precipice."

Raka continued to examine the coal-black cube and grunted, "Tell me something I don't know." The formality of their earlier exchange melting away.

"Well, of course, we know they constantly re-imagine facts - that is the evolution of power - but I'm talking about the very history on which our foundations are based," Neph said slowly.

Raka's eyes moved up to meet the Admiral's. "Go on."

"What if I told you that Mad Galloyde wasn't mad at all? That entire situation all had to do with an unfortunate dealing with the

Grand Precipice. Galloyde never went mad. He never even created a race of evil monsters!"

"Well, he kinda did, on that last one. Just not how everyone thinks," Sarah said, pointing to the cube.

"Oh right, well, yes - he did create a bunch of evil bastards, but definitely not like we have all been led to believe. The truth might shock you. Are you ready?" Neph asked, now completely dropping the formality.

"Go ahead and shock me," Raka grinned back at his old friend.

CHAPTER
THIRTY-THREE

The Captain clicked a button on a panel and asked for the galley. "Bring refreshments. I think we will be here a while," he said through the intercom, looking at his guests.

The cube sat in the center of the table. Raka focused on Sarah and Neph. "Explain to me how that is one thousand souls."

Sarah proceeded to give Raka a brief overview of Earth, covering the basics of their life cycle. Humans lived for an extremely short time. When they died, they would either Ascend or Descend based on the outcomes of their moral compass. Her job was to rehabilitate the ones who didn't Ascend.

"And you were there? On Earth? Were you assigned by the Council?" Raka asked Neph, who nodded and replied, "Correct. I was there." Raka knew not to press his commanding officer for more information.

Sarah continued. "We have a system in place for humans who are incapable of Ascending after multiple attempts. Once we ascertain they are not salvageable, they are cubed like this and sent to another developing planet to be reintroduced into their evolution process."

"They go back to the very beginning? Absolute beginning? How interesting. Fascinating! Who developed that system?" Raka inquired.

"I did," Sarah said simply.

Raka picked up the cube again and studied it closely. "So, this is 1,000 souls of humans who could not Ascend?" He was both in awe and repulsed by the object.

"In a way - yes, and also no," Sarah answered. "That was one person who went through our process four hundred and seventy-nine times. That's four hundred and seventy-nine attempts to live a life on Earth in which they failed to Ascend, although they all belonged to the same consciousness."

Raka's face revealed immediate concern, and his eyes locked with Nephemerus.

Sarah continued, "The reason this cube is more than a thousand souls is because this individual killed in every single one of those lives. Ultimately, he murdered thousands of others, and as a warrior, you are aware that once a life is taken, a part of their life becomes yours to carry."

Raka began to see what Sarah was saying and agreed. "Yes. Yes, this is true. It is one of our core beliefs."

"There are several cultures who believe this, or something very similar," Neph said. "I think she's right. He would possess a portion of each of those lives he took, no matter if they were animal or human. My only concern lies with the consciousness of the same life, even if he went through four hundred and seventy-nine separate trips through Earth."

This revelation surprised Sarah. She wasn't aware of Neph's doubts, but they hadn't had much time to discuss any of this. It was Raka who answered Neph's concern.

"The Etchkaa share one consciousness. Billions of lives spread across a vast planet. Sharing one, immeasurable consciousness, yet we recognize each being as a separate life, a separate soul."

Neph started to respond just as someone knocked at the door. An ensign delivered the requested refreshments, and they all took a few minutes to eat and drink before getting back to the discussion.

"Now we have arrived at my next concern regarding the Ripple. We understand that it appears every few thousand years. If you are here now, I assume you have knowledge of a location - an idea of when and where?" Raka asked, filling his plate for a second time.

Sarah pulled out a small disc from her bag and set it on the table. It was about three inches across and two inches tall, with a lit dome on top. The sight of this tiny object made both Raka and Neph burst into laughter.

"What is that?" Neph exclaimed, pointing to her hologram projector.

"I have never seen one of these in person. I think our museum might have some newer models though," Raka said with a hearty laugh.

"Listen, we don't get all the latest tech on 298 or whatever you call Earth. This is the best I've got to work with!"

"See what I'm dealing with? And you think it's all sunshine and pelerria where I am!" Neph said to Raka.

The Captain shook his head as Sarah pressed the dial on her projector. The room was bathed in a blue hologram, showing the chamber room in clear, readable detail all around them.

"Well at least it works, points for that." Neph ribbed her.

She shot him a look and went on explaining."We received coordinates regarding the time and place we believe the Ripple will occur." She took a long drink of water, mentally admonishing herself. What if she and Tiny were wrong about the code?

"We've been deciphering this code, and this is what we have." She reached into her bag and pulled out a sheet of paper with numbers written on it. She handed it to Raka.

The Captain looked at the paper. "We'll start heading that direction. Admiral - roll or jump?" he asked Neph.

"Roll all the way."

"Excuse me for one moment." Raka stepped out the door to give the orders for the new heading.

Neph immediately took Sarah in his arms. "You're doing great." She hugged him back tightly. He had an incredible calming effect on her, which she wasn't sure was because of his Elget training or just because of him. At this point, she didn't care. She felt her nervous system calm when he was close.

"I want you to know I have no doubt this will open the Ripple," he said quickly, motioning towards the cube. "I just need Raka to understand that we have considered all the possibilities."

"Worst-case scenario, we chuck this into space, it doesn't work, and it ends up who-knows-where. Jess would love that," she said, thinking of Jess' love of panspermia theory.

"That's not the worst-case scenario," Neph reminded her just as Raka walked back into the room and sat down. He examined the hologram and the etchings. Sarah moved the images around the room, expanding on the symbols so he could get a better look at them as Neph made himself busy under a nearby desk. He was looking for something.

"Who drew these etchings?" Raka asked. "How did they get there? Are we sure they are reliable intel?"

"AHA!" Neph exclaimed, emerging from under the desk with a half-full glass bottle of amber liquid. "I cannot believe this was still in here!" He laughed as he took everyone's glass and casually emptied any remaining liquid, then filled each glass halfway with the dark, honey-colored liquid.

"You're both going to need this," Neph warned, as he slid a glass towards Sarah and another towards Raka. He grabbed his own and sat down, unbuttoning his uniform jacket, which he was clearly tired of wearing.

"Before we get started, a toast! To unbelievable surprises!" He held up his glass, which was met cautiously by the other two. They clinked, and Sarah and Raka both took very small sips. Sarah set her glass down while Neph swallowed all of his in a single gulp.

"Sarah, could you please show Raka an image of Tiny, if you have one?" Neph asked. She thought for a moment and then pulled out her other projector. This one was even smaller, but it was in color. She clicked on it, slid through the different images, and stopped on an image of Tiny. She smiled at the sight of her old friend.

Raka dropped his glass and stood up, knocking his chair over as he stared at a much larger image of himself.

"Surprise!" Neph shouted, pouring himself another drink.

Raka's jaw hung open. Sarah twirled the image so he could see all the angles of her friend as she introduced him. "This is Tiny - sorry, his name is actually Thrinythidor. We call him Tiny because…well it's just easier to say and the humans like it. He says he 'finds the oxymoron humorous for the humanoids.' That's a taste of Tiny's humor for you."

Neph got up, picked up the Captain's chair, and sat Raka back down. He righted the spilled glass and poured his friend another drink. This time, Raka drank it all in one gulp, as Neph had just done. He tried to speak but could only stammer. He stopped and stared at Neph.

"Is this why you were there? Did you know?" he finally asked, his voice barely whispering.

Neph slammed down his glass. "Not a fucking clue! Want to talk about a surprise? This - THIS - is who the Council was calling Galloyde's creatures!"

Raka's claws were shaking. "Is he...how is he...does he know... how..." He trailed off as Neph poured him another drink.

Sarah was confused. "I'm not sure what is happening right now. What are you talking about?"

Neph pulled his coat off and tossed it in the corner. He held her head in his hands and stared intently into her grey eyes. "Galloyde didn't create Tiny. He didn't create Bunny, or Seglee, or GilGerg. None of them. Sarah, they aren't demons or monsters."

Sarah pulled away from him and backed up against a cabinet. "What are you talking about? That's not true. Everyone knows he created them because...No, you're wrong. Of course he created them."

"You're right that Tiny is different than the others, Sarah. Tiny is Clorrian. You must see that by now. Seglee is a Yesperarian! That's beyond incredible. GilGerg is a Trillafibit. He comes from -"

"I don't know why you are saying these things. They are from Earth. Everyone knows Galloyde created them. They know he created them!"

"Why, Sarah? Who says that? Sarah, did Galloyde ever tell you he made them? Or did others say that after he was gone?" Neph asked softly. He walked over to her and took her hands in his. "We know who they are, Sarah. That's why Desi and I stopped calling them 'Demons' immediately after we met them. They are species from other planets, other solar systems, other dimensions." He exchanged looks with Raka, "We know exactly who they are."

"I can't believe you actually have the Founders on Earth of all places." Raka paused and then asked. "May I see the Yesperarian? The one you call Celly?"

"Seglee," Sarah corrected him and advanced the images until she got to Seglee.

Raka's face exploded into pure joy. "Oh my! Oh! A Yesperarian! I did not think this was possible. In all my years, I never thought…this is glorious."

Neph grinned, "Oh, you should see her up close! Gorgeous. She flies straight up out of the water, so regal. So agile. Do you know, she ate an entire human whole and then pooped him out! Untouched!" They both laughed at this. Sarah stared at the two of them, unsure of what was happening, but not liking any of it.

"What are Founders? Why are you calling them Founders?" she demanded.

Neph turned to her. "Sarah, you must see it by now. There's no two ways about it. I'm not sure exactly what happened, but I can tell you what I do know. Going back as far as anyone can remember, all life in the cosmos comes from ten original root species. Trillions upon trillions of lifeforms, all rooted back to only ten original blueprints, if you will. From these ten, you can extrapolate any of the life forms in any galaxy - even your humans, modified or not."

Raka took over the story. "When this was discovered, the DNA for each of the ten root species were placed in Corviers - essentially indestructible missiles. The idea was to send them out all over the galaxies as an emergency backup, in case any race was ever eliminated through natural or unnatural means."

"Why not store them in an archive where you would know where they are?" Sarah asked.

"Yes, that would be the intelligent move, and many Corviers were stored, but over time, archives were looted. Power changes, no matter what system you are in. The only way to ensure the safety of all the races was to send these Corviers out to all corners of every dimension, hoping that one day, we could find and retrieve one if and when it was necessary."

Sarah nodded. "Ok, so how many do you have?" Raka and Neph didn't answer; they just stared back at her. "I mean, how many have been found, not that you personally have. That would be weird, I think."

"Sarah," Raka answered. "Until now, no one has ever found a Corvier. The DNA inside - the Founder's bloodlines - have all been lost."

Sarah stared up at the image of Seglee, her eyes filling with tears. "So... so you're telling me they all have family? There's others like them? That...they all belong somewhere else?" She thought of Bunny and how he could have been surrounded by his own kind this whole time.

She didn't wait for an answer. She ran out of the war room before Neph could catch her. She pushed past the guard outside the door, and turned down the first hall she found. She could hear Neph calling her name, but she ignored his calls for her to stop.

The hallways were bare, and each one she turned down looked the same as the one before. She tried the doors, but they needed special badges to access and she had none. She ran as far as she could, trying random doors along the way to see if any would open. Finally, she found one that was unlocked. She closed the door behind her, ran to the corner, and curled herself into a ball. She covered her mouth as she cried.

They all have homes, they all have homes, they all have homes, she kept repeating in her mind as she rocked back and forth, tears flowing down her cheeks.

She didn't hear the door open behind her or Neph walk in, before he carefully slid his arms around her. He sat quietly next to her as she rocked and cried. He held her close and didn't say a word.

CHAPTER
THIRTY-FOUR

Back in Neph's quarters, Sarah took a long, hot shower to recover from the shock. She hadn't spoken to Neph about what he had said about the Founders. She needed time to process all the information. When she finally came out of the bathroom, she was wearing the same clothes he'd worn after his shower the night before - black silk pants hanging long on her and dragging on the floor. She had her hair tied up in a towel and his robe pulled tight on top. He went into his dressing room and found her a long sleeve, cozy shirt to wear. Then he poured her a glass of water and they sat on the couch. She curled up against his side, looking out the windows into space.

"I don't know why I'm upset. I knew the moment I saw Raka." She said after a few minutes. "I wondered if maybe Galloyde based Tiny off of the Clorrians. Last night with everyone at dinner, I kept thinking *'Tiny would love this!'* She turned to him. "You knew, as soon as you met him. You knew."

Neph nodded and kissed her temple.

"He's a little different than the rest. I mean, he's still like five feet taller than all the other Clorrians!" They both laughed, and Neph agreed with a simple "Yep."

"He's so smart too," her voice catching in her throat. "I mean, you met him. He's so smart." Her eyes began to well up. "When he finds out, he's going to be so excited that there's others out there just like him. A whole planet filled with his own kind." Neph handed her a soft cloth as she started crying. "He's going to be so excited."

"Several planets, in different dimensions. Yes - and they all will be very excited to meet him too." Neph agreed.

"Then he's going to leave." Her voice turning high-pitched and wavering. "He'll be so happy and then he'll be gone. They'll all be gone." Her tears now cascading down her face. "But I'm so happy for them you know?"

He wrapped his arms around her and kissed her wet cheek. "Yes, I know." When she was done crying the second time, he took her cloth, now warm and handed her a fresh, cool one. She wiped her eyes, which were red-rimmed and puffy now.

"Do you think Galloyde knew?" she asked, "Do you think he knew that they were the Founders?"

Neph thought for a moment and then nodded. "I do," He responded quietly. "Without Galloyde, I suspect they would still be in tubes in the Corvier and not the living, breathing beings they are today. There's quite a bit I don't know yet, but he must have figured out that Earth's atmosphere was able to support all of them, which is extraordinary."

He paused for a few minutes before giving her a wide grin and squeezing her. "They weren't kidnapped you know. Earth is their home. They were born and raised there. You are their home. You are their family. Galloyde did create them - insofar as taking them from their basic DNA stage and bringing them to life. That's one way of looking at it. But they aren't all alone. They never were."

She smiled and leaned into him. "I know," she sighed. "I just...I don't want to lose them, but I'm also happy that they have their own kind."

"Well, Tiny has to come meet my family. That's a must."

Sarah craned her head around. "I would like to meet them too!"

Neph rolled out a raucous laugh. "Who do you think was at the tables the other night? That was half of them. The other half was in a room across the hall. That's just on this ship. Clorrians have immense families."

She pulled out of his arms. "They were all your family? Obviously I knew about Qualla, but all of them?" He nodded.

"Wait," she said, slowly putting the pieces together. "That was one of your family members who came into your bedroom this morning?"

"Oh that, hah! Nimi - he's like what you would call a cousin. Not a big deal. In Clorrian culture, there's no boundaries like bedrooms or what happens in them. We should be happy they didn't show up earlier!"

She gasped and he pulled her back into him and snuggled against her. "Hey, this ship didn't show up just because I asked nicely. I had some pull to get it here."

She gave him a hard laugh. "Oh yes, *Admiral*, you did. They can't really say no if you're the Admiral of the ship can they?"

"Fleet." He said, putting emphasis on the "t," making it sound like 'fleet-ah.'

"Fleet-ah?" she asked, eyebrows raised. "Admiral of the Fleet-ah? Well, fuck me."

He stood up and scooped her into his arms. "Oh darling, if you insist!" and he carried her to the bedroom.

THIRTY-FIVE

When Neph woke up, he was alone in the bed. He wandered out into the main room to find several chairs and boxes piled high in front of the main door. He chuckled, thinking at least they'd hear Nimi coming in next time. Neph made his way to the kitchen area, grabbing an ogller as he continued his search for Sarah.

He finally found her in his dressing room, looking through the long racks of clothes. He quietly watched her from across the room. She stopped picking through the garments and called out. "I know you're there, stalking me like some weirdo."

"Just watching. You can take anything you want. I don't think they'll care." He took another bite of the purple-hued apple.

"Is this where you live? When you aren't busy being the Prince of Darkness, that is?" She was enjoying herself.

He slowly walked over and sat on an ottoman in the middle of the room. "I don't live here. I think they just bring this stuff out when they need it."

"Wait - you don't live here? This isn't your home?" She pulled a coat off the hanger and held it up to him, judging the look against him. She decided against it and hung the coat back up.

He laughed. "No, no, whenever I am here, they drag all this stuff out. The uniforms, the clothes, all of that. I think it gets all packed away when I'm gone. At least I hope it does."

She furrowed her brows. "They barely had time to pull this all out if that's the case. When's the last time you were here—on this ship?"

"You sound like Qualla now." he said, biting the oggler again. "Probably... mmmm, 400 earth years?"

"Wow," she said, dropping onto the ottoman next to him. "You're so old."

"Get out." He pushed her off the cushion and onto the floor. "You're no spring chicken. Don't talk to me about age."

"*Gasp!*" She feigned horror. "Never ask a lady about her millennias!"

He gestured to the clothes, "See any Overseer casual wear in there? Something for your god-like gal on-the-go?"

"Satan! How dare you!" She made devil horns with her fingers and ran out the other side of his closet, but he was already there and caught her around her waist.

She tried to wriggle away but couldn't. He yelled, "Come on Overseer! Let me see your powers! Unleash thy fury!"

She screamed with laughter as they wrestled. He quickly pinned her on the carpet.

"Ha ha! Lord of the Underwear wins!"

"It's *Underworld*, you freak," she giggled.

There was a knock at the front door. His face fell. "Oh shit. I told Raka to come here to finish our conversation. If you're not ready or up to it, we can put it off until morning."

He stood up and then pulled her to her feet.

"No, no, it's fine," she said a little out of breath. "Let me get dressed, Admiral Underwear, then I'll be right out."

He leaned in and kissed her. "I'll be overseeing you later." He laughed at his own joke and left.

"That was lame!" She cried out, then looked for anything in his closet to put on.

CHAPTER

THIRTY-SIX

By the time Sarah joined them, Neph and Raka were already drinking and smoking something that looked like cigars and smelled delightful. Thankfully, Raka was dressed very comfortably, so the clothes Sarah found didn't look out of place.

She saw that Neph managed to get through her pile of junk meant to slow down any soldiers coming through the front door for an early morning visit. He offered her a drink and whispered, "I like that idea," motioning to the heap by the door. She waved off the alcohol, opting to stay with water.

Raka had brought her things from the war room and placed them on the table.

"I just want to apologize about earlier, Raka. I'm so sorry I reacted that way…" she started to say to him. He held up a hand and stopped her.

"You do not yet know me or my race, although you know my Chriska" He gave Neph a conspiratorial grin "We are made of such thick skin only so it can hold our emotions inside. I shed many tears when you left. This is a great day and also a day of sadness. A brother of ours is out there. He does not know of us." Raka's eyes started to shine. "But he will. And that is a good thing. You will not lose your…what do you call him?"

She looked at Nephemerus. "Well, he was called a Demon for a long time—wrongly as Nephemerus and Desimidor pointed out. He is now called a Regulator, along with the rest of the Founders, but he is my friend. He's one of my best friends."

"Ahh, that's why you took to this raqshaa so well." Raka said.

"Oh shit." Nephemerus groaned, taking a puff of his cigar. "Here we go. Buckle in folks, it's going to be a doozy."

Raka didn't wait to be asked. "A raqshaa means 'horned one,' like a bad seed. A troublemaker. I'm not sure what word you use on your planet."

"Oh we have a few like that, Devil, Lucifer, hmmmm…can you think of any Neph? Help me out here?" Her eyes dancing with delight.

Raka let out a booming laugh. "Perhaps we should call you—"

"Nope!" Neph stamped out the end of his cigar. "Nope, that's enough you two, knock it off, we have work to do. Can't waste time gabbing away."

They moved over to the table and sat down, far more relaxed than earlier. Sarah showed Raka the rest of her charges. Neph and Raka chatting excitedly about which species they were and which planetary system they came from.

"Here's Zhaaniscore or Zana for short. Neph, you and Desi haven't had the chance to meet her yet. She's in hibernation right now in the northern sea. She'll continue to stay deep under the ice crust for the next 150 years before swimming down south, feeding, and returning up north again. Every once in a while she pops her head up above water, takes a look around—but that's pretty rare."

She showed an image of what looked like a swimming brontosaurus. Instead of legs, she had long, slender fins and gills down the side of her neck. "She doesn't have anything to do with operations," Sarah said as she beamed at the image. "She's just out there, doing her own thing. Each time she wakes up, I head out to see her, make sure she's good. She's so sweet, I just adore her." She flipped the image to the next.

"And lastly, here's the Triplets. We actually don't have any other name for them, we've always just called them the Triplets," she realized right then.

Neph tapped Raka's arm. "See it? See it?" he asked, like a kid pulling on his mother's coat. Raka stared at the picture, mouth hanging open. Sarah twirled the image.

"What is it?" she asked.

Raka leaned in. "That's remarkable. How do they move?"

"They run on their paws. Sarah, you use them for tracking primarily?" Neph asked.

She nodded. "They track any human who tries to escape Descend and doesn't willingly return. They have the option…" she glanced at Neph. "They are the only ones who have the discretion to cube any human on their own. It doesn't matter what rep the human might be. It's up to the Triplets to decide."

Raka and Neph exchange looks. "Why? Why were they given that power?" Neph asked.

"Tell me what is unusual about them first and I'll tell you why," she countered.

Raka laughed and took a puff of his cigar. "Oh I like her. She's tough, Chriska. Good! You need that! Hah!"

Neph expanded the image so it showed the Triplet's smooth back. "See here? They are supposed to have wings. Like a bird. Legs and wings. The Triplets are Gulcaries. They can fly, run and swim. They are excellent hunters for all the reasons you use them for, but they are also loners. They don't mix—with anyone. Ever. Except your Triplets are socialized. Absolutely phenomenal."

Sarah was shocked. She tried to imagine wings on the Triplet's back and it wasn't hard. How they would love to fly. She felt herself getting upset, and Neph reached out to touch her arm reassuringly.

"They don't even know they could fly. Perhaps there was an evolutionary leap well after the Founder DNA was catalogued," he said, smiling at her and pulling her in for a hug. "They are perfect the way they are now."

Sarah agreed, thought about how well they get along with everyone in Descend, and decided that her Triplets were more special because they didn't have wings.

"They hunt humans—sometimes for days," she said, getting back into the conversation. "The humans could theoretically make it back into the living population if they found the portals. That's why the Triplets have this discretion. If they get into a situation where it's easier to…stop a human, they have that leeway. And whenever a Regulator eats a human, they decide if they want to cube them."

Now Raka drew a sharp breath. "Does that include Thrinythidor?" Sarah started to agree, but then stopped herself. "I don't think Tiny ever ate a human. Not to say anything negative about the others, but you need to understand that Tiny is exceptionally brilliant. He would struggle with any moral implications of doing that for himself. Interesting. No, I can't say he is unable to produce a cube, but I don't know of a time where he ever has."

"So not everyone *cubes* the humans?" Raka asked.

Sarah shook her head. "Definitely not. GilGerg? He would never. It's not in his nature. I could never ask Clara to do that. She loves scaring the shit out of bad kids, but she couldn't possibly hurt them for real. You see Seglee swallowing humans all the time, but always whole. She's not cubing them." She thought harder about it."It's really Bunny who does it the most, because when I found him, he was trapped, being tortured. It was awful. So he's happy to do that job." She finished quietly.

Neph jumped in and changed the subject. "The cube. How are we thinking of using it? Ideas?"

Raka considered this, "I've heard the same stories as you. A Galactic Ripple appears as a thin shimmer of light—sometimes green, sometimes fiery red, others have sworn it was gold. Sounds like it could be different colors at different times or different Overseers see different colors. I do not know."

Neph looked to Sarah. "When I first heard the stories, I thought if there was any truth to them, the thousand souls that are needed to open the Ripple would be taken from those on the ship trying to cross into it. Then a rudderless ship might end up afloat in a strange destination. It always felt more like a cautionary tale to me—a fantasy." He looked at Raka, "Until my last posting. I met a Traveler who confirmed that the Galactic Ripple was indeed real."

Sarah thought about this. "Can we send the cube out into space alone? Into the Ripple? See if it causes some sort of reaction or an opening we can go through?"

"No harm in that. We can recover the cube if nothing happens," Raka replied.

"We will take the Lander to go into the Ripple. I'll have you stay here on Noneru," Neph instructed Raka.

Raka agreed but added, "You should take some soldiers as well. You don't know what you'll run into."

Nephermerus turned him down, not wanting to risk anyone he didn't need to. Then, turning to Sarah, "Unless you feel we need them?" She agreed with Neph, there was no need to bring anyone else.

"Wait!" Sarah suddenly exclaimed. "You said the Corvier carried ten Founders, right?"

Raka was looking at Sarah's ancient hologram disc and looked up. "Yes, it was ten in each Corvier. Somehow the one that struck Earth either opened on impact or someone found it and opened it up."

"I only have seven. Bunny, Tiny, Seglee, GilGerg, Clara, Zana and the Triplets."

"Eight. There was Kevin," Neph added. "You said you banished one called Kevin."

Sarah's face curled down into a frown. "Right." She sighed. "I did say that...but it wasn't me who banished him. That was Galloyde."

Neph considered this. "That makes sense. I doubt you would have banished a Regulator. Kevin must have been either a Whasook, Thandican, or a Nox. Do you know why Galloyde banished him? Do you know anything about Kevin?"

Sarah closed her eyes, remembering. "He was violent, unpredictable. He was dangerous to the rest of the Regulators." She opened her eyes. "I remember Galloyde saying 'it was as if a human was—" She stopped, mouth hanging open before exclaiming, "Fuck! Fuck fuck fuckity fuck!"

Neph and Raka exchanged looks with each other. Sarah started pacing and talking to herself. "Galloyde said 'Kevin was as if a human evolved into the worst possible version they could be and shot across space—and he was the end-product!' Fuck! How did I miss that?"

"Nox!" Neph and Raka said together.

"Sarah," Neph said, "don't feel bad, there's a lot going on. Not remembering one comment made thousands of years ago is not something to get upset about."

"The Nox are known to be difficult, mean-spirited, short-sighted, rude and a bit dim-witted," Raka said. "But I don't think the entire human race could be like the Nox. If they were, you wouldn't be here—and Nephemerus wouldn't be helping you."

"Well," Sarah sat back down and took a drink. "Some days it's a tough call." She winked at Raka and he gave her a hearty chuckle.

Neph rubbed his face, looking at the images. "So we have three missing Founders—the Nox, a Whasook and a Thandican.

Hopefully Galloyde can fill us in on where they all are once we find him."

Raka said he was ready to turn in after the long day. He thanked Sarah for the information, and Neph walked him to the door. Raka turned to his friend in the hall and said, "Qualla needs to spend some time with you—they all do. Chriska, see your family."

Neph sighed and murmured his agreement. He closed the door and piled the furniture back up inside.

THIRTY-SEVEN

S arah sat on a small chair in front of the wall of windows, quietly taking in the wonder of the cosmos laid out in front of her. Neph finished washing up the plates after dinner and was walking back into the main room when he saw her. He sat down on the floor next to her, so tall that even when seated, he could almost remain eye to eye with her.

Staring out the window, she whispered, "If I fail—if we fail—everyone who has ever lived and died will be for nothing, if I can't get Galloyde back to Earth in time to fix them, it all ends. They'll simply vanish. The Council won't accept them as a species until they reach seventy-eight percent Ascension. Right now, all those billions of souls are in limbo, waiting to join the rest of this—" she gestured to the vast universe. "They'll never reach that if I can't free the souls from the endless loop in Descend."

Neph let out a long sigh. "The Council will never—has never—accepted a species that hasn't met their quota. You're right, all those souls will be lost. It...it won't be the first time that's happened though," he said gently, trying to catch her eye.

Sarah continued to stare out at the black void, dotted with blue, purple, yellow, and red stars and solar systems for as far as she could see. "I know. But—but I can't give up on them, Neph. As infuriating as humans are, they can learn. They can be better, I've seen it. All of this can't be for nothing."

She reached over and brushed a lock of hair out of his face, softly running her fingers through before reaching down to take his hand.

"I need to tell you something important," she said solemnly. "I haven't kept this from you on purpose. You just hadn't asked about it, and I need to be completely honest with you."

He nodded, squeezing her hand. Before she could say anything, he said, "Galloyde is your father."

"What? You knew?" Her face dropped.

"Desi figured it out. It makes sense. Was that it? Do I get a prize?" His eyes lit up, teasing her.

"Guh! I'm over here stressing out about how to tell you and you already knew!" She dropped his hand and stood up.

He pulled her down into his arms. "Don't stress out. I told you we figured out a bunch of things. I've also told you that a lot is at stake. See? You never listen to me and I am technically your boss, you know."

She grunted and pushed with all her weight to roll Neph onto his back. He let her. They tussled on the ground, laughing and wrestling with each other for a few minutes before Sarah managed to pin him, her hair falling onto his face.

"I can't believe you knew. No one's ever known, well except for the Regulators." She said, staring down at him.

"Well, no one knew you were an Overseer and I figured that out." He tried to usurp her by knocking her off balance, but she managed to stay on top.

"How did Desi figure it out about Galloyde?"

"See, this is the downside to bringing a super intelligent—and may I add, a dashingly handsome—Elget to Earth." He tried again to gain the upper position and failed.

She ignored him. "I mean, to me it's obvious, but no one else had ever figured it out."

"I'm sure I would have gotten there myself. I'm pretty brilliant you know—and really good looking. '*Distractingly handsome*,' is the most common description I hear people say, almost too good-looking to be true. Really, sometimes it's a curse. But you needed me so I'm here. That's what you said. You needed me!"

He caught her off guard and flipped her over and straddled his weight across her hips. She was stuck under him as he stretched his arm straight out in the air like a maiden in distress. He proceeded with a high-pitched call,

"Oh Nephemerus, you big, strong, handsome, magical god, please, please, I beg you, please help meeee. I need you Neph, I can't do any of this without you. Save me Nephemerus. You're the only one who is smart enough and handsome enough and brave enough to do any of this! Save me and save all of humankind, you brilliant hunk!" He finished with a broad smile across his face.

"Is that what you heard?" She groaned and tried to wiggle out from under him. "We might need to get your hearing—or your brain—checked."

"That's exactly how I remember it. Don't worry, I'm not just dastardly good-looking. I'm ridiculously smart too." He quickly pecked at her face repeatedly as she tried to block him, giggling at how fast and persistent his kisses were. "That's how I figured out you were an Overseer. That was all me and my huge brain."

"Oh it was, was it? Ok, mad genius. Tell me how you knew." She managed to wriggle just far enough away so he couldn't reach her face anymore.

He started to kiss her neck, more slowly, shifting from annoying pecks to soft brushes with his lips. "Those etchings. They were Clorrian symbols. They told me you were an Overseer."

She gasped and renewed her attempt to flip him over. "You didn't figure it out, you just read it on the wall? That's cheating!"

"Well, I had to read it. You and Tiny only got most of the message and Desi doesn't know Clorrian." He continued to kiss her neck. She started to close her eyes and enjoy his attention when she realized what he said. "Wait, what? Most of it? What did we miss?" she asked.

He stopped and looked at her seriously. "I don't know if I should say." His voice dropping down into a serious register.

She started to worry. "What is it? You have to tell me."

He stood up and pulled her up to her feet. "You should probably know before this goes any further."

She swallowed hard and continued to stare at him.

"The missing part that you didn't interpret…said…*the sexy, handsome Admiral comes in and saves the day!*" He shouted as he swept her into his arms and carried her into the bedroom.

This is something I think I can get used to, Sarah thought as Neph slammed the bedroom door shut behind them.

The morning was oddly quiet when no soldiers suddenly burst into the room and woke them up. The pile of boxes inside the front door was moved slightly and appeared to have deterred any possible visitors. They both dressed and ate early. Before Neph had a chance to discuss the day, Sarah suggested he spend it with his family.

"I'm sure they would love to see you. It's been so long since you were last here. I'd like to go over the etchings, make sure there's nothing I'm missing, since now I know they really *aren't* Clorrian symbols, ugh I should have known." She rolled her eyes and Neph gave her an innocent grin. "I think it's really important you spend time with family though, there were quite a few that didn't get to see you the other night."

He brushed her hair back from her face. "Ahhh, but it was too good a setup to resist— Clorrian symbols. Haha! You bought it right away!" He laughed as he leaned in and wrapped his fingers in her ponytail. "You could come with me and meet everyone. Let Qualla question you endlessly about Earth?"

"That sounds fun, but no. They need to see you. Plus you need to spend time with them. I've been keeping you all to myself, which has been wonderful," she punctuated the last few words with a kiss, "but it's time to share. Go. Get. Go home."

He groaned with a smile and looked around. He came back with a thin, rose gold bracelet and put it on her. "This will alert me if you need me. Just press here," he pressed a small charm on top, "and I'll get an alert here!" He showed her his bracelet. "It works anywhere in the Fleet!"

She looked surprised. "Are you leaving the Cruiser?" she asked, worry creeping in on her face.

"Oh no. No, no. This is a security bracelet. It's just in case of— nevermind. You press it, I'll be back here right away."

She nodded. "Can I press it now?"

"Go ahead! Press it all you like!"

She pressed the charm on her bracelet and watched the light on his appear, vibrate and beep. He held his hand up in a wait-a-minute gesture and ran out the room. A few seconds later she heard him yell, "Do it again!"

She pressed the charm a second time and heard a beep far away. Then her bracelet made a faint beep. Then she heard a louder beep outside the room and hers made a louder beep. The last two beeps were the same volume as he was standing in front of her, grinning.

"Like that? I forgot about that setting. We don't really use that function in any official capacity, but you'll know how far away I am. I'll leave it on that setting. Are you sure I should go?"

"I'm absolutely fine. There's food. I have things to do. I can catch a little catnap— hopefully without the guards barging in on me," she gave him a wide smile, her eyes telling him to go, but making him want to stay. "I'll be fine. I promise," she insisted.

He nodded, kissed her and walked to the door. Just before he exited, he turned and said, "If you need anything, all you do is pick up that intercom. Tell them what you want and they'll get it. Whatever it is. In fact, I suggest you make up something strange for them to do— keep them on their toes. They'll talk about it for years."

She laughed. "I'll be fine."

"Maybe join us for dinner?"

"Maybe. If you get busy, it's ok. Go on, be with your family. Be happy. I just want you to be happy."

He kissed her again, and without thinking said, "Ok, Ishonna." Then he was out the door.

CHAPTER
THIRTY-EIGHT

S arah wanted to go over the etchings one more time to be absolutely sure her calculations were correct. The closer they got to the coordinates of the Ripple, the more doubt plagued her mind. *What if they missed something? What if she got something wrong?*

When the Council had been informed that Galloyde had created "monsters," and they decided they were going to banish Galloyde, they did it in their typical bureaucratic way—meaning the least efficient means possible. First, they put out word that they needed someone who was interested in the new field of "Demonology," and who wanted to work in an intriguing solar system just coming under the Council's oversight.

Galloyde received word of this posting through his trader—a fellow who made infrequent stops way out in the Milky Way, or as he used to say, "Milky out-of-the Way" galaxy. He would bring Galloyde supplies and news from time to time. For Galloyde, it was refreshing to see a friendly face—outside of dealing with the primitives Earth had to offer.

Thankfully the news was timely. Galloyde and Sarah had the chance to create a plan before the Council moved forward with his banishment. Galloyde had Sarah apply to the Council listing, posing as a student of historical study and new cultures from the planet Veris. She sent the Council a résumé that was ideal for the position —not that they had received any other applications for the job.

A Representative from the Council named Codet Bahringers hired her after barely asking her any questions during her interview. He seemed annoyed with the task or with her, she couldn't figure out which it had been. The transmission was weak because they had to use a refurbished communicator that Galloyde bartered for, trading minerals and gems for the bedeviling system that just barely made it through the interview.

Veris has a distinctly green sky compared to Earth's blue, so they took great pains to make sure that it appeared Sarah was indeed situated in a comfortable schoolroom on her forged planet. The Representative barely looked at Sarah. He seemed to be screaming at someone off-camera most of the time. When he did finally look at her, he only asked why she wanted the job, cut her off while was she answering, and then told her to stand up and turn around slowly so he could see her in the camera. She did so and when she was done, he said she had the job. The communicator blew out and they lost contact, but she and Galloyde were convinced she was in the clear.

It wasn't until a few days before Galloyde disappeared that he told her there were other demons, but he didn't say how many. She remembered how scared he looked when he told her to find the all the demons and bring them to Descend.

"If they come back, you have to make sure everyone is inside The Gate or all is lost." He looked desperate. He looked like the mad Galloyde everyone talked about, but he was just her dad. She loved him.

Then one day, she was standing in a field talking with Tiny and Galloyde, enjoying the sun, when a Council Traveler appeared in front of them. Galloyde barely had time to wrap his arms around Sarah to whisper goodbye. The Traveler took Galloyde's arm and they vanished.

Sarah pushed away the memory and pulled Neph's long pants on, adding his cozy shirt and laid down. She felt exhausted from the stress after all this time. Plus she hadn't gotten a lot of sleep lately—both because of her and Neph's nighttime activities and her worry about her dad. She felt like she could fall asleep on her feet.

She had heard overheard Raka tell Neph the night before to make time to see his family. Sarah knew he would be torn, so she capitalized on Raka's request by telling Neph to go visit rather than having him make that decision. He probably would have figured out a way that worked for everyone on his own—after all, he hadn't risen to his military rank by random chance.

Although…she would like to know exactly how he obtained a rank this high as a non-native-born Clorrian, and while serving the Council as an Elget to boot. This was fascinating. She had never heard of an Elget having a second job, certainly not a military career. She wondered if the Council even knew of his ranking.

Neph's time on Iitka with Desimidor under the purview of the Council was certainly impressive. The locals were known to chew up their Elgets or send them packing shortly after arriving. The people of that moon could be extremely hostile. By the time their assignment was over, the Council had been petitioned to post both Neph and Desi there permanently by every significant political member within the small Neba Solar Array. The two Elgets had won everyone over. That took strategy, wits, charm, and hard work.

She didn't think she needed his charm part for her plan, and she certainly didn't foresee this romantic liaison developing between them—but they just clicked. She felt a magnetically drawn towards him. They felt natural together.

While Sarah had little to no options for dating on Earth, she never really felt lonely. Now she felt connected in a way she didn't think was possible with another being. Neph felt like an extension of who she was—even though she obviously still had so much to learn about him.

"Like how he's a Fleet-ah Admiral," she murmured to herself as she pulled the covers up.

She certainly liked being with him, but she just couldn't let it get her distracted. There was still so much to do. Right now though, all she needed was sleep.

CHAPTER
THIRTY-NINE

S everal hours had passed before Nephemerus finally extricated himself from Qualla's quarters, carrying several plates of food and making strenuous promises of more visits to come.

He was greeted by the same guard he had posted outside of his quarters. When he had left for Qualla's, he instructed the guard that no one was to enter the apartment without Sarah's permission. The guard looked confused as this was a new procedure and against traditional Clorrian ways.

When he got back home, Neph dismissed the soldier for the evening and brought the food to the kitchen, where he left the plates on the counter. He then barricaded the chairs, boxes and furniture inside the front door. He didn't want to use assign a guard there all night long, but he also agreed with Sarah's desire for privacy.

Neph opened the door to the bedroom to check to see if she was in there and found the lights were off. It took a moment for his eyes to adjust to the darkness. He started to strip off his clothes and as he got closer to the bed, he saw she was lying down, with the blankets on her, curled up on her side of the bed.

He changed his clothes as quietly as he could, keeping the room dark so he wouldn't disturb her. He slipped into the bed and started to curl up against her when he heard her say, "Do I smell food? Is that something to eat?"

He chuckled and said that Qualla sent him back with plenty of food. She popped up gave him a quick peck on the mouth. "Where is it? I'm starving!"

She didn't wait for an answer and headed straight out to the kitchen. He turned on the lights and followed her. She quickly located the food and unwrapped a large plate of meat. Grabbing a fork that was in the drying rack next to the sink, and without even asking what the food was, she dug in.

"Tell me any big news. What's the headlines? Did you see a lot of relatives? What's happening?"

Neph sat at the counter and rubbed his face. His belly was full, and he was ready for bed. "I have cousins who just had twenty-four offspring. They're all doing really well."

Sarah poured a large glass of water and then unwrapped a second plate, heaped with colorful, odd-looking vegetables and what appeared to be a variety of cheeses.

"Twenty-four offspring? At the same time? Clorrian?" She continued to grill Neph between bites.

"Nope. Cousins—they are actually half Galaadorian. They have litters. So yeah, all at once. Clorrians are uni-births."

Sarah didn't answer as she finished drinking her water.

"Other than that, it was a lot of stories, jokes, pictures, guilt trips—you know, regular family stuff."

She pushed another massive forkful of food into her mouth, and he looked down to see she had already finished the entire plate of meat. Then he saw she was working on the second plate too. Qualla gave him enough food to last over a week, even though they were leaving on their mission in the morning. He'd learned long ago to just take the food Qualla gave him, rather than suffer her wrath.

Now, as she finished the second plate and started in on the third, Neph watched in fascination. He had only known her for a few weeks, but she just ate enough rations to last six Clorrian soldiers for a couple of rotations.

She looked down at her empty plates and laughed. "Hope you did eat enough earlier! Whew, I thought I was hungry, but whoa!" She pulled out the final plate and handed it to him. "Here you go—want me to heat it up for you?"

He waved the plate away, "I ate plenty. You can have it. All yours."

He watched as she contemplated eating the last plate of food stacked high with Clorrian appetizers.

"Maybe I'll save this for in the morning, before we go. Wooooo! Man oh man. That hit the spot!" She groaned and patted her belly for emphasis. "Tell Qualla she knows how to cook!"

"What were you up to all day?"

Sarah smiled and gave him a quick peck on the lips. "Wouldn't you like to know?" She said slyly before answering. "I slept actually, it was nice."

"Wait—all day? The whole time I was gone?"

She laughed. "Just about. I was tired and you've been keeping me up the last few nights. I didn't realize how hungry I was though! Whew!"

She walked past him and headed back to the bedroom.

Neph looked at the stack of empty plates and shook his head, wondering if there was more to what he'd just witnessed, before he slowly made his own way back to the bedroom for some much-needed rest.

CHAPTER

FORTY

S arah awoke several hours later, more refreshed than she had felt in a long time. Neph was still sleeping, so she carefully worked her way out from under his arm and out of bed, trying not to wake him. As she made her way out of the bedroom, she noticed a bright light coming from beneath the door.

She had to shield her eyes as she opened the bedroom door. The entire living room was awash in a silver glow. Each piece of furniture appeared to glow as bright streams spilled through the wall of windows. She pressed her face against the coolness of the glass and closed her eyes, shielding them from the brilliance. She rested there, feeling it reflect against her skin.

The Galactic Ripple was true to its name, as she watched the metallic light rise and wane like a crashing wave at a beach—but without a shore to rest upon. She turned her head, trying to see where it started or ended, but the Ripple stretched further than she could see in either direction.

She suddenly became alarmed. Why hadn't Raka called them? Let them know they have arrived? Then, just as quickly, she remembered—he wasn't able to see this phenomenon. She looked towards the bedroom door. *Neph won't be able to see this either*, she thought sadly.

Sarah sat down in the middle of the floor and stared out at the most beautiful light she's ever seen, entranced. She wondered if the light held her father—and the answers she needed—within its depths.

Neph jolted awake just as Sarah closed the bedroom door. He stretched and yawned, taking a few minutes to get out of bed. He needed more sleep, or at least he wanted more. He grinned as he thought of his family yesterday. They had so many questions about Sarah, especially Qualla. *"You've never brought home a girl before, Mery. Tell us everything."* She drilled him mercilessly. Raka really missed out by not enlisting Qualla for prisoner interrogations, he mused. She could be an excellent asset.

He rolled out of bed, thinking of how they'd arrived on the ship as what? Co-workers? Two people with a shared mission? He never anticipated any sort of relationship between them. Neph walked into the bedroom, clicked on the light and splashed water on his face. He took a long look at himself in the mirror. He hadn't realized how much he felt for Sarah until she leaned in against him at dinner. He finished washing his face, then combed his thick black hair into place.

Whatever was going on between them—he liked it. He immediately felt comfortable with her. They both fell in step together, trusted each other. It almost felt like they had been together for years, not just a few days. He was anxious to see where this new relationship could go, but for now, he needed to focus on the mission. For her sake—and the sake of 8.2 billion human lives on planet Earth.

He walked out of the bedroom and saw Sarah sitting cross-legged staring out the windows. She was on the floor, but her eyes were transfixed, she wasn't moving.

He approached her slowly. "Sarah?"

She snapped out of her trance and immediately jumped up. "Neph!

Neph!" She grasped his arms and pulled him to the window. "It's there! It's really there!" Her eyes wide and her movements quick.

"It goes all the way from as far as I can see there—" she pointed breathlessly to the left, "all the way past there." Swinging her arm to the right. "It's bright white, more of a silver, actually—on the tips. Actually it's kinda translucent, like you can almost see through it, but you can't *actually*. Oh! And it keeps moving! It's - well, it's like a ripple of water. Exactly like that."

He chuckled and nodded, looking out at the black, empty space outside the wall of windows. "I'm so happy you're able to see this. It's going to all work out. This is real, Sarah." He took her face into his hands.

"I wish you could see it, Neph. It's so beautiful," she whispered to him.

He stared at her, studying her bright grey eyes, the curve of her jaw, the softness of her cheek. He moved his hand to the nape of her neck and bent down to softly press his lips against hers.

"I can see all of it through you, my little love," he breathed into her ear. She wrapped her arms around him and nuzzled against his chest.

Sarah closed her eyes—and for the first time that she was willing to admit, she believed her plan was going to work.

CHAPTER

FORTY-ONE

A s they were getting dressed, an alarm sounded in the quarters. Neph picked up the intercom and spoke to the Bridge. Sarah looked out the windows and saw the cause of the alarms. Multiple ships had gathered on the other side of the Galactic Ripple. She wondered if those other ships could even see there was a Ripple as she pulled on her boots.

Gathering their things, they ran to the Bridge where Raka greeted them and led them to the displays. A holographic rendering of the exterior of the Noneru showed a few dozen red lights lined up across from one large green light, with a gap between them.

"Athecierian Cutters, Admiral. About sixty ships that we can see right now, but we don't know how many are—" Raka began to say.

"Cloaked. We don't know how many are cloaked. Why? Why are they here? Is there a skirmish somewhere close by we are not aware of?" Neph asked.

Raka shook his head. "No. They have no reason to be here. In fact, we haven't picked up anyone even remotely close to this vicinity since we put in the coordinates. I would say it's their normal shake down tactics, but they wouldn't be doing this if they knew you were on board."

Sarah raised an eyebrow. Neph replied, "He means because of the political level of my rank. They're savvy that way. They are absolute assholes, but they never get caught red-handed. The presence of the Noneru out here indicates that I'm on board. The Atheciery wouldn't pull their bullshit when an emissary to the Council could confirm their presence." He gave her arm a reassuring squeeze.

Raka pointed to the holographic display and rotated it to show each cutter's location around the Cruiser. "They just showed up all through here, but for some reason, they are keeping formation back here."

"That's because they are on the other side of the Ripple." Sarah offered. "I just saw it this morning," she said apologetically. "We were on our way to tell you when they arrived. Is there a way I can add it on this?" She pointed to the hologram.

A Clorrian technician handed her a pen and mimed what to do. Sarah drew an approximate location of the Ripple relative to the Cruiser right into the hologram. "We're here, and they are taking up position on the other side in a way that appears like they can see it." She finished with wavy lines. "It's a shimmery silver, almost translucent," she said with a slight nod and smile at Raka.

Neph worked his brows, deep in thought. "Sarah, you said that The Grand Precipice worked with the Council to move Galloyde into the Ripple. It had to have been a Traveler who put Galloyde in there. It was a Traveler who told me that the Ripple was real. I'd wager they have a Traveler on board right now—and they have a good idea of what we are about to do."

Sarah looked worried. "Yep, I'd have to agree. That makes the most sense. I don't know how, but they know we figured out a way in."

Neph nodded to Raka and they went into the War Room with Sarah close behind. "Captain, I need to discuss our return trip…"

Neph said loudly while making a whirling motion in the air above his head to Raka.

Raka nodded and loudly replied, "Agreed, Admiral, that will take some planning, but it is the best course of action to return you to Clorria." He shut the door and held up his hand in a *hold* gesture while he went into a drawer, pulled out a small device, turned it on, and walked the room. Neph motioned to Sarah to stay quiet.

Raka completed his rounds with a lengthy check at the intercom and door. He shut the device off with a heavy sigh.

"We're good. The range on this is much further than this room, but at least I know we're clear in here. With all the new recruits and transfers, you just never know if there could be a leak. I'm starting to see why you might have legitimately become Fleet Admiral." He ribbed his friend with a quick wink, but added in a more serious tone, "Let's hope you remember why. The presence of the Atheciery obviously complicates matters and in light of new developments," his eyes flashed towards Sarah, "I'd understand if you decided to take a new course."

"What are you—" Sarah started.

Neph cleared his throat. "Thank you Captain, I appreciate your observation. I would like to have our Landers provide cover as we leave. We'll fly evasive maneuvers towards the other side of Kaarcerus." Neph went to the window and gestured towards the left. "If our Landers can pull attention away and we get clear, we'll be able to launch the cube, hopefully find an entrance and sneak in without the Atheciery noticing." He turned back to the Overseer. "Sarah, does that sound like a reasonable plan?"

She nodded and swallowed hard. "Wait. Will the Atheciery fire on the other Landers? Will they start a fight?"

Raka and Neph exchanged looks. Raka answered. "That is unlikely, but not impossible. We have no quarrel with the Atheciery, and if they aren't being paid to cause a problem, they typically avoid it. Yet here they are, and not by accident. I would say someone is funding this exploit, so I cannot say with absolute certainty they will not fire first. They may use our Landers exiting the ship as an act of aggression."

Sarah moved to the window and stared out at the Ripple, deep in thought. The seasoned Captain read the room. "I'm sorry—I need to confer with my men. Please excuse me for a moment, Sarah. Admiral."

After Raka left, Sarah turned and smiled at Neph. "While I clearly missed this part of your background—an astonishingly large part—you've obtained this rank for a reason. I need you to subtract me from the equation, Neph. I need you to subtract any feelings you have for me. I need you to look at this situation objectively and tell me what you, the Admiral of this ship-"

"Fleet." He corrected her.

"Fleet. Fuck. What you, as an Admiral of this entire fleet, believe is the best course of action? Because," she looked back out the window. "I cannot have you risk so many of your people, of your family, to save just one of mine. We can find another way. There's always another way."

He moved beside her and motioned to the Athecierian Cutters. "They'll always be there," he said softly. "They'll make sure that he never gets out. Now, or in a hundred years—or thousands upon thousands more years. In the meantime, we don't know how much longer the humans have before they destroy themselves."

Sarah wiped her face on her sleeve, unable to hold back her tears, and moved back to her chair.

Neph returned to his seat across from her. "I appreciate your concern for my crew. Before I make my decision, I have a question for you—if I may?"

She dried her face and tried to compose herself. She looked at him, watching her with his kind, compassionate eyes. She couldn't allow him to do this if it wasn't the right decision. After all, wasn't this exactly what she spent all her time teaching the humans? Making ethical and moral decisions? She couldn't ask him to put all his people in danger—risking their world to save hers.

She swallowed hard and sat up straight. "Yes, of course."

"Tell me what you love about them. Any of them. One thing. One story. Anything."

"My demons?" she asked, surprised.

He chuckled. "No, Sarah. The reason why we're here. I've only heard terrible things about the humans. Tell me why you are going to these lengths to save them. Give me one good reason."

"Oh!" It was only then that she realized then that Neph hadn't heard about all the good things that the humans were capable of. Those stories usually went through to the Ascend Operations Tower, and if you weren't actively reading those feeds, you weren't going to see them. Sure, occasionally they would hear some good reports in Descend, but Neph hadn't even found his office yet—much less read any reports.

She took a deep breath and thought hard. One story...just one good story. A good human. Just one. She only needed one. Suddenly, she broke into a huge grin.

"Remember the night you went out with Tiny? To see what it was like to be the Elget of Descend?"

He nodded.

"The next morning, you came in and told this story about Clara and how she was drop-flying a kid. Remember?" She leaned in, still smiling brightly.

He nodded again.

"Ok, well that was Ginnie Roberts. Age eight. A real shit. I mean, truly a monumental little bitch. We Ascended most of her family immediately when she set that fire. When something like that happens, there's no question. We ReCall them before natural death and they Ascend before they feel a thing. We can talk about all of that later. Anyways, you had one part of her story wrong. She didn't kill all of her family. That little fuck had tried to kill them all, but her older brother had escaped out the window."

Neph raised his eyebrows surprised, but didn't say anything.

"Downstream consequences." Sarah leaned back and her smile faded. "We haven't had time to talk about that yet. That's Aramik's territory, but it comes up a lot. Her brother Kenny? He survived the fire, but he was racked with guilt. He had a hard time understanding why he lived when everyone else died. He constantly wished he had died too."

She watched Neph furrow his brow and shift in his seat.

"Hold on, I know you wanted a *good* story, but with humans it's never that easy. Okay, so people come out of the woodwork to take this kid in, they give him a home—a safe home, a loving home. They make sure he gets counseling, tell him it's not his fault, all the things he needed to hear.

A couple years go by and he's living with this great family who adopted him. He's about fifteen years old now. The people who adopted him have three of their own kids—two little girls, not psychopaths, and a boy who is just a year older than Kenny.

"So one day, these two boys are running around through the woods, doing kid stuff when they have to cross a bridge. It's one of those bridges where it's only train tracks—no foot path. The kind with planks spaced way too far apart, so you kinda got to jump to get to the next one? Not easy to cross. So before they decide to try it, Kenny leans down, he listens to the rail, and he hears nothing. Smart right? They both hold the rail, still nothing. They look down the tracks in each direction, which are covered with leaves and sticks, and they see nothing. So they figure it's safe. They cross. Nothing happens."

Neph blinked, and she can see him start to breathe again.

"They run around, do whatever stupid shit kids do. But, then it start to get dark, and they turn around to come home. They get back to the train bridge—only this time they don't bother to check the rails. They don't think anything of it, because hey, these tracks aren't ever really used, right? The older brother goes first and—wouldn't you know it—here comes that *motherfucking train*."

"A *good* story, Sarah. Why the humans should be saved," Neph warned in a low voice.

Sarah dove deeper. "The train is bearing down. There's no way the brother can get off the tracks in time. He can't go forward and make it. He definitely can't turn around and run back before getting killed. Plus, now it's night—and the conductor can't even see those two out there. To make it all worse, the kid *freezes* right there in the middle of the track."

Neph rubbed his temples, and ground his teeth.

Sarah leaned in. "Suddenly, the brother is launched over the side of the bridge. Whoosh. Just flies up and over the railing. Gone! *Total Superman move*, that's an Earth thing. Anyway, Kenny had picked up and launched him over the railing like a fucking rocket. He lands in the water below— and he's fine. The brother, not Kenny. I mean, Kenny was *not* fine. The train crushed him to death—obviously."

Neph let out a long groan. "This is your good story, Sarah?"

She laughed, "Well, it's terrible. I mean—it's so tragic right? Except…it's not. Listen, it's not just that Kenny sacrificed himself for the other kid. It's not even that he chose to do something selfless after what his psychotic sister did—which morally speaking? Serious kudos to him. I mean, gold star right there. But to answer your question—it's the *downstream consequences* that matter here."

She leaned back and sipped her water before continuing. "The brother that Kenny saved ended up becoming a general surgeon. Not in some big, fancy hospital. No, he moved way out to middle of nowhere to help people who genuinely needed medical attention but didn't have any money. They paid him in trades. And chickens. But he made a huge difference to the people who really needed him. He was driven to save as many lives as he could to '*pay back*' Kenny for saving his own. He figured out a way to live on barter so people could still get care. That was how he wanted to make a difference—and he did.

"His sisters were so affected by what happened that they dedicated their lives to pediatric mental health—for *pre-K*! That means for super little kids. They wanted to find and help any mini-psychopaths like Kenny's little sister, way before other families suffered from the same kind of fate. Best part? They found some of my Hi-Reps!" Sarah beamed with pride.

"Their system ended up weeding out some of my fuckers before they had a chance to ramp up! It worked! Oh—and the parents? They set up a scholarship fund in Kenny and his siblings' names. Well...not the little bitch. Fuck her. She deserves every five-hundred-foot drop to the pavement Clara gives her. Hah!"

Sarah collapsed back in her chair with a sigh. "Alright, maybe you don't see it—and maybe this wasn't the *best* story to pick. There's plenty of examples of human greatness that flow into Ascend every single day. Humans saving puppies, doing transplants, lifting cars off babies...but for Descend? *This*—this here—is a great story."

Neph remained quiet, studying Sarah.

She was quiet for a moment before adding, "Look, humans as a whole? On the scales? The entire species? *Awful.* Probably on par with those pricks." She motioned to the Atheciery outside the window. "They can be vicious, cruel, and are way more self-serving than self-aware, but a lot of them get kicked in the face daily and still try to be better people. I think that's says something. Yeah, some of them are just the absolute worst without good reason...but then again, a few of them can be great—really great."

She stared back at Neph. "Well, that's the best I've got. Make your decision. But I ask you to make the best *ethical* decision you can, not an emotional one. I'll respect whatever you decide."

CHAPTER
FORTY-TWO

S arah and Neph walked out of the war room and met Raka outside the door. "Admiral? Any orders for our next move?" he asked, as Sarah glanced at Neph anxiously.

Neph scanned the Bridge and addressed his Captain. "Retrieve the Fleet. I want the entire fold here now. Man all the Landers and have them provide cover." He looked at Sarah. "We'll proceed to Kaarcerus." Sarah's mouth twisted in concern, and she wondered if he was making the right decision.

Neph lowered his voice and asked Raka a question. "Captain, could you please remind me of the Multi-Dimensional Galactic Council Core Belief Value from the Verisian Treaty? I only need to hear the third one."

Raka looked confused at first and then gave Sarah a nearly imperceptible smile. "Of course, Admiral. It states 'Assistance will be given to maintain, defend, or restore the independence and vitality of any Council species, who are unable to intercede on their own behalf, when in danger from natural or unnatural forces, who threaten their existence. Help will be rendered when assistance is requested in any form.'"

Raka paused. "As I remember Admiral, anyone refusing that request for help will be prosecuted for treason per the order of the High Magistrate." Then he winked at Sarah. "That goes for Admirals too."

"Thank you Captain. I do remember all that now that you say it." Neph watched as Sarah's shoulders lowered and relaxed.

"Admiral, how many soldiers are you taking onboard with you? Your security force, or at least the Master-at-Arms—" Raka started to say.

"We won't need additional soldiers, Captain." Sarah answered. Raka looked surprised at this break in protocol and directed his gaze towards his commander.

"Apologies Admiral, protocol states security is required for any—"

"Thank you for the consideration, Captain," Neph interjected. "I believe we are all set. Those orders?"

Raka nodded and saluted. Neph returned his salute. Sarah thought she caught another look flash between the two, but Neph took her hand and they were headed out the door before she could question him about it. He was moving fast, like he had on their first day on the ship, so she had to jog to keep up. Soldiers were shouting orders and running past them. She felt bodies bumping into her as she held her bag tight to her chest and squeezed Neph's hand. They turned down a dizzying maze of bright corridors filled with soldiers, all moving toward their assigned craft. She felt Neph place his hand on her head and guide her through a short entryway door. The next thing she knew, he sat her in a pilot's seat and belted her in. He took the seat next to her and began punching a sequence of buttons on the console in front of him.

She had never seen him look so serious. She remembered Raka saying, '*I hope you remember why you became Admiral.*' At the time, she thought it was a jab—part of their normal back and forth. Now she realized it might be that Nephemerus could have remained content to have stayed in that pilot's seat and never rise to any other rank, much less that of Fleet Admiral. A role that he didn't seem to relish.

The small craft burst forward and she gasped, clutching at the armrests. He reached over to steady her with his free hand as several of the small ships poured out of the Noneru's holding bays and into the unyielding vastness of space. She shielded her eyes against the blinding light of the Ripple, wondering how could anyone see to fly.

Weren't they all going to crash into each other? She glanced over at Neph, who was staring straight ahead with that unwavering intensity. She had to remind herself that he could not see the incredible river of flowing light. Only she—correction—only she and the Traveler—could see what was right in front of them.

CHAPTER
FORTY-THREE

Algetia, once the revered and feared Grand Precipice of Ala Mia had been waiting for years for this moment to arrive, but he still couldn't believe it was finally here when he heard that a proximity alarm had gone off near the Ripple. Initially, they believed it must have been an errant asteroid, but the auditor nearly collapsed when he discovered a Clorrian Cruiser sitting right on top of the very Ripple that held the infamous Overseer.

Somehow, Galloyde had figured out how to send a message outside of his prison. Things had certainly changed in the past few years. No longer the fierce presence at the Muldigals' Council Table, nor the passionate teacher with impossible standards—Algetia was now a shadow of his former self. If he could even remember who that was.

He paced when he heard the news. He didn't know how Galloyde did it, and he didn't really care for the details. Now the Grand Precipice had to prepare for what would happen next.

"They'll always think of him as a lunatic," he mumbled to himself. "Never as a brilliant mind, a scholar, a...a..." What was the word he wanted? It was just out of reach. Then his mind went blank. He couldn't think of what he wanted to say anymore—the words were lost. He shuffled over to the chair and sat, looking down at the small desk covered in papers and the warm cup of tea that just arrived.

"Who do you mean, Sire?" asked his assistant, who just delivered the drink.

Algetia's eyes darted back and forth. What were they just talking about? He remembered something about Galloyde. His favorite, in all the years he had been The Grand Precipice. Galloyde stood head and shoulders above the rest. Algetia thought of how he taught him, all the good times they had, their discoveries, the magic they unlocked, the laughter they shared.

Then Algetia remembered how it all ended. Why it ended, and who ended it.

"Servant," he spat out distastefully.

"What was that, Sire?" asked the young and extremely lazy assistant. A future House Guardian, he imagined himself as, now a glorified babysitter to this aging politician. "How is it that I can I help you?"

"She was nothing but a SERVANT!" The Grand Precipice bellowed and pounded his fist hard against the wooden desk, sending the papers fluttering to the ground.

The assistant nodded absently at the outburst and followed his prescribed orders for when the prisoner acted this way. He deftly removed a small package from his pocket, ripped it open and stirred it into the tea. "Here you go, Sire. This will make you feel more rested." He picked up the cup and guided it to the old man's mouth, giving him no option but to take a drink.

Algetia obliged by taking a sip. He closed his eyes and thought again of Galloyde. His mind cleared for a brief moment and he remembered—how did the Overseer get a message out of the Ripple? Then Algetia took another sip of the tea and the thought was lost. He began to drift off to sleep, his head resting on the wooden desk.

CHAPTER

FORTY-FOUR

As their craft joined the mass of other Landers, Sarah's eyes adjusted to the brightness of the Ripple just as she saw another Clorrian Cruiser appear directly in front of them.

"Haha! There they are!" Neph shouted triumphantly.

Before he could finished celebrating, three more Clorrian Cruisers dotted their field of vision. Soon, everywhere she looked, Cruisers appeared with thousands of Landers now flowing all around them.

"This is your fleet?" Sarah whispered in awe.

"My fleet-ah," Neph enunciated. "Look at that—look!" He pointed to the Athecierian Cutters. They were turning and leaving, quickly. "Hahaaa! Yes! Run away, you cowards. Run away! Hahahahah!"

The intercom came to life. "Admiral, all visible Athecierian Cutters have vacated the quadrant. Repeat, all visible Cutters are no longer detectable. We will be remaining in place until further notice."

Neph copied the transmission and winked at Sarah. "This could very well be the reason I became Admiral. Will you look at that? What a thing of beauty."

Her eyes were still moving from Cruiser to Cruiser, trying to count all of them. "Fuck me," she whispered under her breath.

"Oh yeah, planned on it—but you have to wait until this is over." He flashed her a devilish grin before snapping back into military mode. "Alright, get the cube. We're almost to our entry point. I need you to put that into the release chute I showed you earlier. Do you remember where?"

Sarah fished through the front pouch of her bag and found the cube, then unbuckled herself. She gave Neph a reassuring squeeze on his shoulder as she moved past him to get to the chute. A small access panel was located near the floor behind his seat. Sarah crouched down and opened the latch, swinging the panel open and stared at the cube for one last time, willing it to work. Then she placed the cube inside, closed and latched the panel, and buckled herself back into her seat.

"Ready," she said, trying to sound confident.

Neph checked the instruments, looking for any stray ships following them. "You're going to have to guide me into that Ripple, Sarah. We need to be close enough to dip our nose in. I'll release the cube, which will jettison out in front of us about 1,500 yards, and then hopefully we'll see something—a reaction maybe? Or you'll spot it, but you need to let me know if you do. It might happen quick, so be ready. We don't want to miss it."

Neph glanced over at Sarah and saw she looked pale. "You alright? Having any doubts?"

She said she felt a little nauseous, her breathing becoming shallow. "Just keep moving forward on this course. It's directly in front of us. In a moment, we'll be touching it, but definitely not through it. It's massive—as big as your entire fleet. The Ripple could engulf them easily, just to give you an idea of the size of it all."

He kept watch, one hand on the chute release. She felt a charge flow through her as the Lander slowly eased into the Ripple. She glanced at Neph, who appeared to feel the same charge of electricity.

She waited a moment, then said, "Now!"

He pressed the button, and immediately, a shockwave rocked the ship. Sarah grasped Neph's arm. His jaw dropped, his eyes widening as he tried to comprehend what he was seeing.

The cube had burst into a prism of ice-blue light. The center shone pure white with shards of deep blue light pulsing outward, vibrating against the sides of their ship. They could feel the Lander being pulled into the light. Her hand tightened on his arm as she felt his muscles flex against the controls instinctively, trying to control their approach—to no avail. Neph no longer had control of their craft.

She felt the electrical charge flowing through her increase—from the tips of her fingers, through her hair, down the muscles in her back, and into the soles of her feet.

The prism of light became unbearable to look into and they had to shield their eyes. She covered hers with her free arm. As quickly as it had started, the pulsing on the side of the ship suddenly stopped, and through her shut eyes, Sarah could see the bright light was gone.

Their ship had landed…somewhere.

CHAPTER
FORTY-FIVE

S arah had wondered every day where Galloyde had gone after he was taken by the Traveler. Was he in a prison? Another dimension? Had the Council condemned him to the torturous state in which prisoners are kept physically alive, but their consciousness is frozen on a repeating set of images? Never able to sleep, never allowed to think of anything else. Never ending. Designed to be as inhumane and cruel as possible and the favorite form of punishment of certain Council Leaders.

Overseers, as the name implies, can glimpse the past, present, and future. Not much was known about their powers beyond legend—for a reason. They didn't want to be used as weapons or slaves by any race looking to exploit their gifts.

Sarah hadn't known she was an Overseer until right before Galloyde was taken. She had assumed everyone could see pockets of the past, or would have dreams that came true about the future. She innately knew where her charges were, how to find anyone in Descend by just thinking of them. She would see them, their surroundings, and often, hear their current discussion—enough to know exactly where they were.

It was when The Triplets had cornered a wandering primitive one day, that she saw a vision of the human and their past misdeeds. The bear head roared, and the lion smacked his tongue against his lips in anticipation of a meal. Sarah was struck with a vision of the recent past where she saw the woman lift a rock and bash in the head of another barbarian. She repeated her assault until the man was dead. Another brief glance at the woman revealed that she had a child, and Sarah saw the man in her vision, pick the young child up, toss him several feet in the air, and nearly land in a fire. The man then took the child's food. After the mother checked on her boy, she picked up the rock, killed the man, and fled with her son.

Sarah called out to the Triplets' to stop. They looked at her, confused and disappointed. They had already decided that she was dinner that night—this was before the humans were deemed self-aware and were fair game to any predators.

Sarah ran over to the woman, who was cowering down, thinking that if she didn't make eye contact with The Triplets', they would forget about her. Sarah heard a whimper as she approached—the woman was standing in front of a bush, a bush where she tucked her son behind her.

That was when Sarah realized she saw things others could not. She waved the Triplets off, and let the woman and her son go. Granted, they were eaten shortly after by a mountain lion, but hey—a girl can try to help.

After Galloyde disappeared, Sarah couldn't find any trace of her father using her mind, no matter how hard she tried. Now, knowing he was placed within a Galactic Ripple explained why she couldn't locate him. The Ripple was constantly moving in and out of dimensions, protected by an energy field. Even her powers to locate as an Overseer were useless against the straight-up energy field that formed the Ripple—making it the perfect hiding place.

The craft had landed on solid footing. Outside the windows, they could only see a diffuse grey light. Neph was staring at her, asking if she was alright without saying a word. She nodded, paused, and returned the same look. He nodded. They silently rose from their seats, put on their pressure suits and cautiously opened the Lander door.

The ramp swirled the fine, ashen mist as it lowered to the ground, but that didn't help clear the air well enough to see what was around them. Sarah began to walk out the door, but Neph blocked her with his arm and gave her warning look. He pulled out a weapon. Sarah was alarmed, but relented, knowing this was the only way he would be comfortable proceeding. She followed him down the Lander's ramp as they slowly made their way forward.

"I don't have any mapping capabilities, and it's trying to figure out the air composition, so keep your helmet on until we know more," he said through the communications relay in her suit. "I'm not seeing anyone else out here except for us. We can track our way back to the Lander using this, in case we get turned around in this mist. Turn yours on here." He clicked a button on her left arm, and a display popped up.

She looked all around, feeling strong pull in one direction and pointed Neph that way. In the distance they saw the shadow of a looming structure, but it was difficult to make out any details in the flat light. They started slowly walking toward it slowly, Neph leading and Sarah a stride or two behind. Both of them scanned the landscape with every step.

They reached the base of an ashlar rock wall, stretching upwards sixty feet to a wide parapet that ran along the top edge. The mist curled back and stopped at the wall, as if repelled by the stone itself. Neph checked his display and saw they were still the only two dots in the vicinity.

They walked along the base of the wall for a few minutes before arriving at a large wooden doorway. It was peaked in the center like a medieval gate. There were no windows or holes to peer through. Neph gestured to Sarah and together they pushed the large double doors inward. They opened surprisingly easily, Sarah noted.

Inside, they found an entirely different world than the vast drabness outside the walls. Sarah drew in a sharp breath as she eyed a colorful stone courtyard adorned with tropical flowers growing on lush vines, lazily twisting and climbing the rock walls and over the staircase railings. The walls were tastefully decorated with shelves filled with curios, bright vases and a faded tapestry.

A white marble fountain was placed prominently in the center of the courtyard. The statue was of a young woman carrying an urn, pouring water into the pool as the centerpiece. Her fingers broke the flow of the water as it left the mouth of the urn, separating it into multiple streams. This created a gentle bubbling sound as it landed in the pool, swirling against the edges before returning to the urn to complete another cycle. This was the only sound to break the eery silence—other than the crunch of the gravel beneath their shoes, Neph noticed.

Along one side of the courtyard, sat a small café table covered in a red checkered cloth. The table held an open bottle of wine and a book facedown. Sarah walked past the little table, heading towards the stairway that led up to a second-story deck and a doorway that was closed just above the fountain.

Neph watched as Sarah moved up the stairs and suddenly his heart rate quickened and he felt dizzy. He felt dazed momentarily as the pieces of a puzzle he wasn't even aware he was thinking of, dropped into place. Now he felt sheer terror. "Stop!" Neph hissed. "Don't go up there!"

She turned to see his face was flushed. Was he angry...or scared? She had never seen him like this before. He walked over and took her by the arm. "This isn't safe. You shouldn't be here in your condition. I made a mistake-"

Just then, the door burst open at the top of the stairway. A man with a long, white beard, bright blue eyes and rosy cheeks stepped out and appeared startled as he looked down at the two of them for a moment. Then he let out a deep, booming laugh.

Neph pushed Sarah behind him and trained his gun on the bearded man. He had backed her under the walkway by the time they heard the laughing. She twisted out of his grip and looked at Neph in shock.

"What is the matter with you? That's my father! He's why we're here. Put your gun away!" She checked the display on her suit. The atmosphere read as breathable and she swiftly removed her helmet as she moved towards the stairway.

Galloyde looked down and a small sob escaped his lips. "Sarah! You're here! My lovely girl, I knew you come for me." She raced up the stairs to him and they embraced as Neph looked around the rest of the courtyard suspiciously. He cautiously removed his helmet, still unsure about the air. He then watched as Sarah reunited with Galloyde and walked with him back down the wooden steps.

"Dad, this is Neph—" Sarah started to say, but Galloyde waved his arms towards Nephemerus, beckoning him.

"I know who the Admiral is. You…you, young Merus, are why my daughter could make this journey. Come here. Let me see your face." Galloyde held out his arms widely.

Nephemerus took a reluctant step forward. Galloyde grabbed his arm and pulled him closer, closing the gap, and as he did, Neph felt an instant wave of relief and calmness flow through him. As Galloyde met his eyes, he felt reassured and more confident. He lost any sense of the suspicion he was feeling before.

"Your daughter is extraordinary. I only want to help her." Neph confessed, feeling slightly dazed again. Where did that come from, he wondered.

Galloyde clamped his hand on Neph's shoulder. "Good lad, good. Glad to hear it. We should go. We have much to discuss, but I have been here long and must leave. The others are coming now."

Sarah looked alarmed and started to put an arm around Galloyde who shoo'ed her away.

"Sarah, I am quite capable of walking on my own. Go. Prepare your ship. I will follow. I must find something first though, before I take leave." He told her as he started searching the ground fervently.

Sarah looked to Neph with her jaw tight and her eyes pleading for his help. There was no way she was going to walk away from her father after all she went through to find him. Galloyde was now looking intently around the fountain when an explosion rocked the wooden door to the courtyard.

"Oh, well now, they are already here," Galloyde said, rubbing his beard with one hand and waving one finger in the air with his other hand. "This is not what I had hoped for." He continued to walk with his head down, searching.

Neph ran towards the door and pushed the cart in front of it. On the other side, someone was insistent about gaining entry. Smoke began to fill the courtyard from the explosion. Whoever was on the other side of that door was ramming it with enough force to worry Neph.

"Dad, DAD! We have to go now! What are you doing? What are you even looking for? We have to leave it," Sarah pleaded with him.

"Sarah! I can't hold this door much longer. We have to go, now!" Neph said firmly. "Galloyde, where is your back way out?"

Galloyde kept searching, mumbling, "I don't understand it. It must be right here," he muttered, without any sense of urgency.

The door pushed open just far enough for an arm with a weapon to reach through. Lasers began to shoot all over the courtyard. Neph shot the arm, which dropped the weapon. He pushed the door shut again and held his body against it.

"Found it! Hah!" Galloyde cried out as he picked up a tiny white pebble and studied it before placing it in his pocket. "I could not leave this behind! Can you imagine?" He winked at Sarah. "Over here, come along now, don't dawdle Merus." He shuffled towards the tapestry and pulled it aside, revealing a hidden tunnel. They dashed past the cloth covering and down into the wall of the compound just as the cart broke apart behind them in the courtyard.

They emerged from behind a wall of ivy not far from the wooden doorway. Sarah and Neph each put an arm under Galloyde to move him along as quickly as possible. They hunched down, hoping the mist would provide the cover they needed to make it back to their ship.

"Who was that?" Sarah whispered.

"Athecierians. Must have come through the opening on our tail, cloaked," Neph grimaced.

"Athecierians!" Galloyde cried out loudly, seemingly unaware of the danger.

"Shhhhh!" Both Sarah and Neph hissed as they bent down even lower to try to hide, but it was too late. They had been heard. In the distance, they could hear shouting. Lasers blasted past them.

One buzzed past Sarah and Neph cried out, "Sarah!"

"I'm fine," she snapped at him. "Stop it, they'll hear us!"

Then Galloyde made an odd gasping sound and stopped moving forward. They looked down and saw blood fanning out along his left flank. Sarah ducked down to get a closer look and let out a surprised gasp when an Athecierian suddenly appeared out of the mist, almost on top of them. Neph turned and shot him in the head. Galloyde groaned in pain.

"Can you walk?" Neph asked. Galloyde grunted as he tried to lurch his way forward.

"I've got him," Sarah said putting his arm over her shoulder, but Neph held his hand out to stop her.

"No! You need to get into the Lander, right now! I can't risk you being hurt in your condition. That's an order, go!" he said roughly, pointing towards the ship.

Sarah stood straight up, stepped past Neph, and waved her arm over her head. Two armed Athecierians that were running up behind them flew up and backwards through the air, landing several feet away. Neph looked at Sarah, shocked.

"My condition? What are you talking about? How about you get him into the Lander?" she said, "I've got this."

Sarah walked off towards a large dark shape positioned near their craft. As Neph half-walked, half-pulled Galloyde towards their escape, he saw Sarah approach the dark shape, which turned out to be an Athecierian Cutter. She made a swinging, then ripping motion with her arms. The Cutter lifted off the ground and split into two pieces in front of his eyes.

He couldn't believe what he had just seen. He had been in battles and wars across the cosmos, and he had never seen such a deadly display of might and power. No being had ever been capable of shredding a ship apart through sheer will. If she can do that, what else is she...or any Overseer...capable of doing?

She turned and saw him staring at her. "What are you doing? I already told you to get him inside! Move it." She flicked her hand and, in the distance, he heard another Athecierian cry out in pain.

Neph didn't move, He couldn't. He was trying to form words when he saw a laser graze past Sarah's cheek.

He screamed, "Sarah! get yourself and the baby on the ship, NOW!"

Sarah's face flickered with rage for a millisecond before her eyes narrowed and she strode over to him and growled, "Get it together Admiral, now!"

He shook off his daze and started to move with Galloyde when Sarah grabbed her father, lifted him completely off the ground, and carried him into the ship herself. Neph was speechless. He followed her in and locked up the Lander door as she belted Galloyde into the third seat, then took her own.

He leaned over her seat. "Sarah," he whispered into her ear. "I was just worried about you being hurt. I don't—"

She turned and gave him a murderous look, which stopped him cold. He took his seat and glanced once more at Sarah, who was staring straight ahead, her jaw set. He guided the Lander off of the surface, hoping to find their way back to the Noneru.

As the Lander gained altitude, Sarah placed her hand on his forearm—not lovingly, but firmly, with purpose. She closed her eyes. The mist fell away and Neph could see the entry point from which they arrived through, but it appeared to be closing. He accelerated through the center of the prism and was transported back to where his fleet was waiting for them.

Neph immediately noticed something was very different, as if all of space was much brighter. All of the Clorrian Cruisers were awash in a silver glow. He turned to look out his side window and saw a sea of incandescent streams of light, tumbling over one another like waves on a beach. The size of it was enormous, blotting out all the stars and galaxies in his field of vision.

Nephemerus could now see the Galactic Ripple.

CHAPTER
FORTY-SIX

T he Lander was pulling back into the bay on the Noneru and before Neph could shut down the engine, the door slid open and the medical team boarded. They immediately moved to Galloyde, with Sarah already at his side.

"He was shot here," she said, showing them the entry wound. She had already placed a dressing from the Lander's first aid kit to help control the bleeding. "He never lost consciousness. This happened just a few minutes ago—a few pilns," she adjusted her time frame to theirs, but the medical team didn't ask her any questions or seem to be listening.

Galloyde smiled at her, patted her hand and said "Don't worry, my little Gator. We'll talk soon. Let them do their work." They loaded him onto an oblong hovering stretcher. Once he was in place, a membrane enclosed around him and the team quickly ran off toward the medical bay.

Neph reached out and gently touched Sarah's forearm, holding her back for a moment. "I need to meet with Raka. I'd like you to come with me, but I understand if you need to go with your father."

"I'm going to Medical. You can handle the debrief without me," she said flatly.

"He's going to be fine," Neph tried to reassure her, and moved to pull her in for a hug—when she shoved him back—hard.

"Careful," she snapped, "you wouldn't want to crush the baby!"

"Sarah!" He cried plaintively but she was already down the loading ramp and running to catch up to the medical team. He watched until she rounded the corner and disappeared out of sight. Raka appeared at his side with a huge smile, throwing an arm around his shoulder.

"Ahhh, congratulations, Admiral! A huge triumph!" He noted the despondent look on Neph's face and dropped his own smile. "Or… perhaps I am missing something?"

"Eh," Neph sighed. "The mission was a success, but I made a—I said something out there—" He shook his head. "I let my feelings get ahead of the operation and I don't know, I made a tactical error, Raka."

Raka studied his old friend. He gestured toward the Lander, and they stepped back in, sealing the door. Raka taking the pilot's chair while Neph collapsed into Sarah's seat.

Raka started first. "I'm not sure what you said, but you are aware that you just recovered an Overseer from a Galactic Ripple. Someone who may save an entire species. You did it because it was the right thing to do—and you planned on doing it without knowing you were going to fall in love with that woman."

Neph looked up at him, surprised.

"Oh Chriska, I am not stupid. You two were not a couple when you boarded, but something has changed between the both of you. And my friend, you did not do all of this based on your emotions. I take that back. You do almost everything based on your emotions, which makes you a far better Clorrian Admiral than most of these

Academy raqshaas we have running around today." He let out raucous laugh, enjoying his own joke.

Neph sighed. "I made such a big mistake today. There was gunfire and suddenly I panicked about her getting hurt. I—I said something about her being pregnant—"

Raka's eyes widened. "Is she with child? Am I wrong, and you two have been together longer than I realized?"

"No!" Neph exclaimed. "No, well. That's the thing. I—We haven't talked about it. Alright, when she first came on board, she was drinking alcohol—not a lot of but you know, enough that I noticed when she suddenly stopped. Now she only drinks water. She slept an entire day, and then ate a week's worth of Qualla's food in only a few minutes! She's been nauseous, plus…she cries a lot, like *a lot*. I've never seen her cry before. Never. I don't know. That's all strange right?"

Raka nodded. "That does sounds like she is with child. I can see why you think that, but that is very fast, chriska. Maybe she is sick? Maybe it is something else? Maybe a human sickness? They are very strange creatures, I have heard."

"She isn't human, remember? She just lives there." He rubbed the sides of his face. "I don't think she can catch anything from them. Maybe it's an Overseer thing? I don't know, but come on, doesn't this sound like a pregnancy? We have enough cousins to know how this starts."

Raka nodded thoughtfully, "So you waited to tell her your concerns about offspring until when? Down there, when you were under fire?"

Neph groaned and looked at the ceiling, covering his face as Raka broke out in another round of hard unyielding laughter, shaking the small Lander on its pedestals.

"Ok, alright, that's enough." Neph said, trying to get him to stop.

Raka's laughter only increased in volume and strength. "Wait, wait! You waited until you were being shot at to let her know you thought she was with child? This seemed like the best time to talk about it to you?"

Neph folded his arms and waited for the hysterics to end, pursing his lips, finding no joy in his friends' outburst.

Raka only stopped when he needed to catch his breath. "Tell me, tell me…ahhhh, tell me what you said. What were the exact words you used?" he begged, as he wiped tears from his eyes.

"No." Neph kicked at the floor with his boots.

"You must. You have to, tell me the words." Raka insisted.

"No." Neph repeated louder.

"Ok," Raka accepted Neph's answer. He paused before saying. "I will ask Sarah then."

Neph's eyes bore holes through Raka. "You wouldn't dare!"

"Oh, I would," he returned with a smile. "I'll bring celebration desserts and presents to your room. I'll invite Qualla to come with me. She will be overjoyed!"

"Fuck you."

"And get me with child?" Raka said, starting to laugh again. "No, thank you."

Neph stared out the window. "I said something like, 'I can't risk you getting hurt in your condition.' Galloyde had just been shot and we had an Athecierian running us down."

"Is that all you said, Chriska?" Raka asked his friend, knowingly.

Neph drew in a long breath and pushed it out with a cough. "I might have said it was an order. I did. I said, 'that's an order.'" He avoided Raka's gaze.

"And?" The Clorrian raised an eyebrow.

"And I might have said something like 'get yourself and the baby on the ship.'"

Raka asked breathlessly. "What did she say?"

"She didn't even acknowledge what I said. She told me to get Galloyde inside and she would take care of the others. And she did. Raka, you wouldn't believe what she's capable of. Her powers are beyond anything you've ever heard of…it's a bit…well, let's say I'm glad she's on our side."

"Oh. Shit. Oh shit." Raka repeated, eyes wide.

"Yep."

"You are fucked."

"Yep."

They sat in silence for a moment. "Wait, so you don't even know if she carries a child, not for sure?" Raka asked.

Neph thought for a moment. "Well, no, but come on, I mean, those are pretty clear signs right? She slept like 15 hours straight, and then ate all that food in one sitting? She keeps drinking water instead of any alcohol and she likes to drink, she's a Demon Keeper after all! Anyways, I don't think it could be anything else. Maybe she's pregnant doesn't even realize it?"

Raka shrugged. "You two need to talk. The only thing I know is that you two are paired, so don't mess this up, Chriska. She's the right one for you. Even Qualla likes her. Go write your report." Raka stood and moved to the door. "Are we releasing the Fleet?"

"Keep two, release the rest. I don't know if there are more cloaked Cutters out there. Start rolling towards 7298." Neph sighed and stared out the window into the bay, lost in thought.

CHAPTER
FORTY-SEVEN

S arah watched as the medical team tended to her father. They kept him on the floating stretcher as they provided care via the ports surrounding him. She saw them remove his clothes and toss them onto the floor. She picked them up, and as she did, the little white pebble fell out. If it was important enough to him to get shot for, she should keep it for him. The rest of his bloodied clothes were bagged and sent to the incinerator.

She couldn't get close enough to see what was happening as the Clorrian team moved beautifully around him, like a symphony— albeit a silent one. She heard no audible communication between them. She marveled at how efficiently they moved, working side by side.

Finally, the staff stepped away from Galloyde and the shield around him retracted. He was moved onto a bed, covered by a blanket and appeared to be sleeping. A medical technician approached Sarah and explained they had removed all the injured tissue, but he had some damage to his nerve endings and kidney. They were able to save his kidney, but it would take some time to heal the nerve endings properly.

"How long will it take?" Sarah asked her, "For it to heal?"

The Clorrian considered for a moment. "Two to three rotations, no longer. Go. He needs sleep. We'll let you know when you can visit."

"Can I just stay with him here?" Sarah asked.

The Clorrian looked at her like she was insane. She repeated herself slower so Sarah would understand. "Go. We…will…let you know… when you…can visit."

Sarah nodded and squeezed her father's hand before she left. They didn't know that she just rescued him after thousands of years apart. They didn't know he was an Overseer, and would likely heal himself much faster than they anticipated.

She also couldn't blame them for not wanting someone sitting in the middle of their bay while they tried to work. She smiled at the Clorrian and headed out the door and into the corridor.

She had no idea how to get to Neph's quarters from here. She started to walk in one direction, hoping she would see something familiar. She kept walking down the long hallway and turning at the end of it, then walked some more without seeing anything she recognized. She turned around and retraced her steps, trying to go in the other direction, but soon, the hallways all looked exactly the same. Finally, she stopped someone and asked for directions.

"The Bridge?" she asked the Clorrian soldier. "Which way to the Bridge?" Sarah thought she knew her way from the Bridge back to Neph's quarters. Neph might even still be debriefing with Raka when she got there.

The Clorrian soldier nodded and pointed down one long hallway. She thanked him and walked as far as she could but found nothing to indicate which direction to go next. She found no elevator and no other hallway that led off the long hallway to another route. She walked back in the direction she thought she came and couldn't find the medical bay. Now she was lost.

Sarah sat down on the floor, head in hands. She was exhausted and frustrated. Then her bracelet started to vibrate and beep. She looked down, forgetting she had it on. She heard another low beep. She stood up and moved down the hall. The next beep was louder and the bracelet vibrated on her more strongly. She walked faster, and the next beep became even louder. She broke into a slow jog and at the end of the hall, turned and moved in another direction.

The next beep was a low tone and the bracelet didn't vibrate. She stopped moving and stood still, waiting. The beep was low again. She turned around and retraced her steps, her heart pounding. The beeping sound increased. She moved forward slower this time. She noticed the light was bright on the bracelet. She reached the end of the hall and looked to the left. Nothing. She turned around and looked down to the right. At the end of the corridor running towards her, was Neph.

Sarah broke into a run and threw her arms around him. "I couldn't find my way back, I was lost and couldn't get back to you." She held him tight and pushed her face into his neck.

"I know, I know," he held her tight against him. "I came looking for you and when you weren't in Medical, I knew you would try to walk back on your own." He pulled back from her just long enough so he could look into her eyes. "Sarah. I'm sorry. I'm so sorry."

She nodded and leaned back into his chest. "I don't want to talk about that right now, ok?"

He held her as they both caught their breath. Then he took her hand, and they slowly walked back to the quarters. When they arrived, she headed straight to the shower to rinse off the sweat and blood of both her father and the Athecierians from the battle earlier.

She was letting the steam of the shower fill the bathroom when Neph came in to check on her. He cracked open the door and called to her to make sure she was alright. She didn't answer and hid her face while waving him to come in. Worried, he slipped into the room, afraid she was injured and they missed it in all the commotion. His face twisted in concern as he approached her, standing under the hot water. She was facing away from him, head down. He felt panic start to flutter in his chest when she quickly turned and grabbed his shirt and pulled him into the shower with her, attacking him with a flurry of kisses.

CHAPTER

FORTY-EIGHT

After taking a long, hot shower, they dressed and went out to the kitchen. Sarah pulled out the last plate of Qualla's food and heated it up. She gave Neph a sly grin as she slid it over to him, placing the utensils next to the plate and then pouring him a tall glass of water. While he ate, she went over to the liquor cabinet, poured a small glass of kasyli, and sat down next to him.

She locked eyes with him and without saying a word, slugged back the drink and slammed the glass down. She leaned over and whispered, "Wow, would you look at that? Guess I'm going to be a shit mother, huh?"

Neph groaned. "Ok. Let's talk about it."

"Talk about what?" she asked with a gleam in her eye. "What is there to talk about? Oh wait, what was it you said? How you made the wrong decision to bring me out there in 'my condition?' Or when you ordered me to get into the Lander? Was there a small infant somewhere out there that I overlooked, Neph? Had you seen a baby crawling around on that Ripple, or do you possibly think I might be pregnant?"

He pushed his plate away before answering. "Look. I admit I handled this poorly. I should have talked to you about my concerns—"

"Concerns? Concerns! Aha, oh I get it. We had sex and of course you must have instantly impregnated me because you have god-like sperm. You're oh-so-powerful, you're the great Nephemerus os Clorria! Have sex with me and have my babies instantly! I must have missed that part of your bio. Wait, am I already showing? Was that the giveaway? Tell me, what that it?" She took his hand and made him rub up and down on her flat stomach.

"No!" He yanked his hand back. She gave him a playful smirk as she poured another drink and slugged it down.

"Come on, Sarah. Let me explain."

She gestured that he had the floor.

He led her to the couch and sat down with her. "When we first got on board, we both were drinking and having fun...lots of fun." He smiled and tickled her. She giggled and curled up in a ball, slapping his hands away until he stopped.

He sat back and continued to explain. "I noticed you were drinking a lot of water—well, only water. Which I figured was because of that!" Pointing to the clear mead. "That can do a job on your stomach, so I didn't think much of it, but then you slept an entire day away, which I thought was a bit strange—"

"Because I drank water and slept all day after you kept me up all night with sex-a-thons, so naturally I must be pregnant? Seriously?" Her brow narrowing.

"No! When you ate five days' worth of food in ten minutes along with...you know, well, you know..." he said, his voice drifting off.

She leaned in close to him, noses almost touching. "No, Nephemerus, I don't know. Please tell me why after three rotations you think you made me pregnant. Say it. Say it out loud. Succinctly." Her eyes burrowing into his.

He swallowed hard. "Well, thinking about it now, I'm not so sure-"

"I bet you're not." She snapped and flopped back to her spot on the couch.

"I've never seen you, uh, well on Earth you're always very controlled and in control and in charge and on top of things and you know, you can be, you know - a little scary. I told you sometimes you can be scary."

"Go on." Sarah had one eyebrow raised slightly.

"So here, things are different and you know, obviously they are different and you react differently, and for good reason and sometimes you…you have good reasons, really good reasons—" He rambled aimlessly.

"I'm going to stop you from this agony right now, darlin." Sarah drew in a long breath. She counted each of the offenses on her fingers. "Just so I get this right, you think because I drank some water to rehydrate, because the circulation system here is dry as fuck, and because I took a long nap after we had a couple all-night sex sessions and I didn't get any sleep for two days, and because I ate a big meal after those all-nighters, and then because what? What? Because I've been crying? Neph, was it because I cried when I found out that almost everything I knew about my life was a lie? Oh well, when you put it that way, of course I must be pregnant. That is the only possible answer. Good job. You're a real detective."

Neph stared at the ceiling, not answering her and trying not to make eye contact.

"It's so obvious, I wouldn't have known if you didn't point it out to me, and then—whoop!—One day a baby is going to just shoot out of me. What would I do without you here to tell me about my body? Hey, when do we start picking out baby names? Did you tell your family yet? Should I bake a cake for the party?"

"Sarah—"

She got up from the couch and started pacing in front of him. "How dare you endanger *our* child on the Ripple like that?" She went to the liquor cabinet and this time, didn't bother with the glass —she slugged the kasyli straight from the bottle.

"Neph, why didn't you explain to me that I was pregnant before we went down there? I guess I'm too stupid to know how any of this works right?" She slugged back another mouthful of the potent alcohol.

"I also don't understand why you haven't made a ship-wide…no wait, Fleet-ah wide announcement! I mean, you're the new Admiral Daddy. Wait! Does our baby have other sisters and brothers?" She paused to take another long pull from the bottle, wiping her mouth with the back of her hand, continuing to pace.

"What am I saying? You naturally impregnate anyone you have sex with, so *of course* our baby has tons of siblings. You probably have babies in every single dimension, am I right?"

She dropped the now-empty bottle on the carpet and burped.

"Fuck," Neph moaned.

"Nope. Can't tonight honey. Got a bun in the oven, remember?" Sarah stormed off into the bedroom and slammed the door behind her.

CHAPTER

FORTY-NINE

Neph washed the dishes and finished his report on Galloyde's extraction. Then he sat on the couch, alone in the dark for a long while. He was worried. Was his relationship with Sarah going to be over before it even had a chance to start? Just because he assumed something that, now in retrospect, was so stupid? Why did he even think of it?

He went over the encounter again in his mind, admonishing himself for telling her—no ordering her—to get in the Lander. He closed his eyes thinking of how she didn't even respond to him when he told her to get to safety. He thought of how quickly and easily she was able to stop the Athecierians. Did she know she could do that? Did Galloyde? Are all Overseers able to rip ships in half?

He had never even met an Overseer before Sarah. There were less than a dozen known to exist in all the Universes, and at the moment, he had two of them on his ship. No wonder she had asked him what he knew factually, versus the rumors or stories. Either the other Overseers weren't as powerful as she was or they don't let anyone see what they were really capable of doing. If they had, tales of their strength would have spread wildly out of control—or worse, they might become weapons against their will for some of the more unscrupulous races.

His mind turned back to Sarah. She was certainly confident on the Ripple. Effortless, he thought. If she could rip a Cutter in half, what else can she do? Well, she did say they didn't need to bring any soldiers with them, now he understood why.

He stood up and walked to the windows, staring out at the shimmer of the Ripple he could still see in the distance. Perhaps traveling into the Ripple was what allowed him to see it now. His mind whirled at what an incredible gift it was—to be able to see what only a handful have ever witnessed.

He looked at the closed bedroom door. He longed to lay down beside her, but he also dreaded it. He didn't want to fight. He understood how angry she was—and rightfully so. This wasn't about assuming she was pregnant; it was about not communicating with her after he had asked her to be truthful with him.

He cautiously walked over to the bedroom and his hand hovered over the handle, positive it would be locked. He considered not finding out and just sleeping on the couch. His hand pressed the handle—it opened. A sigh of relief escaped from his lips.

He cracked the door and saw the light was left on in the bathroom. He found his second pair of long pajama pants neatly folded on the counter waiting for him. He glanced into the bedroom and saw his side of the bed had been turned down. He changed out of his clothes, turned off the light and gently slipped under the covers, careful to move as little as possible. After a moment, Sarah rolled over and tucked her arm around him, laid her head on his chest and said, "You have to talk to me Neph. If something is on your mind or bothering you, just talk to me, no matter what it is. We have to trust each other."

He kissed the top of her head and said he would. She looked up at him with her clear grey eyes, smiled and pulled herself up to him and whispered, "well in that case, hold on—because now it's my turn to put a baby in you!"

And that night, she did her best to try.

CHAPTER
FIFTY

I n the morning, Sarah wanted to know how and when Medical would contact her so she could go see Galloyde.

"Maybe I should just go and check in on him?" she offered after finishing her breakfast. "Just to see if there's any change?"

"Nope, you don't want to do that. Trust me," Neph warned. "They will send a message. They aren't chatty or hospitable, if you haven't noticed. Just wait until they message you."

"Oh, well, how will they message me?" Sarah looked around for a monitor or display.

"Right over here." Neph led her down a short hall and into a room she hadn't noticed before. Inside was a small office with a beautiful, ornate desk, two plush office chairs, another bar cart and a large black-and-white image of Nephemerus receiving an award at a ceremony on the wall. The image almost appeared to be three dimensional as Sarah went over to get a closer look at it. When she did, she noticed a glass case filled with medals that sat below the picture.

"Oh! Are these yours too?" she asked, squinting to read what was written on them, but it was in another language.

"Nope, I think those belong to the maid. Come over here, I'll show you the message center." Neph tried to pull the second chair around the desk so they both could sit next to each other but the chair was too large. Instead, she sat on his lap.

He held his hand over a triangle that was inlaid into the desk and a display appeared in front of them. He waved his hand over the triangle until he found what he was looking for.

"Here we are—Messages. Looks like we have...ahh, oh shit. One hundred twenty-one messages since we left Earth. All from Desi... nope. Make that one hundred nineteen from Desi, one from Jess and one from someone named Luis."

Sarah drew in a sharp breath. "Can you open the one from Luis first? I just need to know if everything is ok!"

Neph waved again and Luis' face appeared on the screen. He was smiling and waving. "Hello Miss! I mean Sarah! We are good! I'm sending this because the Ascend Elget came by to visit and said I should send you a message and tell you everything is fine, and it is. Everything is fine. Bunny is good! Everyone else is good. Of course they miss you. Ok, I hope you are having fun even though it's not a vacation, but you still need a vacation, but you're busy saving the world. See you soon. Oh, and this is Luis. Bye. Oh, and the Ascend Elget asked to have Satan call him please. I think he really needs to hear from him. Ok, bye now."

Sarah was smiling from ear to ear. "Thank you, I was just worried something might have happened. Alright, go on."

Neph picked the first message Desimidor sent. His bright happy face was in the screen with Jess and Aramik in the background waving. "Hello! Just wanted to send you a quick message. You just left, but we wanted to wish you good luck again. We are all sure you'll get the job done. You and Sarah will make a good team. Please let us know how things go. We'll be waiting. See you soon." The transmission ended.

Neph picked the next one. It was just Desi this time, it looked like he was in his office in Ascend. "Hello Nephemerus. I wanted to just send a quick hello. It's been about three days now. It's hard not to worry. I'm sure you and Sarah are well on your way to the Galactic Ripple and have a good plan in place. Please be safe." He paused. "We hope to hear from you soon." The transmission ended.

Neph skipped down a few. It was Desi in the conference room by himself and pacing back and forth. "Nephemerus, seven days have passed and still no word. I don't know if you have told Sarah that Galloyde is her father yet. Be gentle with this. You can be abrupt sometimes. Maybe just direct, but you need to be careful with this. She might not know her mother was a Replicator. I do hope you two are getting along. Just try to be nice, Nephemerus." He stopped pacing and looked at the camera. "And get back to me already, I'm starting to worry!" The transmission ended.

"Wait. What is a Replicator?" Sarah asked.

Neph leaned back in his chair and ran his fingers through his hair. "Remember how The Grand Precipice had an arranged marriage?" she nodded. "Well, there's no way his blood could mix with any other race. Sacrilege!" He put his hand over his forehead and feigned fainting. "Can you imagine diluting the magnificence of that royal asshole? A Replicator is someone who does exactly that—she carries a baby with the DNA of the father but doesn't add her own. It is up to the father what DNA is added to the child for their offspring. That way they can design their child with whatever is in fashion at the moment. Most of the times, these pious pricks add a sterile base, so that only their DNA is present Which is how I knew that you must also be an Overseer."

"Ooooh, so when Galloyde ran off with Olethia. Their offspring could only be another Overseer."

"See? I'm so brilliant." Sarah laughed, ruffled his hair, and kissed his forehead.

He waved on to another message. Desi was back in Ascend Operations with Jess looking over his shoulder at the camera, but also eyeing Desi with deep concern. "Hello Nephemerus. Hope you are busy with the mission. I'm sure you are, since it's been two weeks since you left here and we are anxious to hear if you found the Ripple and Galloyde. Anxious to hear anything at all." Jess bumped Desi. "Oh! We are good. We are all fine. Everything is running smoothly. Tell Sarah her Regulators are performing exceptionally well. No one has been eaten." Jess bumped him again. "That was a joke, of course."

Neph looked at Sarah, "I should have checked in. I forgot how much time passes on Earth during a rotation. It's about nine Earth days to each Rotation here, so to them, we've been gone for almost a month already."

"Wait, it's nine days to one of ours? It only feels like a day up here."

Neph grinned. "Yeah, it's crazy, it all has to do with the planet and their orbits. When I was on Iitkaa? It was almost 35 days to one rotation. Desi had to leave once for a Council meeting and it felt like he was gone for years."

He skipped down a few more messages and opened one at random. Apparently Desi was in the middle of another manic explanation, back in the conference room and pacing again. "I do believe that once we locate all 10 root species and return them to here, we can kickstart the original DNA strand and perhaps fix where Galloyde may have made his transient mistake. But we need him, it's dire that we get him back here." Desi looked into the camera, his facial expression somber. He looked pale and sickly, "But I fear you are lost, my dearest friend, and will not return." The transmission ended abruptly.

Neph clicked on Jess' message which was next. Her face came up, overly animated. "Hello Nephemerus! I have confirmed the data access ports on the Noneru, and I am hoping you receive this in good health and expediency. Please respond as soon as you receive this message. Desimidor needs to hear from you. I cannot stress this enough—he needs to know you are alright. We would also like to know that Sarah is safe as well. We all seriously need to know that both of you are alive and well. Please respond as soon as possible. Like right now. Absolutely right now. Thank you."

He waved to the last message Desi sent. His face appeared in the screen, extremely close up. He looked hectic. "Are you even getting these? Why haven't you answered me? I need you know you are still out there. It's been weeks. I keep sending these and everyone thinks…" He stared off the camera. "I'm sure you're fine, but I'm worried and it's hard to keep up a brave face. I think maybe it's all my fault. I should not have let you go on this—this…" he faded away but didn't shut off the transmission. It just continued as he stared blankly off to the side of the screen.

Sarah's face fell. "Oh no. Oh no, how did we not -"

"No, no. You didn't even know about this system, but I did. Shit. Shit, shit, shit." He punched on the display and waited. There was a trilling sound and then a breathless "Hello?" They saw a disheveled Desi come into view. He was in his apartment in Ascend.

"Hi Desi!" yelled Neph, as if he was walking into a party. "How are you, my friend?"

Desi stared into the display in disbelief. "Nephemerus?"

Neph nodded. "Look! Here's Sarah! Sarah, say hello! Look it's Desi!"

"Hi Desi! I'm so happy to see you! We have great news!" Sarah gave him her biggest smile and waved to him like she was in a parade.

Desi was so close to the display, they could only see part of his face. "You're both still…alright? You are coming back? I…we thought you were gone. Lost. We all thought it," he whispered, like he was telling a secret.

"Oh Desiiiii!" Neph called out. "Come on buddy! Sarah wouldn't drag me all the way out here just to lose me right? She loves me too much, don't you honey?"

She ignored him. "Desi? Desi? Are you ok?" Sarah asked. She could see Desi looking around his room now for something before looking back at them with tears in his eyes.

"I thought you were both gone! Why didn't you—why didn't you answer me?" His voice rising into a high pitch.

"Comms were down, buddy. Solar…problems." Neph stalled. "Just got them back up. Terrible. We called as soon as we could. Hey, we got good news for ya. Are you ready?"

Desi nodded, wiping at his eyes.

Sarah leaned in closer to the display. "We have him, Desi. We are heading home with Galloyde. We'll be back real soon ok?"

Desi started to cry audibly.

"How soon?" Sarah whispered to Neph.

Neph cleared his throat. "Dez? Hey Dez? We're going to jump back once we stabilize the trans…fig…omm…miters." He looked at Sarah. She nodded at the screen. "So we'll be back on the planet right with you in four, maybe five Earth days tops. How's that?"

Desi sniffed, then blew his nose, wiping away a considerable amount of snot. "Of course. Yes, of course. No hurry. Take your time. We are fine here. I'm just happy the mission is a success. I knew all along you two were fine."

"Good man. I'm going to call back shortly and let you know more of our plans if you don't mind? Just to give you some more details if you're ok with that?" Neph asked.

Desi feigned disinterest. "I'll try to be available when you call."

They said goodbye and shut down. Sarah looked at Neph. "I feel so bad for him! For all of them!'

"Ehh, don't be, we got Galloyde." He pulled her in tightly against his chest. "We succeeded. I'll call him in a little bit and smooth things over a bit more. By the time we land, he'll be fine. At least your beasts are behaving!" He wiggled his eyebrows at her wildly.

Sarah gasped and pushed him away. "My beasts? Excuse me, but my Founders are…Galaxy Royalty! You! You, sir, are the beast!" She got up and pointed at him, "Get thee away Leviathan!" She ran screaming and laughing out the door.

Neph chased her and caught her before she even reached the kitchen. He tossed her over his shoulder and called out. "Gotcha! Guess you're the maiden of Satan now!" She screamed with laughter as he spun her around several times, taunting her. "Apologize to the Devil. Say it. Say it!"

"No! NO!" she yelled. "Put me down Lucifer! I'm the mother of your children!"

Neph continued to swing her around while she squealed with laughter when they both heard, "Children? Mery? Have you neglected to tell me something?"

They both looked up to see Qualla standing at the door to the quarters, watching them.

"Mery, you are going to have babies?" Qualla bounded down the steps into the main room at the two of them. Neph let Sarah down off his shoulder, and before he could say anything else, Qualla held both of them in a firm embrace. "I'm so happy!"

"No, no, it's a joke." Neph tried to say, muffled by her arm covering his face. Sarah was buried further below. There was no chance anyone could hear her denial, squished down below them.

Neph expertly moved Qualla's arms away and managed to pull Sarah out of the vice grip of his adopted Clorrian mother. "It was just a joke we say to each other. It's Earth humor."

Qualla stared at Neph and then Sarah. "Is this true?" she asked Sarah.

Sarah swallowed hard. "I'm not pregnant Qualla. I'm sorry to mislead you. We were just joking."

Qualla frowned. "Mery! Ishonna, but you can be so stupid." She tutted at him and looked back at Sarah. "You need to eat?"

Sarah grinned and winked at Neph. "Yeah, Qualla, I'm starving. Whatcha got?" She followed Qualla into the kitchen and helped her unload several plates of food she had brought with her. Qualla explained what each dish was, and Sarah told her how she loved all her cooking.

Nephemerus took a seat at the counter. "Is there enough food there for me? I'm hungry too." He shot back at Sarah, who stuck her tongue out at him.

Qualla grabbed his face. "Too skinny. How come you never eat? Always running around this one. He never eats."

"I know," said Sarah, mimicking the same action and taking hold of Neph's face as soon as Qualla let go and walked away. "Too skinny. I'm always saying eat, eat, eat! If I've said it once, Qualla, I've said it a thousand times. Boy, am I glad that I'm not the only one telling him this." Her mouth wrapped upwards in a fiendish grin as Neph pulled out of her grip.

"Ohhhkay, you two can work on this. I'm going to go call Desi back. Oh wait, I think that might be him calling now. I better run. Busy, busy, busy. Qualla, thanks for stopping by. T'shonka. Sarah, my little love." He glared at her comically. He clasped his hands together as he backed out of the room. "I'm so happy you two have this time together," he said sarcastically as he disappeared into his office.

Over the next hour, Sarah followed Qualla around the kitchen, asking how she prepared many of her dishes, what Nephemerus liked the most, and about life on the ship. Qualla had just asked Sarah about her family when Nephemerus rushed out of his office.

"Medical just messaged. He's awake! You can go!" Sarah apologized and said she had to leave. Neph paused to press his forehead against his mother's. "We'll be back soon. Ishonna." he said to her before running out the door after Sarah.

CHAPTER

FIFTY-ONE

T he Medical bay was only a few minutes away from their quarters. Sarah must have gone pretty far in the wrong direction considering how long it took them to walk back the last time. When they arrived, Galloyde was seated upright in bed. There was one other patient in a bed nearby. The staff nodded to the Admiral when he entered but did not salute, Sarah noticed. She and Neph made their way to each side of her father's bed.

He greeted her with a huge smile. "My little Gator, how are you sweetheart?" She leaned in and embraced him.

Neph started to back away, and Galloyde called to him. "No, no, you stay. Pull up a seat there." Neph saw the chair he pointed to, moved it next to the bed and sat down.

Sarah did the same on the other side, then held her father's hand, beaming up at him. "We found you, I can't believe we found you!"

Galloyde laughed heartily. With his white beard and twinkling eyes, he had an astonishing resemblance to the humans' caricature of Santa Claus, Neph mused. Another fairytale where someone watched your every move to measure good and bad deeds. These humans loved the notion of mythical beings constantly watching and judging their actions.

"I spent a great deal of time dream-walking in Thrinythidor for you to be surprised to have found me, although I am thankful he was such a hospitable host," Galloyde said smiling. He looked at Neph. "Clorrians are not as well known for their telepathy as they are for their ingenuity, strategy, and emotional intelligence. Long ago— long, long ago, they read the thoughts of their enemy as easily as you can read emotions as an Elget. That was what made them nearly unbeatable. This skill is still present in the modern-day Clorrian, but not as celebrated, but I have been, let us say, 'out of the game' for a fair bit of time."

Sarah considered this. "Tiny is a Founder and clearly Clorrian, so that's why you could access him?"

Galloyde took in a deep breath. "Ahh, so you know. The Founders." He nodded quietly, deep in thought.

Sarah waited for a moment before saying, "I just found out. It was Neph and Desimidor, Earth's current Elgets, who told me. They aren't like the others Elgets though—"

"No, they are not." Galloyde interrupted. "I know exactly who they are." Nephemerus looked intrigued. "You are very much part of this plan," Galloyde continued, "just as Thrinythidor has been, and Desimidor. Even that soul who had four hundred and seventy-nine lives on Earth, whom you needed to open the Ripple, is part of all of this. Many moving parts had to happen to get here, to this very moment." He looked to Sarah, eyes shining with tears. "But it was never, never part of the plan to leave you, my dear."

Sarah swallowed and choked back her own tears. "Dad, we have to talk about what is happening. There's so much going on that I don't understand, and Neph and Desi are working a lot of it out, but there are still so many missing pieces."

Right then, a Medical Technician walked in to check on Galloyde. He didn't say a word, just gave a slight nod and kept moving when he was done checking the connections and the readings on the instruments.

"We have a little while longer, but the medical team will kick us out soon. Plus, you should get your rest. We'll get back to Descend within a rotation." Neph said.

Galloyde closed his eyes for a moment and squeezed Sarah's hand. "There is so much to tell you, so much you should have known already." He opened his eyes and locked eyes with Neph. "Merus, thank you. For coming to get me. For bringing your Fleet. For taking care of my daughter."

Nephemerus was taken off guard by calmness washing over him. "Yes, of course. You're welcome. I'd do anything for Sarah…and for the good of the humans too, I guess." He faded on the last part, trying to downplay the confession he just made.

"What do you need to know the most right now?" Galloyde asked, putting his hand over Neph's. Sarah could see Neph's deep brown eyes dart back and forth, trying to choose just one of several burning questions he had been waiting to ask.

"What were the Athecierians looking for on Earth?" Neph asked.

Galloyde smiled slightly. "That is not what you want to know the most. I will give you the answers you deserve to know. Ask me the question you want to know the most, Merus."

Neph sat back and ran his hand through his thick hair, wide-eyed. He cleared his throat and sat straight, holding Galloyde's gaze. This time, he didn't think about it at all. "Why did you do it? Why did you break natural law?"

Sarah's jaw dropped, but she remained silent. She watched as Galloyde considered. "Now that is a good question," He nodded thoughtfully. "That is a question worthy of a man of your station."

Galloyde inhaled deeply, and both Sarah and Nephemerus were drawn in. The room seemed to contract and the air felt heavy. He looked straight ahead as he spoke to them. "There has not been one single rotation that has passed where I have not asked myself that exact question. Why did I interfere with the natural order of evolution? We know that all primitive species live. We know that they will all die. That happens again and again until they evolve into a state of self-awareness. Eventually, they Ascend and are able to move onto higher consciousness, joining the rest of us. Well—many of the races at least, not quite all."

He paused, remembering with a slight smile on his lips. "There were so many humanoid species then. All so wondrous and fascinating. Whether they were meant to survive or you knew they would falter, the sheer amount of evolution, luck, and environmental factors involved for these tribes to survive up to that point was staggering. Perhaps I was biased from being a witness, a bystander to history. Perhaps I was simply...in love." He looked at Sarah and then to Neph knowingly.

"That changes your perspective, when you are in love. Olethia and I had traveled all over the continents. Watching the tribes as they roamed, as they learned to hunt better, built more sophisticated tools. Some excelled and others...ehhh, not so much. And we were fine, celebrating the wins of the populations that were going to thrive and accepting the losses of those whom nature deemed unworthy. That is the very purpose of evolution, to pass on the traits of strength, intelligence, and harmony to ensure the survival of the species."

He sighed and then coughed. Sarah grabbed his water off a nearby tray and he took a long drink. Neph caught a look of disapproval from the Medical Technician watching from a distance.

"You mention the very purpose of evolution. We all learned in Ala Mia to observe and follow the natural law, which is to never, ever tamper with evolution. You did. You chose to ignore our number one directive," Neph challenged.

Galloyde sighed. "You are right. I did. There is no denying that. I recognized weakness within this one small tribe. I saw they would not share their food with one another. They would steal. They lacked empathy. They were lazy. They were aggressive towards one another with little to no provocation. In retrospect, it is so easy to discern these deplorable traits in the creatures that now inhabit Earth."

He paused but Neph pressed. "Exactly. You caused that." Sarah gave Neph a warning look and he toned down his accusation. "I don't understand why. Surely you must have considered the outcome of your actions. Evolution knows better than any of us do, even better than an Overseer."

Neph sat back and avoided Sarah's gaze, but kept his eyes on Galloyde.

The elder Overseer sighed, lost in his own thoughts. "You are correct again Merus. Without my interference, would the human race have reached a collective higher consciousness by now? Be part of the Muldigals? Maybe even be seated at the Council? Would they have been far more advanced with more technology, culture, and languages like the others of their ilk? I can say without reservation that without these…evolutionary mistakes holding back society, they most certainly would have."

Then Galloyde stared back at Neph, brows knitted tightly together.

"There will never be a clear explanation as to why I did it, Merus. I want to say that at the time, I had truly believed this tribe would overcome their faults. They would adapt the strategies of the successful tribes. They would learn sharing meant survival. They would see empathy and cooperation as strengths to be replicated, and that community was necessary for group survival. I had no reason to believe this, I had no proof or scientific algorithm that would support my theory. I simply had hope that they would find their way. The truth was that I was deeply in love and I saw the world not for what it was, but for what I hoped it would become."

"You interfered," Neph breathed out in a low voice, repeating his earlier statement to Sarah back in the chamber room in Descend. "You interfered, and that's against the rules."

Galloyde hung his head. "I did. I connected their dots. I added what was missing within their DNA to allow them to cheat nature. I decided to change what evolution knew better to leave missing. They populated the world with their broken genetic coding. They found a way to thrive despite their abysmal behavior...They became a cancer, a parasite on the rest of humanity. They affected the positive communities and dragged all of mankind down with them."

He fell silent again.

"The Council did not have to banish me," he whispered. "Their mere existence is my greatest punishment."

Neph looked at Sarah with regret shining in his eyes.

"Dad, how about you get some rest ok? I'm coming back early to see you. I don't care what they say—I'll be here. Just try to eat something and get some rest."

Galloyde nodded and laid back. "I'm so happy to see you, my little Gator." He gave her a big smile.

She hugged him and kissed his cheek. "I've missed you, I love you so much, Dad."

Neph spoke to the head of the medical team as she said goodbye to Galloyde. She saw the medical technician didn't say anything to Neph, but this time managed to give him a slight salute as Sarah heard Neph say sternly, "Do you understand me?" Then Neph gave the technician a formal salute, turned on his heels and they walked out.

In the hallway, he wrapped his hand around hers and squeezed. " I'm sorry. I know that was upsetting." Neph leaned against her. "I wasn't expecting that. All that regret... I don't know what I expected, really."

They started to walk back to the quarters as he continued to talk. "All the stories I've heard—everything is based on him being Mad

Galloyde, crazy, out of control—and none of it is true. I mean, not even close."

He stopped and leaned against the hallway wall. "I just believed all the stories, and I never do that. Why did I blindly believe everything? Every one of those stories were lies." His face twisted in anguish.

"Hey, hey!" Sarah reached up and caressed his face. "The story about Galloyde and his monsters has become legend. Trust me, I know. Thousands of years it has been out there. Even if we start telling the truth today of what really happened—"

"Sarah, we can't say anything right now—" Neph interrupted.

"No, I know, but I'm saying if we tried to change people's minds, to get the truth out there, people wouldn't believe the real story. They'd rather believe the lie. They would rather believe in the monsters."

Neph took her hand and kissed it, then kissed her forehead. They began walking again.

"I'm his daughter and even I thought he created my dem—my Regulators. They all believe he created them. You thought it was true because that was what people put in front of you each day as factual."

Neph opened up the door to his quarters, Sarah stepped in, and he closed the door and proceeded to pile up boxes and furniture on the inside. The one time he forgot to do this and Qualla busted in, he chided himself.

"I know. I just—I think what bothers me is that, if I was in his shoes, I could see myself doing the exact same thing." Neph said in a low voice.

Sarah leaned against him, looking into his deep, soulful eyes. "I think that a lot of people might, if they knew the whole story. Well, maybe not if they knew the outcome! I mean, talk about downstream consequences! There's so many jerks out there now!"

He smiled down at her. "But without those jerks, we wouldn't have met."

She pulled away and looked at him. "Wouldn't we though?" She walked away without saying more as Neph pondered her remark.

Qualla had left food for them with a note telling them both to eat.

"I talked to Raka. He's going to step it up so we get back to Earth a bit earlier. Desi was better when I talked to him the second time. He said they have been trying to work up a "back-up plan" in case we didn't find Galloyde." Neph scooped the stew out of the pot with a ladle, cooling it with his breath before sneaking a bite. Once approved, he filled a bowl and sat at the counter.

Sarah thought for a minute. "Hang on. How come it took us three full rotations to reach the Ripple, but we can get back to Earth much faster? Wait. All your ships jumped to the Ripple when they met us. Why didn't we just jump to the Ripple? Why aren't we jumping back to Earth?"

Neph nodded as he took a long drink. He was stalling. She waited while he kept sipping and drinking, she pulled the glass out of his hand. "Well?"

He coughed from chugging cold water. "Oh, yeah! There's a great explanation for that, and I'm going to tell you what it is. Right now." He spooned another huge scoop of stew into his mouth and started chewing. Then pointed to his mouth and rolling his eyes, showing how good the stew tasted.

Sarah waited as he chewed. He was almost done when he got up. "Hang on…got to get some water. Wash this down."

"You're fucking kidding me. Do you need a nap first? Maybe a foot rub before answering me?"

"Oooh doesn't that sound nice!" He grinned and took another long drink.

She pounded the counter once with her fist. "Nephemerus os Clorria!"

"Alright, alright. You're forgetting when we first boarded, we didn't officially meet with Raka until early in the second rotation. You didn't give him coordinates to where we needed to go until the end of the second rotation. So technically, we arrived at the Ripple in really just over one rotation. Now, heading back, Galloyde needed medical attention. If we jumped, then he would just have to stay in Medical to complete his healing anyways. He needs three to four rotations to heal so why not roll back?"

"Roll? That's roll instead of jump? When Raka asked you to roll versus jump, that's what he means? Ugh, why didn't I catch that before?"

"Because you were distracted by my incredible charm and good looks." Neph wiggled his eyebrows erratically.

Sarah looked away, feeling herself start to laugh, but didn't want Neph to see. "Yeah, that must have been it."

Neph confessed, "I'll admit, I might—just might have wanted to spend a little more time with you before we got back to Earth and it all goes back to like before."

"What? What are you talking about? Do you think this will change between us when we get back?" she asked, suddenly a little worried.

"I don't want it to." He pulled her closer. "I don't want that at all, but Earth is your home, not mine. What if we get back and maybe you don't want—"

Sarah pulled Neph in and kissed him deeply before nuzzling against his neck. "The only thing I don't want is to be without you."

CHAPTER
FIFTY-TWO

That night Neph dreamed of Earth—but not of the Earth he had already seen. This was one where the constellations were in the wrong place. The mountains had not completely formed and the humans didn't have their cities, roads and buildings yet.

Neph could feel he was there, but he was also not there.

As in most dreams, Neph knew on some level this could not be real, yet he felt the wind against his skin, smelled something burning in the air and stood on the rocky ground. He felt a stone sharp enough to cut into his foot bite into his boot, but could not look away from what was happening right in front of him.

Galloyde was running up a hill, along a steep path towards a beautiful woman with long, flowing hair that shone like copper in the sunlight. She looked frightened as she bounced a small child on her hip. The child was facing away from Neph, but couldn't be older than a toddler. The child was pointing back down the hill towards Galloyde. Smoke was billowing all around them. Every few seconds another explosion would rip into the surface and rain down mud, rock and debris around them. There was nowhere for them to take cover in the open field.

Further down the hill, Neph saw Tiny and Seglee chasing behind Galloyde. Their eyes turned upward towards the sky. Neph looked up and, as he did, all the light from Earth's sun was blotted out as an Athecierian War Ship creeped across the landscape, dropping an astonishing number of bombs. Seglee launched herself past Galloyde, beat her wings hard, and landed next to the woman. She opened her beak and the woman placed the child inside gently, as if putting the child to sleep in a cradle, nodding her head and trying to say comforting words. Galloyde continued to yell, waving his arms wildly as he ran closer. Seglee closed her beak and took off just as a bomb landed exactly where she had been standing.

Exactly where the woman had been standing.

Neph heard a scream of anguish and saw Galloyde fall to his knees. Only a crater remained where the bomb had struck. Tiny reached Galloyde and scooped him off the ground, and continued to run, shielding him from the explosions. Neph searched the darkened sky for Seglee and felt the ground shake with another explosion—then everything went black.

Neph woke up with a start. He was sweating, his heart pounding rapidly in his chest. He felt like he couldn't catch his breath. Sarah was deep asleep next to him. He climbed out of bed and made his way to the bathroom. Once inside, he closed the door, hands shaking. He was overcome by emotion. He fought to stop himself from wailing out in grief. He sat in the dark, trying to comprehend what he saw. He finally took a towel and held it to his mouth to dampen a low cry as he shed heart-rending tears. He can't remember the last time he felt this upset by a dream, but none of this felt like a dream.

This felt like a memory.

CHAPTER
FIFTY-THREE

S hortly after Neph had left the bed, Sarah sat bolt upright at the same time that Galloyde sat upright in his bed in Medical. Both had called out "Athecierians!" upon waking. Neph came running out of the bathroom, alarmed to find Sarah yelling. He thought she was just having a similar bad dream, like the one he just had, until she jumped out of bed and started to get dressed. She was fully awake and needed to get to Galloyde.

"Call them, call them and tell them not to give him anything. I have to talk to him, they are coming! They're coming! They're coming!" Neph watched as Sarah ran back and forth. He wondered if she was still in some dream state until she stopped and looked right at him.

"Neph! The Athecierians! They didn't leave on their own, they weren't running away from you. They are heading to Earth! We have to go!"

Neph thought about what happened at the Ripple. Even with the arrival of the Clorrian Fleet, the Athecierians would have responded in some manner, instead of simply leaving. Had they been a diversion? Was there more to this?

In the Medical department, Galloyde awoke with the same start and was trying to fend off staff who thought he merely experienced a bad dream. They wanted to sedate him and would have succeeded had the Admiral not called and demanded he not be medicated. The attendant was unsure how the Admiral could be aware of the patient's status, but promised not to give him any medications until the Admiral spoke to the Medical Physician.

They entered the Medical department moments later. As soon as Galloyde saw Sarah, he shouted,"Athecierians! Sarah, they are heading to—"

"I know! I know, I saw it too." She rushed to his side and threw her arms around him. "How much time?"

He shook his head, looking worried. "I don't know. I can't see it anymore. I used so much energy just to survive on the desirihia. I'm still drained."

Sarah nodded and said to Neph. "I need to contact Luis and Desi. It's an emergency." She turned back to Galloyde,"Dad, we only have seven of the demons—I mean, seven of the Foun—um I mean the Regulators. We only have seven! What do we do about the others?" She looked suspiciously at the staff who was listening to their conversation.

Galloyde looked at her panicked. "What? Only seven? Where are they now?"

Neph motioned for the medical team to leave immediately. They did as he requested. He followed them to the door to make sure no one was within earshot, and when he was sure they were alone, he returned and motioned to Sarah that it was safe. She pulled a chair up to one side of the bed; Neph did the same on the opposite side.

"Zana—she's in hibernation. We have Bunny, Tiny, Clara, Seglee, GilGerg, and the Triplets. I don't know where Kevin was banished to and I never found the other two."

Galloyde closed his eyes as he let out a long sigh. "The Nox."

Neph chimed in. "We know that leaves a Whasook and Thandican that are unaccounted for."

Sarah said, "We need to know where they are so we can get them in The Gate before they show up! And Dad...Zana—she can't fit in there. What do I do about her? She's way too big, I don't know where to put her." Her eyes started to fill with tears.

Galloyde placed his hand on hers. "Shhh. It is alright. She will be fine. You said she is in hibernation?" Sarah nodded. "Good, she will be down near the core of the planet. She will be untouchable. Absolutely untouchable—even to those devils." He winked at Neph. "Present company excluded."

This made Neph burst out with an unexpected laugh. He covered his mouth and Galloyde reached over and grabbed his arm with his other hand. Immediately Neph felt that calmness wash over him again. "I know you are no devil, Merus, I tease."

"Dad—" Sarah started.

"Where is the dagger?" Galloyde continued. "Let me see it."

Sarah blinked rapidly. "It's on Earth. It's with someone I trust. He'll put everyone in The Gate until we get there."

Galloyde's face darkened for a moment as he read his daughter's thoughts. "Sarah. This is no job for a human to do." He studied her face. "But I trust you, I know I left you without many options."

Galloyde turned to Neph. "How quickly can you get us to Earth? Also, any of those ships that were outside the Ripple able to join us as well?"

Neph said that he would take care of it and went to relay his orders to Raka.

Galloyde turned to Sarah. "The Whasook and Thandican should be fairly easy to pick up in time—perhaps before the Atheciery get to Earth—if they have not wondered off too far in the past few millennia. Both are extremely territorial, so I am hoping we get lucky."

"And Kevin? The Nox? Dad, we can't let the Athecierians get even one of the original bloodlines. They'll just sell them to the highest bidder—or worse."

Galloyde stared off in front of him, deep in thought. "The Atheciery were never supposed to be like this. They were one of the first species to Ascend and yet…" He fell away in thought before snapping back. "The Nox! Sarah, I don't think we can get to him."

Neph joined them again and sat back down. "We are jumping right now. You will feel a slight sensation, like you need to cough. Then we will be just outside of Earth's orbit, beyond detection. Do we know where the other three Founders are located yet?"

"Yes. Two of them should be easy enough to pick up with a ship a little bit larger than the shuttle you picked me up in. The last Founder—that Nox…I fear will not be possible. I put him in the worst place I could think of." He looked at Neph. "I banished him to Ala Mia."

Nephemerus jumped up and knocked his chair back. "No!"

Sarah looked up at him. "Why? What is it?"

Nephemerus paced back and forth, mumbling, "No, no, no, no, no, no, no, no, no."

She looked at Galloyde. "Why? What does that mean? Wasn't Ala Mia your home? Wasn't Mom from Ala Mia? I don't understand!"

"Your mother was never Ala Mian!" Galloyde harshly retorted.

Neph stared at the floor, still mumbling, "No, no, no, this can't be."

"Couldn't we just jump to Ala Mia and grab him—"

"NO!" Both Galloyde and Neph shouted.

Neph tried to quickly explain to Sarah, "Ala Mia is the home to the Elgets—where they live and train—it's also the home planet of the Grand Precipice, Algetia. While it is best-known for this, it also has the lesser honor of being the home to Radimus. An asylum built by the Council. Designed to be absolutely inescapable. There are no guards in Radimus, because there are no rules to enforce. There are no cells for the inmates, no meals, no therapists, no medications, no one to help. Those who reside inside will never, ever be released. Once you go in, you fight to survive against one other with no hope of escape. For eternity—or until you die."

Sarah gasped.

"There is no way to take anyone out of Radimus," Neph whispered. "Its a fate worse than…than—"

"It's the worst fate in the cosmos." Galloyde finished. "Or close to it. I should know."

"Alright, let's focus on the other two. We can pick them up and get them back to The Gate. Neph, do you have a ship we can use to reach them?" Sarah asked.

Neph explained they could use a type of ship called a Sweeper to recover the two remaining Founders on Earth.

"It has cloaking capabilities for working close to the surface. It isn't as advanced as what the Athecierians have, but it has enough to fool any human technology easily enough. Plus it's large enough to pick up a Whasook. There's no way a Lander would work for that!"

Galloyde and Neph both chuckled at the thought.

"Ok Dad, we need those locations. I know it's been awhile, but can you remember where they were last? Maybe there's a way we can track them?"

Galloyde nodded. "Like I said, they are each quite territorial. I am sure the Whasook is still in Lake Hazan. You will be able to locate him quickly if he is still resides there.

"As far as the Thandican, I know exactly where she is. She lives within Ball's Pyramid, She will not have moved from there. I would say she is safe, but if we can, we should try to retrieve her. I cannot say for sure if she is far enough down to be safe if they come for her. I say we should try to get them both in The Gate."

"Ok, so we are heading to the coast of Australia and then northern Canada. You're sure we won't be seen?" Sarah asked Neph. He assured her again they would be safe.

"The Sweeper's cloaking technology will appear like a cloud to anyone who happens to be looking in that direction. I'm guessing both of these locations are fairly remote though?" Sarah and Galloyde agreed. "The Sweepers allow us to move quickly and transport large cargo while going undetected." Then he addressed Galloyde. "You'll have to stay here until your kidney is completely healed. There's no two ways about it. Do not go against the Physician's orders."

Galloyde considered this. "I'll stay as long as the Athecierians don't arrive. If they do, I must be sent to Descend. To The Gate."

Neph looked at Sarah. She nodded in agreement; he did not.

"We don't have much time." Neph answered. "I need to make preparations with the Captain. Sarah, could you get anything you need from the quarters? I'll have the guards bring you to the Sweeper once you are ready. I would like to leave as soon as possible."

He started to leave and turned back to Galloyde. "I'm going to do everything I can to help save the humans in my role as Elget as assigned by the Multi-Dimensional Galactic Counsel. As Fleet Admiral of the Seventh Division of the Lisceraa Defense Force, I'll do everything I can within my power to protect planet 7298 from a hostile invasion."

He paused, glancing at Sarah only briefly before continuing. "And as an Vecurasian raised by Clorrians, who is very much in love with your daughter, I don't know what is coming next. I do know that I cannot and will not let them take you away from her again." He stepped closer to the bed. "If that means I have to hide you somewhere in this galaxy or the next so they don't find you, I'll do it. I will not allow her heart to break again. So no, I will not promise to bring you to the surface when they arrive. I will not lie to you or to your daughter. I hope you can find it within yourself to trust me to make the right decision when the time comes."

Neph turned and curtly nodded to Sarah and walked out the door. Sarah looked shocked. Galloyde took a moment to absorb what he heard, then squeezed his daughter's hand and smiled.

"He loves you. Merus has a good heart. He will keep you safe, my little Gator."

"Yeah, I think he's certainly going to try. Dad, just rest and get better ok? I'll see you soon."

Galloyde smiled and closed his eyes as Sarah turned and dashed out the doors to get back to the quarters. This time, she knew exactly where she was going.

FIFTY-FOUR

S arah made her way back to the apartment and grabbed her things quickly. She took anything Nephemerus might need as well. She tossed it all in her bag, slung it over her shoulder and ran back out the door to the guard who was waiting for her. The guard walked with her in a new direction and finally they arrived at a large, bustling center, where soldiers and large crates were being moved back and forth. He told her to head down a long ramp, and the Admiral would be waiting at the bottom.

She found the ramp and made her way into a massive landing bay, far larger than where the Landers were kept. Inside this one she found several towering ships. She stood there, staring up at the massive crafts all lined up, one after another. She couldn't even gauge their true size—they all seemed to rise up thousands of feet.

She was admiring the ships and marveling at how many the Cruiser could hold when she heard someone calling her name. She saw a female Clorrian soldier, trying to get her attention and repeating her name. Sarah waved back and walked over to her.

"The Admiral requested that I escort you to The Bibbly. How are you enjoying your time on the Noneru?" The soldier asked, with a cutting jab in her voice.

"Excuse me?"

"I believe you saw the rest of our fleet recently. We have Heftu and Tegreta with us in orbit right now, but we are on the Noneru, which, of course, is the Admiral's cruiser." The soldier said condescendingly.

"Oh! Oh right, we are on the Admiral's ship," Sarah emphasized the word 'ship' repeatedly. "Well this ship is lovely. I'm sure the Admiral is proud of this ship, as he is of all the ships in his fleet." The female soldier didn't respond and brought Sarah in between two large crafts. The space was cluttered and no one was around.

"Here we are. The Admiral is inside. It was so wonderful having you onboard. Till the stars burn out." The soldier smiled and pointed up towards a small, dark entrance. She left before Sarah could say anything else.

Sarah saw a set of narrow collapsible steps leading up to this entryway and wondered why it didn't have the wide entry platform like the Landers had. She climbed the unsteady steps and didn't see anyone at the top. She noticed right away this didn't look like the other ship. It was crowded with tools, compartments, and large equipment. There was only one long, extremely narrow corridor. She must have to go further up, she thought. Sarah continued moving through the narrow passage, trying to find anyone else. She stopped when she had gone as far as she could.

This doesn't seem right at all. What if I'm on the wrong ship? She considered pressing her bracelet to locate Neph, but decided to look for another way out instead. She traced her way back, looking for another set of stairs or a ladder that led upwards. Surely everyone was above her? This must be the belly of the ship, she thought. Nothing here appeared to look like anything on the Lander.

She was almost back to where the stairs were when she heard

Neph's voice in the distance saying, "She was supposed to be here by now, so where is she?"

"I'm right here! Hello! I'm here!" Sarah called out as loud as she could over the din of the bay. She rushed to the stairs and climbed back down to the platform.

"There you are!" He walked over to meet her. "I was getting concerned." Then he lowered his voice. "Was there a reason you were in the mechanical overhead?"

Sarah glanced up at the stairs and could see that the Sweeper's entry platform was next to the overhead. The female soldier had distinctly pointed to the wobbly stairway which was close to the ship. Just over Neph's shoulder, she saw the soldier watching her with a wide, satisfied smirk on her face. Sarah took a look at Neph in his Admiral's uniform and understood what just happened.

She bit her lip and gave a gruff laugh. "Oh, you know me. I just wanted to get a lay of the land." She turned her body so the soldier could get a clear view as she reached up and gently brushed her fingers along the side of Neph's neck, over his sideburn, running her nails through his thick hair before dropping her hand down onto his epaulette, brushing it off as if some dust had gathered there. She shot a smirk back to the soldier, who looked away, angry.

"Sorry about that darling, I'm ready." She gave him a doe-eyed smile.

Neph, who rarely missed a thing, held out his arm for Sarah to take as he leaned over and whispered, "Care to tell me what that was all about?"

She slid her arm through his as they walked up the platform and into the Bibbly. She whispered back, "Oh it's nothing. Turns out that Whasooks and Thandicans aren't the only ones who are territorial."

CHAPTER
FIFTY-FIVE

The Sweeper was a considerably larger ship than the Landers, as Sarah found herself running after Neph yet again. She thought it differed very little from the larger Cruiser-class ship, other than the fact that it fit easily inside the Noneru. She kept up a light jog next to him. How can he move this fast? He was talking to a Clorrian Commander she didn't know. She wasn't able to listen to their conversation because she was focusing so hard on not losing Neph down a side corridor.

They reached the Bridge, where she could stop and catch her breath. She was in good shape, but his extra foot of height and apparently years of military strutting had her at a disadvantage whenever he decided to enter into his hallway sprint. Maybe I'll have him run Bunny next time he needs it, she mused.

"Ball's Pyramid, I want atmospheric cover and let me know when we are in the area," Neph ordered the Commander.

The Commander nodded. "Yes Admiral." He looked nervous, clearly not used to reporting directly to the Fleet Admiral.

Neph motioned to Sarah and they found a similar room off the Bridge to talk in, but this was not for battle planning. It appeared to be for an officer respite. Neph automatically took the seat behind the desk, and as he sat, he paused, looking at Sarah and started to offer her the seat. She laughed and waved him to sit down.

"This is your ship. Your fleet-ah. Don't be weird."

"You're weird." He countered. He put his elbows on the desk and rubbed his face.

"There's so much to do. We don't have much time."

"Right." Sarah took off her bag. "Look, we have to recover the Thandican first. Hopefully that'll be quick, but I really need to talk to Luis right now. You also need to know about The Gate, and that's going to be a lot of information. We also have to figure out how to get the Nox back."

Neph nodded. "Let's split this up. You call Luis. I'll speak to Desi and explain the situation about the Nox. We'll brainstorm about that while you talk to Luis?"

Sarah nodded. "I also need Desi to know about The Gate so let's kill two birds with one stone—ugh, that's a terrible saying, now that I think about it. After I get done with Luis, I'll get on with you two and explain what I need to. Hopefully we can get it done before Ball's Pyramid. If not, it'll have to wait until we head to Lake Hazen."

Neph agreed and brought her into the next room to set her up on a display. He hailed Descend, and Nexar answered. Neph left as Sarah asked for Luis. A moment later, he appeared—all smiles. Sarah was not.

"Luis, get them in The Gate. The Athecierians are coming. I don't know how long you have. We are alerting Desi and support now. Get Tiny to help you. I'll signal you when I arrive."

Luis looked alarmed and then quickly regained his composure. "Yes, Sarah. I will. I will contact you when it's done. Wait, there's no way to contact you, is there?"

Sarah shook her head. "Just move them in there now. Neph and I are back on Earth, but we have to do something first—we'll be there soon." She paused and swallowed. "We talked about this. I know you can do it. I trust you. The most important thing is get everyone inside The Gate. It's the only place the Atheciery can't get to them —" her voice started to crack.

"I have to go. I will see you when you get here." Luis cut off communication. That was precisely the right thing to do.

In the next room, Neph was explaining to Desi that they were back in Earth's atmosphere, but they needed to recover two of the three missing Founders before returning.

"We should have the Thandican and Whasook shortly and be heading back to you."

Desi furrowed his brow. "How are you transporting a Whasook? That is not a simple matter."

Neph explained they were using a Sweeper for the job. "There's a lot more I need to tell you—that we need to tell you. Sarah will join me in a minute, but we think the Atheciery are heading towards Earth right now, as we speak."

"What? Why? Do they think Galloyde is here? Oh, well of course they do. Who else would have broken him out of the Ripple? Yes, that was a little short-sighted of us. Oh, do you think the Grand Precipice hired them to bring him back or were they permanently assigned as guardians? I'd bet both."

Neph watched as Desi answered his own questions. Neph was used to this and tried to intercept Desi's running dialogue. "They were at the Ripple as we entered it. The Atheciery followed us in."

"No!" Desi gasped. "How? No, no, don't tell me—tell me later. Wait, were they just a diversion? No, they needed to see exactly who it was who recovered Galloyde, of course."

Of course. Well, that's one burning question answered, Neph thought.

"So they are on their way here, do you think this, or you know with certainty?" Desi inquired. He actually waited for Neph to answer this one.

"Sarah and Galloyde are certain. They both saw it in their dreams, it makes sense—they wouldn't have left the Ripple the way they did if they didn't have another plan."

Desi nodded slowly. "Overseers. Two Overseers. They see. That's what they do. They don't know when the Atheciery would arrive do they? No, of course not—you would have told me already. Well, let's be glad they can't jump. Alright. So you already jumped back and you're recovering the Founders immediately. Why? What do the Founders have to do with the Atheciery and Galloyde?"

"I can answer that," Sarah said as she entered the room. She pulled the chair around and sat down where Desi could see her. Neph got up and swapped places with her so she was directly in front of the screen.

Then she told the Elgets about The Gate in Descend.

CHAPTER
FIFTY-SIX

"There is this longstanding belief in many of Earth's religions that there is a gate to Heaven, where upon dying, you will meet a pleasant gate keeper by the name of St. Peter. If he calls your name, you are granted permission to enter into what they call Heaven, where all your deceased relatives and animals will join you for eternity. Welcome to the Pearly Gates," Sarah said with a flourish, introducing the Elgets to the idea of entryways into the afterlife.

"Then there's Hell's gate, where humans are said to be kidnapped by demons and dragged kicking and screaming all the way down into the underworld for an eternity of torture. If the Gates to Hell are unlocked, demons will escape and destroy mankind."

Desi interjected. "Sarah, do any animals on Earth believe in the afterlife? Do they build altars or hold ceremonies? Since this belief extends so far that animals can go to this heaven, then isn't it reasonable that some would go to Hell? By that logic, wouldn't the humans expect to see other animals with equal or higher intelligence quotients practicing religious ceremonies to ensure their entry to a Heaven as well?"

Sarah laughed heartily. "Desi, stop trying to make sense of any of these religions. Let's remember that the humans still believe they are the only intelligent life that has ever existed, anywhere in the universes, even though they haven't finished exploring all of their own planet yet. They have no idea how many other species are right under their noses that are far more intelligent than they are. Humans remain so primitive in their thinking that if you can't build a skyscraper, then you must not be smarter than they are."

Desi groaned. "That level of narcissism is impressive on a galactic scale. I'm not sure how they are even classified as 'self-aware,' when they don't understand where they rank in intellect or observation of other species. How is it not obvious to the humans when higher-intellect forms of life refuse to play along with their strange rituals? The Council really needs to tighten their guidelines on what 'self-aware' really means. I apologize, go ahead, please continue."

She pulled out her holodisc and turned it on. "Desi, I appreciate you trying to understand the little barbarians, and some of them do get it, and they Ascend. For the others, it's easier to believe in myths instead of taking responsibility for their own behavior. To be fair, some of their religious structures are beautiful, and many have helped hold communities together during a crisis. But let's not pretend logic has always been their strong suit. Hey, will you be able to see this alright?" He nodded from his office in Ascend. He could see Sarah's hologram set up on the table.

"This is the map of Descend," she explained. "The irony of all of this is that despite the fictional lore, we actually do have a physical Gate in Descend. Here is the center of Descend, and over here," she pulled the hologram upwards to show several levels of underground tunnels. "The Hi-reps are housed in here. Then it all goes down into this section before it leads to the Chamber room. Can you see it?" A small room along the bottom of all the tunnels could be seen in the hologram. Both Elgets nodded again.

Sarah rotated the diagram so they could see from another direction. "The Chamber is part of the Old Passages. These were created by

Galloyde. He made this when The Athecierians first came to Earth about 250,000 years ago."

"And you call me old?" Neph said under his breath.

"Now is not the time," Sarah warned. Desi looked perplexed for a moment, then continued to listen closely.

"Anyways," Sarah continued, "Galloyde had escaped with Olethia, my mother. When the Grand Precipice apparently sent The Atheciery to come get her and Galloyde, they were unsuccessful—"

Nephemerus drew in a sharp breath.

"What is it?" Desi asked.

Neph's face went dark, remembering his dream. "Your mother. Sarah, what happened to your mother?"

A tone buzzed right at that moment and the Commander stepped in. "Admiral, we are in the vicinity. We will be over the target in 4 pilns." He quickly took his leave after giving a brief salute.

Neph looked at Desi. "We have to go get this Thandican. We'll pick this up as soon as we achieve the target and we are on our way to our second location. Wish us luck."

Desi did and ended communications.

Neph steered Sarah out of the room and back to the Bridge, where they examined the surface of Ball's Pyramid on the main screen. It looked like the tip of a steep mountaintop, jutting out of the water. Inaccessible by boat, the sharp outcropping of rock in the sea was ideal for the Thandican. Neph was grinning from ear to ear. He ordered the Commander to ready a "Stinger" for the operation.

"Galloyde was right. I bet your Thandican didn't move. What an ideal, remote location. Nearly impossible for predators to attack. If there is open space inside that volcano, she could be thousands of feet below the surface. How can we reach her though? We're going to need climbing gear and—"

"You forget, "Sarah said, "when I found my Regulators a long time ago, I got them all back to Descend without any gear, without 'Stingers' or 'Sweepers.' I'll be fine. Don't worry, just get me close to the surface, that's all I need.

Neph rolled his eyes. "Just because you didn't have the gear back then doesn't mean you can't use what we have today. We are in a time crunch. Let me help you with our retrieval equipment, get the Thandican, and move on with our mission."

"Ahem?" The nervous Commander coughed. "Admiral. We are over the target. The Stinger is ready for you…" He looked back and forth between the Admiral and Sarah while letting the sentence dangle out in front of him.

Sarah glanced at the location, rising out of the water. What if the Thandican wasn't there? What if— She shook the thought away and smiled up at Neph.

"After you, Admiral," she said, patting him on the butt. He sighed again, but the smirk she caught on his lips betrayed his feigned annoyance.

CHAPTER
FIFTY-SEVEN

L uis had a plan. He had mentally run through this plan ever since Sarah first asked him to carry this out for her. Once he knew the exact steps to take, he repeated them daily in his mind, so if he was ever asked to execute them, they would become second nature to him.

He had the dagger on him, but unlike Sarah, he kept it under his clothes and hidden from sight. He reached for the dagger in the small of his back, just to make sure it hadn't moved. He had to start with the Regulators who were the furthest away, so that meant the Triplets. As he started in that direction, he spotted Tiny just up the walkway.

"Tiny, un momento." Luis called to him.

No longer exhausted from being up all night, consumed with creating or interpreting etchings, Tiny found himself having plenty of energy and enjoying long conversations with Desimidor about the history of Descend. He was just returning from the Ascend Operations Tower when he heard Luis calling to him, his voice serious.

"Hello! Good news, I heard that Sarah and Neph—" Tiny began to greet Luis.

Luis cut him off. "Thrinythidor, it's time."

Tiny stared at Luis who had never used his full name. Luis was only going to use his name for one distinct purpose, if it ever was needed. He felt his own smile fall from his fade. He couldn't help but ask in a weak voice, "How long do we have?"

"No idea. Go. Now."

Tiny nodded. He turned and started his own part of the plan. Except unlike Luis, he didn't have to think of the steps—he remembered them.

FIFTY-EIGHT

T he Stinger looked like an oversized drone, Sarah thought. She hesitated getting inside—correction, onto it. This looked like less safe than riding on a paper airplane.

There were 2 seats mounted on a tubular frame like in a hang glider. Three rotating blades formed a triangle above the safety bar on the top of the craft. The Stinger seemed to have less structural framing than a ride on your average traveling amusement park attraction.

Neph stepped onto the flimsy contraption as if he commuted with one every day. He sat down on the side that had a singular joystick coming out of one of the steel tubes. He looked up at her, waiting. She glanced around, looking for a helmet or pressure suit for when they would inevitably fall out of this child's toy. She saw none, and Neph called to her to join him as he clicked a lap belt over his legs. One singular lap belt. Who could ever say Clorrians didn't have a dark sense of humor?

She grimaced as she stared down off the deck, calculating if a free fall might be a safer way to get down to the surface. She resigned her fate and stepped onto the Stinger, sitting down next to Neph.

He leaned over and clamped on a second bungee lead that wrapped around her wrist. She saw that he wore one as well.

The entire machine was absolutely silent, which didn't comfort Sarah as they left the Sweeper's platform. At first, she thought the Stinger's blades simply weren't working as they were careening towards the volcano below. Then Neph pulled them out of their dive and gradually took them on a leisurely reconnaissance flight around the rocky outcropping.

He pointed at the side of the pyramid and she saw the shadow. She gave him a thumbs-up. He flew as close as he could to that spot and then pointed the nose straight upward. She felt a small bounce and then a bump. The Stinger latched onto the side of the volcano. She could hear the landing gear driving itself into the rock. She looked at Nephemerus, who was grinning wickedly at her.

She shaded her eyes from the sun and yelled, "Good job!"

"I know!" he yelled back. The wind whipped past, making it hard for either of them to move easily. He swung out, using the Stinger to provide a foothold on the side of the mountain. She did the same on her side. As she did, she saw how deeply the landing gear was embedded into the rock face. That's handy, she thought.

Neph climbed to a spot up above her and found a flat area. She hugged him when she pulled herself up and he just laughed.

"I should just pitch you off from here and save myself the trouble," he grinned at her.

"You like the trouble," she shot back.

"Oh I do. I love the trouble."

They pushed themselves against the rock face and made their way into the shadow. At first they saw no opening, no crevice leading down inside. Then Sarah moved a little further along and reached behind a boulder.

"I'll need you to move. Get over to the side, that way!" she pointed past Neph. "Then crawl up and hang on to that rock, really tight!"

He nodded. When he got into his spot, she looked down the mountain at the Stinger. Then back to Neph, up at the sun, and back to the boulder. She picked up a smaller rock, then struck the boulder with it. First, small pieces clinked away harmlessly down the side of the rock.

"Whoa. Remind me not to get you really mad!" Neph teased as Sarah kept staring at the boulder. She put a hand up, warning him not to move. The rock wall under them rumbled and shifted.

"Hang on!" she yelled.

Rocks began to tumble down all around them. Neph was too far away to shield Sarah, but he could swear he saw her smiling as she watched the boulders bounce past her. He saw one hit a few inches from her head. Right before it was about to hit the Stinger's front end, the boulder suddenly turned 90 degrees in the air and flew in an entirely different direction. He looked back at Sarah, who was flicking her wrist back and forth. With each flick, another boulder would cast off to the left or right, easily avoiding the Stinger. After a few minutes, the avalanche slowed to just a few pebbles. Sarah crawled up to where the boulder had been, now peering into a small hole in the side of the mountain.

"Are you ok?" she called to Neph.

He pointed further up Ball's Pyramid. "Looks like it opened up there too."

She agreed. "Yeah. I need some oxygen in there. This has been sealed for quite a long time. We don't want too much to get in though; I don't want to disturb anyone else."

"Wait, what? Who else? Who else is in there, Sarah?" By now, Neph had made his way over to the opening in the rock face.

She had already tied a rope around her legs and waist in a makeshift harness and was sliding into the small hole before answering his question. She turned her body around and rested her hips against the side of the hole, her legs swallowed by the pitch black below.

"Darling, I don't want to fight, but at some point, you're going to have to accept that there are situations that I am uniquely qualified for, and this is one of those situations. I can either find this Thandican quickly, or *we* can look together and it'll take a lot longer. Will you please trust me?"

"Just come back to me."

"Oh, you're not getting rid of me that easily." He heard her laugh as she pushed herself off the edge and fell backwards into pure darkness.

CHAPTER
FIFTY-NINE

Luis found the Triplets and began the chain of messages. The Triplets would inform Seglee, who would then access The Gate through an underwater cavern. The Triplets would find Clara, and they would all proceed to The Gate together.

Luis would go find GilGerg and secure him with the Descend Support team. Tiny was responsible for Bunny, just in case Bunny was feeling stubborn. Only Tiny had the brute strength to physically "convince" Bunny to follow orders if he decided to refuse. Luis doubted it would come to that. Bunny knew Sarah was gone. He had been on his best behavior since she left; everyone had. Nonetheless, Luis would feel the most relieved when Bunny was safely in The Gate.

Once Bunny was secured, the Ascend Elget and Support staff would be asked to join, and then The Gate would be locked. This meant no new admissions. No human could enter Ascend or Descend. Recently deceased souls would be left without any destination, this had never happened before. Luis tried not to think about it. If he was being asked to lock The Gate, he was going to lock it.

He was making his way back through the levels when he saw Chronny. Luis directed him towards The Gate, but when Chronny tried to ask a series of questions, Luis waved him away and moved to the next classroom. Everyone knew to follow this one order without any pushback.

Finally, he looped around to the break room and found GilGerg eating a snack out of a knocked-over trash bin. Luis had been a pillar of strength until he saw his furry friend run and crash into him in pure, unadulterated delight. Luis knelt down and hugged his companion.

"Yes, yes, my friend, I've been busy. I need you to come with me. Right now, it's important. Yes, there will be food. Come right now." Luis took a deep, steadying breath before walking back out the door. He had to get back into the frame of mind that got him this far.

Get them in The Gate. Keep them safe. Get them all to safety. Lock The Gate. Luis repeated this refrain to himself as they made their way through the corridors and down to the Old Passageways. He walked until he knew he was well inside the perimeter, then he performed a head count. Then he counted everyone again. And again. And once again.

Then Luis took a deep breath and locked The Gate.

CHAPTER
SIXTY

In the pitch-black darkness, Sarah felt the click of The Gate's lock inside her. She erupted with a visceral cry. They were inside! They made it. Even though it was coal black all around her, tears sprang into her eyes, making any chance of seeing any hint of light that might be coming from above completely impossible.

She squeezed her eyes shut and looked deep within. Bunny, Tiny, Clara, the Triplets, GilGerg, and yes, Seglee were all within the cavern. She scanned their perimeter, all the way around, under the cavern, and through The Gate. Intact. Luis. Exhausted. Fingers wrapped bone-tight on the dagger. Everyone was inside. Everyone was safe.

She shifted her gaze. "Alright, now where are you, you fuckers..." she mumbled. Her father flashed in her mind. He was looking too, she realized. Of course he was. He had felt The Gate lock just as she did. He was doing the exact same thing he taught her to do. They searched together and found their quarry, The Atheciery, almost immediately.

That's their war ship. You don't remember their war ships, Sarah. They've been here before. Her father's voice rumbled in her head.

Suddenly they both saw there wasn't one single war ship, there were two? No, there were even more. Sarah was trying to count, while she could hear Galloyde counting.

Sarah then saw glimpses of irate beings—all different species— attacking each other within closed quarters. It was in a building that seemed abandoned and heavily damaged. There were walls that were missing, broken windows, and sections of floor that had been blasted away. Screams punctuated the night air. Sarah shivered at the vision, quickly and then began to seethe with anger. One name is pushed into the forefront of her mind. *"Kevin."*

She shook off the images of what must have been Radimus, and pulled her mind back to the Athecierian War Ships. She counted seven of the enemy ships before what must have been Lake Hazan took over her mind.

A massive freshwater lake stretching over 46 miles long and nearly 7 miles at the widest point, buffered by mountains and glaciers on every side. The lake stood as an oasis in the sea of snow and ice. An enormous creature erupted through the frozen surface, taking in air at the northeast corner of the lake. Fish flopped onto the ice next to the creature's head. He glanced down, then dove into the ice, swallowing the fish and the ice ledge together as he disappeared back into the murky depths.

"There's no way he can even fit in there." She whispered in awe. "That lake can't be deep enough for him unless…" She saw underground feeders connecting Lake Hazan to the north, flowing into the Arctic Ocean. She smiled as she watched the Whasook lazily cruise the bottom of the lake, enjoying the shoal of fish he cornered, bite by bite.

The Whasook was the size of a fin whale with legs the size of sequoia trees. No wonder they would need a much larger craft, Sarah thought. Then Galloyde pointed out a key bit of information to her. She listened to him explain how to transport the Whasook with a smile on her face.

Sarah acknowledged this tip from her father before her mind flashed to Nephemerus, who was waiting high above for her, peering into the darkness.

He was staring into the black hole, unable to see any sign of Sarah. A cool breeze from below was blowing his hair back, revealing the strain on his face. His neck muscles taut, his eyes narrowed. She could feel his rising sense of panic. Then she saw the rope he had brought with them, still hanging from a bungee on the Stinger. Neph glanced down the mountain to gauge how quickly he could get it and come back—

"Stop!" She shouted at him in her mind. Above her, Neph jumped back, shaken. He looked around, to make sure she hadn't emerged from another point and then accepting that he heard her in his head.

"Ok, I'll stay right here," he called into the darkness.

Sarah felt a sense of calmness wash over her like a spring shower. Her breathing slowed as she relaxed. She held out her hand and focused on the image of a tiny purple flower with the yellow center that grew in the harsh elements along the rock face of Ball's Pyramid. She hovered in the darkness, letting go of all the images flooding her mind, letting go of all her worries and concerns. She let go of everything except for the image of that one tiny flower.

Sarah heard the buzz of a tiny creature near her ear and the fluttering of its wings against her face, her ears, neck and then on her hands.

Breathe, Galloyde reminded her. *Focus on the flower.*

She took another slow deep breath in and exhaled slowly. She repeated this again and then again. At the end of the third breath, the Thandican surrendered herself into Sarah's hand.

"Time to go my little friend. I promise I'll bring you right back here when it's safe again." She softly whispered into her hand.

CHAPTER
SIXTY-ONE

S arah surfaced quickly, popping her head out of the hole and into Neph's anxious grasp. "They have seven warships. They are just over one rotation out. The Gate is locked. Dad showed me the Whasook. He's in the northwest corner of Lake Hazan. Oh, and look at my new friend!" She held her hand out and opened her palm, shielding the tiny creature from the sun and wind. Inside, a scaled bird with a tiny, needle beak, no bigger than her pinkie finger looked up, her glimmering silver body and bright red eyes shining in the sunlight.

Neph's eyebrows shot up. "You got all that while you were down there?"

"Isn't she gorgeous?" Sarah asked, beaming over her new Regulator.

Neph kept his head back. "Yeah, but you might want to be a little more careful with those guys. That's the root Founder to the Kirlally. They are exceptionally dangerous."

Sarah already had dropped the Thandican into her shirt pocket and tucked it in safely. Neph's jaw dropped. "You m-m-might not want to do that—" he stammered.

"Let's get going!" She shouted back at him and began to scale down the mountainside to their craft.

Once seated back in the Sweeper, Neph warned her to hang on as they took off, bouncing backwards into a short freefall before he engaged the engines and returned to the Bibbly.

Once aboard, Sarah placed the Thandican in a locked cage in a locked room that Neph had insisted upon. They set course to Northern Canada and went back to his Admiral quarters. He didn't have quite as many rooms as he did on the Noneru, but it was still stunningly appointed, she noted.

"How many ships within a ship do you have?" she asked, taking in the smaller footprint of the quarters, which were still the size of a massive penthouse suite.

"Later. Seven warships? You're certain?"

'Yes. Both Galloyde and I saw them."

Neph nodded silently, processing this information. "Alright. We have three Cruisers now, but as big as they seem, they are no match for even one Athecierian warship."

Sarah was alarmed. "Wait. You don't have anything—"

He held up his hand. "I didn't say that. Don't forget, we are Clorrian. A race whose entire history is mired in the glory of war. Every ship is meant for battle, even that Stinger. That was designed to physically rip out the guidance or life support systems in enemy ships. We have Battleships and Airships. One Airship could easily handle all their warships, but unfortunately, they cannot jump. They are essentially floating cities, no—floating planets. Their immense size makes it impossible for them to jump like the Cruisers can. Our closest Airship is at least three rotations away. The Battleships are just over two rotation away, but The Atheciery will be here for almost eight Earth days before our ships arrive. That'll be too late."

Sarah pondered this. "What are the capabilities of the Battleships against the Atheciery warships? Also, won't the humans see an actual battle?"

They both changed their clothes, preparing to go to the lake. Then Neph called the Bridge to receive an ETA. They would be at the northernmost Canadian lake location in 30 pilns.

"Clorrian Battle Ships can handle two, maybe three warships each. I could order ten to this location, but it won't help if they aren't here in time. Unlike the Airships, Battleships are much smaller, but their weapons systems are so cumbersome, they don't have the capacity to fit in the jump technology—although I need to seriously reconsider changing that for future builds.

"As far as the humans, if the Atheciery want war, the humans will absolutely see what's happening. They won't be trying to hide their attempt to wipe this planet off the map. We need to locate and capture a Whasook, transport both Regulators to The Gate and still figure out how to get the Nox." Neph collapsed back into his chair. "Fuck...Fuck!" he repeated for emphasis.

Sarah grabbed two glasses off a cart located against the far wall. The Clorrians always had alcohol stocked in these rooms, she noted with amusement. She poured two amber-colored drinks and handed one to Neph before she sat down. "We can't reach Desi now that he's in The Gate, so we have to figure out a plan, but I think I've got a way to do it."

Neph leaned forward and sniffed the glass before taking a sip. "Hit me."

Sarah slugged her drink without hesitation and slammed her glass down with a sly look. "You and Galloyde said there's no way to storm in and get Kevin right? Too many prisoners, too unpredictable?"

Neph nodded. "Death wish. Not a possibility, even with a hundred Clorrians and plenty of time, I wouldn't do it, couldn't do it. The worst of the worst are in there. Even if you could get in, you can't get out. It can't be done."

Sarah tipped her glass and rolled it along the bottom edge. "But they do get in. They get sentenced. They are put inside of there somehow."

"Yeah, of course, but that's the Council. They use a….ooooh. Oh, fuck no."

Sarah grinned. "Oh, fuck yeah. Everyone has a price and you said you knew one!"

"No! No! No, no, no. I said I knew a Traveler. I didn't say I knew a suicidal lunatic who could Travel."

Sarah pushed back from the table and began to pace. "Listen. I can locate that Nox anywhere in that facility. From right here, with Galloyde's help. We get a Traveler to pop in, grab him, then pop back out. We need him in The Gate—for everyone's benefit. Without him on Earth and safe with the others, there's too much risk of something going very wrong. So let's do this. It'll be a snap, no problem."

"Oh, ok then, no problem," Neph rolled his eyes. "Let's break down your concrete plan, shall we? First, we have to find a Traveler who's actually insane enough to willingly Travel into Radimus without Council approval, because I'm sure no one has ever considered doing that before. Second, we want to try to kidnap a Nox who is a fucking lunatic on his best day, thinking he is suddenly going to play nice? A Traveler is going to pop up in his face and this Kevin character is going to say, 'Hi there, chum, thanks for the ride. I'll just go along easily and not try to kill you?' Right. Lastly, I don't even know if there is a Council lock or perimeter alarm or barrier on that place, so that Travelers can't do this exact this sort of thing to begin with. If a Traveler can't jump back out, there's no way to do this."

Sarah walked over to Neph's side of the desk and leaned over his chair, and smiled. "So what I'm hearing, is that you're saying you love my plan, think it's our best shot, and you'll reach out to your contact? Great!"

"That is not at all what I said!"

"That's so odd because that's exactly what I heard," Sarah said, smirking as she sat back down in her chair. "I'll reach out to Galloyde and see if he knows anything about the security system at Radimus. If this works, we can just pop in, pop out, and have the Nox on Earth in just a few hours. Easy." She leaned back and put her boots on the desk.

"What the—" Neph started to say.

"Unless you have another hashed out plan? Do you? What's yours? I'd love to hear it. We have less than two rotations until The Atheciery turn Earth into a pile of ash, so what'cha got?"

"Fuuuck." Neph finished his sentence.

"Of course darlin, but keep your mind in the game right now. We have to save an entire species first."

CHAPTER
SIXTY-TWO

S arah contacted Galloyde and asked if he knew of any security measures that would prevent someone from leaving Radimus. Neph reached out to his Traveler contact and asked to meet on Earth. They were soon interrupted by the Commander, who informed them that they had reached their destination.

"We are over the target. How would you like to travel to the surface, Admiral?" the Commander asked, the last few words almost in a whisper, remembering the near brawl his question triggered just a few hours ago.

Neph didn't look up from his display. "Put the Sweeper down in a clearing next to the lake. Maintain cloaking, switch to terra concealment. I'll take a Lander down ahead of you."

"Copy, Admiral." The Commander nodded and whirled away.

"Gotta get going, Dad. We need to pick up the Whasook," Sarah said to the display on a second screen in the small office.

Galloyde looked well-rested and healthy. He had cleaned up and changed clothes. He must be nearly all healed, Sarah thought. I bet he's been giving the medical staff a rough time now, she smiled to herself, thinking of how rigid they all are in there.

"Did you talk to Merus about transportation yet?" Galloyde asked her, grinning.

Neph closed his display and looked over. "Hello there, Galloyde. We have the Sweeper. We are prepared to hoist the Whasook all the way to Descend if we need to. Our cloaking abilities can extend up to 10,000 feet beyond our craft. Which reminds me, will he need to enter via Seglee's route? Is there enough room?"

Galloyde looked back to Sarah. "Guess not. Talk soon, little Gator. Good luck!" Galloyde cut off his communications.

Neph looked at Sarah. "What was that about?"

Sarah shook her head. "I think you might be learning a new thing or two about Whasooks very soon." She laughed. "I need to get out on the water. Can you help me do that?"

Neph looked puzzled. "On the water? Oh no, I don't recommend that. You'll be too exposed. We need to lure him out of the lake and then somehow wrap a harness around him. Maybe we can trick him into stepping into it. Even then, it's going to be difficult if he really fights us. Unless you think you can convince him to load easily into the cargo bay?"

Sarah listened to Neph talk through different approaches as she walked with him toward the Landing Bay. He continued to theorize different scenarios as he walked up the platform and into the Lander, assuming she was following him. It wasn't until he saw her walk by outside as he took the pilot's chair that he realized she hadn't boarded with him.

Sarah found a long, flat metal sheet. She was judging the weight of the object when Neph poked his head back out of the Lander and asked, "What are you doing with that?"

"I need it for on the water. Do you think this will float?" she asked him, but didn't wait for an answer as she started to haul it up the platform into the craft.

He helped her bring it on board and tuck it away. They strapped into their respective seats and took off. This was a far more controlled flight than the last one they took as they made their way down to the lake's edge. Neph made one pass over the lake, but little could be seen through the tumultuous, dark water. The ice was receding in most areas, but the water appeared black to the naked eye. He found a spot along the northwest edge and cleared the Sweeper for landing. The Bibbly came in and took a position on higher ground, dwarfing the Lander. In front of their eyes, it looked as if it had disappeared, blending in with the mountains, trees, and snow around the ship.

Sarah was already outside and dragging the makeshift skiff out of the Lander and heading toward the water. Neph jogged to catch up to her, their breath condensing into white puffs in the frigid air as they spoke.

"Are you sure about this? If you get bumped and go overboard, or if something happens, I'm telling you—you don't want to be out there with a Whasook coming out of the water!"

Sarah pulled up the ends of the metal in a sharp curve, making a canoe out of the flat sheet before tossing it out onto the water. She stood on a rope she had tied to it to prevent it from floating away. She watched Neph with a half-smile and said nothing as she continued to put on her gloves and prepared to leave. He looked out at the lake and then back at where the concealed Sweeper had landed.

"Why do I already regret what I just said?" he shouted as the wind picked up. "I'm thinking you already know something I don't, and I'm just going to look stupid in a few minutes."

Sarah kept the same smile on her face and motioned him to come closer to her. When he did, she pulled his hood up and tied it tight to keep him warm. Then she gave him a quick kiss. She turned, got into her little boat, and started to push off with a long plank she had decided to use as an oar.

She turned back to shore and squinted at him. "You're too handsome to look stupid, but I think you have the right instincts! If you want to see something pretty amazing, you're welcome to join me, Admiral." She winked at him and gave another hard push off the shallow footing with the makeshift oar. The little skiff pushed further out into the water.

Neph paused for a few seconds before he jogged through the shallow water and clambered onto the concave shell. She didn't even look back at him; she just kept rowing. He sank down low and spread his body out along the bottom of the boat, trying not to tip them over. She continued to row as he watched them get further from shore and into the deeper, black swirling water.

Once Sarah was about a half mile from shore, she sat down cross-legged between Neph's legs and stopped paddling. Because of his long, lanky frame, Sarah doubted if Neph could stand up in this boat if he tried—it was simply too small. He stayed in his position as she sat between his legs with her eyes closed. A moment later, a low rumble emitted from her. The frequency was pedantic, rhythmic, and grew in intensity.

At first, Neph found the humming soothing, but as it became louder, he realized it made their tiny boat vibrate. He looked over the side and, despite Sarah no longer rowing, the water continued to ripple away. He looked further across the lake and saw large sections of the ice drop into the water and disappear.

He used the sides of their craft to pull himself more upright as Sarah sat squarely between his legs. He pulled her backwards and into his chest to protect her from whatever was coming. He could feel his heart vibrate from the sound emanating from her. The sound felt as if it was echoing from inside him, from under their boat, and rolling down from the tops of the very mountains that surrounded the lake. He closed his eyes and squeezed her tight as the noise became deafening.

For just a moment, Neph was truly afraid for both of them.

Suddenly, the sound stopped. The chanting ceased, and she turned to look at him, her finger pressed to her lips in a "shhhh" gesture. Her half-smile returned, and she motioned to the water. The ripples that had been moving away from them were now moving toward the boat. Neph's eyes grew large with alarm, and Sarah squeezed his leg to reassure him. That did little to calm him as the head of a Whasook rose out of the water right next to their flimsy metal craft. Sarah giggled with pure glee as the head and neck continued to rise for another 80 feet.

Neph whispered faintly in her ear. "Don't make sudden movements."

She nudged him with an elbow playfully and turned around. "Don't be silly. Why are you acting like you're scared?"

The Whasook's head lowered down on the opposite side of their float and stared right at them. His eyes were larger than their entire bodies. Sarah pushed herself upwards off of Neph's knees and stood up. She faced the Whasook's nose and put one open hand straight up in the air and made a small whirling motion. The Whasook made a single dip of his massive head and then leaned in over the boat.

Water poured over Sarah and Neph as the Whasook's head passed over them. Neph let out a high-pitched yelp, positive they were going to be eaten whole. Sarah leaned out of the boat and pressed her free hand against the flat of the Whasook's nose. She appeared to be rubbing his giant nose in a circle.

Neph heard the same humming sound Sarah had made before, but now it was coming from the Whasook. She continued to make the circles against the wall of his snout as the sound became louder, thrumming out of the water and coming at him in all directions. He glanced over the sides and noticed the waves now were larger and hitting their tiny craft even faster. When he looked back towards Sarah, he had to blink a few times. He could have sworn the Whasook was now half the size.

Neph stared at the head of the creature, then at Sarah, who was looking over at Neph, laughing and then smiling, and then back at the Whasook. He pulled himself up again, pressing his back into the rear of the boat as carefully as possible, without tipping them over. Neph looked up the long neck and thought the creature must have sunk back into the water, he thought. That was why he looked so much smaller.

Sarah continued to make circles on the nose, which at this point looked like the size of a hippopotamus' nose. That can't be right, Neph thought as he looked back toward shore. That looked the same. He looked at Sarah—she looked the same. He looked at the Whasook again, who was now the size of a large dog.

Sarah had stopped with her circles and sat back down and grabbed the plank. She held it out, and a miniature version of the Whasook swam onto it. She pulled it on board and set it in front of her. It was the size of a small kitten.

She turned around to Neph with a wide smile. "Pretty cool, right? Told ya you'd learn something new today!"

He was pale and shaking as he pulled his coat in tight around him. Sarah started to row back to shore. He made sure he kept an eye on the Whasook the entire time, but it had curled up in a ball on her lap and appeared to have gone to sleep.

"Dad was pretty sure not too many other species knew that Whasooks can change their size. It's so they can move through underwater passages that might cave in or freeze over time. It's pretty handy if you think about it. When you brought up their size and transporting him, that's when it occurred to him—just force him to reduce his size. Easy!"

"Easy!" Neph grunted. "What happens if he suddenly pops back to full size and kills us all? How long can he stay like that?"

"Oh, he can stay this size for years if he wants. It also works for hibernation if the food availability is low. I mean, if you think about it, the evolutionary leap here is genius. He can even go smaller than this! His caloric intake is infinitesimal compared to his size when you first saw him. Then think about if he needed to fight? Boom, back to big boy mode. Such an impressive species, right?"

She looked back at him, her face glowing with pride. "Well, you know them better than I do. I can't imagine a whole planet—maybe a whole solar system—of these guys! Wow! If they have this type of evolution at the Founder stage, imagine where they are now? And this is just one trick that Dad knew about. I bet there's tons of others." She looked over her shoulder again at him. His face twisted in a snarl as he stared at the wrapped-up Whasook, who was now purring on her lap.

"Hey, what's the deal?" she prodded Neph. "What's that all about? He's not a Demon, you know. Don't be so judgy."

Neph looked at her, so excited about her newest Regulator. "You're right, I'm sorry. The Whasooks of today are mostly known for being a bit more aggressive. They eat first, ask questions never. So when I saw you put yourself so close to its mouth—"

"His mouth. This is Bob," she said with a straight face.

"Bob?"

"Bob. Literally Bob. That's it. Not even short for anything. I asked. He said his name is Bob, and be nice please, he understands every word you are saying."

Neph digested this for a moment. "When I saw you so close to... Bob's mouth, I thought you were going to be eaten. I know you're a Demon Keeper—erhm, Regulator wrangler. I know, I... well, I guess I don't really know anything you are capable of doing." He looked down at his freezing hands. "Sometimes I just forget, and I just want to jump in and keep you safe."

"From Bob," she said flatly, pointing to the purring, kitten-sized Whasook, who looked adorable curled up in her lap.

Neph sighed. "Yeah, from Bob."

They were close to shore. "I get it. I appreciate what you're saying. Listen, without you, I never would have found Bob—or Bezel. That's the name I'm going with for the Thandican. None of this would be possible without all you have done. I understand that. I just need you to trust me when it comes to these guys. We are a team. We work together. Right?"

He pulled her into him and hugged her tight. "Always, my little love."

CHAPTER
SIXTY-THREE

As they boarded the Sweeper, they were met by the Commander, who was ready with the cargo bay doors open. Sarah stood there grinning with Bob wrapped in her scarf. She handed Bob to an officer and told him that the creature needed water and sliced herring if they had it.

The officer cautiously took the two-pound Whasook and looked at the Admiral, who followed up with, "You heard her. Get to it."

Neph walked up the platform with Sarah and took her hand. She noticed his was ice cold. She looked up at him and saw his skin was pale. "Are you ok?"

He nodded slowly and turned down a corridor to head toward the bridge, but started to lose his balance. "We have to get to Descend, we should get…" he trailed off.

The Commander caught up to them and informed them that the Atheciery were less than a rotation away. He asked for orders but stopped when he saw the look on Sarah's face.

Neph just stared forward, unseeing. Sarah felt his face, his ears, then the back of his neck. They were ice cold. She turned to the

Commander and gave him the coordinates to Descend and then in a low voice added, "I need you to send hot food, liquids mainly, to the Admiral's quarters now. Help me to get him there. Discreetly, if you can, please."

The Commander nodded and motioned to two nearby soldiers, who immediately came over and stood at attention, awaiting orders. The Commander stated simply, "The Admiral needs to retire to quarters. Quietly. Now." The soldiers nodded and stepped to each side of Nephemerus, dwarfing his tall, lean frame. At a casual distance, they appeared to be walking close and guarding him, but Sarah, who was right next to Neph, saw his feet lift completely off the ground. They moved quickly through the hallways. She went to follow, hearing the Commander say he would be awaiting an update. She promised she would and ran after the guards.

As they rounded the last corner to the Admiral's quarters, she saw the Medical Physician, Dr. Wyseth, standing outside the door, looking passively displeased. The soldiers went by the doctor and entered the quarters without stopping. Sarah paused and motioned for her to follow inside. The soldiers had sat Neph on his bed. He was gray and cold to the touch.

Sarah threw a blanket over him as she started to explain to the physician, "We were on the lake. He was lying on the bottom of this metal skiff. I think he lost too much body heat." She looked at Dr. Wyseth. "Hot bath, warm liquids? Let me try that first for him, unless you want to do something more now?"

"No, just you," Neph whispered and reached for her arm. He grasped her wrist and squeezed with all the strength he had left.

He's scared, she realized. Sarah started stripping off his boots and socks as fast as she could. She ran into the bathroom and turned on hot water to run for the bath. Dr. Wyseth did a quick exam on Neph as Sarah answered the door and retrieved a tray of food from the guards. She thanked them and brought the tray into the bedroom.

The physician watched her. "You can try your way. Do what only you can. If he doesn't significantly improve quickly, I'll have to bring him to Noneru for further treatment." Sarah agreed and walked the doctor out of the bedroom and to the front door.

"And you'll have to order him to do it," Wyseth finished saying, her face expressionless.

"Order him? He's the Admiral, a Fleet Admiral. I don't think—"

"And you're the Overseer. He won't follow anyone's orders except yours. Try your way first, but hurry. He's half-Vecurasian by birth. He needs to stay warmer than most species. Try to remember that he is not the same as you or me."

With that, Dr. Wyseth turned and left the quarters. Sarah ran back into the bedroom and stripped off the rest of his clothes. She helped him into the bathroom and eased him into the bath. The water was warm, but as soon as he got in, she turned the water on again, much warmer. By now, he had lost all color in his face, neck, and chest. His dark eyes looked sunken, and his hands were ice cold to her touch, even in the hot water.

She helped him drink a cup of warm broth. He didn't protest and tried to take the nourishment. He wasn't able to bend his fingers to hold the cup himself, so she slowly tipped it back, letting him sip some of the clear broth in, give him a chance to drink it down, then repeated until he was done.

Then she pulled her clothes off and slid into the water behind him, making sure she could reach the faucets and the rest of the food. She filled a small cup and poured it over his hair and shoulders repeatedly, leaving the hot water tap on, and the drain open, making sure the water didn't cool down. She could see Neph trying to flex his hands and toes.

"It's alright, shhhh, it's okay, don't force it. Here, try some more." She gave him another cup of warm broth. This time, he could grasp the cup between his palms as she continued to pour the hot water down his back, shoulders, and arms.

Neph continued to shiver. This isn't working, she thought. Then she remembered what Wyseth had said. Do what only you can.

Sarah grunted at her own stupidity as she wrapped her arms around Neph's chest and her legs around his hips. She closed her eyes and breathed into his ear. "You're warm again, just relax, you're warm again." Heat flowed into his body as the water temperature increased. Inside, he felt a blossom of warmth flow throughout his core.

The muscles in his body slowly loosened. The cup dropped onto the floor and his full weight rested back against her body. The water was shut off and the drain closed, as they simmered in the hot water. She combed his hair away from his face with her fingers and continued to cup water over his chest and arms, keeping him warm.

He reached up and wrapped his hand around her arm, his fingers now warm, eyes still closed. She heard a faint thought rise from him. *Ishonna, Ishonna, Ishonna.* She kissed his temple and murmured softly in his ear as they laid in the water until the fog began to clear from the mirrors.

CHAPTER

SIXTY-FOUR

S arah helped Neph to bed, where he fell asleep nearly immediately. She tucked him in, dressed herself, and left the bedroom. She found the intercom was in the same spot as the Noneru. She picked it up and asked for the Commander. There was a pause and soon, she heard his voice. "Yes, how can I help?"

"Commander, I'm pleased to report the Admiral is feeling much, much better. I wanted you to know as soon as possible. Have we arrived at those coordinates?"

"Thank you, I appreciate the update," the Commander responded. "We have been in place for the past 40 minutes in Earth time. We remain cloaked. The Atheciery continue to close in."

"Thank you, Commander. Neph—" she caught herself. "The Admiral will let you know the next move shortly."

"Of course. In the meantime, do you need anything? I can call the galley, or do you need to speak with the Medical Team?"

"I don't want to keep having you call the kitchen, Commander. I can do that. As for Dr. Wyseth, that would be helpful. Just let her know the Admiral is resting and feeling much better. He will return to the bridge shortly."

"Understood." The communication ended. Sarah clicked the line and heard a new voice. She asked to speak to the galley. When she was connected, she asked for hot food to be delivered for the Admiral.

She checked on Neph, who was still sleeping deeply. She sat down on a chair facing the bed, thinking of her tiny room on the Noneru, which seemed like it was such a long time ago. *I bet he purposefully put me in that broom closet,* she thought. *No, he didn't know things would turn out like this between them,* she chided herself. She was an Overseer, and she didn't see any romantic connection to him in all the plans she made to bring him to Earth and help rescue her father.

Sarah had done her research on Desimidor Vas Qulas Zyrla and Nephemerus os Clorria while they were still Elget Trainees on Ala Mia. She needed to have the right Elgets on the Earth rotation when she executed her plan.

Desi had been an easy choice right away, with his background, temperament, and lineage, but Neph had never even been on her radar originally, she mused. It had been a Merkvestor named Laja Sinari who caught her eye for the second Elget spot. His family hailed from the Borgell system and gained their wealth from building and selling interplanetary transports. Not only did they have Clorrian connections, they were tied into virtually any race who had access to jump ships, legal or not.

Laja's decision to join Elget training on Ala Mia came as a shock to his family, as they assumed he would take his place within the family dynasty. Yet Laja was born with remarkable Elget capabilities, and along with his gift of intuition, magical range, and fighting prowess, he possessed a strong sense of cosmic altruism that both his family and many of his fellow kind did not share.

Sarah believed Laja's innate strengths and connections would make him a perfect fit for her plan. Just as she prepared to write to the

Council to make her request, she discovered Laja had left his training.

She learned of this from Aramik, whose job included storing and updating Earth's information in the Muldigal Library database. In order to stay somewhat connected, Aramik managed to develop a rudimentary feed to the Library. He received occasional updates from the Council that his friends would forward to him. Although Earth should have had an open line of communication with the Council office, the planet's location within a black hole prevented most information from coming through. His feed was sporadic at best.

All of the Council planets had an inherent interest in the Elgets on Ala Mia. The Elgets were a direct connection to the Council, and strong relationships were built from the early days of the Elget Trainees to when they would eventually take their seat at the Council Table. An Elget Trainee who willingly abandoned schooling on Ala Mia was unheard of—and news indeed.

Sarah's mind raced, as she hadn't considered an alternate for Laja. Her gut reaction was that Laja was the ideal candidate, just as Desimidor had been. Granted, she had started her research for the right Elgets nearly five centuries before she would need to make her request, but she wanted to pick her team and see how they performed in their roles well before they arrived. This way, she could gather as much intel as possible prior to their arrival. True intel, not the rudimentary, bland Introductory Packet the Council sent out to each Operations Center before the Administration changeover every couple thousand years

She watched Nephemerus turn over and reach out toward her side of the bed, searching for her. When he didn't find her, he pulled the covers up high over his shoulder and returned to a low, rumbling snore.

How did she decide on him? Her mind wandered for a moment, and then she remembered. She had been talking with Jess about possible candidates in the classes that had graduated recently. Jess asked her if she had reviewed everyone else in Laja's class, and Sarah scolded her. Of course she had.

Then, as Sarah picked up her notes, they dropped to the floor, and Nephemerus' information slipped out, away from the bulk of the others. She looked at it and realized she hadn't vetted him. Jess had returned to her station, and Sarah didn't want to admit she missed someone and give that droid the satisfaction of being right. Sarah returned to her office and looked into him, which was not easy. His official information was sparse and not easy to track, but once she started connecting the dots, he became the obvious choice as Laja's replacement.

Had Jess known she'd overlooked Neph and slipped his information into her bag? Sarah now considered this possibility. Jess was literally a computer—she would have noticed Sarah not mentioning Nephemerus' name in the list of candidates... No! His information was already in her notebook. She had clearly just overlooked him because she was hyper-focused on Desi and Laja.

But how could she have been so careless to have missed him? She wondered about this as he snorted and let out a strangled cry, clearly dreaming now. Her mind flashed through the images of a long, dark laundry chute located deep within the Noneru, the etchings carved on the wall in Descend, then to the face of a very young Nephemerus, sitting at a school desk, turned around in his seat and talking to an equally young Desimidor in a small, quaint classroom.

"Dad!" she said out loud.

Neph stirred in his sleep.

Sarah realized that she didn't pick Neph—Galloyde made that choice. She stood up and started pacing. Galloyde saw the connection, probably better than she did; he probably already knew Neph was going to be an Admiral for the Clorrians, then blocked it from her. She had been able to see Neph as a pilot, but she never saw him as a high-ranking officer, certainly not an Admiral. Her father had also mentioned he knew exactly who Desimidor and Nephemerus were when he met... *Merus. He calls him Merus. Why?*

Then there was the question she had been purposefully avoiding. Why would an Admiral of the Clorrian Fleet be moonlighting as an Elget for the Muldigal Council?

That made no sense. Both are high-ranking positions within his culture. Elgets are known and respected throughout all of the Universes and dimensions—but so is being a Fleet Admiral for one of the most prominent species in the cosmos.

The two roles were diametrically opposed. One is a peacekeeper role, a representative for the Council. Once Neph was done with the Earth assignment, he would most likely start brokering new peace accords with Council planets that have become disenfranchised over the centuries. He could even be moved straight into political strategy on Kentron, the physical location of the Council within the Tengelly System.

Sarah began to pace. Neph's other role was one of the highest-ranking officers in the Clorrian military—Fleet Admiral. Sarah had no idea how a non-Clorrian could achieve this, but despite him not being born a Clorrian, he held the title with respect and honor. He didn't appear to hide his role as Council Elget from his family or his officers.

Yet the fundamental nature of the Clorrians is that they are a battle-prone race. After having conquered all of the planets within their solar systems, they became one of the very few species to develop the ability to jump from one point to another—the sole reason being to further the glory of the Clorrian empire. They did not shed blood needlessly; they were not savage, but tactical. They could be harsh and unyielding. A perceived enemy was unlikely to win against the Clorrians in most battle situations, based on historical outcomes. She would be hard-pressed to find two such opposite roles to play, so why would Neph be doing this? What does he have to gain?

She felt her heart tighten and heat flushed her cheeks. What else was she being blocked from? Who else in her life had been put in front of her, beside her, to serve another? Does she have any control over her life? Is she just a pawn to be moved around by others for their own satisfaction?

"Fuck!" She yelled out and kicked the wall.

Neph grunted and slurred a nearly indecipherable, "Sarah?" then rolled over and continued snoring.

She sat back down in her chair and took three long, slow breaths. She didn't have time for this right now. She'd search out her answers soon enough, but her focus right now was to she would give Neph the few minutes of sleep he needed before they returned to Descend.

CHAPTER
SIXTY-FIVE

N eph couldn't speak. He could feel Sarah moving around him, but he struggled to keep his eyes open as she helped him into a bath and ran water over his body. He remembered getting out of the skiff and walking toward the Bibbly before everything went dim. He heard her voice speaking to him, but she sounded so distant. His ears were ringing, and he was so tired.

Finally, he began to feel sensation in his arms and legs, like pins and needles. His chest stopped hurting, which came as a relief. He hadn't realized how much pain he was in. No bed had ever felt so soft or warm as the one he was in when he finally laid down and drifted off to sleep.

He felt as if he were slipping into an unconscious state. A feeling of calm and peace surrounded him, not unlike what he felt when Galloyde had taken his hand. He was in a dream—or was this a memory?

He seemed to remember this place, as if he had been here before. It was quiet, except for the sounds of animals chattering in the distance. A light breeze brushed the leaves in the stand of trees nearby. He heard the bubbling of water traveling down a stream off to his right. He started to walk down the well-trodden path leading toward the sound of the water splashing when he heard the sudden squeal of a child's laughter.

Twisting along the thin, dusty trail, he saw a little girl running down the hill. With a head full of white-blonde bouncing curls and chunky legs, she appeared to be just a few years old.

She shrieked again and pumped her legs furiously as she rounded the corner, bright grey eyes shining with pure delight as she ran past him and headed straight for the water. Not lagging far behind was Galloyde. His face unburdened with lines, his blue eyes bright, and the lack of the bushy white beard made him appear far younger than the man Neph met on the Ripple. He too was laughing and running, playfully chasing the child.

Neph watched as the child turned sharply, then ran upstream toward a huge rock face. Suddenly, Neph realized where he was. He was in Descend, next to Seglee's lake—except the lake didn't exist yet. Just this bubbling stream of water and lush forest. Neph braced himself as the little girl continued to race full-bore at the rock wall. *She's going to knock herself clean out*, he thought. He gasped loudly, wanting to warn her, but couldn't find his voice.

"Sarah! Don't you do—" Galloyde warned.

Then she was gone. She simply disappeared. Galloyde stopped running. He just stood there and let out a deep sigh, followed by a hearty chuckle. Shaking his head, he turned and walked back up the path. Neph went down to the water where the little girl had disappeared, and as he got closer, he saw in the shadow of the rock, a small pool had gathered, and it appeared to be a few feet deep.

She swam under, he realized. *She ran at it like a hellion, then dove straight under.*

"That's my Sarah," he murmured proudly to himself, before turning away and running up the hill after Galloyde. He had already returned to the task at hand, completely unfazed about the whereabouts of his young daughter. Galloyde had rigged a cart and strapping system to attach to either Bunny or Seglee. In the cart itself sat a massive boulder. As Neph got closer, he saw chunks of the rock had already been chiseled away.

Galloyde was busy carrying tools from a work area near the cart into a small cave entrance. Neph tried to imagine where all of the buildings in Descend would be located, but he was struggling to find landmarks to orient himself. Then he realized that the cave entrance Galloyde was using was located several floors below ground level. *It was inside the caverns*, he thought. That's why he was having trouble imagining present-day Descend—this was all underground when Neph arrived on Earth.

He watched Galloyde walk into the cave entrance and followed him. The tunnels were well-lit from a huge combination of bioluminescent fungi Galloyde had planted along the walls. Neph couldn't help but smile at the varieties he passed as they made their way deeper underground. These plants were beautiful and efficient; he wondered why they weren't still in use in the tunnels today.

The passage ahead widened, and Neph could hear water rushing by, but couldn't discern if they were over or under the stream.

The passageway inside was huge—at least 40 feet wide and over 30 feet high. What caught Neph's attention were the large stones Galloyde had piled up in the middle. They were broken open, and the residue inside was glowing bright white. Eiracore.

Galloyde was taking the molten core of an asteroid, forging it in the air, and creating an intricate blockade at one end of the tunnel. Neph watched in wonder as the iridescent lava rose out of the stone, rotated in the air, spinning into thinner strands, then weaved into a pattern. Galloyde repeated this step over and over again, and each time, Neph became mesmerized by the process.

When a planet becomes unstable and either explodes from a collision with another cosmic entity, excessive volcanic activity, or chemical reactions deep within its core, the outer plates separate and the molten core becomes a projectile. As the magma cools, a hard outer shell is created while protecting a pocket of 2,000-degree lava deep inside. The magma remains perfectly preserved as long as the outer shell remains intact—until it is opened and the white-hot lava is accessed. This core could be theoretically shaped, if you had a mold that could withstand the heat. So far, no one in all of the Muldigals could find a way to shape the molten core into anything useful before it cools into a useless lump. Until now, Neph noted, as he watched the Overseer easily weave the Eiracore into an incredible masterpiece.

So this is The Gate, Neph watched in wonder. *This would be impenetrable to anyone.* There was no weapon, no army that could destroy Eiracore. Even if they had all the weapons, with all the tools, for all of eternity—no one could break into this fortress.

Neph smiled at Galloyde's ingenuity. The person he spent his entire life thinking was a madman, he now realized was an absolute genius. The one thing he didn't understand was why. Why did Galloyde need to build this Gate in the first place?

CHAPTER
SIXTY-SIX

T here was a knock at the door, and Sarah found it was the food she ordered for Neph. In addition, there were dry, clean clothes for both of them. She smiled—something from either the Commander or the physician, she guessed.

She put the food in the little kitchen and returned to the bedroom. This time, she laid down on top of the covers, fully dressed except for her shoes, anxious to get going. She slid under his arm and put her head on his chest. He pulled her against him drowsily, and after a few moments, he woke up.

"Hey," she whispered, "are you back with me?"

He looked at her and then looked around the room. "Yeah… what happened?"

She pulled the covers up around him as he turned on his side to face her. "It's my fault. I have to be more careful with you," she said, brushing his cheek. "Next time, no cold-water fishing for you." She kissed the tip of his nose softly. "We have to get going if you feel alright though. Are you ok to move?"

Neph drew in a long, sharp breath, tested his legs, and stretched his arms. "I feel pretty good. Uh! Wait!"

Sarah looked alarmed. He looked concerned and then felt his chest. "Hang on, wait," he said. Then he laid flat on his back, hand across his heart.

"What is it? Do you need the doctor?" Sarah leaned over him, careful not to put any weight on him.

"Aaaaauuggh," he groaned, jerking his body back and forth.

She leapt up and started for the door when she felt her legs being pulled backward. Before she could react, Neph flipped her over and was on top of her. "Gotcha!" He gave her a long kiss.

When he finished, he started to chuckle at his joke—then saw tears running down her cheeks.

"Hey! Hey, I was just kidding around," he said, brushing her tears away with the back of his knuckles. Sarah gave him a weak smile, but her eyes remained filled with worry.

"It's going to take a bit more than cold water to kill me, my little love." Brushing her hair back, he whispered, "Hey now, it's alright, don't worry. I'm here. I'm not going anywhere."

"It's all my fault," she whispered back. "I was so focused on the Whasook. I didn't think about the cold water, or how you could have…"

Her eyes welled up again, poured over with a fresh river of tears. "I teased you to come out onto that lake with me. I didn't think. I just wanted you to see. You would have been fine if I made you stay in the ship."

"Made me?" he laughed. "Sarah, first of all, I never would have stayed in the ship, you know that. Second, I've survived a lot worse than this—but I'm sorry I scared you." He kissed her on each cheek. "I'm here. I'm fine. Sure, maybe I lost a few toes because you seduced me into joining you on that metal death trap, but I'll learn to walk without them."

She shoved him hard in the side.

"Ooof. See? Totally fine." He brushed her chin softly with his lips before moving down to her neck. "I'm not some little fragile human, Sarah. It's going to take a lot more than a tiny chill to kill me."

She ran her hands through his black mane of hair, whirling her fingers into locks, trying not to think of how cold he had been just a short time before—how she thought, just for a brief moment, that she could lose him.

Neph stopped kissing her neck and looked into her eyes, studying her face. She had been deeply frightened, much more than she was saying. He could feel her fear buried deep inside. He waited for a moment to see if she was going to share that with him.

She remained quiet, choosing to focus on keeping her warm body against his, her mind distantly thinking of wrapping him in several extra layers of clothes for when they next left the ship.

He gave up on the idea of her sharing her fear with him and instead decided to wiggle his eyebrows wildly at her. "You can't get rid of me that easily, you know."

Sarah burst into laughter. "Hey," she said, pulling him down onto her, "that's *my* line."

CHAPTER
SIXTY-SEVEN

Galloyde was frustrated with the medical team. He felt fine —he felt better than fine. His body felt stronger than it had in, well, centuries. Now that he wasn't using his energy just to survive, he felt renewed. Now he could easily see the Athecierian War Ships—their location, where they planned to rendezvous, even what they were eating if he focused hard enough.

He just needed a way to escape these overzealous medical attendants. He understood they were following orders, but he had to get to Earth's surface. The Gate had been locked, but the Atheciery were just less than a third of a rotation away, and he wanted to make sure they were prepared.

Yet Sarah had left a human in charge of The Gate. A human! Of all the choices she had available to her, she could have chosen the Gigla android, or one of those ReTrainers. Anyone but a human. Despite his concern, he trusted her decision. When he started to prod her mind, he found her resolute. Galloyde relented when he saw the level of conviction about the one she had chosen to entrust the dagger to in her stead.

He paced the Medical Bay. They must have the Whasook and Thandican by now. *Why hasn't Merus sent word to release him to the surface yet?* He closed his eyes and searched. He found Merus—his color grey. Sarah was worried. Worse, she was scared. Merus was freezing. She was moving quickly, trying to warm him in conventional ways.

Of course, Galloyde sighed. She could have warmed his core immediately using her powers, but she apparently panicked. She was blinded by her love. Galloyde couldn't say he wouldn't have made the same mistake in the same situation. He had, in fact, made a similar mistake long ago.

Granted, he would have insisted on getting the Whasook by himself and avoided this entire situation—but that boy would never leave his daughter's side. That was why Galloyde had chosen him. Loyalty was Nephemerus' greatest quality, along with a fair amount of intelligence. Sure, he was also well-connected, kind, curious, skilled —but that fierce loyalty was what landed Merus on his greater journey, and partly why Galloyde had been so intrigued with him in the first place.

He allowed himself a small smile. Not even his rebellious daughter could keep that Vecurasian boy on land in the middle of the Arctic.

Merus was not born a cold-blooded Clorrian, but rather as one-half of the warm-blooded Vecurasian. As he lay at the bottom of that metal skiff, purposefully shielding Sarah from the temperature of the frigid water, he placed himself into harm's way. That was stupid, but kind, Galloyde grunted. Merus was not aware that Sarah could not be harmed by cold or heat. Another power of the immortals— of the Overseers.

Galloyde shook his head. They needed to focus on the Nox! Without that piece of the puzzle, everything they had done up to now was in jeopardy of failing. All the Founders needed to be in The Gate, to stay protected. If even one of them fell into the enemy's hands, unspeakable multitudes of solar systems could fall into oblivion— not to mention their immediate plan to save humanity would become a fool's errand.

Suddenly, Sarah flashed in his mind. She had a solution. She was trying to get him back to the Earth's surface, with plans on reuniting with him there. Good. He wanted to get out of there. Almost on cue, the door opened, and a medical assistant brought Galloyde clean clothes.

"The Admiral has sent word that you will be joining him on the surface shortly. These will be more suitable for you." She turned and left. Galloyde looked at the two shirts and legged bottoms with pockets. Again, he found himself smiling. How handy those would have been to wear all those years he toiled on the Earth's surface before.

CHAPTER
SIXTY-EIGHT

N eph pushed a massive amount of food into his mouth just as Sarah came out of the bedroom. "Alright, I think we are all set. We need to get to the surface with Dad. I already sent word to get him ready, but you'll need to give the final approval to the Physician before they let him go. She's going to want to question you anyway, make sure you're alright. Oh, and did you contact your Traveler friend so they can make the run for fucking Kevin?"

Neph nodded as he tried to chew and swallow far too much food. Sarah watched in amusement. She leaned against the counter, grinning as he tried to chew, but the more he chewed, the worse it got.

"Gee, honey, you took an awfully long nap today. Now you're ravenous. Something you need to tell me? Actually, now that I think of it, you seemed a little snippy the other day. I'm thinking you must be pregnant! Is that it?"

Neph's eyes went wide, and with his mouth so full, he couldn't swallow and couldn't speak. She came around the counter to his side with a malicious ear-to-ear grin. "You know, I shouldn't be so quick to assume. I don't even know—maybe the men from your planet carry the babies. Now that I really think about it, maybe you weren't cold at all today. Maybe you fainted because you got a big 'ole litter in there!" She poked his belly in a few places. "Hiya kiddos!"

This was too much. He spit out the huge lump of food he was trying to swallow and started to gasp.

Sarah pointed to the half-chewed glob of food on the counter and said, "Ew, is that how you feed your babies on your planet? Like little birds with pre-chewed food?"

"Stop, stop!" he coughed, waving his hands in surrender.

She shouted at his stomach. "Hellooo babies! What'cha hungry for? Do you want some potatoes next?" She loaded up a fork and made a zooming sound toward Neph.

"You're such a freak," he groaned, but opened his mouth. She delivered the potatoes, and he took them gladly.

"Yeah, but I'm the momma to your freak baybehs. How many can you carry, anyway? Ten? Twenty?" she asked, putting his fork down and pouring him another glass of water.

He didn't answer. He ate one more bite of food, then drank the rest of his water before looking at her. "Are you ready to go?"

She nodded, and they left, heading toward the Bridge.

CHAPTER
SIXTY-NINE

T iny stared at the etchings. The chamber was located at the very end of where The Gate was protected by the Eiracore. He stood there, hoping something new would jump out at him—something he hadn't seen before, something that would help.

"I don't think you missed anything," he heard a familiar voice behind him. He turned to see Desi standing in the doorway.

Over the past several weeks, he and Desi had covered a number of topics—from his memories of Galloyde and The Atheciery, to the creation of The Gate, the implementation of the Elgets who served on Earth from the Council, all the way up to when Tiny started waking up to these etchings carved by his own hand. Together, they deduced a great deal that made sense and were able to fill in a number of small gaps that Desi and Neph had from their conversations.

The other great concern was what to do in case Galloyde couldn't save the humans. Thankfully, before they were locked in The Gate, they confirmed that Galloyde was on his way back—although they didn't know if he had an answer to how to fix the problem with the humans. That little tidbit would have been helpful, but when word came down that it was time to go into lockdown, there had been no time to ask questions.

Of course, there would be no way to communicate outside of The Gate. The Eiracore was impenetrable in every possible way, including radio, sonic, and ultraviolet waves. Truly, nothing could get in—or out. They were protected, but they were also prisoners of their own making.

Desi and Tiny originally deduced that Galloyde built The Gate to keep Sarah safe from the return of The Atheciery. They were not aware that she had handed her dagger over to Luis. Once inside, they witnessed him place the gold dagger into The Gate's lock and make an elaborate gesture. When he did, the Eiracore glowed bright blue, revealing itself from deep within the walls, floor, and ceiling of the cavern for as far as they could see down the Old Passage. Then the glow dimmed and faded, only remaining visible at The Gate. The light felt comforting as it pulsed through the detailed ironwork, once in a while giving a slight hiss as a spark would fall carelessly to the ground.

The spark held no heat and did not burn, as GilGerg found out. He liked to chase them and tried to catch them like snowflakes as they sparked off the tips of the bars. When GilGerg opened his mouth, Chronny caught sight of his teeth and felt like he was going to faint again. Each time, Chronny took it better than the one before and just gave GilGerg a thumbs-up sign before walking to the back of the cavern to recover. No one else paid GilGerg any mind as he chased his blue sparks.

Once The Gate had been locked, Luis continued to keep the dagger safe on his person. He didn't fear anyone inside The Gate trying to steal it from him—he was more wary of it being taken as he approached The Gate itself, as if an unseen force might snatch it from him. Desi could see Luis' knuckles clench around the handle tightly each time he was in sight of the larger passageway.

Desi asked to see the dagger once. Luis obliged, but only to look at it —not pick it up or take it from his possession. Desi noted the jewel in the base of the dagger. It was an unusual cut and color. He asked Luis if he knew what the stone was, and Luis shook his head.

"I asked Miss… Sarah the same thing, and she only said it was not of this Earth. When I asked what that meant, she said Galloyde told her it was important the stone never leave here."

Tiny and Desi contemplated this. Was the stone so important that Galloyde built The Gate to protect it? What could that have to do with any of the Founders?

CHAPTER
SEVENTY

Sarah and Nephemerus walked quickly toward the entrance. Looking around, they didn't see anyone else in Descend. They stared at the building that sat over the cave that housed The Gate for a few moments. Then they moved quickly again.

Luis was pacing near The Gate. His heart was unsettled. He wasn't sure when he was going to see Sarah again, but for some reason, he felt like she was late. Not being able to communicate was much harder than he thought it might be.

He had been staring at the dagger when he thought he heard a sound in the passageway, just outside of The Gate. He was alone, and he strained to see into the darkness. He cleared his throat and deepened his voice. "Hello?" he called out gruffly.

No response.

His heart began to beat faster. His hand gripped the dagger so hard it felt like the handle could cut into his skin. He heard another scuff in the darkness—but now much closer. That was not his imagination. Luis stepped back further from The Gate entrance, and as he did, he felt something large land on his shoulder and then cover his face. He started to cry out when he realized it was Tiny's claws.

Tiny gave him a silent signal to stay quiet and listen, which Luis could barely make out in the dim blue glow of the Eiracore. They were at a definite disadvantage. Inside The Gate provided illumination, so they could be seen by anyone outside, whereas any intruders could easily stay shielded in darkness.

"Hello?" a familiar voice suddenly called out. Luis looked at Tiny as both their jaws dropped.

"Hello? Is anyone there?" the woman's voice called out again.

Before they could say anything, Desi rushed past them. "Sarah? Sarah, dear girl, is that you? We're here! Right here! Everyone, it's Sarah!" He quickly ran toward The Gate, and Tiny took giant steps to catch the back of Desi's jacket and stop him right before he got close to the metal barrier.

Standing there, right at the edge of the dim glow of the Eiracore, were Sarah and Nephemerus. They stood just a few feet back from the entry of The Gate, arms at their sides, staring at the three inside.

"Sarah! Nephemerus! You're here! You're safe!" Desimidor cried.

"We told you we would be back. We have to hurry—unlock The Gate now," Neph said evenly.

"Yes, yes, of course." Desi looked at Luis, who didn't move. Luis was staring at Sarah. She stared back at him and pulled her lips back into a perfunctory smile.

"Let us in. We need to hurry," she said, in the same even tone that Nephemerus used. "Before they get here."

Tiny pulled Desi further back from The Gate. Luis took a step backward as well.

"Luis, what are you doing? Just open it—" Desi demanded.

Luis looked at Desi and shook his head. He looked out The Gate and asked, "Before who gets here?"

Sarah stepped closer. She wasn't smiling now. She looked at Tiny, then to Desi, as if she was seeing them for the first time. Then she looked at Luis and repeated in her monotone voice, "Hurry. Open The Gate, Luis."

Desi wrestled away and lunged toward Luis. "It's Nephemerus and Sarah! What are you doing? Just open the gate!"

Tiny grabbed Desimidor and turned him around, grasping his shoulders. "Stop! It's not them."

Nephemerus stepped forward. He did the same slow scanning motion and then locked on Desi. "Open the door. Do you want them to get me? I'm your friend—trust me."

"Yes, Luis, open up. Now. Hurry." Sarah continued to smile coldly, her eyes unblinking. "They are coming. Let us in." She took a step closer to The Gate.

Luis took a small step back and raised the dagger. Both Sarah and Nephemerus grimaced as The Gate glowed bright blue light, illuminating the two on the other side.

"Do me a favor, chica—touch The Gate for me," Luis said, his voice wavering. He gestured with the blade. "Go ahead, put your hand on it."

He waved the dagger toward The Gate, and the bars glowed bright white. Sparks flew outward and cascaded down onto Sarah and Neph like raining fire. Sarah let out a blood-curdling shriek and was quickly joined by Nephemerus. The two of them turned into a whirling dark cloud and vanished. Desi fell to his knees and began to cry. Tiny leaned down to comfort him.

"Sarah warned us that there might be things trying to get in," Tiny explained. "Things that we don't understand. They can't pass into The Gate unless we open it. That wasn't our Sarah. That wasn't your Nephemerus."

Desi stared into the dark passage. "I don't understand. What was that? She knew our names."

Luis came over to Desi. "You said my name. That's when she used it. She almost sounded like Miss Sarah, but not completely. They can't touch The Gate. Sarah told me it won't feel right in here." He pointed to his chest. "She was right." He swallowed hard. "I don't know how many more times I can do that though."

Tiny and Desi stood, and they all formed a large hug. They agreed it was best to share this information with everyone.

They gathered everyone into the Chamber room, leaving Tiny to guard The Gate. They decided to have patrols by the entrance and agreed not to use anyone's names until confirmation was made on the real Sarah's return.

That night, everyone slept by The Gate entrance—scared, but united together.

SEVENTY-ONE

On the Bibbly, Sarah gathered Bob and Bezel from their respective holding rooms. She placed Bezel back into her front pocket, where the Thandican nestled in, safely tucked away. Bob liked being carried like a small dog. Sarah put him in her shoulder bag with a soft towel under him, and she left the top flap open. She swung her bag around behind her so he could pop his head out and watch what was happening.

Neph was on the Bridge while she made her rounds. He contacted the Noneru and confirmed that Galloyde needed to be sent to the surface.

"I didn't realize how much time I wasted. The Atheciery are a quarter rotation out—that's going to give us two, maybe three Earth days if we're lucky," Neph said, as he moved quickly around the Bridge of the Bibbly. The Commander coughed.

"Something you'd like to add, Commander?" Neph asked.

"No, Sir!" the Commander quickly responded. He turned away and then turned back and opened his mouth, thought better of it, and then started to turn away again.

"You better say it if you ever want to become Captain. Let's hear it," Neph growled.

"If I say it, Sir, I definitely won't become Captain."

Neph stared at the Commander. His burning intensity was a notable change from the lighthearted officer he was when Sarah was at his side.

The Clorrian Commander blinked rapidly, drew himself up to full height—towering over the Admiral—and said, "Sir, I disagree. You did not waste any time. It is astounding you are standing right now considering the state you were in when you arrived back on this ship. You may not be Clorrian, but your heart is as strong as Tèciken the Great. I will follow you into this battle with The Atheciery and any other you ask of me. I am proud and honored to serve as your Commander."

Neph's expression did not change, and the Commander's eyes started to dart back and forth, realizing the mistake he had made. Neph took a long breath in and slowly let it out, letting the young Commander simmer in self-doubt.

"Is that all you have to say, Commander?" he asked coldly.

The Commander dropped his head and nodded. Why did he say anything? Now he's going to be stuck doing rotations out in the OaB or further. Why?

Then he heard a low chuckle and looked up to see Neph grinning at him. "Tèciken the Great? Oh, I like that one, Grally. Tèciken, hah! Wait till I tell Raka that one. You compared me to Tèciken! He'll never get over it." Neph reached up and grabbed the Commander by the shoulder and shook him with a laugh. It was the first time the Fleet Admiral had ever used his name.

Neph ordered Commander Grally to return to the Noneru once he left with Sarah on the Lander. Just then, Sarah arrived with her charges in tow. They said goodbye and headed to the Lander Bay.

Neph told Sarah that the Traveler stated they would hear them out, but wasn't committing to the mission just yet. Neph also wanted Galloyde there. While Neph was still worried that The Atheciery would try to kidnap Galloyde, his presence might convince the Traveler to make the trip to Radimus. Sarah agreed.

They boarded the Lander and made the short trip down to the surface. As they were landing, they saw Galloyde's transport arrive at the same time. They walked over to greet Galloyde and found that Raka had brought Galloyde himself. This gave Neph a chance to update his Captain on the latest situation while Sarah and Galloyde looked over their new Regulators.

"Oh, look at him! What a gem!" Galloyde exclaimed as she handed over the Whasook.

"Oh, yes. Hello, Bob, I'm Galloyde. Very pleased to finally meet you. Yes, it is a bit warm here, but not too bad. The fish? Well, it has been a little while since I have fished here, but I remember it used to be mainly cod, salmon, and oh, yes, the alewife certainly! Hah! Oh, you are right about that, Bob!" Galloyde laughed heartily.

Sarah smiled politely as she pointed to her pocket.

"Right, right, we will talk more about that. I definitely have more questions for you too, Bob." He handed the Whasook back to Sarah, and she tucked him back into her bag.

Then she carefully reached into her pocket and retrieved Bezel, who shone brilliantly against the bright sunshine of the morning.

A slight whirling sound could be heard as she handed her over to Galloyde, but right before he took her, the Thandican flew straight up in the air and hovered right in front of his nose. The whirling sound became much louder.

"Oh!" Galloyde laughed. "Why, look at you! Just wonderful!"

Neph and Raka saw this movement from the Thandican from where they were standing.

"Galloyde, be careful," Neph cautioned. "Move very slowly."

Sarah could hear the restrained concern in his voice. Oh no, she thought, poor Neph is going to lose it. She tried to catch his eye, but both soldiers were locked in on the Thandican. Galloyde was still chuckling and chatting away when Bezel suddenly flew straight up, then directly behind Galloyde.

That was the breaking point. Neph and Raka broke into a dead run.

"Look out!" They both cried.

"Oh shit," Sarah mumbled. "Hey fellas, it's really ok——" she tried calling out, but it was too late.

Galloyde stepped aside quickly as the two soldiers dove into the spot he was just standing. They hit the ground and each other, landing in a twisted pile. Galloyde smiled down at them. On his shoulder, whirling and almost whimsically laughing along, sat Bezel.

"Ah, hey fellas, so what you two just witnessed was a greeting dance. Thandicans do that when they meet one of their own kind. You two wouldn't have seen that before because you're not an Overseer or a Thandican, but thanks for the concern," Sarah said, trying not to laugh as she helped them stand up.

"Well, I have seen a Kirlally attack before, and it looks pretty similar," Neph said, brushing off the dirt. "It's awful. Really awful to witness," he added as he walked a wide path around Galloyde, his eyes never leaving Bezel.

"I would like to thank the both of you for not saving my life from my little friend. I appreciate your vigilance, Raka, Merus. I would like to remind you that the Regulators are on our side. They work with us, and we with them," Galloyde stated diplomatically, before turning toward Neph—who Sarah swore took a step behind Raka.

"Where is your friend, this Traveler?"

"I am here," a voice said from behind Raka's Lander. They turned to see a thin figure standing in the shadows.

"Urisca!" Neph cried out in excitement. He stepped out from behind Raka to greet his friend. As the Traveler stepped into the light, Sarah saw they were wearing an ornately decorated robe covered in symbols and modulating color blocks changing form and shade. The robe covered the Traveler from their head, down their arms, and all the way to the ground, pooling at their feet. You could not see what was underneath at all.

Fascinating, she thought. She wanted a closer look at their robe and to learn more about them, but they all had to move quickly—the Atheciery were almost there and there was no time to waste.

CHAPTER
SEVENTY-TWO

They sat outside while Neph introduced everyone and gave a brief overview of how he met Urisca when he was younger, before he had attended Elget training on Ala Mia.

"I was still a pilot then, and Urisca wasn't officially employed for the Council yet—"

Raka made a scoffing sound. "I am sorry. Forgive me. I was led to believe that the Council created... erm, raised the Travelers. I didn't know there was a time in which Travelers were considered freelancers?"

Urisca's hood nodded up and down slowly. Their voice was deep, modulated, and slowly paced. "You are correct. The Galactic Council does indeed create and rear my kind. We spend deca-rotations learning all the galactic maps, routes, and dimensional pathways before we are placed into service. We are genetically altered to withstand repeated temporal disturbances without the benefit of a ship to protect our bodies. There were many of my kind who went before me who suffered for the greater good. I am the product of the evolution made by correct decisions, adjustments, and improvements."

Urisca turned to Galloyde, their hood swinging in his direction. "Something you are intimately familiar with, I believe?"

Galloyde didn't have a chance to respond before Neph cleared his throat and said, "Urisca, I cannot thank you enough for joining us today. Our situation is not entirely our own—it belongs to all of the cosmos. This human species stands at the precipice of extinction. We have been asked to help. Per the Verisian Treaty, we are bound to do so."

Urisca considered. "Then why would you be asking me for assistance, Nephemerus? Why are you not requesting this assistance directly from the Muldigal Council?"

This time Galloyde responded, and quickly. "Because we all know the Muldigal Council does not care if the human species lives or dies. These humans are still mortal, having not completed their Ascension yet. They are not yet an official Council planet, so they will not intervene—as you know... or knew, when you were still in their employ."

This caught Urisca's attention. Galloyde continued. "As a former Traveler to the Council, you are aware that if we brought this matter before them, they would laugh it off. They provide Elgets to Earth, yes, but that was simply out of pressure from the surrounding systems and to appease the Quadrant Representative. The Council has not provided adequate supplies or the standard ground support. I think we even have an android here that is over 100,000 years past their service date? Would any of the other colonies have to deal with that, Urisca? No, I am certain they would not. No, no—the Council is simply waiting and hoping for the humans to self-destruct... with my so-called 'experiments' along with them."

Then Galloyde leaned in close to the Traveler. "But what they do not know is that a Corvier hit this little hidden planet. They do not know that a full complement of Founders survived. If they did know that, they would suddenly care very much, Urisca. That is something they would care about deeply. But then, I would not need to tell you that... if you still worked for the Council."

Galloyde sat back and stared into the hole of the dark hood. Urisca remained quiet.

Sarah spoke next. "His name is Kevin. Well, we call him fucking Kevin because he's a Nox and he's—"

"An asshole, as all Nox are," Raka finished.

"Yes, he is an asshole," Sarah agreed. "He's in Radimus. We need him back. We need you to go get him and bring him here."

Urisca looked at Sarah. "Why?"

"Excuse me?" She wasn't prepared to let a stranger in on their whole plan, but Neph nodded at her and reassured her mind that his friend could be trusted.

"You will have to tell me why. If you want me to take someone out of Radimus, I have to know why I am doing it." Urisca stated diplomatically.

Sarah looked to Galloyde, who nodded, and then to Raka, who did the same. She took a deep breath. "We believe that we need all of the original Founders here on Earth so Galloyde can save the humans."

Urisca stood firm. "Why?"

"Why do we need all ten Founders here?" Sarah asked. The hood dipped in a nod. She answered, "The Gate is the most powerful if all the Founders are here."

"Why?" Urisca pressed.

Sarah sighed and looked to Neph. He jumped in. "Because we don't want the Atheciery to kill all the Founders, Urisca!"

"Why?"

Everyone let out a collective groan.

Galloyde responded. "You want to know why I want to save the humans?" Urisca nodded. Galloyde took a moment. "Because it is my fault they are going to destroy themselves. In order to fix my mistake, I need that Nox."

"Why?"

"Fuck me," Neph breathed. The hood of the Traveler swung to Neph's direction, but his body remained completely still.

"Sorry, but we are in a time crunch. Galloyde just needs that fucking Nox. We have The Atheciery coming to burn this place to the ground right now. We have to get this done. They can guide you right to where he will be. You can pop in, then pop right out—"

"Why?" Urisca repeated.

"We can't get into the entire story right now, Urisca!" Neph rocked from one foot to another, impatient with his friend.

"No, no, no," Sarah said, calming Neph. "He's not asking about The Atheciery. I think he wants to know why Galloyde needs the Nox to fix the humans."

"I need his blood," Galloyde stepped in. "His genetic code, his DNA. As you said, Urisca, you are the product of 'evolution made by correct decisions, adjustments, and improvements.' The humans that are here on Earth right now are not. The lineage I tampered with is the result of unwanted evolution caused by my poor decision. I need to make an adjustment, and that Nox can provide the root DNA code to make the improvement. With all of this, I can change the entire species and help them avoid self-destruction."

Urisca looked away from Galloyde and the others and appeared to be thinking. "The Nox DNA will reset their genetic code. You will have the same problem in approximately 400,325 years. You are not fixing this problem; you are merely delaying it."

Galloyde let out a loud guffaw. He stood up and walked over to the Traveler and clamped his hands on their shoulders. "Excellent! Excellent calculations!" He looked pleased. "Tiny and Desimidor arrived at the exact same conclusions," he said, as he tapped the side of his head and winked.

Galloyde continued. "There will be an additional modification, an improvement to this formula which will prevent the humans from self-destructing again so quickly. You are entirely correct. The Nox DNA would provide the blueprint to reset 98.271% of that genetic bridge I performed all those years ago."

He sat down next to the Traveler and looked at each person at the table as he spoke. "This time, we have to add another species' blood to make sure the humans not only survive, but also ensure they can all finally Ascend as well."

Galloyde explained the rest of his plan to the Traveler, who listened patiently. At the end of Galloyde's explanation, Urisca walked away from the group and found a spot high on the hill, staring out towards Seglee's lake. Their robe glowed brightly as the symbols flowed from one square to another, blocks of color lighting up and fading, then lighting up in another block. It was beautiful and nerve-racking at the same time.

Sarah paced. Neph and Raka conferred, and Galloyde closed his eyes and rested his chin on his chest.

The robe slowed and eventually stopped its hectic display of colors and symbols. The Traveler returned and addressed the group. "I have considered your proposal. Your mission is honorable. Your intent is true. The mistakes you may or may not have made," they said, directing the words at Galloyde, "in the past are worth the risk you are all willing to take. But I cannot take the Nox out of Radimus for you."

"What?" Neph exclaimed.

"Can I ask why?" Sarah asked calmly.

The Traveler nodded. "He was placed there for a good reason. He is dangerous. If he is returned here, he will continue to be a danger to all of you—to everyone he was a danger to in the past. Right now, he belongs in Radimus."

"But we need his—" Neph started to say, but Sarah put her hand on his chest and stopped him.

"Wait. He didn't say he wouldn't help us. He said he couldn't take him out of there."

If they could see the Traveler's face—if they even had faces—Sarah imagined it would be smiling.

"Indeed. I will get the blood you need from the Nox. I will bring it back to you, but I will not endanger any of you in your mission."

"You bloodthirsty bastard, get over here!" Neph laughed and lunged across at his friend. Sarah watched Neph hug the Traveler ferociously, in a one-sided embrace. Finally, Raka pulled Neph off so they could continue planning.

"Ok, so next step—where do we get a syringe fast so you can get the blood?" Raka asked.

Galloyde pulled one from his pocket. "I took this from the Medical bay," he said, his eyes gleaming. "Just in case we needed it."

With little time left before the Atheciery were due to arrive, Sarah, Galloyde, and Urisca walked toward the water, leaving Neph and Raka behind to check on the status of their enemy.

The two Overseers explained that they would be able to find the Nox within Radimus, so they could show Urisca exactly where he was.

"How?" the Traveler asked.

"Like this." Sarah smiled at him as he heard her voice clearly in his mind.

Is this how you knew I was no longer with the Council? Urisca thought, but did not say aloud. They heard Galloyde chuckle in their head, but saw he was not making any sound.

Urisca nodded. "Will you tell me before I leave, or is it easier to tell me when I am there?"

Sarah and Galloyde exchanged looks. They held hands and closed their eyes. They responded in unison:

"Nox." Galloyde and Sarah both said directly into Urisca's mind.

Sarah and Galloyde reached out with their free hands and each took ahold of the Traveler's gloved hands. An image appeared clearly in the Traveler's mind: a Nox walking along the top floor of a building. Bars along one side. Crumbling walls. A hole where a window used to be.

Urisca disappeared from Earth and appeared in Radimus, standing behind the Nox.

The Traveler slid a thin arm around the Nox's neck, catching him by surprise, and whispered into his ear at the same time. As expected, the Nox swung outwards, screaming. When Kevin turned to punch at whomever was holding him, he saw no one was there.

Kevin felt something wet on his neck and reached up to touch it. He saw blood on his fingers. Outraged, he howled and punched the wall. A Toomatian trader just happened to turn the corner right then—and fucking Kevin jumped on him and started to bite at his face.

Urisca reappeared on Earth in the exact same spot he'd left less than a minute before.

"Here you are. Put it to good use," Urisca said, handing over the syringe of blood to Galloyde. "For the record, thank you for protecting the Founders for as long as you have." Then he looked to Sarah. "You as well."

Then Urisca was gone.

CHAPTER

SEVENTY-THREE

The Athecierians watched the Traveler and the Overseers gather together. The Traveler disappeared, then reappeared with something small, handed it to Galloyde, and then left again. The Atheciery had two cloaked Cutters nearby, each carrying eight soldiers. Not nearly enough to take on the Clorrians, who had three Cruisers currently in orbit. Soon, though, their War Ships would arrive—and then they could finally destroy this entire planet and never return.

Stupid barbarians, so far away. It was ridiculous that they had to come all the way out here to deal with these fleas.

But why were there two Overseers all the way out here? Surely this was why the new Precipice brought them. They remained hidden, fearing detection from Mad Galloyde, while they watched and waited.

CHAPTER
SEVENTY-FOUR

Raka confirmed that the first War Ship was now less than five Earth hours away.

"What is the status of our fleet?" Neph asked.

"Our Airship is well over a full rotation away. Our Battleships are closer, but the first to arrive is still two Earth days from now. We could try to make a stand with the three Cruisers, hope the Airship arrives in time, but I wouldn't recommend it. If you wish, we can have the fold jump here, but the chances of survival are—"

"No. I'd rather you, Heftu, and Tegreta back down. I'm not endangering the entire fold. We shouldn't engage that many Athecierians. If we can delay them on the surface, maybe we can buy time for the Battleships," Neph decided, deep in thought.

Raka considered this. "Delay them? What if they show up shooting?"

Neph shook his head. "No, I highly doubt that. They wouldn't come all this way just to start a war. No, they'll want Galloyde back. I think we can delay them for a bit. Raka, there's something else we need to discuss. Once I'm inside, I won't be able to communicate with you, so I'll need you to take command of the Fleet."

Raka studied his old friend. "Admiral. Nephemerus. Are you sure about all this? Please, consider your family and the Fleet. You could take Sarah, even some of these humans with you. You should return to the ship. If you fight from above, you'll have a stronger advantage."

Neph nodded in agreement. "I know. Trust me, I'd take her and all the others and hide them in another dimension if I thought I could get her to go." He looked at Raka. "It's not just about her or the Founders—it's the entire planet at risk from those winged fuckers. We have to do this."

Raka nodded slowly. "I will accept your command... temporarily." He punched Neph in the shoulder, hard. Neph wasn't expecting it and reeled backward.

"What was that?" he cried out, cradling his shoulder.

"You've gone soft, Chriska. Be strong like a Clorrian. I will not carry your body home."

Then Raka turned and walked into the Lander and left, waving goodbye only to Sarah as he closed the Lander platform.

Sarah saw the end of this exchange as she was walking over. "Uh, so is everything ok with you two?" She reached up and touched his shoulder, which was tender. "What was that about 'carrying your body'?"

"It's an old Clorrian battle saying. It's supposed to be inspirational. Basically: fight hard enough so you come home able to walk on your own—otherwise, you'll be left to die on the battlefield, alone and forgotten." Neph moved his arm back and forth to make sure it wasn't damaged.

"Huh. That's what Clorrians use for inspiration? That's really heartwarming. Here, let me have a look."

He let her look and winced as she squeezed the muscle.

"We have less than five hours. It's just us until the Battleships come. We should get in that Gate." She ran her hand up around his shoulder again; he could feel how warm her touch was.

"There we go. That should do it. Let's not have anyone carrying any bodies today, alright? Ok, let's go." She kissed his cheek and squeezed his hand. Neph noticed the pain was completely gone from his shoulder.

As they walked over to the cavern, they saw Galloyde staring off into the distance. Sarah called out to him to join them. He answered her in his mind.

The Atheciery are already here.

SEVENTY-FIVE

T hey walked together down into the tunnels, and as they got closer to the entrance, Sarah stopped and listened closely. Then she whistled a high-low, high-low pitch.

Nothing. No response. They walked a little closer until they could see the dim glow of The Gate. She whistled again, high-low, high-low.

She heard a whistle in return—low-to-high, low-to-high again. Sarah grinned and waved Galloyde and Neph to follow her. They walked up the passage toward the entrance to find Luis standing there with Tiny and Bunny, all three looking extremely serious, their bodies tensed as the three approached.

"Hi! Oh man, I missed you guys so much! Is everyone ok? Are you alright?" she asked with a wide smile, her eyes lighting up as she saw her friends.

"Where's Desi?" Neph asked. "You kicked him out already? If you did, I get it—he's such a pain in the ass," he said, laughing at his own joke.

Tiny and Luis looked at each other and didn't say a word. Bunny shifted from one leg to the next, growling and drooling.

Galloyde nodded. "Ahhh. Desirihia."

Sarah snapped her head around and looked at him. "What? What do you mean? Are they…?"

"No, no," he said. "Not them. They think we are the desirihia. The Atheciery must have beat us here."

Sarah went up to The Gate and grabbed the bars with both hands, leaning her entire body against it. "Luis! Babbling brooks sometimes breach into swamped streams but debilitated dams can never return to running rivers."

"SARAH!" Luis yelled. He jumped forward and grabbed her hands. Bunny let out a howl of joy.

From the shadows, Desi stepped out and reached through the bars. Neph grabbed his friend's hand.

"It's you. It's really you!" Desi whispered. "Not that smoke thing."

Galloyde looked at Sarah. "If they just did a desirihia, they must be close. Get inside quickly."

"Luis, let's rejoice inside. Step back, please."

Luis nodded and asked everyone to stand back from The Gate. They obliged. Sarah waved her arm as The Gate dissolved in front of their eyes.

Sarah ushered Neph and her father through and turned around, waving her hand again. The Gate reappeared. She held out her hand, and Luis handed her the dagger.

The light through the metal pulsed once more, glowing much brighter with two more Founders and two Overseers contained inside. Sarah went to sheath her dagger on her thigh and quickly realized she wasn't wearing her holster. Luis had been keeping the dagger tucked in his belt, and he didn't have it on him.

She started to look for a way to hold onto the dagger when she saw goo dripping onto the ground in front of her. She looked up to see Bunny standing there. Hanging at the end of one of his very long talons was her leather holster. She smiled up at him as she took the holster. "Thank you, my love." He gargled, and more goo dribbled down his body as he lumbered away.

Sarah strapped the holster to her right thigh and sheathed her dagger. Ahhh, that felt good. When she looked up, everyone was hugging each other, welcoming them back home. The Regulators were overjoyed to see Galloyde. Neph quietly made his way over to Sarah and discreetly wrapped his arms around her.

"We made it," he whispered in her ear, slyly brushing his lips against her cheek as he did it. "So am I to believe I'm second in your heart to the drool monster?" She laughed and playfully pushed him away.

Standing there, her heart was full as she watched her father reunite with his long-lost 'creatures.' As she looked from Neph to Desi, to Luis, to Jess, Sarah realized that everyone she loved was inside this Gate—and now, the bloodthirsty Atheciery were coming for them.

It was time to fight, but even she didn't know why.

SEVENTY-SIX

After a brief rejoicing, everyone moved to the center of the tunnel to discuss the next steps. This was where Seglee could see everyone from her cavern. Her head craned up from below through a small opening in the rock, and she rested her chin on the floor of the passageway. Tiny asked about the desirihia.

"What was it that we saw?" he asked Galloyde. "They looked just like Sarah and Nephemerus, but slightly off. Their voices weren't exact, but in the tunnel, it was hard to tell."

"And they refused to touch The Gate!" Luis added.

Galloyde nodded. "Ah, that was a desirihia and most definitely the Athecierian trying to get inside The Gate. That is something they picked up from Overseers, I am afraid. I hope not from me, but they certainly have witnessed me using it in the past. A desirihia is a mirage, an illusion, except it can feel very real, and can be deadly. If you had let them inside, they would have attacked you posing as Sarah and Neph."

He thought for a moment. "I do not know how they have developed this power. I survived by creating a desirihia on the Galactic Ripple. An Overseer can create anything they wish from their surroundings, so I created the atmosphere, the building, and all that I had inside. That is how I ate, drank, breathed the air. Tiny, you said they disappeared like smoke?"

Tiny nodded.

Galloyde looked at Sarah gravely. "Perhaps more of an illusion than a full desirihia, made more believable in the low light down here. A complex desirihia is impossible to discern from reality and not easily accomplished. An illusion is more likely, but still very difficult to spot. You all did well to recognize it. The Atheciery will utilize these types of illusions to trick you, to get inside your head. Trust your gut. The Atheciery cannot touch Eiracore, well, at least not this Eiracore."

Desi stepped forward. "Because of that jewel in the handle?" he asked. "Is that what we are protecting in here? Is it the dagger, or the jewel? Is it Sarah or...yourself?"

All eyes turned to Galloyde, who returned their gazes, one by one. He motioned for everyone to sit.

"We have such little time, but I will get through this as quickly as I can." He looked at Desi. "My daughter was correct in choosing you. You are indeed brilliant." Desi beamed with pride, and Tiny gave Desi a friendly clap on the back.

Galloyde stood in the middle and created a whirling ball of light between the palms of his hands. "I will show you what happened, in glimpses. I ask that you let me show you what I can, then ask questions after. I will warn you, this will be upsetting for many of you, if not all." He glanced toward Sarah briefly. Neph inched over closer to her.

The ball of light formed into a three-dimensional image. Neph gasped. It was the scene from his first dream with the woman and the baby. Exactly what he remembered. In the dark, he felt Sarah reach for his hand and squeeze, but his heart rate didn't slow.

They all watched his dream play out, right up to the final explosion when Sarah cried out.

"That didn't happen! My mother was here, in here. I remember her! Dad. Why are you showing this? That's not what happened."

"Sarah," Galloyde said weakly. "The Atheciery came looking for us by order of The Grand Precipice. We fled to Earth. I was not found somewhere else and banished here. This was where we were hiding. It took them thousands of rotations to find us. Here on Earth, millennia passed. We watched the humans grow and evolve. Some lived, many more died." He looked at the image hanging in the air, of the war-torn countryside. Then he looked to Tiny, sitting quietly with tears streaming down his face. Seglee let out a long singular wail at the memory in her cavern under them.

Sarah crawled backwards until she was against the wall. "I remember mom here and you built this when I was what? 5? She was here, inside of here. She would play with me outside. She was here. She didn't Ascend until I was... I was 8? 9?"

Galloyde moved closer. "That was all a desirihia, Sarah," he whispered to her.

Neph moved over to Sarah and held her tight as she started to cry. Nexar, Gilgerg, and Desi tried to comfort Tiny and Seglee, who were also grief-stricken.

Galloyde suddenly called out, "Enough! I told you all this would be difficult. They are coming here as we speak. We need to move through this now." He regained his composure and continued. The next scene showed much of Nephemerus' second dream of The Gate being built. Instead of watching the scene, Neph rocked Sarah and whispered to her that she needed to be strong for her charges. They would deal with all this together after they fight The Atheciery. She stopped crying and focused back on Galloyde.

"The Grand Precipice knew he could not kill me. Taking my love, my Olethia, from me was his punishment. While he did not care for her, he knew me and my past enough to understand that killing her would be worse than killing me."

The image Galloyde was showing everyone froze on Sarah as a small child, standing with Seglee and Tiny.

"What he did not know then, and what the Atheciery did not see, was our child, Sarah. Seglee hid Sarah in the lake, undetected, while they searched for me. Thrinythidor had kept me safe until they left." He paused. "I knew they would be back, so I had to create an indestructible defense—a fortress. I knew Algetia would never stop, even after taking my love. Olethia and I had found an asteroid that caused immense damage to this planet thousands of years before, so I brought a piece of it back here. Inside, I knew I would find the Eiracore I would need. I just needed a power source."

"The stone," Desi breathed, eyes wide.

The ball of light turned into the image of the stone on the dagger. "This stone fell from the crown of an Athecierian General during their attack. It is called a Hiseth. Rare. Powerful. I suspect this is how they can perform illusions. I found the stone after their attack —actually, Sarah did."

Everyone looked at Sarah, who was watching the images blankly. She was taking it all in, stony-faced. Emotionless.

"I will never understand the insatiable appetite Algetia had for revenge. He did not love Olethia. He had no feelings for her. To be crass, he simply could have had her replaced with another Replicator and not have even noticed the change. She was there to serve a function for him. But with me..."

Galloyde took a moment and started again. "He was the closest thing to a father that I had ever known. Algetia and I shared a bond. I will always believe we were close. I know we were. That bond is why he grew to despise me, and unfortunately, he used our bond to discover all of you."

The image in the circle now showed each Regulator: Seglee, Tiny, Clara, GilGerg, the Triplets, Kevin, Zana, Bob, Bezel, and lastly, Bunny.

"While he is not an Overseer, his skills as an Elget are well beyond the normal training." Galloyde focused on Neph. "He should never be underestimated."

Galloyde redirected himself back to the rest of the group. "I built the Gate to protect all of you. You all are the most important species in all of the universes. You are the Founders. Your bloodlines are the root of life on every planet, in every dimension. Without you, worlds are lost. This Gate is to protect you from being harmed—not to keep you in, but to keep those who would harm you out."

There was silence in the cavern.

He went on. "When I saw he was coming for me, Sarah took over, to protect you, at all costs. All costs." He took a moment, tears springing to his eyes. "You may come to hate me, despise me, thinking I kept you from your homes. From your own people, from your worlds." Tears flowed from his eyes. "You would be right to do so. I have thought about all of you—even those I had yet to know," he said to Bob and towards Sarah, who had Bezel still tucked away in her pocket. "The only thing I was certain of was you all had each other, and this way I could protect all of you here."

The floating orb now showed the Gate. "Out there, I cannot protect you. Out there, if you were separated on different planets, I could not protect you. Out there, if someone tries to harm you..." He stopped and stared at the ground, chest heaving. "If you are angry with me, know I kept you here—"

"We—we kept you here," Sarah called out softly.

Galloyde looked at her gratefully. "We kept you here for your own protection because you are so important, beyond all measure."

"Well. Fuck me," said Desi, breaking a long silence which followed. "I got that about as wrong as you can get it. I'm done guessing for today!" He was met with nervous laughter that was the stress reliever everyone needed right then.

After a brief moment, Neph asked, "I don't understand why now? After all this time? Why not attack here while you were in the

Ripple? I would have seized that moment, knowing you weren't here. Or at least do it as soon as you left, before your replacement could prepare for an attack."

Galloyde nodded. "Yes, good thinking, Admiral." There was murmuring to this response, and Desi's face curled into a questioning look at the military reference of his fellow Elget.

"Although everyone assumed that I did create a race of horrific beasts on Earth, the Atheciery descriptions of a Clorrian and Yesperarian were not missed by Algetia, and I believe that is how he deduced that Founders must be on Earth," Galloyde continued. "I have to assume the Grand Precipice was hoping to eliminate or sell the Founders, so he sent the Atheciery back to collect his prize. That is when we all lived inside of here for a bit. Sarah, do you remember that time?"

"I'm not sure what I remember anymore," Sarah mumbled.

Galloyde did not bother to address this and looked to Clara. "You remember?" Clara dipped her head in affirmation. Galloyde asked the Triplets if they remembered, and they bowed each of their heads in affirmation.

"Good. Yes, the Atheciery returned with a significant number of their warships, prepared to take the Founders and destroy this little planet." The images showed dozens of Athecierian warships hovering over Earth. "At this point, Algetia was already starting to lose his grip on reality. In an ironic twist, while I was being called 'Mad Galloyde' for supposedly creating all of you, my pursuer was —and still is—losing his mind." Galloyde paused. "I wish I could enjoy that bit, but in fact, it is simply a huge loss. He has a brilliant mind. Cruel, but brilliant."

He snapped out of this thought and returned to the images, which moved from the warships surrounding Earth to Athecierians cowering from the glowing Gate.

"The power of the Hiseth was more than even I had hoped. I was looking for a source to activate the heat of the Eiracore so I could mold it into what I needed—to create an iron cage strong enough to hold back those who wish to attack. For reasons unknown to me, the Athecierians are unable to even touch the Eiracore when it is powered by the Hiseth. That stone has tremendous power." He looked to Bunny. "Tremendous power…" he trailed off.

Bunny opened his mouth with a long moan, and copious amounts of goo spilled out. Luis stood up to move away, but patted Bunny on the arm with a smile before leaving. Bunny tried to wipe up the mess with his talons, unsuccessfully.

Neph leaned into Sarah. "What's that about?" She looked at him, and she whispered she would tell him later.

"As long as we remain within the Gate, which surrounds this entire perimeter—including the cavern below—we remain untouchable to the Athecierians. They could drop a bomb directly on top of the cavern, and the Eiracore will protect us. When they returned to find they could not access the Founders or myself, they left. That was when the Grand Precipice began working on a plan to separate me from all of you."

"Well, to follow up on Nephemerus' question, then why not attack here when you were on the Ripple, then?" Desi asked. "It seemed like the appropriate time. They didn't know an Overseer was here. A Council Representative asked Sarah to take over for you. Presumably not knowing she is an Overseer."

"Codet Bahringers was definitely not aware of my abilities when he interviewed me," Sarah said. "I made sure he was under the distinct impression that I was a student from Veris and was interested in the history of Galloyde. He did say that I was replacing Galloyde, but not that he was being banished. We already knew that part, so we were a few steps ahead, but we did not know when or where they were planning on sending him. They were able to shield the destination from both of us."

Nephemerus' eyes went wide. "Codet Bahringers? He hired you on behalf of the Council?" Neph looked at Desi, who was equally alarmed.

"Yes, that's the one. He was clear with me that Dad was being removed. We already knew the Grand Precipice was planning something and figured the Council was involved but—"

"The Council, yes, but you're absolutely positive it was Codet Bahringers who you spoke to? Was he with a Traveler? How did you meet with him?" Neph grilled her.

Galloyde interrupted. "Merus. Not now. That is not the focus right now. You will have your time. We need to continue. Where were we? Oh, why now? Yes. When my daughter and Merus rescued me, the Atheciery came directly here. An Overseer was not in residence to lock the Gate. Yet, as you have all witnessed, an Overseer is not required to do so, and Luis performed admirably under immense pressure, especially in the face of the enemy." Luis blushed and stammered a thank you as everyone gave him a quick round of applause.

"I do not believe they came here of their own will. This time, I do not believe it was my nemesis Algetia who sent them here either. Rather, I believe this was orchestrated at the direction of the object of your fascination, Merus."

Nephemerus drew in a sharp breath and looked at Desi, saying nothing.

"It does not matter who sent them or why right now," Galloyde continued. "They are coming. To be blunt, they will try to take all of the Founders—for control and for power. It is as simple as that. With your bloodlines, they can sell you to the highest bidders. Manipulate species. Change entire worlds." The images in the ball of light showed current species morphing into new species.

"The reality is that I cannot die, and Sarah cannot die," Galloyde said in a quiet voice. Sarah kept her eyes forward, purposefully avoiding looking at Neph. "Yet many of you can," Galloyde continued. "And I fear that if you do, it will be an unspeakable loss —not only to our family here, but to the tens of thousands of species who descend from your DNA. Worse yet, some of you may not be able to Ascend."

There was a long silence.

"This is not a battle for you to fight. When the Athecierians come, you must stay in here where you are protected. Under all circumstances, stay in here. Your survival is far too important for the entirety of the cosmos to worry about dealing with the likes of immoral and unjust mercenaries. Worlds will fall if you do not stay inside these walls. Do you understand? Tell me you understand my words. Tell me you will stay inside."

The Triplets let out three separate cries, followed by howls from Bunny, Clara, Seglee's scream, a loud rumble from Tiny, thrumming from GilGerg, a chattering from Bob, and a high-pitched buzzing from Sarah's pocket. The Founders' reluctant acceptance was heard.

CHAPTER
SEVENTY-SEVEN

After the meeting broke up, Sarah was walking into the Chamber room when she felt a hand on her arm. She turned to see it was Neph. He led her down to the end of the room, past the fireplace, where they pressed themselves into a dark corner and he pulled her tight against him. She buried her face into his neck.

"You cannot go out there," she whispered.

"If I knew I was going to be stuck down here, I would have stayed with my ship, my crew. I can attack them from above. Why didn't you tell me?" he started to say.

"No. No, you have to be here. In here. I need you here. With your military experience, just in case... in case they somehow get past us. Listen, if they breach through the Gate, there's a way out through Seglee's cavern so you don't get trapped..."

"Sarah." He held her face. "Please don't ask me to do this. I can't stand by while you're in danger. I can't do it."

She kissed the palm of his hand and reached up to trace her finger along the side of his neck. "There's a way out through Seglee's cavern, but only if you are somehow breached. She will show you where to go. Neph, I need you to remember that I can handle myself out there. Remember on the Ripple?"

He remembered her picking up the Athecierian Cutter and ripping it in two as if it was paper. She didn't even break her stride doing it.

She leaned against him and brushed her fingers lightly along his collarbone. "They must be protected. Galloyde and I will deal with the Atheciery. We cannot die. If you were out there, I'd be distracted, you know that. Don't do that to me."

He kissed her, holding her tightly, feeling frustrated. "I can't just wait in here, not knowing what is happening out there," he whispered in her ear. "I can't even talk to Raka. My Battleships—"

"Will be here far sooner than expected," she cut him off, her eyes sparkling.

Neph let out a laugh. She covered his mouth and issued him a stern hush.

"Seriously?" he asked, unable to hide his relief. "Sarah, our Battleships against seven of their warships? Then it's no longer a fight. That's like Bunny against—"

"Don't say GilGerg, because he's far tougher than you think!"

Neph paused. "I was going to say Bunny against a deer, but now I'm slightly worried about that furry mop."

Sarah giggled. "Just don't mention GilGerg to Chronny. He still hasn't recovered, but I mean it, Neph. Please, promise me you'll stay in here."

Neph promised and picked her up off the ground, kissing her one more time. As she sank back down to the floor, she pressed her lips against his ear. "Ishonna, Neph. Ishonna, Ishonna."

They broke their embrace just as Desi walked into the chamber with Galloyde at his side. They were late in pulling themselves away from each other, but both her father and the Elget pretended not to notice.

Galloyde motioned to Neph that he would like to speak to him, and they moved over towards the center of the room, while Sarah walked toward the door with Desi.

"Sarah," Desi said, glancing between her and Neph and smiling his approval. "Is there anything I can do for you while you are out there, dealing with all of this?"

She thought for a moment. "I know you and Tiny have been brainstorming. What have you come up with?"

Desi's face lit up. "Oh yes! We have ideas, but we must tell you together. I know there isn't much time, but perhaps there is something that might help you? Maybe not, but let us see."

She turned to leave with Desi, but not before catching a glimpse of Neph with her father, deep in discussion. They both looked serious. Sarah was sure her father would be warning Neph to stay inside the Gate and keep everyone safe, but just as Sarah stepped out of the room, she felt a harsh pang of concern. That wasn't what they were talking about, but she couldn't get a clear vision of what they were saying.

Before she could turn back around, Desi took her arm and led her into the passageway.

"Ahh, there he is. Thrinythidor!"

Tiny saw them and joined the two of them. Desi explained that Sarah wanted a recap of what they had been working on. They quickly explained that when she and Nephemerus left, they decided to proactively work on any issues they could see as a possible problem until her return.

"The first concern was where to put the humans when and if we had to go into the Gate," Tiny explained. "I was telling Desi the history of Descend, and the Gate is obviously a large part. Protocol doesn't allow for humans to join us here during attacks. After all, when the Gate was built, Descend didn't exist. We didn't have to worry about humans back then."

Sarah agreed. The humans were a living species on Earth but were not yet self-aware, so there was no system for their afterlife in place yet.

Tiny continued. "The original passageways extend beyond the Chamber. Although the Gate's protection ends at the Chamber room, the entire structure is quite strong. We moved the humans into all the lower levels once you sent word. They have to triple-bunk in some of the lowest levels, but they have food, water, and supplies. If the Atheciery try to use the same type of bombs as before, the humans shouldn't feel a thing in those levels. If they use new technology… well, they are dead anyway."

"Literally. I mean, they are already in Descend." Desi shrugged his shoulders.

Sarah struggled to contain an outburst of laughter. "Oh GOD, Desi! You're their Almighty Lord and Savior! Where's your never-ending compassion?" she managed to get out between choking laughs. "You sound like you should be taking over Neph's post!"

"Actually, we have discussed that. After all, no Elget is officially posted to Ascend or Descend. Aramik said some Elgets have traded positions in the past, and really, I find Descend quite fascinating! I think I'd prefer a more hands-on approach too. I'd like to talk about that more later with you," Desi said, eyes wide with excitement.

Sarah was grinning and watching Desi and Tiny. She could not have imagined these two working so well together—but then again, she hadn't seen Neph becoming so important in her life.

"Next, we felt we had to solve the issue of the humans who wouldn't be able to enter this realm once the Gate was sealed," Desi continued.

"I would love to hear about this as well." They all turned to see Galloyde in the passageway behind them, listening patiently. He gave them a small smile. "I had decided at the time to seal all portals leading into this plane in the event the Gate was locked. This was to prevent any aggressors from breaching into the world of the humans, which of course they could circumvent, but if anyone came all this way, it would most likely be for one of us and not for a human. At least closing the portals would slow them down."

Desi anxiously nodded his head in agreement. "Yes, yes. We absolutely saw your logic in doing that. We also struggled with how to deal with all the people who, well, died while the Gate is locked. Especially for an extended amount of time. Ironically, it was the humans themselves who solved that problem."

"Oh, well now, this has to be good," Sarah said, eyebrow raised.

"Galloyde, are you familiar with any of their stories? Erhm… any of them that actually stem from you, the Founders, and the Atheciery?"

For a moment, Galloyde considered this, rubbing at his chin. "I know they romanticized those winged psychopaths. They loved to carve their likenesses everywhere—in the caves, on rocks—they drew them every place they could find. The humans were so enamored with their pale skin and those wretched wings. They collected the feathers every chance they could. They even portrayed the Atheciery with their weapons, with blood still dripping from them in their paintings. Yet they continued to adore them." He sighed, shaking his head. "I should have realized right then that perhaps that particular group of humans were too barbaric to push into Ascension."

Desi looked at Tiny, then back at Galloyde. "The early drawings? The cave drawings originally showed the Atheciery with weapons and blood?"

"Oh yes. They were incredibly accurate. They used clay and animal blood. Not too many of these paintings have survived over the years, although there's still a few intact under the ice, near the poles. As I told you, the humans were smitten by those Athecierian wings. They re-traced over them with fresh paint or charcoal to keep their images fresh, for countless years. Eventually, they simply stopped tracing over the weapons and blood—but not those abhorrent wings."

"Now you," he gestured to Tiny. "The humans saw you and your fellow Founders as well. I hadn't separated us onto this plane yet. They saw you, but they had no reason to fear you, because you are nothing to be feared. Do you remember?"

Tiny nodded. "They lacked language skills. Some would point. Some would try to attack—the aggressive ones. Others would hunt from afar. Not much of a threat with their sticks and blunt rocks. Most just ignored us. Never a real threat, especially once the Triplets joined us. That cleared out all the humans in this area." He smiled. "But once in a while, there was a nice one."

"Pretty much like now—they really stick to a pattern," Sarah said dryly, as they all had a little laugh.

Galloyde continued. "They drew pictures, but with limited skills. I am assuming they made up stories to go along with those pictures. Are these the stories you are referring to?"

Nodding, Desi explained to Galloyde as briefly as he could that one of the beliefs the humans had involved a god, with tales of angels and demons. This deity would perform miracles and oversee the day-to-day struggles of every individual soul, intervening with miracles and other unexplainable phenomena.

Galloyde burst out laughing. "They think I am one of their gods? Hah! Why would they even think that?"

"Well, Dad, to be fair to their very limited views, you did create a whole little subspecies. There is an argument to be made there," Sarah pointed out.

"Oh, daughter, I object. I have never created anyone except for you. Humans evolved through natural selection. All I had done was connect a missing strand of their DNA. Nature most certainly would have intervened and eliminated that group of humans had I not interfered. This mistake haunts me, and I deeply regret it, but these DNA gaps must be obvious to their scientists by now? They must realize this when they study the past and see where there was a distinct intervention in the evolution of one genus of humans, while other tribes did not have this—this 'miraculous' leap," he said, stealing Desi's word, "to surge forward and evolve. Surely this has been discovered and studied? Humans now use rudimentary science. They use logic, correct?"

Tiny sighed. "That's a really long story—"

"For later," Sarah interjected. "Desi, what are you doing while the Gate is locked?"

"Oh! Yes. Well, in one of these stories, they created this place they like to call 'Purgatory.' It's basically neither in Ascend nor Descend. A waiting room of sorts. So we decided we can borrow their concept and create a place for those who pass away while the Gate is locked!"

Galloyde's eyes lit up. "Yes! Of course, you can create a separate plane, just like this one, where they are held until we can address their situation." He looked at Desi and Tiny. "Brilliant. Simply brilliant. This is done? You have already completed this?" Galloyde closed his eyes briefly and said, "Oh wait, I see it now. Excellent. Just excellent work, the two of you."

Tiny and Desi beamed with pride. Sarah watched as they nudged each other in camaraderie.

"Ok, we should get going," she said. "Anything else you need us to know right now?"

Tiny and Desi exchanged looks. "It can wait until after you are back," Desi said.

Galloyde then handed them the syringe filled with the Nox's blood.

"Hold this for me. This is the solution to saving the humans, so I implore you to keep it safe. You will need to create the solution if there is an unforeseen issue—"

Tiny interrupted. "What do you mean?"

Galloyde grabbed his claw and Desi's arm at the same time with frightening speed. He closed his eyes, and for a moment, none of them spoke. When he released them, they all nodded solemnly toward one another.

"Do you both understand the gravity of this?" he asked Desi and Tiny. They were still speechless from the breadth of information Galloyde pushed into their minds, but they each managed a slight head nod. "Good. I trust you both. Let nothing stop you from making this happen." He walked away from their trio and joined Sarah.

"I think my daughter is ready to take care of some old business. Am I correct?"

"Almost." Sarah went over to Bob, who was getting attention from Luis and GilGerg.

"Excuse me, I need to borrow this fine fellow if you don't mind." She picked Bob up and carried him over to where Seglee could sneak her head through the floor. Neph and Galloyde followed to see what she was doing.

She called out to Seglee, who popped her head up right away. Sarah let her get a good sniff of Bob and explained Bob needed to join her in the lake below.

"I need you to watch each other's backs, Seglee. Bob, I'd like to ask that you choose an appropriate size once you feel the layout of the cavern. The fact that the Atheciery made it all the way to the Gate entrance is a problem. I want to make sure they don't attempt any other breaches. If you see someone in the water who doesn't belong there, Bob, you know what to do."

He raised his tiny head and let out a baby-sized yowl, then made a chomping motion.

Neph chuckled menacingly. "Oh, he knows what to do. That's what they love to do. Eat first, ask-questions-never. Right, Bob?"

Bob raised his head again and made a chomping motion, more vigorously this time.

"Ok, be on the lookout down there. Watch each other's backs. Be safe." Seglee graciously nodded her beak, then withdrew her head back down into the cavern below so Bob could slip past. A moment later, they heard him splash into the water. Shortly after, they heard a deep, rumbling yowl, which made the ground shudder underneath their feet. Sarah nodded to Neph and Galloyde. "Now I'm ready."

CHAPTER
SEVENTY-EIGHT

T he two Overseers walked out of the Gate quickly, not allowing for any fanfare. Sarah turned and waved her hand, making the Gate reappear as they stood on the other side of it again. She let her eye catch Neph's one last time, and he smiled at her and nodded.

Brave face, she thought. He's worried, even though he knows his ships will arrive soon.

She walked upwards out of the caverns with Galloyde, who was already in her mind.

You would be just as worried if places were reversed, her father reminded her. She said nothing. He already knew her feelings, so no response was needed.

They walked up the cavern passageways, looking for any movement in the dark. Shadows that didn't belong, shapes that were too dark that lay in the crevices, waiting. Perhaps a glint of light that might appear in the wrong place.

There were sixteen Athecierians who were nearby, waiting for their reinforcements to arrive to lead an attack on her family in her home.

As far as they knew, the Atheciery had watched Raka get into the Lander, return to Noneru, and then saw all three Clorrian Cruisers retreat out of Earth's orbit, none the wiser to the impending attack.

Obviously, the Clorrians wouldn't abandon the planet—not with a Fleet Admiral still on the surface. The Athecierians wouldn't fall for that. But just as the Clorrians could track the Athecierian warships, the Atheciery could track the Clorrian Battleships and Airship as well.

Or, at least what they perceived to be those ships.

CHAPTER
SEVENTY-NINE

C odet Bahringers leaned over the railing on the Katska, the lead Athecierian warship, his fingers digging into the metal, his face twisted into a grimace. Finally. He could end so many of his problems in one place. He was minutes away from destroying Galloyde, his monsters, and finally killing one of his tormentors.

He moved over to the Captain. "Well?" The Captain looked displeased at the constant interruptions.

"Again, we are on the exact same course, at the same arrival time of—"

"Don't tell me that! I'll have you in Radimus for speaking to me like that. Do not tell me that! Do you understand? Answer me, answer meeeee!" Bahringers shrieked. Each of the Athecierian pilots looked down and away, trying to avoid any eye contact with the belligerent, ranting madman.

The Captain continued in the same tone of voice. "As I was saying, we will arrive in 10 pilns. It's also important to know we are tracking several Clorrian Battle Ships that entered the Quadrant heading towards—"

"I don't need to know the traffic report, you insipid idiot! Just fly this saaaaad excuse of a ship!"

"Yes, sir," the Captain gritted his teeth. "If you would like to head to Departure, we are preparing your Convoy. The fighters are at the ready now... Precipice Adjunct."

Codet Bahringers closed his eyes and hissed. He pushed his voluminous robes out, as if trying to make his unusually short stature seem larger, then he whirled on his feet and left the Bridge. When the doors closed behind him, the Captain let out a sigh of exasperation.

CHAPTER
EIGHTY

D esi sat in the Chamber room, quietly thumbing through his diary—something he had started during the long days when Neph and Sarah were out of reach. He enjoyed hearing Tiny's stories about the humans, and their idiosyncrasies. Journaling their accomplishments was one that Desi was particularly intrigued in and to his surprise, one that he found useful in trying to ground himself as panic increased in the absence of hearing from his fellow Elget.

Tiny had given him a leather-bound diary he found. It was engraved on inside the front cover with, "To Chaz, we are so proud of you - Love, Mom and Dad." The only entry was a scrawled, "This sucks, I wanted a car," on the first page. The rest of the journal was in perfect, unused condition. Desi tore out the ironic page from the ungrateful Chaz, and began to journal his experience on Earth.

He found the practice of writing to be liberating and soon he carried his diary with him everywhere. He collected leaves he found interesting, Frath's recipe for chicken noodle soup, and a few holos from when he was a student at the Elget Academy.

He was staring at one of the images taken on his first day in Ala Mia. It showed seven fresh, young faces, all looking at the camera, with seriousness and pride. On the back was an inscription of the event.

ALA MIA – Elget Class #47

Student Roster – Kia Aspwall, Bassi Tinnl Wirve, Desimidor Vas Qulas Zyrla, Codet Vir Bahringers, Laja Sinari, Nephemerus os Clorria.

Head Master – The Grand Precipice, Algetia of Ala Mia.

He closed his eyes and thought about his time there, organizing his thoughts to share in his journal.

The class began their semester the same way as all the others had in the past. Scouts had either found the Elget candidates via school or training grounds, who had submitted possible candidates—or, on rare occasions, legacy families who would submit an applicant directly.

For this class, there were two legacy applications. Desimidor Vas Qulas Zyrla, the seventh confirmed Elget of his house. His family and his own abilities were already well-known and highly regarded in many circles. His entry to Ala Mia was a formality, but Desi never treated it as such. He studiously went through each step of the admissions process as if he were trying to win his seat. This lack of entitlement was surprising and viewed as commendable by the staff, who liked him immediately.

The second application came from Codet Bahringers. He claimed to be a fourth-in-line legacy Elget, although he lacked any innate signs of talent. The first Elget connection was distant and questionable, and one in which he couldn't show actual proof of relation.

The second Elget relation Bahringers insisted upon using as a qualifier had no formal training at Ala Mia, and was not known by anyone at the school. There was also no confirmation of their skill—or that they even existed. Without official recognition from the Muldigal Council, no one had the right to call themselves an Elget. An Elget was, by definition, a formal Representative of the Multi-dimensional Galactic Council. Claiming to be an Elget without formal recognition would mean death, so no one had ever falsely asserted this claim.

Codet's parents were the kind of people who always owned or ran a business in whatever you were doing. It didn't matter what field or industry—you could count on them to be better at it, have more of it, and be making far more money at it than you were... according to them. So when the school inquired about their Elget connection, they threatened to pull their generous funding if Codet wasn't allowed entry into training.

When questioned on any of his Elget relations after admission, Codet refused to speak about the subject—a stark change from his earlier insistence on forcefully telling everyone about them during the admission process. His wealthy family and connections insisted that his claims were valid. Eventually, the admissions Board relented —not being able to prove any of his claims were false, but also not being able to prove they were true either.

For students Aspwall and Wirve, they were both successfully scouted from the OaB solar system. Aspwall was a late-bloomer, but could manipulate the moods of those around her—a useful tactic in negotiations and peacekeeping matters. Wirve was meek and shy, preferring to hide herself behind people or things wherever she went—unless a non-sentient entered the area. Then she became their voice, and all her shyness melted away. Her voice and posture would assume theirs, which was impressive to witness coming from her slight form. She was a valuable voice for societies wanting to be more responsible toward their fellow lifeforms who had yet to reach a level of self-awareness where the Council would finally recognize them. Wirve stayed tied at the hip to Aspwall throughout all of their Elget training, despite not knowing each other at all prior to arriving at Ala Mia.

The last two students were Laja Sinari and Nephemerus os Clorria.

Both came to the school with questionable backgrounds, yet both possessed undeniably strong Elget skillsets.

Laja was a Merkvestor, hailing from the Borgell galaxy—his family renowned for their vast empire of shipping transports, and even more so in how their business was run. The Sinari's operated with more tactical ruthlessness than most regimes. They had no competitors within their dimension and the next seventeen dimensions parallel to Borgell. If anyone wanted a ship, you paid the Sinari price tag—one way or another.

He addressed this concern outright on his application, stating he wanted a different life and to use his skills to build worlds for others. He was persuasive and convincing in his words, but the risk of impropriety with such ties to a family such as his was a threat to the very nature of what the Muldigal Council was meant to represent.

Yet Laja's skill in connecting the motivations of others by their past, present, and future actions was a remarkable and rare trait. To deny him entry to Ala Mia based on his family relations would be wrong if he truly wanted to serve. Instead, the Admissions Board decided to take additional measures. Laja was visited by three esteemed Elgets, each of whom probed his mind to determine if his intentions were true. Each time, they returned to Ala Mia with the same answer—his intentions were genuine in his heart. Laja Sinari was admitted to the program.

Nephemerus entered the program at approximately the same age as the other students, but he was far more worldly. He also had to deal with the concern of the Admissions Board in being allowed into the school—not from a poor family connection, but the lack of any family connection. He would only say he was from Clorria and refused to answer any questions regarding his family, any possible Elget relations, or even where he had lived throughout his life. The only reason they entertained his application was because he received a sponsorship from the Rear Admiral of the Ubinia Fleet. This was the first time the Admissions Board had ever heard from Clorria. What made it all even more curious was that Nephemerus was not a blood-born Clorrian.

The Admissions Board decided to have him go through the same process as Laja Sinari, to ensure that his intentions to represent the Council were true and genuine. When Nephemerus was interviewed, those same mind probers saw nothing at all but a grey wall. When pressed on this, Nephemerus—still just a young child—confronted these esteemed Elgets by saying he knew they were looking around in his mind and he didn't appreciate their intrusion. This amused the Admissions Board.

They informed Nephemerus that the Elget interview would be a condition of his entry to Ala Mia. After all, they needed to know who they would be sending out to manage these planets. The Elgets they trained had to be responsible, kind, and trustworthy. They couldn't be "like Mad Galloyde, could they?" Nephemerus relented and agreed to meet with the mind probers again. During that interview, they weren't blocked. Only this time, they saw scenes of bright sunshine and pelerria, a yellow field flower found in the high mountain regions of Clorria. When the Elgets pushed his mind further, they would see their own worlds—with incredible clarity. He even went as far as to bring one Elget back to the time of his own birth.

They reported this back to Admissions, and Nephemerus was promptly admitted to the program. The Board had no choice. They had never had an Elget student recall a memory from another Elget before. They were more curious than annoyed. Correction—Algetia, the Grand Precipice, was curious, which made Nephemerus an automatic admission.

The room assignments were supposed to be random, but since Aspwall and Wirve refused to be split up, the remaining four decided who to room with on their own.

Desi and Nephemerus had struck up an interesting conversation about Jaffer's Third Inversion Quandary, and no one else wanted to be caught in those types of discussions, so they were automatically paired together.

That left Laja Sinari and Codet Bahringers. Even if Laja had a questionable family background, everyone felt it was cruel to make him Codet's roommate. But Laja was fond of listening to low-frequency vibrations. He said he found the sounds calming. Since rooming alone wasn't an option, Laja agreed to be Codet's roommate, knowing he could quite literally tune the annoyance out.

It had taken only half a rotation for the students to realize that Codet was a serial liar. No one wanted to be associated with that—especially in a program that hinged upon your integrity.

Their hope had been that the school would remove Codet due to his constant lying. Codet was considerably shorter in stature than the rest of the students, but no one cared about his height. No one except Codet—another trait that made being around him deeply uncomfortable. He always found a way to accuse you of hating him based on his height, rather than recognizing his own abhorrent behavior.

Classes soon began, and the more everyone tried to include Codet in any activities, the more he would refuse—and the harder he pushed back. He would then blatantly accuse them of being jealous of him and holding him back from his "inherent greatness." The teachers witnessed this behavior firsthand and informed the Grand Precipice.

Soon after, Codet's father arrived at Ala Mia to retrieve his son for the one-way trip back home. The day did not go by without fanfare, as accusations of favoritism, extortion, nepotism, and worse were called out loudly by the Bahringers family to anyone within earshot. They packed up their son and completed their visit by screaming about what a sham of a program the Elget training had turned into, before getting into their transport and leaving Ala Mia.

Algetia listened to the concussive tantrums of the Bahringers with mild amusement from his balcony. He had canceled classes and let the other students have the day to relax and recover from the trauma of dealing with their classmate. He was displeased that Bahringers was even allowed into the program. He had vehemently opposed it, and as the Grand Precipice, his decision should have been final—but he received word from the High Magistrate of the Council. They wanted Codet to attend, and Algetia was 'strongly urged to comply.'

As he listened to the grousing fade down below, he chided himself for not telling the High Magistrate to go mind his own business, and that Algetia would mind his.

It was shortly after this incident that the Sinari family showed up at the school unannounced. Laja's parents insisted he come home, having heard the program was unfit and no longer as respected as it once was. The school tried to intervene, attempting to show his parents Laja's impressive test scores. They wouldn't even look at his accomplishments as they haphazardly packed their son's possessions. Algetia made a rare appearance within the dorms to speak to the parents, to explain the misunderstanding and convince them to let the young Merkvestor continue his studies.

His parents refused to listen to the Grand Precipice and dismissed him as if he were one of their employees.

Wirve was in the next room and debated using her power. She could calm his parents and help change their minds, but Aspwall convinced her that since she wasn't an Elget yet, she could get into trouble—or worse, lose her own spot—if she tried to help.

Laja's parents ended up taking him home. Everyone was devastated, not only by the loss of great talent, but knowing the kind boy's dreams were shattered. Laja had the habit of talking to teachers, groundskeepers, cooks, and delivery people about how one day, he would be an Elget and travel all over the multi-universes to help others.

His face lit up when he described new initiatives he wanted the Council to consider, and how he was going to be able to help so many. When the conversations would come to an end, he would just smile, turn his low-frequency tones back on, and walk off into the woods humming to himself, peaceful and happy.

His unwelcome departure was a stark contrast to the collective relief everyone felt when Codet was finally removed from the campus— after just a few days of his terrorizing everyone. The loss of Laja Sinari left a hole for the remainder of the program.

Desimidor had received one letter back from Laja near the end of their training. He had sent many, keeping in touch as he had promised he would, but only received a single response back. It had merely said,

"I am honored to have met and gotten to know you, Kia, Bassi, and Neph for the time I had at Ala Mia. I will treasure each of you within my thoughts. You will always be part of me. – Laja."

Any letters Desi sent to him after that one were returned unopened, so he stopped writing to him. As the fire burned low, Desi smiled, thinking of his time there, but soon that smile curled down into a frown, remembering what happened after and why Codet Bahringers was such a threat, to him, to Neph, and to everyone in The Gate.

CHAPTER
EIGHTY-ONE

Algetia pulled himself up onto his trembling legs. His body was betraying him, just as everyone else had betrayed him. His simpering attendant jumped forward, offering to help him sit back down.

"Get off of me!" he bellowed. "If I wanted to sit, I wouldn't have tried so hard to get up. Why must I be surrounded by dullards and lackeys!"

The attendant stepped back, glancing down at the hard marble floor and thinking how nice a quick fall would be—to shorten this assignment. This frail, insane Elget had been the bane of his existence for what felt like endless rotations. The ruthlessly cruel inmate required guards, servants, and physicians—to what end? Why was he so important?

The attendant sneered at the Elget, who was clutching the heavy drapes and looking out from the balcony. Normally, he wouldn't be allowed near the open door, but what was he going to do? Fall? He wished. If a fall on this hard marble didn't do the trick, maybe a fall from the tower would. No one would complain. He would even push the old goat over the railing himself, if he was sure he would get away with it.

The bones of the Elget's hand worked back and forth under the paper-thin tissue of skin, trying to steady his teetering, while his other hand was clutched in a fist against his bony chest. Long, thin wisps of hair blew back in the wind. The attendant's bored expression grew into one of curiosity as the Elget inched himself closer to the railing.

He really should pull him back into his chair, but the attendant was also hopeful—wishing for this rotting, decaying, foul creature to fling himself over the side of that balcony, ending this painful misery for both of them. The sheer joy from the thought of this erupted into a giggle, and the attendant had to bite it back before anyone could hear.

A sudden gust of wind arose and tried to push Algetia back into his room. He angled his skeletal frame against the wind, pushing forward, and when he made it to the railing, he shot the hand he held against his chest straight out and opened his fingers.

A brilliant flash of green lit up the night as the elder Elget hoarsely shouted into the wind. Then his body went over the railing and disappeared into the darkness below.

The wind continued to howl and blow into the room, ripping through the heavy drapes and sending sheets of paper dancing through the air—until the attendant snapped out of his daze. He pushed himself past the wheelchair and out onto the balcony. Far below, on the cobblestones, lay the Grand Precipice—now dead. His open hands were empty.

The House Guardian ran to the side of the old man and demanded to know what happened from the gathering bystanders. Guards gathered as well, and soon the medical staff—but it was far too late. Algetia's lifeless eyes stared up at the attendant as the news of his death spread from hushed murmurs into strangled cries of disbelief.

The medical tender shook her head as her own medical assistants draped a sheet over the body. The House Guardian looked up at the balcony and pointed. He said something to his guard. A moment later, the attendant was being forcefully escorted down the stairs to join the bloody scene outside.

"Tell me what happened. Now," the House Guardian said gruffly, backing the attendant up against the wall. "Be fast. Speak!"

"I—I, uh, he..." The attendant stumbled over his words, his eyes taking in the white sheet covering the Elget, now absorbing a wet maroon stain and spreading. He felt faint.

The House Guardian grabbed the front of the attendant's shirt and pushed him upward against the wall. "Tell me what happened, boy!"

"He got up, out of his chair. He was so fast. Faster than I ever saw him move before. Before I could do anything, he jumped over the… the…" The attendant started to cry. He would not be blamed for that prick's death. He tried to hide his face and lack of tears.

"What else?" the House Guardian sneered into the attendant's face. "Did he do anything? Say anything? What else happened up there, boy?"

The attendant's mind raced. The House Guardian knew if you were lying. He always knew. He would find out. He always did.

"He did say something. He got up and there was a green light, and he shouted something. There was a green light. He was holding a green light and then he disappeared."

The House Guardian let go of the attendant, letting him slide to the ground, where he continued his theatrical display of grief.

The House Guardian walked around the body, inspecting it for clues, looking for anything close by. Then, to the attendant, "You said he shouted something right before he fell. Is that right?"

The attendant confirmed with a nod.

"What was it?" the House Guardian asked.

"It was hard to hear because of the wind, but I could have sworn he shouted, 'Galloyde.'"

CHAPTER

EIGHTY-TWO

S arah and Galloyde walked out of the Descend campus building that stood over the caverns and found no one waiting outside. There were no Cutters, no Athecierian soldiers gathered to fight. No War Ships hovering above them. Nothing at all. They continued to walk away from the center of Descend and out towards the fields, looking for any signs of an encampment. Occasionally, they would stop and briefly scan the horizon to see if they could sense anyone close by. There was nothing.

Galloyde and Sarah had spoken of using their powers to jump the Clorrian air and battle ships into Earth's orbit, but without being on board or able to even see those ships, it was easier said than done. The Clorrian Air Ship was a third the size of Earth's moon. The Overseers decided to fold space into smaller pockets between the points where the ships were currently located and Earth instead. Sarah had told Neph the truth—his ships would be here far sooner than reported—but it was still hard to say exactly when they would arrive.

In the meantime, they maneuvered space debris into shapes that suspiciously mimicked an Air Ship and placed it just outside of

Earth's orbit. Unless they could physically see the debris, the Athecierian radars would assume it was a Clorrian Air Ship and hopefully keep their distance.

The biggest question was why the Athecierians were coming back yet again. Despite warning the Founders not to leave the Gate and stating the Atheciery were here to collect them, neither Sarah nor Galloyde knew the Atheciery's true intentions. Were they here for Galloyde? Were they trying to get the Founders? No matter what the answer, it was not truly an Athecierian's battle. They were mercenaries—and rather lazy ones at best.

Since the Atheciery's last failed trip to Earth, no one had bothered to hire them for any worthwhile work, so they had become a fixture at Galaador, devolving from blood-thirsty guns-for-hire to hedonistic and melodramatic pool boys. Wealthy benefactors enjoyed the novelty of having an Athecierian on their arm while visiting the party planet. With their chiseled bodies, porcelain skin, beautiful features, and lack of intellect, the wealthy were quite willing to pay for the time of the unemployed mercenaries to engage in more leisurely pursuits.

Since no one respected Athecierians as a cosmic rule, turning into playthings-for-hire didn't faze any of them. They had no leadership or moral center to guide them. They would steal, kill, or decimate anyone in any place for a price. When that market dried up, they switched to serving umbrella drinks, using their wings as sunscreens, and performing foot massages for the same price. Whether they were slaughtering the unlucky or performing a couple's massage, the work made no difference to them—as long as they got paid.

Yet here they were, returning to Earth on their third run. This planet had been their largest and longest-running failure. Perhaps they were trying to reclaim a sense of integrity by finally achieving success on this planet. Both Overseers dismissed this notion, knowing that the opinions of others held no value to the Atheciery —only money mattered. Someone must have hired them to return to this remote planet.

They had walked into the fields, nearing the point where Sarah's mother placed her in Seglee's beak to save her during the first Athecierian attack. This is where Galloyde's affectionate term "my little Gator" originated. Seglee had cared for Sarah in those early days after her mother had been killed. The giant bird would dive down under the lake, letting Sarah sleep nestled in her beak, safe and warm, the water swirling outside, soothing and calming the little baby. When Galloyde came to the lake, Seglee would swim up to the surface and open her beak so they could visit.

Sarah would be lying inside, swaddled in her blankets, safe and sound. She reminded Galloyde of the little birds that perched in an alligator's mouth, plucking out food between the dangerous reptile's teeth. He was calling Seglee an alligator, asking her, "How's my gator today?" when he came to check on Sarah. When Sarah grew too large to fit in Seglee's beak anymore, she would run around, clamping her arms together and shouting she was an alligator. Hence, he started calling Sarah his "little Gator," and the precious nickname stuck.

The father and daughter climbed up a small hill and looked back towards Descend, making sure no one was following them from behind. No one was there. They sat on the grass and carefully scanned again, looking for any sign. Were there any cloaked ships? Those approaching warships should be—

There! Both Sarah and Galloyde caught sight of them at the same time in their minds. Approaching fast from just beyond the fifth planet of this solar system. All seven ships had already passed Jupiter and were approaching Earth on a direct course. They would reach them in just a few moments.

Galloyde stood and looked up into the blue sky. Sarah stayed seated, eyes closed to keep watch.

The Athecierian Warships split formation. Two of them went past Earth and towards the second planet in the solar system. Two more War Ships stayed just at the edge of Earth's orbit. The remaining three ships entered Earth's atmosphere at incredible speed. One flew directly to the northernmost pole, the next remained high in orbit within the atmosphere, and the last headed directly toward Galloyde and Sarah.

It was easy for the Athecierians to spot and move through the portal to Descend. Galloyde was unable to prevent any intergalactic visitors from coming into that particular Descend plane because it belonged to the Council. Since there were countless reasons for different ships to access a planet, the Council had put a permanent entry point in place.

Galloyde saw the familiar shadow cover the field. The warship blotted out the sun and cast them into darkness. It took them a moment to adjust their eyes to the change in light. It was hard to see exactly how large the ship was above them. They both realized too late that it wasn't stopping where they were. The ship had merely entered the atmosphere at their location and was moving past them toward the center of Descend.

The Overseers had wanted to pull the ship back into the field and away from the Gate. Now they were at a disadvantage. They turned back toward Descend just as several bay doors opened under the ship and Cutters poured out.

They watched as the smaller craft formed an elaborate pattern around the ship. They weren't shooting any weapons yet, but it was a clear show of force. Galloyde and Sarah continued down the hill, making their way back toward Descend, running as quickly as they could. The Cutters continued to fly complex patterns until the two Overseers were nearly out of the field. Then the small crafts broke away and flew directly toward Descend.

"I am starting to think they might not want to have a chat with us first," Sarah said to Galloyde. He agreed as they continued to hurry back. They watched a Cutter turn, then come back directly toward them, firing its weapons.

"Well, I would certainly call that unfriendly fire," Galloyde said, flicking his hand as if he were shooing away a bug. "Especially since they are unwelcome guests." The Cutter lurched sideways and burst into flames, falling out of the sky.

The other Cutters followed suit and began firing upon the two Overseers in the field. Sarah and Galloyde took cover behind a large rock, but they had the Warship itself hanging directly overhead. Each Overseer was handily sweeping Cutters off to one side or the other, careful not to have them create an impasse that would prevent them from leaving the field—a task that was beginning to get more difficult, as all the aircraft were piling up. They were running out of room to push the wreckage.

"I think we need to back up. Pile them up in the open, way over there." Sarah pointed further out into the field.

Galloyde looked at where she was pointing. "That's a good spot to dispose of them, but it puts us right in the open."

Sarah thought for a second, then looked at Galloyde. He nodded in agreement to her silent suggestion. They let a few Cutters fly over them and then crashed them, one by one, into one tall pile. Then they ran behind that pile, taking cover.

"Nice thinking, I like it." He winked at Sarah.

"You taught me the same technique when you were felling trees one year. Same principle—Hey! Got 'em!" She flicked her wrist as two Cutters flew by, lasers burning the pile of debris they were using as cover. Each Cutter was tossed aside as easily as she had dispatched the falling boulders on Ball's Pyramid. They crashed and burned to one heap, expertly driven there by Sarah's will.

Galloyde had already started working on another pile of Cutters and moved toward it to take cover. Sarah began to wonder why none of the pilots chose to return to the Warship, retreat, or even eject. With a 100% fail rate, it was fascinating to see such dedication from the Atheciery—who had never shown loyalty or commitment to any cause in the past. Anyone who hired the Atheciery was gambling on having any of them actually show up or stay when a battle erupted. They were essentially independent contractors. If they decided they didn't want to do the job anymore, they simply left or didn't show up. They held no allegiances.

So this didn't make any sense—that they were willing to die for a cause that was still a mystery.

Sarah glanced into one of the destroyed Cutters. She confirmed there was indeed an Athecierian pilot at the helm. She saw his wings wrapped around the back of his seat and his alabaster skin peeking out from under his helmet.

Do you think they are under any type of mind control? she posed this thought to Galloyde, who was now quite a distance away, working on another pile of dead Athecierian pilots and their ships.

Money. Everything they do is for money. No other cause, he answered coldly.

Sarah couldn't imagine how much money could justify certain death. She took no pleasure in killing these mercenaries, but she was not going to allow anyone near the Gate.

Sarah. She heard Galloyde call her from behind another burning pile. He was almost across the field now. *The Warship, Sarah—take down that Warship.*

She looked up. It was so large from one end to the other, she couldn't even see all of it from her position. The Cutters were simple, small. She could wrap her mind around them. Something of this size? She'd never tried anything of this magnitude.

Maybe I can if you help me? She answered him, but Galloyde didn't respond. *Dad?* She tried again. She pushed her mind. She could feel him but… what? She felt something hectic happening. Something wasn't right. She tried again, pushing hard with her mind. *Dad!*

I am with you, my daughter, he answered her. *I am not as strong as I once was. Creating the desirihia for all those years left me weak. I cannot take down the ship. You can do this. Focus, Sarah.*

Sarah was mindlessly piling up Cutters left and right as they crashed all around her. She turned and put up a barrier surrounding her from oncoming shots so she could focus on the task at hand.

Sarah looked around. Where could she push the Warship to land if she was successful? She didn't want it to drop directly down on top of herself, Galloyde, or Descend. Looking past the growing piles of burning machinery, she saw a patch of open land. If she could break up the ship and make it fall in that direction…

Something was off. Her father felt distracted. Was he overwhelmed? She couldn't place the feeling.

Do it now! Galloyde commanded.

She let her mind wander up into the ship, through the bay doors, past the Cutters, into the main engines, onto the floors. She spread her mind outward, corridor by corridor, taking in all of the rooms at incredible speed. She took deep breaths as the ground beneath her rumbled from the gunfire. Her mind traced through the thousands of spaces, through the electronic panels, room after room, pulling it all toward her. She drew another deep breath as her hands opened and rose into the air. She felt her heart rate match her breathing.

She sparked a fireball through the core of the ship, causing an explosion. She closed her fists and heard the shriek of metal crushing and whining under the strain. She was doing it! She focused hard on ripping the ship apart, starting right in the core.

Then a face appeared directly in her line of vision. A terrible, haunting face. A menacing face.

Sarah gasped and opened her eyes. She looked up and saw the War Ship slowly tilt to one side. Engines fired and the metal groaned in protest, but the massive ship remained in the sky.

Dad! she called him. *Did you see that face?* Her father didn't respond.

Who the fuck was that? Her mind raced. She remembered seeing that face before but couldn't remember where or who it belonged to. She turned and ran from her position out in the open and dove behind a pile of burning Cutters.

The Warship had righted itself just as she saw a Clorrian Battleship enter the atmosphere, high above her.

Her heart leapt for joy. Yes! She thought of Neph and how he said the Athecierian Warships didn't stand a chance against his Battleships. She laughed in pure delight as she dispatched a few more Cutters before turning to watch the Clorrians dispatch the Atheciery.

Her joy quickly faded as she watched the Battleship enter Earth's atmosphere at an impossible angle and speed. It wasn't slowing down or changing course. The Clorrians were going to crash. Suddenly, the back half of the ship burst into flames.

Sarah heard a wail of anguish behind her. Turning, she saw Nephemerus running down the path, through the field. His eyes were wide as his ship plummeted straight into the ground, a few miles away. He didn't even see her as he ran past, transfixed on the explosion.

Sarah heard a heavy thudding sound and then the metallic click of latches from high above her. She looked up to see the Warship was aiming its weapons. A high-pitched whirling sound filled the air as Sarah spotted a line of Cutters bearing down on Neph. She jumped into the pathway to protect him.

DAD! she screamed out to Galloyde, who didn't answer. Where was he? What was happening? She threw a protective shield around Neph and turned back to the Cutters. She was able to destroy all but one as it flew past her and fired upon him. She saw that the ship's gunfire would have struck Neph if not for her shield.

The shield protected him from the last Cutter—but not from the Warship. The whirling sound was from a laser gun mounted below the ship. She watched the muzzle target Neph as he dodged between the burning piles of wrecked Cutters as he ran down the path. Before she could warn him, the laser fired.

He was hit directly.

Nephemerus was killed instantly.

His body vaporized into ash.

Sarah dropped to her knees. She uttered a low groan before falling forward onto the ground. She stared ahead at the spot where Nephemerus had existed just a second before. She could not draw breath. She laid her head down on the ground, closed her eyes, and wished she could die.

CHAPTER
EIGHTY-THREE

"**S**ARAH!" Her father was pulling on her arms. His voice wasn't in her head. He was standing in front of her, yelling. "Get up!"

Sarah looked at him, looked around the field, and slumped back down on the ground, staring up at the ship. *They killed him,* she thought. She couldn't speak.

Galloyde grabbed her arms again and yanked her upwards. "Get up!" He dragged her behind a pile of flaming metal. She didn't answer him—she couldn't, even if she wanted to. Her heart had stopped beating when Neph was killed.

"Are you hurt? Sarah? SARAH!" he desperately pleaded with her as he ripped Cutters out of the sky and slammed them to the ground, now grunting with the effort he needed to do so.

Finally, Galloyde grabbed her shoulders and shook her violently. "Sarah! Listen to me. They are going to get into The Gate. They will kill everyone there. You have to stop them. They will kill all of them like they killed Nephemerus."

She blinked. She looked at Galloyde. He looked desperate. She looked up into the burning red sky, now blackened from the smoke of the downed Battleship. She felt her heart beat once in her chest.

"They will slaughter Bunny, Sarah. They will take him away from you. You will never see him again. They will slice him up and sell him for parts. They will do the same thing to Tiny and Seglee and every single one of them. Sarah, you must take that ship down now!"

She felt a few more erratic beats deep in her chest. She felt dizzy and nauseous. She slowly shook her head and tried to stand, then started to fall. Galloyde caught her and steadied her on her feet.

She felt as if her body had been ripped apart and sewn back together. Her heart tried a few more beats, still wildly out of tune.

She glanced up at the Warship hovering over her, taunting her. She thought of Nephemerus running—

"Sarah, NOW!"

Her heart began pounding in her chest now. Loud and persistent, increasing in speed. She could hear her own heartbeat pounding in her ears. She saw the spot where her love had been taken from her. Unbridled rage coursed through her veins. She raised her hands, her lips pulling back in a twisted grimace, as she grabbed the edges of the ship in her mind and crushed it as easily as she was crushing a tin can.

The ship began to fold in on itself, bursting into flames. The Warship was torn into massive sections and fell to the ground, adding to the burning haze of the Clorrian Battleship. Other pieces imploded mid-air and rained fire down all around Sarah and her father.

She then turned her mind to the Athecierian ship sitting at the north pole and repeated the same crushing maneuver, even faster. She growled and contorted her face as her hands mimicked the ripping motions that sent the ship bursting into flames. She let out a howl as she tossed the remainder of the ship down into the ice shelf, burying all of the crew and ship deep underground.

Her teeth still bared, Sarah moved her mind onto the ship above them in Earth's orbit. She hissed and bit hard into her own lip as she pulled that ship apart—choosing not to crush it, but instead to yank it open. She spun the two halves into a fiery avalanche of twisted metal as it entered Earth's atmosphere. Enormous sections broke away and burned, adding to the fireworks as the two halves of the ship fell for miles, eventually landing in the depths of the Indian Ocean.

Sarah's face was unrecognizable as she moved her focus onto the two War Ships that had been in Earth's high orbit. They were preparing to leave the solar system, having lost communications with the first ship. They had just passed the red planet and were thrilled to leave Earth and all this nonsense behind them. Sarah flicked her wrists and crashed them into each other, leaving no sign of their existence except for shards of space debris.

One Athecierian Warship was sitting unknowingly behind Venus, simply not paying attention to the happenings all around them. Sarah ripped this one right down the center, like a sheet of paper. For those aboard, death was quick and unexpected. She left the two halves of this ship floating in orbit around that planet to serve as a warning to others who wanted to come to her home and threaten what was important to her.

Then Sarah searched for the last ship—the one with that face—but she couldn't find it. They had already fled.

Sarah fell to the ground, and everything went black.

CHAPTER
EIGHTY-FOUR

She heard voices in the dark. Whispering. Worried. Concerned. Then Sarah remembered—and the tears began to flow. She couldn't pull in any air into her chest. She started to choke as she gasped, trying to breathe.

"Shhh, shhh, it's ok, it's ok." She heard a voice tell her calmly.

Her tears blurred her vision. She couldn't speak. It was never going to be ok again, she thought. She let out a deep, painful wail as more tears flooded her vision.

"I can't... I can't!" She heard someone snap, their voice close by.

Then she felt her hand being held gently. "Sarah. It's me. It's Desimidor. I'm here, my dear." He squeezed her hand. "Sarah, would you like to sit up?" She shook her head no.

"That's fine. You stay just like that. You stay just like that then. That's fine." His voice was calm and soothing and kind. His warm hands cupped hers. His kindness only made her want to cry harder.

"It's not... it's not fine. It's never going to be fine ever again," she whispered, and she let out another deep moan, filled with grief and heartache.

"That's enough! Stop this! I said stop this now!" she heard someone hiss in the distance. Several voices were talking in hushed tones. The loudest was farther away. She couldn't hear any of them clearly.

Desi took a deep breath. "Sarah. I need to tell you that you saved us all. The War Ships are all gone." She didn't answer—her sobs continued as she held her arm over her face, tears streaming down and onto the couch. She was lying down in the chamber, Desi sitting on the floor next to her. Galloyde stood in the distance, watching.

Desi continued. "Sarah. Sarah, what I tell you next... you need to hear. Please. Please sit up for me."

She uncovered her face, which was bright red. He helped her sit up, readjusted her blanket, and gave her a glass of water. She tried to take a sip and coughed, trying to catch her breath. A fire was burning in the tall stone fireplace. She couldn't see Galloyde standing behind her in the room.

Sitting down on the couch next to her, Desi proceeded slowly. "This next part is hard and will be difficult to understand, but know this first—none of this was done with ill intent." She looked at Desi questioningly, then back at the fire. A new wave of tears erupted. He patiently waited as they rose and waned.

"Not everyone knew. And not everyone who knew wanted to do it. I need you to know this. It's important. Sarah. Hear me." She stared at the fire. He wasn't sure if she heard anything he was saying. "Sarah? Sarah?"

He stood and walked away. Galloyde nodded at him as he left. Galloyde sighed and walked over. He sat next to Sarah and put his arm around her, pulling her tight against his side. "My little gator." She stared at the fire, numb.

"I love you so much. More than you could ever know. One day I hope you will give me a chance to explain myself." He kissed her on the head, stood up, and walked out of the room.

Sarah continued to stare into the fire, fresh tears streaming down her face. Her vision blurred. She was staring so hard into the flames, she thought she saw someone walk out from them.

She wiped at her eyes and saw Nephemerus standing in front of her.

She blinked away the tears—and his image was still there. Imagining him there only made her explode in another wave of grief. Her body racked back and forth as another round of sobs engulfed her, knowing he was lost forever.

She finally slumped over onto the couch and stayed that way, her face pressed into the cushion. She lay there trying to catch her breath.

Then Sarah felt her head lifted, and someone sat down next to her. She rested her head on their lap and closed her eyes. When she opened them again, her face was dry.

Her hair had been brushed back, and the fire had died down. She was still lying on someone's lap.

She looked up to see Nephemerus smiling down at her.

ACKNOWLEDGMENTS

The writing was easy. Putting it all together to publish? Not so much. Without the people listed below, you would never have met my Demons. I'll try my best to thank you all, but words on a page can never express my gratitude for all your encouragement, guidance, patient listening, and sage advice.

First and foremost, to Georgia Hesse, who read and re-read DESCEND at lightning speed, sharing such incredible wisdom. The hours spent discussing the world of Ascend and Descend, the moral compass, and sharing your ethical beliefs not only shaped this book —but my own life. Thank you.

To Dianne Rothenberg, my constant cheerleader. Your unyielding belief in my talents when my own wavers is the bedrock of confidence I needed to bring these musings from my Mac to the world at large. You make a difference every day, and I always look up to you. Not physically—let's not get crazy here—I'm still an inch taller when you don't have your heels on. But you know what I mean.

To Amy Benoit, my friend who has indulged my wild imagination— for any and every subject—without judgment and never insisting that I conform to society. Your kindness and support have meant the world to me.

To Barb Hassan, your enthusiasm and optimism have buoyed me through all my spiraling. You've always been a true friend to lean on, and without your support, I certainly wouldn't have been able to bring my fantastical world to fruition.

To Margaret Owens, who has always stated with unwavering conviction that I <u>am</u> a professional writer, and who shares my penchant for the world outside the one we live in day to day—my deepest gratitude. Now pack your bags, we need to board our flight.

To Michael van Koetsveld, thank you for the opportunity to be a writer—a real writer. My joy in our friendship is boundless, and your words of encouragement buoyed me through to the completion of this book.

To Noel Davila, who is always a positive light in my life. Thank you for answering all those panicked texts, weighing in on the silly pen names and artwork, and for showing—not telling—me how excited you are in my endeavors, as I am in yours. I will always be thankful for your friendship.

To Geri and John Russo, my neighborhood-Italian-surrogate parents and security agency—thank you for always believing in me. You have no idea what that has meant to me. I love you both.

To my Beta Readers—Carl French, Judy French, and Christopher Dea. Thank you for taking the time to read a multitude of raw, unedited manuscript pages while providing invaluable feedback.

To my Guild of Unwritten Words community—you are the reason I truly believed I could publish a book. Each month, I am astonished at the level of writing, support, and abundant optimism that flows from each of you, no matter where we are in the process. Tamra Pica, I'm so thankful we found each other. I cannot wait to see what project we finally collaborate on—and when we do? Watch out! It'll be out of this world. To everyone else in the group—and I can't name you all without panicking that I'll miss someone—please know that you are the role models, you are the success stories that kept me going.

To my Alpha Readers, without these three wordsmiths listed below, this book would be an incoherent mess of rambling words without meaning;

To Loren Benoit, I deeply appreciate your willingness to jump into a genre that isn't your bread and butter. Your observations and feedback were invaluable.

To Erik Shimizu—Wow. Just wow. You will never understand the impact and the joy you brought me with your review. I'm still gobsmacked by the level of detail you provided. I stake a claim on you, and will always be sending you my latest manuscript. In fact, I should strike your name from these acknowledgements, because you are my secret weapon and I don't like sharing! Hah!

To Ed Burns—from listening to my endless stories about scientific discoveries and weird facts that are (probably/absolutely) related to my story, to taking the time to share your insights and thoughts on my pages, I deeply appreciate all your effort. Your 'Ed-its' were right on point. You lit up my blind spots, and your advice made my story better. For that, I cannot thank you enough.

Oh! And thanks to Klaus! My ever-vigilant German Shepherd. Without him, the world wouldn't have met Bunny. After all, Bunny *is* Klaus—his sharp teeth, protective nature, and kind heart.

Lastly, I need to thank my parents, Dave and Kathy Lyon. Their love for reading gave me a lifetime of adventure. I thank them for giving me Tolkien to read when I was eight years old. That was either a sign of their belief in my reading comprehension—or their desire to make me stop running around and sit in my room quietly for hours on end. Either way, it opened up the door to my wild imagination. Thanks, Mom and Dad. I love you, and I miss you.

GLOSSARY

CHARACTERS

479 — Evil human who lived four hundred and seventy-nine times on Earth.

Air Pilot Sutobi — Lander pilot.

Algetia — The Grand Precipice. Husband to Olethia. Lives on Ala Mia.

Allmar — House Guard for the Grand Precipice of Ala Mia.

Aramik — Research Assistant and Elget Transitionary in the Ascend Operations Tower.

Bassi Tinnl — Elget classmate at Ala Mia. Came from the OaB system.

Codet Vir Bahringers — Council member who first hired Sarah.

Commander Grally — Commander of the Bibbly.

Desimidor Vas Qulas Zyrla — Ascend Elget 17. Firvian and Clorrian bloodlines.

Frath — Chef at Devil's Cup.

Galloyde — Banished for creating unnatural life on Earth. From Terevia.

Jess — Gigla Android. Computer analyst in the Ascend Operations Tower.

Kia Aspwall — Elget classmate at Ala Mia. Came from the OaB system.

Laja Sinari — Merkvester from the Borgell system. Classmate of Neph and Desi.

Luis — Surrogate father and back-up Demon Keeper.

Nephemerus — Descend Elget. Vecurausian/Balksen orphan.

Nexar — Purple-eyed Harivasker. History teacher and ReTrainer from the Dalubar system.

Nimi — Cousin to Nephemerus.

Olethia — Galloyde's love. Algetia's wife through arranged marriage.

Professor Chronny — Hi-Rep ReTrainer. Morality and Ethics teacher.

Qeraa and Liro — The first two Elgets on Earth.

Qualla — Neph's adopted mom.

Raka — Captain of the 7th Lisceraa Force and Neph's best friend

Sarah — Demon Keeper of Descend.

Urisca — Traveler for hire.

Wirve — Elget classmate at Ala Mia. Came from the OaB system.

DEMONS

Bezel — Thandican species. Silver-scaled bird with a needle nose.

Bob — Whasook species. Eats first, asks-questions-never.

Bunny (Brohyramier) — Garakith species. Sarah's favorite and Descend's largest Demon.

Clara — Galonnow species. Specializes in scaring children. Long hair, fuzzy ferret body, wide head.

Gilgerg — Trillafibit species. Luis' sidekick and genuine goofball. Descend's mascot. Lovable furry creature who is very sensitive, so he's usually not called in for scaring humans.

Kevin — Nox species. Most human-like Demon. Aggressive and dangerous.

Seglee — Yesperarian species. An underwater Demon who will swallow humans whole.

The Triplets — Gulcaries species. A lion, bear, and eagle's head on one body. They track humans who believe they can run away from Descend.

Tiny (Thrinythidor) — Clorrian species. The most intelligent Demon. He and Sarah share a deep connection. Tiny is incredibly huge (although still smaller than Bunny) and has a turtle/pangolin appearance.

Zana (Zhaanicore) — Billirock species. A swimming brontosaurus. In hibernation for 150,000 years in the North Sea. Not part of normal operations.

PLANETS

Ala Mia — Elget training planet and home to Radimus.

Balksen — Planet where inhabitants are very warm-blooded.

Borgell System — Home system of the Merkvester. Laja Sinari is from this system.

Cartika — Galloyde's desert planet where he went to the Bazaar.

Clorria — Homeworld of the Clorrian race.

Dalubar System — Nexar's home solar system.

Earth — Located in a black hole in the Milky Way system. Isolated.

Enceladus — Saturn's moon.

Firvia — Desi's home planet.

Galaador — The cool, happening place. Everyone wants to go there.

Gigla — Technological center of the multi-dimensional universes.

Iitka— Where Neph and Desi spent 1,200 years working together in a similar Elget gig.

Kaarcerus — Planet near where the Galactic Ripple formed.

Kentron — Center of the 3rd Dimension. The Muldigal Council has a physical presence here.

Losinnia — Planet with the Muldigal Data Repository Library.

Milva — Planet destroyed by Athecierians. Neph's parents died there.

Neba Solar Array - Asteroid belt that is home to the moon planet Itkaa.

OaB System — Region which several Elgets reside.

Ogiolo System — Ala Mia is located in this system.

Pockula — The site of an uprising that Neph handled while serving with Desi.

Tengelly System - Kentron is located in Tengelly. The Council's physical location.

Terevia - Galload's home planet

Toomot - Trader/Merchant planet - Ruffians. Neph was taken here as a boy

Vaqa - Far away planet

Vecuraus Galaxy -Birthplace to Nephemerus

Veris - Green-sky planet which Sarah posed from as a student of demonic studies

TERMS

Ascend — Humans who die and whose consciousness is ready to move to a higher level of learning.

Atheciery — Mercenaries. Beautiful, but destructive. Ruthless.

Balksen — Neph is half Balksen on his father's side.

Chriska — 'Brother' in Clorrian.

Clorrian — A warrior race known for deduction, strategy, and intuition.

Corvier — Impenetrable missile holding the 10 root species.

Council Traveler — Individuals who can travel anywhere within the Muldigals.

Cube - The vessel which holds the Consciousness of a unredeemable life.

Descend — The place where humans who need to ReTrain go. Exists adjacent to Earth and accessible by portals.

Desirihia — Oasis-like place, but real enough to see, eat, and survive in.

Dream Walking — Communication through dreams by an Overseer.

Eironcore — Impenetrable iron made from lava found within an asteroid.

Elgets — Administrators sent from the Muldigal Council to oversee primitive planets.

Etchkaa — Alien life form that shares one consciousness.

Firvian traits — Cunning and a universal sense of truth.

Firvian Volle — Delicacy that Desi loves from his home planet.

Heftu and Tegreta — Joined Clorrian Cruisers under the command of Noneru.

Higher Consciousness — The level of Ascension where a species becomes part of the cosmos.

Hiseth — Green stones found in the Sotlopitis Sector. Power in mineral form.

Hiva — Slang for Clorrian scum.

Ishonna — 'I love you' in Clorrian.

Jaffer's Third Inversion — An unsolvable equation.

Kasyli — Clorrian mead; clear, cinnamon-scented, and highly potent.

Katska — Lead Athecierian Warship.

Kirlally — Descendants of Thandicans. Feared by Neph and Raka.

Lupa — Six-legged camel found on Cartika.

Merkvestors — From the Borgell System. A full quadrant in another dimension. Ancient society with a massive collection of solar systems. Former seat of the Muldigals.

Mirreáge - Adaptor for species to translate language and physical attributes.

Muldigals — Multi-dimensional Galactic Council located in Kentron.

Noneru — Admiral's ship.

Overseers — Beings of immense power who can see the Ripple. Few exist.

Pelerria — A yellow wildflower found in Clorria.

Piln — Unit of time used in space travel; approximately one minute.

Quadrant Representatives — Individuals responsible for the solar systems within their assigned quadrant.

Raqshaa — Clorrian term for scoundrel or "horned one."

Recusuvo Wars — Wars that killed Neph's parents.

Repetition — The number of times a human has died, returned to Descend for training, then returned again to Earth, repeating the cycle.

Rotation — One space day, equal to about eight Earth days.

Ryhol-Mist — Inhalant drug found on Galaador. Hypnotic in nature.

Till the Stars Burn Out — Traditional Clorrian farewell.

Tèciken — A legendary Clorrian warrior.

T'Shonka — 'Thank you' in Clorrian.

Ubinia Fleet — Fleet whose rear admiral sponsored Neph's entry to Ala Mia.

Vecurasian — Neph's mother was Vecurasian.

Version Treaty — Cosmic agreement intended to protect Council planets.

www.ingramcontent.com/pod-product-compliance
Lightning Source LLC
Chambersburg PA
CBHW020509020726
47493CB00001B/248